LIGHTLESS

LIGHTLESS

C. A. HIGGINS

DEL REY

NEW YORK

Lightless is a work of fiction. Names, characters, places,
and incidents either are the product of the author's imagination
or are used fictitiously. Any resemblance to actual persons,
living or dead, events, or locales is entirely coincidental.

Published in the United States by Del Rey, an imprint of Random House,
a division of Penguin Random House LLC, New York.

DEL REY and the HOUSE colophon are registered trademarks of
Penguin Random House LLC.

Library of Congress Cataloging-in-Publication Data
Higgins, C. A. (Caitlin A.)
Lightless / C. A. Higgins.
pages cm
ISBN 978-0-553-39442-9 (hardcover : alk. paper)—ISBN 978-0-553-39443-6 (ebook)
1. Women engineers—Fiction. 2. Terrorists—Fiction. 3. Space
travelers—Fiction. I. Title.
PS3608.I3645E68 2015
813'.6—dc23
2014037514

Printed in the United States of America on acid-free paper

www.delreybooks.com

2 4 6 8 9 7 5 3 1

First Edition

Part 1

THE ZEROETH LAW OF THERMODYNAMICS

If two systems are in thermal equilibrium with a third system, they are also in thermal equilibrium with each other.

Chapter 1

INITIAL CONDITIONS

When there was something wrong in the *Ananke*, Althea knew.

The *Ananke* was a special ship. The *Ananke* was a miracle—a miracle of engineering, a miracle of physics, a miracle of computing. The *Ananke* was beautiful, its gravity-producing mass nestled in its center, contained by a cage of sparking magnets, with the rest of the ship curling out over that core, the lights of windows studding its black spiral like bioluminescence. When it drifted through black space, it looked like an extinct creature of Terran ocean depths, a creature out of time and into space. The *Ananke* was Althea's in heart if not in law, and Althea knew her every inch.

For that reason, when there was something wrong in the *Ananke*, Althea knew.

"Scan of the filtration system reports no abnormalities," Domitian said from behind her. The crew of the *Ananke* was so small that even the captain had to aid with System-mandated tasks. He sat on the opposite side of the control room, running scans on the other end of the U-shaped control panel. The room was narrow enough that Althea could have turned around, stretched out her arm, casting its shadow on the dull metal tiles, and touched his broad shoulder with the tips of her fingers.

"Right," Althea muttered, her eyes tripping from line to line on the code scrolling up the screen.

"Did you finish the atmospheric check?" Domitian asked, his voice a low rumble.

"I'm running it again."

Domitian said, steady, solid, "Is there something wrong?"

Althea didn't answer him, only continued to scan the results displayed before her. "I'm okay," said the scans in the language of math and code, but they were wrong; she knew it.

Althea became aware of movement behind her, the scraping of a chair against the metal of the floor, the sound of Domitian's boots against the deck. She felt him lean over, hand braced against the wall. The underlighting from the display made his craggy cheeks covered with gray stubble look rough like old stone.

"Show me what you're seeing when you see it," he said. "The System wants a report of anything that might be wrong."

Althea knew. That was why she was running this scan again—for the third time, not that she would tell Domitian—on the faintest feeling of something being off. The System kept order, kept peace, and something that great could not be *afraid*—yet the System had sent down a mandate for increased security, and if there was enough cause for the System to enforce these kinds of countermeasures, Althea was worried enough about her ship to run the scans a third time on a distant suspicion.

"Do you think it's that terrorist?" Althea asked as the scan scrolled on.

She felt rather than saw Domitian glance up at the ever-present surveillance camera in the corner of the room. The *Ananke* would record everything that camera saw and then send a copy to the System. All ships did, System or not; all locations on planet or off, public or private, did the same.

"It's not for us to speculate," Domitian said. "Just make sure the *Ananke* is fine."

The orders to increase security had come on the heels of a System-wide raise of the terrorism threat level. Althea didn't think it was too great a leap to connect the two, but Domitian was right. They probably were not supposed to know.

Althea saw the error before she consciously recognized it. "There," she said, and paused the scan. It was small, and so it had passed by too fast for her to notice twice before, but now that she saw it, it was glaringly off, glaringly wrong, clearly stitched together with two disparate pieces, as if someone had sewn the head of a man to the body of a dog. Someone else's code had been inserted into her own. Whoever had done it had been skillful. Anyone else wouldn't have noticed; Althea almost had not.

She read it through.

"It's the docking bay," she said, and then rose, knocking into Domitian's chest in her sudden urgency. "Someone's boarded."

Domitian was moving before Althea had finished the last word, checking his sidearm, any signs of paternal patience vanished from his face.

"Go to the armory," he said tersely. "Arm yourself and take the spares as well. Then join me in the docking bay. Lock the control room after yourself and be on your guard."

"Should I wake Gagnon?" Althea had to half chase him; he was already out the door.

"No time," said Domitian, and then he was stalking down the hall with his gun out, one hand ready to fire, the palm of the other beneath to brace it.

Althea took a breath; adrenaline was making her hands tremble.

Then she did as she was ordered and let training take over. She locked the door to the control room, sent an advisement to the System of their situation, went to the armory, and took the three guns inside to prevent the intruders from gaining any extra weaponry, clipping two to her belt and taking just a single magazine of ammunition, which she thrust into the frame of the gun she'd chosen for herself with only the faintest tremor still in her fingers.

Then she headed back up the *Ananke*'s single long, winding hallway, the spine of the ship, feeling the pull of gravity lessen the farther she got away from the ship's lightless core. It was because she knew the *Ananke* so well that instead of going directly to join Domitian in the docking bay, she paused in front of the door leading to the physical location of the *Ananke*'s mission data banks.

If someone wanted access to the most highly classified System information that the *Ananke* knew, this was where they would go.

Althea took a breath, flexed her hand around her gun—brought up her other hand to brace it—and then pushed the door inward, bursting into the data repository, a steely dark room filled with computer towers flashing dim blue lights.

On the opposite end of the room, bent over the room's one direct computer interface, stood the figure of a man.

"Don't move!" Althea said, and he raised his hands in the air.

He was slender, on the short side but taller than Althea, with pale blond hair cropped close. He was wearing cat-burgling clothes, a tight black turtleneck and fitted black pants with black boots so well worn that they didn't creak as he slowly straightened up, black-gloved hands upraised. Althea stepped carefully into the room, eyeing the corners for accomplices. It would be difficult for anyone to hide among the densely packed wires and data towers, the neurons of the ship that covered the steely gray of the walls and even stretched to the gridded ceiling, but Althea would take no chances.

The man started to turn around. Althea snapped, "I said don't move!"

The man completed the turn, and Althea was briefly struck silent. The most brilliant blue Althea had ever seen had been in the sky of the equatorial region on Earth, where she had gone for a brief vacation from her studies. That did not compare to the brilliant color of the man's eyes. His appearance in the *Ananke*'s data banks was as unsettling as if the one who had been the most beautiful of God's angels had stepped out of the ether onto the *Ananke* and started to fiddle with the computer.

"It's always a pleasure," said the stranger, and his accent was strange and shifting, Terran now, Martian then, a trace of icy Miranda in the vowels, "to be held at gunpoint by a beautiful woman."

He smiled at her. He had a smile like a wolf.

The sight of that smile loosened Althea's tongue. "Who are you?" she said.

"A passing traveler."

"What do you want with my ship?"

"*Your* ship?" said the stranger, with keen interest, but before Althea could respond, her name was barked down the winding hall of the ship.

"Althea!" It was Domitian.

"In here."

She heard not one but two sets of footsteps and saw Domitian shoving another man in front of him. There were only three crew members on the *Ananke;* this man was not one of them, and with a sinking heart Althea realized that he was a second intruder. The new stranger was taller and darker than the blue-eyed man, with a fringe of brown hair hanging into his eyes. He had one arm tucked up against his chest, his other arm holding it in place, and Althea's eyes lingered on the swollen portion of his forearm, oddly bent, that indicated a violent and recent break. It was nothing a session in a System medical brace would not heal in a matter of days, but it had to be painful.

At the sight of him, the blue-eyed stranger's jaw grew tighter, then grew tighter still when Domitian shoved him ungently forward to join the blue-eyed man at the back of the room. Seeing them together, the familiar way they traded glances, Althea realized that they knew each other. They must have boarded together.

"Empty your pockets," Domitian said with his gun trained on both men. "Turn them out."

The man with the broken arm scowled and seemed about to protest, but the blue-eyed man, with his expression inscrutable, immediately turned out his pockets, letting a knife, a few small tools, and a variety of data storage chips clatter onto the floor like flakes of steely snow. The man with the broken arm followed suit, with similar items appearing but slender twisted bars following. For a moment Althea could not think what they might be and wondered why he was carrying twisted bits of wire. Then she realized that breaking into the *Ananke* would require more than picking electronic locks; it would require opening physical doors as well. The bits of wire and metal must be lock picks. She lifted her gun back up.

"I want them in separate rooms," Domitian said to Althea in his calm, even voice. The two men watched him closely like dogs sizing one another up. Althea was faintly relieved to have been excused from the blue-eyed man's attention. "One in the ship's brig, one in the storeroom nearby."

"And what if we don't go?" the blue-eyed man asked.

"Your friend tried to resist me," said Domitian. "I snapped his arm. What do you want me to do to you?"

The blue-eyed man smiled, white teeth showing.

"I mean if we think getting shot would be better than going into your brig," he said, clarifying with a show of false politeness that perfectly matched his Terran accent.

Althea's hand twitched around her gun. For a moment she was afraid Domitian really would shoot him or order her to fire.

She was not the only one; the man with the broken arm was very tense, as if he were getting ready to move suddenly. Domitian didn't do anything for a breath of time, his face as cold and set as stone, but then his gun twitched very slightly, the angle of its trajectory changing from the blue-eyed man to the chest of the man with the broken arm.

The blue-eyed man scrutinized him for a moment longer, then glanced at his friend and nodded very slightly. Domitian led the way out of the room, the two strangers following and Althea keeping to the rear, her finger slipping from the trigger guard to the trigger and back again.

There was no trouble putting the strangers in their cells. Domitian must have judged the blue-eyed man to be the more dangerous of the two, and so he ended up in the *Ananke*'s one genuine cell, and the injured man in an empty metal room with the door locked from the outside. Both rooms were near the very lowest part of the ship, in the very last part of the *Ananke*'s spiraled hallway, where the gravity and the tidal forces were at their strongest. It made even Althea, accustomed to the *Ananke*, dizzy to stay too long down there.

As soon as the door had shut behind the blue-eyed man, blocking his disquieting gaze, Domitian turned to Althea and said shortly, "Wake Gagnon; send him to join me. There may be more intruders. You go back to the control room. Lock yourself inside, update the System on our status, monitor the computer and the cameras. Find out their identity. We'll communicate via the intercom, but keep chatter to a minimum. Clear?"

"Yes, sir," Althea said, and left.

Gagnon, the supervising scientist on board and the final member of the *Ananke*'s three-person crew, was, like most scientists, not a morning person. He answered the intercom in a tone that suggested that he was contemplating the manner of Althea's untimely death but was roused rather quickly when she told him about the intruders.

"What?" he said, his voice crackly and thick with static, filtered through the machine. "How did they get on board?"

"They hacked the *Ananke*'s computer and tricked her into letting them board," said Althea, sitting in front of a vast screen, most of which was taken up by the tiled video displays of a hundred or so of the *Ananke*'s thousand cameras. The part of the screen Althea was focused on, however, contained direct access to the mind of the ship and a message she was writing to be sent to the System.

"How the hell did they do that?" Under other circumstances, Althea would have been flattered by Gagnon's incredulous tone; at the moment, it only annoyed her.

"I don't know yet," she said, and attached photographs of both prisoners, stills from the video feeds, to the message along with her write-up and sent it. The *Ananke*'s cameras sent their footage of the inside of the ship to the System at regular intervals, but the manpower involved in monitoring the constant solar system–wide surveillance was so great that it was possible no one was watching the *Ananke*'s footage live. The truth was that with the increasing violence in the outer solar system, the System's resources were overtaxed. It was not something the System wanted its citizens to know for fear that certain sects would take this as a chance to be even more unruly, but Althea knew it. She and the rest of the crew always had to act as if they were being watched, but sending a report would generate a faster and more certain response.

Gagnon, fortunately, took warning from her tone and didn't pursue the subject. "And Domitian wants me to do what?"

"Search the ship with him in case there are any more," Althea said. "I have your sidearm; you'll have to stop by the control room to get it from me."

When she glanced up at the tile showing the footage of Gagnon's room, she saw that he was just sweeping his long red hair back into a ponytail and zipping up his uniform jumpsuit, scrubbing a hand across his unshaven chin and leaving the stubble be.

In the video, he stopped at the intercom beside the door and punched the button. In unison with the movement of the image on the screen, his voice came from the intercom at Althea's elbow: "I'll be there in a moment."

Now that Althea knew what the intruders had done, it was a simple matter to track it down and undo it. Here in the control room, with the entire ship arrayed before her in its code and in its cameras, she was nestled next to *Ananke*'s cerebellum.

Gagnon arrived to get his weapon, briefly breaking into her almost meditative state.

"Where's Domitian now?" he asked, buckling it to his waist, towering over Althea on her gray padded chair.

"Docking bay. When you see him, tell him that the camera feeds from the docking bay when the intruders boarded are completely corrupted; I can't access them."

Gagnon nodded and leaned forward to look at the video feed from the docking bay; tall and thin, he leaned right over her without pushing into her space. "That's their ship?" he asked, pointing at a large ship shaped like a Ferris wheel parked on the *Ananke*'s deck. Though it was tall, it was dwarfed by the vast cavernous emptiness of the *Ananke*'s hold. "Nothing special. Too massive to have a relativistic drive; standard centripetal gravitation model. Transport and living quarters, not weaponized."

"So?" Althea demanded.

Gagnon's hand clapped down on her shoulder. "So they're probably thieves," he said, "not saboteurs," and with a quirked smile, he left her alone.

She let out a breath after he was gone and tried not to be too reassured by Gagnon's certainty. She couldn't let herself relax until she had seen with her own two eyes that no one had done anything permanent to her ship.

While she worked, Gagnon and Domitian started their sweep of the ship. Whenever one finished sweeping a room, he would tell the other one over the intercom.

"Clear," said Gagnon.

"Clear," said Domitian a moment later, his deeper voice rendered staticky and scratchy by its passage through the ship's wiring. The *Ananke*'s dark core was harsh on electronics.

The more Althea looked, the more it seemed that Gagnon had been right: the men were thieves, not saboteurs, and their interaction with the ship's computer had been solely for the purpose of getting on board. They had deceived the computer—and Althea—so well only because they were so practiced at coercing ships' computers into allowing them to board.

Still, she went through all the important processes, checking, just to be *sure*.

"Clear," said Domitian.

A polite chime from another part of the enormous screen caught Althea's attention. The System had responded to her message. There were files attached to their response, one labeled MATTHEW GALE and the other LEONTIOS IVANOV.

"Clear," said Gagnon.

The message itself read:

The intruders have been identified as Matthew Gale (of Miranda) and Leontios Ivanov (formerly of Earth). They are known thieves and work together. On occasion they have a female accomplice named Abigail Hunter (of Miranda) [no photograph available]; perform a complete check of your vessel's premises. Attached are the files for the two identified intruders. Read all flagged items and respond accordingly.

It was not signed. A single person must have typed it, but it had not come from that individual but rather from the System as a whole. The typist, whoever it had been, had been nothing more than the fingers to type it.

"Clear," said Domitian.

Althea hit the intercom. "The System has identified our two intruders," she said.

"Clear," said Gagnon, and, "So who are they?"

"I haven't read their files yet. The System says they usually work together on their own, but they might have a third accomplice, a woman."

"Names," Domitian demanded, as always terse.

"Matthew Gale and Leontios Ivanov," Althea said, glancing back at the screen to be sure she got the names right. "The woman they might be working with is Abigail Hunter."

"Ivanov?" said Gagnon. "That sounds familiar."

"No chatter," Domitian said. "Althea, read the files and report to us. Gagnon, this room is clear."

"Yes, sir," Gagnon said a little more smartly than was wise, and Althea opened the files.

The first file that opened was Matthew Gale's. The image was immediately familiar to her as the man with the broken arm, although he clearly had been younger when the photo had been taken. Even though the photograph was a mug shot, he was smiling a crooked smile at the camera, looking fairly cheerful about his apparent incarceration. He hadn't changed his appearance since the photograph had been taken; his brown hair was still just a centimeter away from dangling into his eyes in the front, and he was still clean-shaven.

Althea looked to the next file, already knowing who it would be.

Leontios Ivanov was the name of the man with the wolfish smile, but the man in the photograph and the man she had surprised bent over her computer were so different in affect that she might have doubted that they were the same man but for the blue of their eyes. He was even younger in his photograph than Gale was in his, wearing a brilliant blue high-collared shirt like the ones that were fashionable among the Terran elite, his handsome face as blank as a mask. The man in her hold had been as graceful and controlled as a wolf hunting was; the man in the picture was nothing more than rigid, stiff.

Ivanov's file had more flags than Gale's did. She told herself that was why she started with his, and not Gale's.

The first flag she encountered was POTENTIAL TERRORIST CONNECTIONS.

She hailed her crewmates immediately, checking Gale's file while she did. "Both our intruders are flagged for terrorist connections."

"You don't think maybe they were more than thieves?" Gagnon asked.

Althea thought nothing for sure right now; she only feared. Before she could respond, Domitian said, his deep voice calming, "We'll find out why they're here in time. Read the files all the way through, Althea."

Althea obeyed. The files clarified the terrorism flag, indicating that both Ivanov and Gale probably were connected to the terrorist called the Mallt-y-Nos, but before Althea could really take this in, it went on to say that the System believed the two men were only tangentially connected to the organization, if at all. Ivanov and Gale were hired thieves, grunts, nothing more. It was far more likely they were on the *Ananke* to rob her than to destroy her.

But why try to rob the *Ananke*? She was clearly not a merchant vessel. The *Ananke* was not designed for cargo but for scientific experiments. Perhaps they had hoped to find valuable scientific equipment on board—they would not have had any luck; the ship's extremely valuable scientific equipment was the ship itself—or perhaps they really had come on to destroy her.

Wondering would get her nowhere. Althea continued to read through Ivanov's file to the sound of Gagnon and Domitian announcing "Clear" as they checked each room.

The next tag said, GENETIC PREDISPOSITION TO ANTI-SYSTEM VIOLENCE.

Althea got back on the intercom.

"Ivanov's the son of Connor Ivanov," she said. "That's why you've heard of him, Gagnon."

"Connor Ivanov, the man who destroyed Saturn?" Domitian asked.

"Yes, him," said Althea. She had not yet been born when Connor Ivanov had declared Saturn and its moons independent of the System and begun a civil war; she had not yet been born when he had lost control of the moons almost immediately or when the System had come down like lightning from a wrathful god and restored peace forever. But she knew the story. It was a proud tale for System citizens to tell one another, how the System protected their peace and their safety without flinching, without defeat.

Gagnon sounded triumphant. "That means his mother is Milla Ivanov. Doctor Milla Ivanov. The astrophysicist. *That's* how I know his name."

"Discuss this later," said Domitian. His voice was absolute, like the fall of a gavel, and stopped Althea before she could mention that she'd been to several of Doctor Milla Ivanov's lectures before, too.

Leontios Ivanov looked a good deal like his mother now that Althea remembered her, and it seemed he had inherited her intelligence as well. From his father it appeared that all he had inherited had been heavy System surveillance. Althea could tell exactly the kind of man he was from his file: Terran, rich, intelligent—blessed. He had been at the top of his class at the North American branch of the Terran University. The System had sought to employ him.

Except that there was one more tag on his file, the oldest of the tags, and it read MOOD DISORDER.

At the age of nineteen he had tried to kill himself and nearly succeeded.

Althea looked back in the file at his blessed life and then back at the bare, sparse details of the attempted suicide and did not understand.

But sitting and wondering would get nothing done. For the moment, she dismissed her curiosity and moved on to Gale's file.

"Clear," said Gagnon.

Gale had many of the same tags as Ivanov—from what Althea could tell, they had started working together ten years earlier and had never stopped since—but his list of crimes stretched back much further than Ivanov's, back to when Gale was still a child in the foster system. Gale's file was straightforward; there was no incongruity of attempted suicide. Without disparagement she saw someone: lower class, from the outer planets, a problem child. It seemed strange that the two men would partner up.

"Clear," said Domitian.

The oldest tag on Matthew Gale's file was labeled FLIGHT RISK. For a moment, she did not understand what she was reading; then comprehension struck her like a bullet.

"Domitian, Gagnon," she said, interrupting Gagnon's announcement of "Clear!" He and Domitian were hardly halfway down the *Ananke*'s central hall; they were far away from the two prisoners in their cells. "Gale is an escape artist. Gale's the one in the storage closet."

She glanced up at the tiled video displays and sought the one of Gale's cell. It was up near the top, far out of her line of sight when she had been reading the files. In the image she could see Matthew Gale, with his broken arm bent up awkwardly against his chest, hand stuck into the neck of his shirt to brace it and hold it partly still, kneeling in front of the door and picking the lock. The heel of his boot had been twisted to the side, exposing a hollow place within; that must have been where he had kept the picks.

Althea turned back to the intercom and was about to warn Domitian and Gagnon, but before she could, Gale shoved his boot back into place, stood unsteadily up, and swung open the door; the sound of the *Ananke*'s pealing alarm rang out throughout the ship.

"Gale?" Domitian asked with tension in his voice that was like anger.

"He just picked the door to his room," Althea shouted back over the sound of the alarms. She had to find the display of the camera in the hallway outside Gale's cell to see what he was doing next. "He's in front of Ivanov's door now."

"Stay in the control room; we'll handle this," Domitian said, and in the corner of her eye she saw them leave the rooms they were sweeping and take off running down the hallway. She heard their boots thunder past her door as they ran, and she sat and opened the videos showing Gale and Ivanov, turning on the sound, unable to do anything but watch.

Gale was fumbling with one arm broken, holding some picks in his teeth, having trouble getting leverage, getting torque. She watched him drop a pick and heard the quiet sharp exhalation of what must have been a swear, too low for the camera to pick up.

There was a camera in Ivanov's cell. Through that camera, Althea saw Ivanov rise from the cell's slender cot to come stand before the cell door, his face as expressionless as it was in the picture on his file.

Up in the main display of camera screens, Gagnon and Domitian ran down the hall, passing from one camera's sight to another, appearing at seemingly random places in the mosaic of images, only to leave each image again a moment later.

"Mattie," Ivanov said quietly, with the static sound of empty air making it hard to hear. Althea turned up the volume and listened.

Gale seemed to be determined to ignore his partner in crime and continued to try to force the lock.

Gagnon and Domitian were getting closer.

"Mattie," Ivanov said again, louder, and knelt down so that his face was level with the one opening in his cell door, the food slot. Gale still ignored him.

"Matthew Gale!" Ivanov said, so suddenly loud that Althea startled, and Gale stopped trying to undo the lock to slam his hand, open-palmed, against the door. Ivanov didn't flinch but waited, and Althea watched his hands flex into fists.

Gagnon and Domitian were almost in sight of the two. They were blocking the only way up to the docking bay or the escape pods; they were armed and hale, and Gale was unarmed and injured. He would be captured soon, Althea assured herself, and continued to watch, silently urging Domitian and Gagnon to run faster.

Gale opened the food slot, and Althea saw the two men staring at each other through the narrow opening.

"Go," Ivanov said, and Althea watched Gale hesitate, looking up the hall to where he must have known pursuit would come. "Go," Ivanov urged when Gale still knelt there and looked in at him, and Althea felt a curious uncomfortable churning in her gut.

Domitian and Gagnon would catch Gale soon, she told herself, but somehow that did not help the churning, which felt almost like the beginnings of guilt.

Finally Gale seemed to decide.

"This is for Europa, Scheherazade," he said, and let the food slot cover fall, clanging shut. Then he rose to his feet and started to run just as Gagnon and Domitian came into sight, still far distant.

In his cell, Ivanov leaned his head against the door across from where Gale had been, and Althea closed that window and instead focused on following Gale as he ran down, down, down to the very base of the ship's spine. She watched him pull up short at the downward curve of the ceiling that terminated the hall, looking around as if for some way out. Farther up the hall, still quite distant, Domitian and Gagnon still pursued. Gale had nowhere to go.

All throughout the *Ananke* there were computer interfaces in the hallway, separated by about thirty feet. Such frequent access to the computer was necessary in a ship so large with a crew so small, but it meant that there was a way to access the computer at any point on the ship, including at its very base.

Matthew Gale bent over the computer terminal nearest to him and began to type.

"What?" Althea said aloud, and rose to her feet without anywhere to go. "No, no, no," she muttered, and looked to see where Domitian and Gagnon were—they were there, they were running, they were getting closer but weren't close enough yet—and then back at Gale, who was frowning with concentration and still typing. If Althea could connect to the specific interface he was working from, she could try to stop whatever he was doing, but first she would have to find out which one it was. The interfaces weren't numbered in order, and she'd have to force access; he'd probably stop her, but if she could just delay him from doing anything, Domitian and Gagnon could catch up to him and stop him—

Before she could do anything, every screen in front of her—the hundred video feeds, her connection to *Ananke*'s bowels, the still-open files on Gale and Ivanov—went black and still, dead with the lights, leaving Althea blind in the dark.

When the *Ananke* came back online a few minutes later, the lights flaring on with a suddenness that nearly blinded Althea again, she knew that something was wrong in the computer.

"Damn it, damn it, damn it," she muttered as the screen brightened slowly and the videos from the cameras blinked on and off, black spaces in the grid of video. "Come on, Ananke."

The screen glowed featureless, white.

There was a screen in the corner of the room that played System official news at all hours of the day. It could not be turned off, but Althea had long since muted it, finding that it interfered with her concentration. Even when it was muted, subtitles streamed across the bottom of the screen endlessly.

Now, jolted by the sudden shutdown and restart of the ship's systems, the screen blared to life.

"Twelve insurgents were caught this morning in a residential home on Triton," said a beautiful woman with emotionless eyes and a crisp Terran accent; the volume was too high, and her voice slammed into Althea's head like a physical blow.

"God *damn* it," said Althea, and briefly abandoned her post to dash the few steps across the room and lunge for the mute button.

"Surveillance in their residence recorded discussion of treasonous sympathies," said the screen.

"Althea!" It was Domitian's voice on the intercom.

"I'm *coming*," said Althea, though she knew he could not hear her, and punched the mute on the news just as the newscaster said, "Interrogation commences in—"

Althea spun back around to the interface by the camera screens and hit the intercom. "Did you get him? What did he do?"

"He's not here," Domitian said, and Althea looked up at the grid of videos, which was studded with empty places where the *Ananke* should have been receiving signals from cameras and wasn't. One of the few visible displays showed the base of the ship's spine, where Althea had seen Gale last, bent over her machine; now Domitian and Gagnon stood a few paces apart in an empty hallway.

"That isn't possible," said Althea. There were no rooms that far down in the ship, no doors for him to hide behind. The hallway did not continue on or loop around itself; it simply ended.

In the video, Althea watched Gagnon spread his arms out and look up at the camera, demonstrating the emptiness of the hallway for her benefit.

The computer screens sizzled with static again, went black, then sharply turned back on.

"Gagnon, what does the screen on the terminal down there say?" Althea demanded. The interface Gale had used had to show some sign of what he'd done.

"Gale is our priority right now," said Domitian. "Althea, are there any other ways to leave the base of the ship or places to hide?"

She hardly listened to him. The screen before her kept flickering like murmurs in a heart. "He's done something to the computer," she said. "It's bad; I need to fix it."

"He didn't have enough time to do anything," Gagnon said.

"I'm coming down there," Althea said, and ignored Domitian's immediate "Althea, stay there!" as she left the control room, locked the door behind herself, and started running down the *Ananke*'s hallway.

She passed Gagnon halfway down.

"Domitian's pissed," he warned as he passed her. It was all he had time to say; Althea did not slow down. Doubtless Gagnon had been sent to take the position she'd abandoned.

If something happened to the ship because Althea had not been fast enough to care for the computer, they would all be in trouble. She did not slow down.

Domitian was waiting for her when she arrived, his gun out, his expression black. "What the hell were you thinking?" he demanded as she ran past him to kneel in front of the machine. "Disobeying a direct order?"

"There's something wrong with the ship!"

"I don't care; you obey!" Domitian roared, and Althea flinched. The screen before her showed nothing but the smooth blankness of an empty workspace; Gale had covered his tracks.

"What if Gale had gotten to the control room and found it empty?" Domitian demanded.

"He couldn't have," said Althea. "There's no way . . ."

"He's not here right now," said Domitian. "Until we know how he could have escaped, we have to assume he could be anywhere on board this ship. Leave the computer and think. Are there any other ways out of here?"

"There's the hallway," Althea said, still kneeling in front of the machine but leaving it alone for the moment.

"Gagnon and I were in the hallway. What else?"

She tried to think past her immediate knee-jerk reaction that there was no way out. "There's the hatch to the core."

She turned to look at it, a heavy hatch near the extreme end of the hallway, set into the floor. Althea could see that it was still locked from the outside.

"What else?" Domitian asked.

"I don't know—"

Domitian walked past her to the hatch and, still with his gun in his hand, undid the latches sealing the hatch shut and gripped the handle. With a grunt of exertion—the gravity this far down made the hatch very heavy—he lifted the hatch and looked down. Althea walked over to stand behind him and look over his shoulder.

Right below them both, trying to pull them down, was the *Ananke*'s beating heart, the electromagnets that caged it humming with electricity, arcs of plasma and reddened photons following the swoops and curves of magnetic field lines and fighting the impossible pull of the mass cradled in the center of the ten-story-radius hollow sphere that was the rib cage of the ship.

If Gale had fallen in or jumped, he would still be visible, his body shredded and stretched and dead, frozen in time just above an event horizon so small that Althea wouldn't be able to see it from this distance even if it could be seen—because the heart of the *Ananke* was a black hole.

If Gale had thought to hide in this enclosure, clinging to the highest part of it, he would not have been able to resist the pull of the *Ananke*'s heart, and Althea now would see him dead down there as well. There would be nothing to hold on to, anyway; the only protrusion inside the hatch was the dead man's switch inside its clear plastic cage, which would shut down the computer if it was flipped and leave the computer solely under manual control.

But there was no one there. Gale had not gone into the *Ananke*'s core.

Domitian closed the door and sat back on his heels.

"What else?" he asked again, and Althea knelt once more before the computer screen.

"I don't know," she said, and urged the computer to open whatever had been closed last. She would see what Gale had done.

"He didn't vanish, Althea," Domitian said.

A window opened on the screen. It took Althea only a moment to recognize it.

"The maintenance shafts," she said.

"What?"

"I don't know how he even knew . . ." She had no idea how he'd known about them; they were vestiges of the ship's construction, made, sealed, and forgotten except for emergencies Althea never expected to happen. They had not even occurred to her as a method for Gale's escape, and she couldn't imagine how he'd persuaded the program to run. The shafts were airless and frigid, uninhabitable unless the program was running; the program itself was well concealed and responsive only to Althea's clearance level. He must have hacked into the program quickly: the maintenance shaft doors could not be opened unless a certain bare minimum of habitability had been achieved, and although the process was very swift, it still took a certain amount of time, time that would have been valuable when he had Domitian and Gagnon running down the hall toward him—

"Althea!" Domitian barked.

Althea collected herself and tried, for Domitian, to speak quickly.

"There are maintenance shafts throughout the ship," she said. "They were shut down after the ship was constructed, but they still exist in case I need to use them for a big repair. He shouldn't have known about them, but somehow he did. He ran the program to make them habitable again."

"He's in the maintenance shafts?"

"Yes." Althea left the computer to run to the back of the ship, to the metal-paneled wall. "There should be an opening—"

It fell open at her touch.

"—here," she finished, and turned to see Domitian checking his gun once, efficiently, then heading for her with a grim expression.

"Where do those shafts go?" he asked, kneeling down beside her to look up into the narrow space.

Althea took a breath. "Everywhere," she admitted.

"I'm following him in," said Domitian, and leaned forward to crawl into the tunnel just as the *Ananke*'s alarm began to wail.

Domitian was on his feet and going for the intercom before Althea could even process the sound. "Gagnon!" he barked.

"An escape pod has been launched," Gagnon said, sounding tense. "Gale?"

"Do the maintenance shafts go to the escape pod bay?" Domitian asked Althea.

The maintenance shafts went everywhere. They were lucky, Althea thought, that Gale had gone for the escape pods and not for some sensitive part of the ship. "Yes," she said.

"Scan the pod," Domitian said into the intercom. "Confirm Gale's inside."

"The ship's been affected; the sensor readings might not be accurate," Althea started to protest, but the two men ignored her.

"The *Ananke* recognizes one life-sign," Gagnon reported. "Gale's on board."

"Can you fire on him?" Domitian asked.

"I've been trying to start up the *Ananke*'s weaponry system, but it's not responding." Gagnon sounded frustrated. He was never patient enough with the *Ananke*; Althea itched to go up there and coax the shell-shocked ship into obedience. She might be able to do it fast enough to hit the escape pod before Gale was out of safe firing range.

"Keep trying, but even if you can't, we're between planets and outside the usual trade routes," said Domitian. "The escape pods have no mode of propulsion, and if he turns on the distress signal, the System will pick him up. Either he'll starve to death or he'll be captured again."

"Yes, sir."

Gagnon cut the connection. Domitian turned to Althea. "How did Gale get out of his cell?" he asked.

"He picked the lock," Althea said, remembering the video. "He had picks hidden in his boot."

"With a broken arm he picked the lock," Domitian muttered, and then seemed to snap out of his distraction. "Confiscate Ivanov's boots. We don't know what he might have hidden in there."

"Ivanov's in the cell," Althea protested. "There isn't a lock to pick from the inside."

"He could have something else hidden. Confiscate Ivanov's boots. Then you can continue to work on the computer, but I want you to stay by his cell. There's a computer interface near it; work on that."

"But—"

"I have to finish sweeping the ship," Domitian said. "There still could be a third intruder. With the way these people have been manipulating the computer, we need to check manually. Gagnon needs to monitor the control room. Are you going to disobey me again?"

Althea went. Domitian jogged past her up the hall after relaying the same information to Gagnon, and so she was alone when she reached the blank steel expanse of Ivanov's cell door.

The hallway there was choked with wires and pipes that covered the walls and twined through the grates that made up the ceiling, separating the hallway from the blue-white fluorescent lighting above. The lights hummed and whined at frequencies almost too high for Althea to hear. Ivanov's door was indeed almost directly across from a computer interface. This was less by design, Althea knew, than by coincidence; the interfaces were spotted at even intervals up and down the hallway. The wires and pipes of the walls had to bend around the shapes of the computer interface and Ivanov's cell door, distorting like light around a black hole.

Althea stopped in front of Ivanov's door, took a breath, and pulled the gun from her holster, opening and closing her fingers around it until she was comfortable. Then she said through the door, "Put your back against the opposite wall and don't move."

There was no sound of movement from within the room.

Althea hesitated, wondering if she should open the door anyway, but caution won out. She debated going to the computer terminal and trying to coax the *Ananke* into showing her the camera footage from inside the cell, but she doubted it would work and she wanted to obey Domitian quickly. She thought about calling out again and decided that would only make her sound weak. That left her with only one option. She dithered about it for a moment, hoping that Ivanov would speak up from inside the cell, or move, or do something to confirm that he was there, but still there was nothing. She crouched down to eye level with the food slot, as Matthew Gale had done fifteen minutes before, and lifted the slot to look into the cell.

Leontios Ivanov was seated on the floor across from the door. His back was against the opposite wall. She suspected he had been sitting there this whole time and simply hadn't bothered to move or reply when she'd spoken. When he met her eyes, he raised his eyebrows at her expectantly, as if she were taking up his time.

Althea let the slot clang shut so that he wouldn't see her scowl. She pulled a key from the tool belt around her waist and checked her gun again before unlocking the door. When she opened it, she immediately trained the gun on Ivanov.

He was still sitting and only glanced down at the gun, unimpressed. Then he looked back up at her.

"Give me your shoes," Althea said.

"Do you know what that thing does?" Ivanov asked instead of obeying. He nodded at the gun.

Althea narrowed her eyes. "It shoots," she said.

"Yes," Ivanov said with a trace of exasperation, "obviously. But it's not an ordinary gun, is it? Do you know what that particular type of gun does to the human body?"

Althea stared at him and brought her other hand over to hold the gun with both hands.

"It's designed for use in spaceships," she said. "The bullets are designed for wholly inelastic collisions. It won't ricochet if it's fired in an enclosed space like a ship. So I can shoot you if you don't do what I tell you and not worry about hurting my ship."

"'Your ship' again," Ivanov said with the same flash of interest Althea had seen back in the data room, and her unease grew. "But that's not what I was asking. Do you understand what that particular type of gun does to the human body?"

Althea opened her mouth, about to say yes, of course she knew, she had been trained, but Ivanov interrupted her.

"It hurts," said Ivanov. "All that kinetic energy from the bullet moving goes into the human body. It keeps none for itself. That bullet will create a miniature explosion in the target's flesh—organs will rupture, muscles will be shredded, blood vessels are more than torn, they're burst. If you fire that into a man's torso, it will liquefy his guts."

Althea stared at him in silence for a long, long minute.

"Give me your boots," she said at last with the gun still trained on his heart.

Ivanov did not move, watching her as if testing her; then he did move, bending forward to unlace his boots and slide them off. He tossed them toward her gently when he was done, and she kicked them out into the hallway and closed the door on him, his feet slender and pale and vulnerable against the steel floor as he sat against the wall between the narrow cot and the toilet in a dark cell the size of a closet.

She locked the door behind herself and called Domitian to let him know she had the boots.

Althea worked on the computer for some time without much success. Something Gale had done, some virus he had infected her ship with, undid every change she'd effected, and the errors seemed to propagate out like ripples in a pond. Several of the cameras refused flat out to work. The computer would obey her normally for some time and then without warning execute a random operation that had no reason and no connection to what she had been doing. It was as if every operation on the machine had become a little bit more chaotic than before.

She was so absorbed in the computer that she almost didn't notice Gagnon's arrival.

"Althea."

"What?" she asked flatly, keeping her eyes on the screen in the vague hope that their interaction would be fleeting enough that he wouldn't break the focus of her concentration.

Gagnon leaned in and spoke in a low voice, as if he did not want Ivanov to hear.

"Domitian wants you," he said. "He needs your help up in the control room."

"With what?" Althea asked.

"Repairs" was the cryptic response. Gagnon then said, "I'll stay here and guard Ivanov until he sends you back down."

Althea's concentration was well and truly gone now. She reluctantly closed down what she had been doing and headed up the hall. Gagnon leaned against the wall to watch the door to Ivanov's cell.

Domitian, when she joined him, was standing in front of the holographic terminal in the corner of the room, right at the circular edge of its raised platform, staring at it with the expression of a man who had run out of ideas. His eyes darted to the door once when she entered, but when he saw it was only Althea, he resumed the lost stare she was used to seeing on other people's faces when confronted by technology.

"What is it?" she asked.

"The ship is clear," Domitian said instead of answering immediately. "I located the hatch to the maintenance shafts that opened into the escape pod bay; Gale hadn't shut it behind him when he escaped, so I sealed it, then shut down the habitability program as you instructed— the computer reports that the maintenance shafts are completely sealed and uninhabitable again. And Gagnon managed to access the footage from when the men boarded; only the two of them disembarked. But while Gale was escaping, the System tried to contact us. We received a communiqué, top priority, from a System intelligence agent by the name of Ida Stays."

Althea didn't know the name, but when it came to intelligence agents, that wasn't a surprise. Like every sensible person, she tried to stay out of situations in which she'd need to meet one, and like every sensible person, she tried not to be seen looking too closely into their activities.

"And it's a hologram?" Althea asked, coming to stand beside Domitian and look at the holographic terminal. It was wide and tall enough for a person to stand inside it, but the floor of the terminal was raised and its ceiling lowered to accommodate the diodes that would create the hologram. At the moment it was dark, dead.

"Yes," said Domitian. "There's no text portion."

Sometimes very high security transmissions wouldn't have a text portion so that they would be protected from espionage. Althea walked over to the computer and attempted to access the holographic terminal.

At first the terminal flatly refused to turn on. There was no reason for that, so Althea relentlessly tried again and again, and eventually—without any reason—it did turn on with a low hum. The diodes glowed, brightened, and then stuttered.

"Play most recent message," Althea said, her voice projected with confidence so that the machine would hear and understand even as she frowned at the unusual stuttering of the diodes.

At her words the machine rallied, lighting up again, a form coalescing and then shuddering once more, the visage and shape of a slight woman created by the interference of light coming together and then twitching, jerking apart. Patches of dark and light appeared where there should be none, the ordinary human form appearing briefly monstrous, deformed. Then the whole thing went dark, the premature hologram vanishing.

Althea exchanged a glance with Domitian. On the bright side, she supposed, now he would certainly believe her when she told him that the ship's computer needed her attention.

Althea hesitated, looking at the holographic terminal and at the unopened message on the screen at her fingertips, then decided to fall back on the age-old solution for all mechanical problems before trying anything more complicated.

She ended the program for running the holographic terminal—stopped it dead—and then turned it back on again.

The diodes glowed, red and cold.

"Play new message," said Althea.

An uncertain flicker, and then that misshapen woman appeared once again in the terminal. Her head was offset through an accident of filtration, her knee disconnected from her thigh. The recording began to play, distorted and groaning, whining, a harlequin baby born and screaming like tangled steel wool being wrenched into straightness. It was wrong, it was horribly wrong, something terrible put forth from Althea's beautiful machine. Even though she knew it was nothing more than an accident of corruption in the ship's systems, the hellish mistake in the terminal made her hands shake and her skin crawl. But just as Althea was reaching out to turn it off again, the horrible image glitched once more, then flashed into perfect life. Domitian didn't seem to have been affected by the distorted figure but stood with his back straight, looking at the holographic image as if he were really in the presence of a superior instead of a superior's image.

The woman in the holograph was petite, slender, and flat, with a strong sharp jaw for someone so delicate, light-skinned with black hair chopped rigidly short, sweeping down to brush the underside of her chin. Her shoes were practical and professional but with a sharp little black heel, and her skirt was fitted and black. Her blouse was loose and flowery, a touch of charming, innocent femininity that contrasted with the rigid lines of the rest of her garb. Her lips were colored like bruises, a red so dark and deep that it touched into purple.

Althea had known women like this woman before. This was the kind of woman who preferred the company of men to the comfortable logic of Althea's machines, who looked at Althea with her awkwardness and her impatience and her wiry tangled hair and smirked among others like herself behind their hands.

Althea looked to Domitian to see if he had experienced the same instinctive dislike but saw nothing of the kind on his face. He was only watching Ida Stays's hologram with close attention.

Of course, she thought to herself, the System was watching; the System was always watching. She turned her attention back to the hologram.

In the hologram, Ida Stays had no chance of meeting the eyes of either Althea or Domitian; instead, she gazed directly ahead, most likely into the camera that had recorded the message.

"To the crew of the *Ananke*," she said, "detain Leontios Ivanov and Matthew Gale. Take extra precautions in their detainment; they are known for escaping System control. They are crucial to my investigation and the safety and security of the System. I have been granted access to your current location, and I will rendezvous with you at System Standard Time 1700 hours. Do not let Ivanov or Gale out of your sight and wait for me to question them. Ida Stays; end message."

The woman vanished; the diodes went dark.

"That's in an hour," said Althea. "What do we do?"

"Nothing," Domitian said. "We can't pursue Gale; even if we could, we have no means of capturing him. I have already updated the System on our situation, and when Miss Stays arrives, I will handle it.

"Until then," he continued with his eye on something above and behind Althea, where the camera displays were, "I will be interrogating our prisoner."

Althea's heart jumped. "Let me come."

Domitian gave her a strange look.

"I want to find out if he knows what Gale did to the computer," Althea said. "They work together; there must be particular tricks they use all the time. This is one of those tricks; I know it. I just don't know what, or how advanced, or what it's supposed to do—"

"I'll question him," Domitian said. "You stay here, monitor the control room, and work on the computer."

"You wouldn't know what to ask," said Althea, without really thinking it through.

Domitian, fortunately, was always patient with her. "What would you ask?" he said. "Would you give him a list of the computer's problems and ask him which of his and Gale's 'tricks' it's likely to be?" Althea said nothing, as clear as if she had admitted it. "You can't give this man any information, Althea. In his position he survives on his information. Telling him something he doesn't need to know is the same as putting a weapon in his hand. I will ask about the computer, and you will stay here. Understood?"

He held her gaze until Althea dropped hers. "Yes, sir," she said.

When he left, closing the door behind himself, she turned to look at the grid of camera images. In them she found the footage of Ivanov's cell, where from above she looked down at Ivanov still sitting with his back against the opposite wall and his bare feet crossed at the ankle.

It was standard to interrogate a prisoner until a satisfactory explanation of the reason for his presence was obtained. On most ships, that interrogation would be followed by imprisonment. On ships like the

Ananke, a System-sponsored research vessel with military applications, an interrogation would be followed by execution.

It was fortunate for Ivanov's sake, Althea supposed, that she and Domitian had heard the message from Ida Stays before Domitian had had time to interrogate him.

The files on Matthew Gale and Leontios Ivanov were still open on her abandoned workspace. Althea dragged them to the side, but her next step in attempting to fix the ship involved a long period of waiting, and so, with only the slightest twinge of guilt, she opened the video showing Ivanov's cell and skimmed through the two men's files while she watched Domitian walk down the *Ananke*'s long, winding hall.

Looking at the men's files, Althea became more certain that whatever virus had been put in the machine, if it had been some preprepared disease, as it must have been to be so complicated and so swiftly created, Gale couldn't have created it alone. He had never even graduated from lower school, much less gone to university. But Ivanov had gone to the North American Terran University and studied computer science. Althea didn't believe that Gale could have fooled her computer so completely himself on the spur of the moment. Ivanov must have helped him design it; maybe Ivanov had designed it himself. Gale had just taken their design and applied it so that he could escape.

That meant that whatever virus was infecting her ship, Althea thought, Ivanov knew how to fix it.

On the video screen, Althea saw that Domitian had reached Ivanov's cell. Without a word, his face still and set as stone, he opened the door. Ivanov didn't move even though he had to crane his head back to look at Domitian's face.

"We know who you are," Domitian said, his low rumbling voice poorly picked up by the cameras, so that Althea had to lean forward to listen. "We know who your companion was."

Ivanov cocked his head to the side. The camera in his cell was positioned above where Domitian now stood, and so Althea could not see Domitian's face clearly but Ivanov's face was nearly head-on.

He was smiling, insolent, amused.

"What we want to know," said Domitian, "is why you are on board."

Ivanov took a beat longer to reply than was normal. Althea's fingers were tight around the edge of the control panel.

"Simple curiosity," Ivanov said. His accent had changed. No longer

sharply, purely Terran or broadened by the traces of an adopted Mirandan drawl, it had something of Jupiter in it, faintly similar to Domitian's accent. "We were flying past, and by pure chance we saw your
strange ship."

Ivanov's eyes flickered up and straight into the camera. Althea knew
he couldn't see her, but she was made uneasy nonetheless and was relieved when a moment later he looked away.

"You don't expect me to believe that," said Domitian.

"I don't expect you to believe anything I say," Ivanov said, "but I'm
telling you the truth. Mattie and I were on our ship, headed for Mars,
when our path intersected with yours. We wouldn't have even found
the *Ananke* if we hadn't nearly run into her. Now, men like us, when
we see a ship this magnificent—"

Domitian interrupted. "If you're hoping for rescue, none is coming.
Gale was killed trying to escape."

Althea supposed Domitian was telling the truth in a way; Gale
would be dead soon from asphyxiation or starvation unless he was
picked up by another ship, and with no one looking for him, his escape
pod probably would never be found.

Ivanov went very still in exactly the position he had been in, his
head cocked slightly to the side. His face showed nothing at all.

Then his face relaxed back into the insolent amusement he had
adopted against Domitian.

"You know, the first rule of interrogation is to get the subject's trust,"
Ivanov said. "You just lost it."

"I killed Gale, and I can kill you, too," said Domitian.

"Then why don't you kill me?" Ivanov asked. "You could shoot me
in the docking bay. Fire that gun there"—he nodded at Domitian's hip
and the weapon resting on it beneath Domitian's heavy hand—"right
into my chest. And I fall. And then you leave and open the air lock. My
body, my blood, all the mess goes flying out into the solar wind. Maybe
I'm already dead, or maybe you're a bad shot and I'm not dead yet, so
I get to drown in my own blood and suffocate in a vacuum both."

Ivanov seemed to be watching Domitian very closely. What he was
looking for, Althea didn't know. But his manner unsettled her.

"So then why don't you kill me?" Ivanov asked. "Oh," he said, feigning coming to a realization, one finger lifting to point toward the ceiling. "That's right. You've just told me. You can't kill me unless I tell you

what you want to know." He smirked at Domitian. "You're not very good at this."

"I don't need to find out anything from you," Domitian said. "Gale is dead. Once you are, too, the threat will be neutralized. But if you tell me what I want to know, I'll reconsider killing you."

"Thanks." Ivanov had a deft sense for sarcasm.

"Answer me. Why did you and Gale board this ship?"

"I already told you," Ivanov said. "Curiosity. Nothing more. What answer are you expecting?"

"I want the truth," Domitian warned.

"And I'm giving you it," said Ivanov. "We'd never seen a ship like the *Ananke* before. It's something different. It's almost an organism instead of a machine, the computer is so powerful. Mattie and I both have a professional interest in computers, and in any case, we figured there would be something valuable on board."

"Did you come on board," said Domitian, "on orders of the Mallt-y-Nos?"

Althea thought she saw Ivanov flinch. "I'm a thief, not a terrorist."

"Then you know her."

"Not personally." He was wary.

"You know of her."

"Everyone does."

"Tell me what you know about her," Domitian said.

"Just that she's a terrorist." He paused, then lowered his tone as if telling a ghost story, with only a fine edge of sarcasm to spoil the effect. "I know enough about her to avoid her and her hounds. Do you know what her name means?"

"No."

"It means 'Matilda of the Night,'" Ivanov said. "In mythology, the Mallt-y-Nos was a noblewoman who loved so much to hunt that she said to God, 'If there is no hunting in heaven, I will not go.' And so God damned her to hunt forever as part of the fairy host. The sound of her shrieks and howls drive her fairy hounds to hunt the souls damned to hell, hunt them down and drag them there."

His voice had lowered, hushed, and Althea strained to hear.

"They say that the louder the sound of her hounds' barking, the farther away they are," said Ivanov. "And so, when the howling is the quietest, only a whisper, that's when the hounds are right beside you."

The beep of the *Ananke*'s computer, indicating that its scan was done, was so loud and sudden after Ivanov's soft story that Althea jumped and swore.

"I don't care about fairy tales, Ivanov," she heard Domitian say as she leaned away, and she kept half an ear on the interrogation while she dealt with her injured machine.

Domitian said, "Tell me what Gale did to this computer before he escaped."

"I don't know," Ivanov said, politely acidic in a way that was very Terran. "I was locked up in a cell."

"You must have some idea," said Domitian. "The two of you must have contingency plans for situations like this."

"Contingency plans for being unexpectedly captured on a secret military vessel with a superpowered computer of a kind neither of us have seen before?" said Ivanov. "Shockingly, no."

"Enough," said Domitian, and, to Althea's frustration, moved on. "I want you to explain what Gale meant when he said, 'This is for Europa, Scheherazade.'"

Ivanov hesitated.

"Ivanov," Domitian said when the silence stretched for too long.

"Which would you like first?" Ivanov asked. "The Europa part or the Scheherazade?"

"I don't care," said Domitian, "so long as you answer the question."

"Scheherazade," Ivanov said, "is an easy answer." He smiled, brief and charming. "When Mattie and I are traveling between moons and planets, that's a lot of space and not a lot of things to do. So sometimes I tell stories. One time I told Mattie the story of Scheherazade and her thousand and one nights, and Mattie thought it was funny how she told stories for so long and I did the same thing. So sometimes he calls me Scheherazade."

"A nickname," said Domitian.

Something flickered over Ivanov's face, like an impulse to laugh, suppressed. "That's what I said."

"It's affectionate?"

Ivanov shrugged. "It's just a nickname."

"And Europa?" Domitian asked.

"You've already checked up on times Mattie and I were on Europa, of course," Ivanov said, and Althea winced, because with the computer in the state it was in and with securing the ship, Domitian certainly had not had the time. She started trying to bring up the file; Domitian would want to look at it when he came back up. He also would know, once he saw the file open, that she had been listening to the interrogation, but Althea knew that his annoyance with her wouldn't last.

"And so you know," said Ivanov, "that a con went wrong on Europa last time Mattie and I were there. We were robbing a ship called the *Jason*—a System ship, but the crew were pirates and extortionists in their spare time. The System doesn't care what their ships do as long as they keep the System's people quiet and under control."

He had the rhetoric of a terrorist for all that he claimed not to be one.

"Mattie was caught by the crew of the *Jason*," said Ivanov, his measured tone growing more and more distant with every word, "and I left him."

"You came here together," Domitian said.

Ivanov very nearly rolled his eyes. "Obviously, he escaped. The point is that I left him there. We kept working together because we make a good team, but that established something: each man for himself. I left Mattie on Europa, and so Mattie left me here."

The file on Europa finally had opened. Domitian queried something else, but Althea didn't hear. She was too busy reading and rereading the first few lines of the report.

Eight years ago—longer than she would have guessed—eight years ago, the report said, the *Jason* had been found drifting in orbit around Europa, unmanned, its computers wiped.

All the System could determine was that Matthew Gale and Leontios Ivanov, under alias, had been recorded in interactions with the ship's crew some days before.

The ship was unmanned, the report said, because the entire crew had been murdered.

And all Ivanov had said was, "Mattie escaped."

Domitian was done with their prisoner when Althea looked back over at the feed, leaving the tiny cell and locking the door, while Ivanov sat in the same place with his back against the wall and his slender pale feet crossed at the ankles.

What kind of man are you? Althea wondered, looking at Ivanov with his handsome face and his Terran accent and his murderer for a partner, and it wasn't until Domitian was halfway back up the hallway, leaving Gagnon to guard Ivanov's cell door, that her attention was drawn away from the video by the sound of an incoming message.

It was from the System: high security clearance. Althea opened it.

Ida Stays was ready to board.

Part 2

THE FIRST LAW OF THERMODYNAMICS

The amount of work done in one direction is the same as the amount of heat transferred in the other, or, the internal energy of an isolated system is constant.

Because of this, a perpetual motion machine cannot exist, and all systems come to an end.

Chapter 2

PRESSURE

Ida Stays was always right.

The System Intelligence Agency as a unit did not believe that Leontios Ivanov and Matthew Gale were anything more than occasional hires by the Mallt-y-Nos, separated from her by many go-betweens; they did not know her name and had never seen her face. But Ida had known that the meeting of the Martian representatives would be targeted even before the Mallt-y-Nos had struck. Ida had known that Ivanov and Gale would be captured soon. And now, Ida knew that Gale and Ivanov could tell her the terrorist's name.

Soon everyone else would know that Ida had been right about that as well.

The movements of Matthew Gale and Leontios Ivanov—both known and suspected and plotted out even as far as their first meeting ten years ago—started to show a correspondence, beginning around five years before, with the known and suspected movements of the Mallt-y-Nos. There was the snag, of course: the Mallt-y-Nos's movements could not be known for sure, and there were inconsistencies with the two men's course even in a best fit.

But there was more than the facts that Ida could marshal and present to her superiors, more than the numerical equation of guilt she could construct, more than anything else: she *knew*. She knew with solid and certain instinct that Matthew Gale and Leontios Ivanov knew the Mallt-y-Nos.

Her superiors had consented to the interrogation in the end, though it had been a near thing and they had imposed on her certain restrictions for reasons of the *Ananke*'s security: if it was possible that Ivanov and Gale knew of some immediate threat to the *Ananke*, the System required that the two men be kept on board the ship to be readily at hand for the dissolution of such threat; therefore, until the ship was certain to be out of danger, the interrogation could happen only on board the *Ananke*. Whether they posed a threat to the ship was part of what Ida had come to determine, and until she had reason to leave, she was content to conduct her interrogation on board for the convenience of it: with no transport time required, she could begin the interrogation immediately; there was no extra hassle of the increased security required for the transport of prisoners. Her presence on the *Ananke* had a time limit—Ida had only until the ship reached Pluto on its course, two weeks' time away—but Ida knew that if she did not have something to show for her efforts by that time, she would have more concerns than where she should conduct the interrogation.

But running out of time was of little concern to her. She was right, of course, and she would get confessions from Gale and Ivanov or both. To consider otherwise was impossible.

And to be proved right when all others doubted her—that was the best kind of glory anyone could have. Ida looked forward to it.

She had been approaching the *Ananke* for the better part of an hour; it first had appeared in her viewscreen as nothing more than a tiny spot of white, indistinguishable from the background stars. Now she was near enough for voice communication thanks to the speed of her ship's relativistic drive. Ida reached over in her bland little shuttle—System standard issue—and hailed the *Ananke*, saying in her most pleasant tone, "Ida Stays hailing *Ananke*, please come in." She always thought it was best to lead with a caress.

A static-filled moment, then a woman's voice said, "One sec." Brusque, Terran with a trace of a nasal Lunar accent; Ida mentally reviewed the crew on the *Ananke*. There were only three, she recalled, as strange as that was for a ship this size. The woman's voice she'd just heard must have been the voice of the only female crew member, the mechanic, Althea Bastet.

Ida waited patiently. The silence stretched out just long enough that her patience started to turn to impatience, but at last a man's voice came on.

"The *Ananke* apologizes, Miss Stays," said the man. Willem Domitian or Rufus Gagnon, then; the Terran accent suggested the scientist, not the captain, although there was no way to be certain. "We're stretched a little thin at the moment. I'll help you dock and board."

"Thank you," said Ida, still sweetness; she did not know the politics of this crew yet.

Another pause, and then the man—Gagnon?—spoke again.

"Usually we'd just have you maneuver in front of the main doors, then the *Ananke*'s computer would dock you itself," he said, sounding a little strained. "Unfortunately, we're having some computer difficulties right now."

"That's quite all right," Ida said. "I know how to fly a ship."

Gagnon sounded relieved. "The main doors will open in a moment."

Ida looked at the viewscreen, which was showing the seashell shape of the *Ananke* growing larger and larger as she drifted closer. At the termination of the ship's spiral, there were two long, flat panels forming the spiral's edge; as Ida watched, they slid slowly open, exposing the inside of the ship like a wound being stretched wide.

She steered herself into that wound, careful to compensate for the gravity of the *Ananke*. It was a simple task but a slow one; distances were vast in open space.

The mission of the *Ananke*, whatever it was, was a state secret. Ida had pushed her luck to be granted access to the ship; she had been denied knowledge of its purpose. The gap in her knowledge was a weakness, an annoyance, but in the end it hardly mattered. Gale and Ivanov doubtless had boarded the ship to sabotage it; knowing that the ship was System and military was more than enough explanation for that impulse. Ida gladly would take advantage of the ship's paranoia to interrogate Ivanov and Gale on board, uninterrupted by the tedium of arranging a prisoner's transport.

Of course, no doubt the crew cared a good deal about the ship and its secrecy and would resent her arrival, so Ida would have to step carefully.

There was already another ship in the docking bay, one that Ida recognized immediately from surveillance footage and police images:

the *Annwn*. Gale and Ivanov really were here. Their ship stood dark and hollow in the *Ananke*'s bay.

Gale first, Ida decided. Everything she'd heard about him indicated that he was the weaker. He'd be less able to lie to her effectively, more likely to bend and break. It was lucky Gale and Ivanov had been captured together; they could be used against each other very effectively.

The hold had repressurized; Ida opened the doors of her ship. On the far end of the vast hold, a pair of glass doors swung open and a man stepped out, tall and imposing most likely, but he seemed small and insignificant so far away and beneath the *Ananke*'s high arching ceiling.

Ida walked toward him, calm, confident, sure. She did not show the way her heart pounded with excitement. Gale and Ivanov, here, now, and hers.

The man was indeed tall and broad, with graying hair and a craggy face. He had piercing gray eyes and wore a System uniform impeccably, and Ida knew at a glance that he was the captain of the ship, Domitian.

Ida smiled at him and held out her hand. She'd remembered to put on her darkest red lipstick, and she knew its effect.

"Captain Domitian," she said pleasantly, still striding forward, and he took her hand in a firm grip and shook it, the corners of his thin lips turned down. "I'm Ida Stays. I'm pleased to have come on board."

Domitian hesitated, and Ida knew at once, with a sudden chill that left her roiling excitement frozen in her gut, that something was wrong.

"Miss Stays," he said, diffident and polite, in a low rumble of a voice, "I'm afraid there has been a problem."

The last thing Althea wanted to do was talk some arrogant Systems agent straight from Earth through the relatively simple task of landing in the *Ananke*'s hold.

"One sec," she said when Ida Stays hailed her in a high sweet voice that Althea didn't like at all, and she immediately got on the intercom to Gagnon.

"I need you to come up here and help someone board," she said, censoring herself at the last second when she remembered that Gagnon was standing in front of Ivanov's cell, guarding it. "I'll take your place. I need to focus."

A pause. "Okay," said Gagnon, agreeably enough. "But I can't leave Ivanov, so you need to come down here first."

Althea glanced at the few working camera images. She could see Domitian just striding into the frame in one of them, still heading up the *Ananke*'s hall at a walk.

"Fine," she said, and left her station, locking the door behind herself out of habit and jogging down the hall toward the cell. She passed Domitian on the way. He said, "Althea?" as if he thought he might have to spring into action right away, but she only said, "Gagnon will explain!" as she dashed by. The control room couldn't be left unattended for very long, especially not with Miss Stays waiting.

She reached Gagnon in a matter of minutes, breathing hard when she did.

"Domitian will explain?" he asked with a glance at Ivanov's cell, and Althea nodded and felt only a very little bit guilty about leaving the two men to figure it out. Gagnon was soon gone, and Althea got comfortable in front of the computer terminal by Ivanov's cell and prepared to devote herself to the study of her ship, uninterrupted, for a few hours.

She had not counted on Ivanov.

"The captain said you're still having trouble with the ship," he said after the sound of Gagnon's steps against the metal-mesh floor had rung away into silence.

From behind the brushed steel of his locked cell door, his voice came disembodied, like the voice of a ghost or a god.

The unfulfillment of an unanswered question nagged at Althea's nerves like an unclosed parenthesis, and so after the opened silence stretched for a long minute, she said tersely, "Yes."

"Then I should apologize," Ivanov began, but Althea snapped, "Stop talking, Ivanov."

On the screen before her, the *Ananke* opened at her touch like an infant outstretching its arms, and Althea resumed her search through the ship's systems.

"Call me Ivan," said Ivanov, and Althea did not trouble herself to respond.

For a few blissful breaths she was left alone, just long enough that she let herself relax and start to fall into the machine, the world around her falling away in importance until there was nothing left—nothing important—but her and her ship.

Ivanov said, shattering her concentration like a dropped glass, "I wanted to apologize on behalf of my friend."

Althea gripped the edges of the keyboard so hard that the tips of her fingers went white. "Do you?" she said.

"Of course," said Ivanov. He seemed not to notice her warning tone. "Mattie wouldn't have wanted to hurt your computer. We came on board because we were admiring it, and we wanted to get a better look at it. Mattie has a great respect for beautiful things—he likes to take them, make them his, not destroy them. He wouldn't have hurt your machine at all, or he wouldn't have intended to."

It was a strange apology as apologies went, but Ivanov sounded genuine, entirely sincere. For a moment Althea hovered on the edge of half belief, her grip on the keyboard gone loose.

Then reality came back to her, and she remembered all she had read about the man locked away out of her sight, and she bent back over the screen once more.

"Shut up, Ivanov," she said, and got back to work.

Fury was a dangerous emotion because it was self-indulgent. Fury didn't want to ensure that it got what it wanted; fury only wanted to rage, and rip, and tear, and make another hurt in proportion to fury's strength.

Ida Stays took measured steps back and forth across the floor of the docking bay in front of Domitian and tried to control her fury.

Gale was gone. Suddenly, the two weeks she had been allotted seemed a short time. She had had Gale, had had *both* men, and then, through the incompetence of others—

Ida breathed in and out, her respirations as slow and measured as her steps. Domitian was standing in precisely the same place he had stood when he had told her of Gale's escape, his back straight, his eyes directed straight ahead, waiting for her reaction. She glanced at him and continued to pace and to breathe while she considered what she would say.

Some wrath was expected. She was allowed to cut into him. She only had to consider first precisely what she would say so that the System, watching on the ship's cameras—if the camera in the docking bay even worked!—would not see anything untoward about her, so that they wouldn't suspect anything from her except a healthy frustration and a healthy expression of her frustration. She was risking her career enough simply by interrogating Gale and Ivanov; she did not need to risk it any more with unsuitable displays of rage.

She glanced again at Domitian, who stood without a muscle moving, waiting for her judgment. Another reason to control herself: she wanted him on her side.

She halted her pacing and decided what to say.

"Do you understand why it is so important that I speak to these two men?" she asked.

Domitian's focus slid down from the far wall to settle on her face. "I know a little, ma'am," he said.

A good answer. It did not admit ignorance, but it did not attempt to prevent her from continuing her explanation, as she clearly intended to.

"And what do you know of the Mallt-y-Nos?" she asked.

"She's a terrorist, ma'am."

There was softness in him, Ida judged, despite his scarred face and bloodied past. She aimed for that softness. "The Mallt-y-Nos is more than a terrorist," she said. "She's a murderer. She uses her rhetoric as a way to cover up all the innocent lives she's destroyed. Nine months ago the Mallt-y-Nos severed surveillance on Ganymede—it took the System a month to bring it all back online. During that time there was looting and rioting, the destruction of several System buildings—chaos. And because we had no surveillance, we will never catch all the people responsible and we can never be sure that some of the people we disposed of for the safety of the System weren't innocent. And you know about Mars: fifteen System representatives dead with a single bomb, as well as everyone else in that building. Some worked for the System. Some were tourists. Men, women, children."

Domitian's lips were set in a hard line. She was having an effect.

"The Mallt-y-Nos," continued Ida, and resumed her steady stalking back and forth, "destroyed a System military craft out by Neptune headed to quell rioting on Triton, which she also doubtless started. The Mallt-y-Nos is a bomber first and foremost: the fastest, brightest kind of murder with the highest amount of victims. Half a dozen minor bombings are attributable to her before the System came to know her from the Martian attack, and doubtless there are many more we don't know of—government buildings, military compounds, banks, one of which put Ceres's economy into a depression for months after its destruction—she's targeted them all. She is a poison in the System, a disease, a virus, and if we don't find her soon, she may infect every part of it. And now we know that she is planning another attack. That attack could even be on a ship like this one. Do you understand?" Ida asked, speaking each word like a strike against Domitian's stillness. "Do you *understand* why she must be found?"

"Yes, ma'am," said Domitian.

She stopped again to take another breath, to consider him before moving on to the next stage of her performance.

"Matthew Gale and Leontios Ivanov are currently our best leads on the Mallt-y-Nos," Ida said. Domitian's expression hardly changed, but Ida saw the confusion nonetheless; doubtless he had read the two men's files and had seen that the System did not share her opinion.

Ida moved, turning to square her shoulders parallel to his, and said plainly, "What I am about to tell you is classified information. Matthew Gale and Leontios Ivanov know the Mallt-y-Nos. They know her name. They know her face. They can tell us who she is."

Domitian's chin had lifted slowly in understanding.

"And you," said Ida, calm and controlled, her fury bubbling over into cruelty, "let one of them get away."

Domitian took it.

He stood there and took it, and Ida let the silence stretch, aching and agonized. She was outwardly cold and still and pleased inside that he had bent so easily at her sharpened words.

Domitian said, "However I may assist you, Miss Stays, I am happy to do so."

He had broken. He was humble. Ida relented, and Ida smiled.

"You are in a position to help me a good deal," she said. "For the time being I will be conducting the interrogation on board the *Ananke*. If it is feasible, for the safety of your ship and the expediency of my interrogation, I will leave before then, but most likely I will remain on board until the *Ananke* reaches Pluto. I have with me all the equipment I need. I only need a room."

"We have rooms," Domitian said, and led her out of the docking bay and into the *Ananke*'s hall.

They left the vast, echoing docking bay and stepped into a narrow, wire- and pipe-choked hall where there was not quite enough space for her and Domitian to walk abreast and fluorescent lights flickered overhead. Computer terminals every ten yards or so glowed among the tangled pipes, with dark holographic terminals sunk into alcoves in the walls beside them, and the whole effect was almost claustrophobic, as though Ida were walking through the veins of some great creature meant for blood and not the steady click of her low black heels.

"The rooms I'm going to show you won't be used until we've passed Pluto," Domitian explained, and his low voice seemed louder and fuller outside the echoing emptiness of the hold, "once the experiments begin."

"Are all the rooms identical?"

"No, ma'am."

"Then I'd like the one that's the largest," said Ida. "The most imposing."

"I was just about to take you there, Miss Stays," Domitian said. "May I ask how the interrogation will proceed?"

"I assure you that my interrogation will in no way impede the running of your ship," Ida said immediately.

"I was only curious, Miss Stays."

Again Ida was pleasantly surprised by him. She said, "Legally, I am not permitted to use truth drugs until after I catch him in a lie that directly impedes my investigation. So I will begin by simply conversing with him." She had little doubt she would be able to catch Ivanov in such a lie, and without much effort. Ivanov would be chained to a chair for hours at a time, filmed, and attached to a polygraph; the psychological effects of that alone would trip him up eventually. But even more than that, Ida had studied him, had watched selections of the years' worth of footage of every moment of his childhood up to the age of twenty, had studied the sparser footage of the last ten years, when he had been working actively as a con man. She understood how Ivanov thought, how he worked. She knew how he lied.

"I will, and I think soon, be authorized to use the Aletheia," she said, and thought of the truth serum sitting in little glass vials in a little box in her little ship. "But I hope to break him without needing to resort to drugs that way."

It was more satisfying in the end to break someone with nothing but words.

They had come to a door. It was no different from any of the other doors they had passed, but Domitian had stopped beside it, waiting for her to finish speaking, and so it had to be the one. "Is this the door?"

"Yes, ma'am," Domitian said, and reached for the handle. Ida reached out and laid one hand on his, noting abstractly that her hand was small and her fingers slender against the weathered skin of his strong hand. She saw that he noticed it, too.

"Before we go in," Ida said with a gentle smile, "I want to assure you that I will not attempt to interfere with your authority on this ship. I am simply here for an interrogation."

"Thank you, ma'am," Domitian said. He had gray eyes. She smiled more widely, and he opened the door.

The room inside was vast and empty and white. Ida took one wondering step into its wide brightness, the entire thing nearly half the size of the *Ananke*'s hold and so much brighter; each of the identical white panels that made up walls and ceiling and floor was lit from behind, and the whole room was as bright and blindingly white as if that could hide the fact that it was entirely empty. She was small in that room, small and exposed, and a camera blinked at her from the corner, the eye of the ship—of the System—watching.

She turned to Domitian and did not have to feign pleasure now.

"It's perfect," she said.

There was some sort of awful arrhythmic drumming sound coming from behind Althea, slightly muffled, and its inconstancy jarred her thoughts out of code and drew her attention from the computer to the closed cell behind her.

Briefly abandoning her interrupted work, Althea accessed the video stream from the camera inside the cell, which, fortunately, continued to work, and peered at it. In the image before her, Ivanov had moved to sit on the narrow cot with its flat bare mattress. His shoulder was pressed against the wall out of necessity, the cot was so narrow, and Althea found the source of that uneven, frustrating pattering in the drumming of his fingers against the wall.

Althea stared at the image for a moment longer, expecting to see some sort of explanation of the action, but Ivanov continued to drum against the wall without apparent aim.

Finally unable to endure it, Althea snapped, "Ivanov, stop that!"

The drumming cut off abruptly, but Althea still saw his hand twitching against his thigh as though he would have liked to continue. Perhaps it was a nervous tic. Ivanov said, "I thought I told you to call me Ivan," and his voice was light, amused, almost teasing, and that did not match with his expression at all.

Althea scowled and closed the video window. She tried to remember where she'd left off in her work before that damned tapping had drawn her out of it, but then, cautious and quiet, the tapping started again.

"Ivanov!"

"Sorry," he said. "It's boring in here."

Althea could not have cared less. She said nothing in the hope that he would do the same.

That particular tactic failed, as it had failed every time during their brief interactions thus far. "Maybe I could help you try to figure out what's wrong with the ship," Ivanov suggested.

It was tempting, but Domitian had ordered her not to, and so Althea did not give it a second thought. "No."

"Mattie must have installed the virus at a specific computer terminal," Ivanov mused, as if he hadn't heard her. "If you look at that terminal, you should probably see traces of whatever he did."

"I already looked at that terminal; I'm not an idiot," Althea snapped. "Shut up. I'm trying to work."

"I'm trying to help," Ivanov countered.

"Well, I can't leave my place to guard you anyway," said Althea, firmly. "So shut up."

Ivanov laughed.

"What do you think I'm going to do if you leave me alone?" he asked. "The door is locked. I have no picks and couldn't pick it from the inside anyway. There's a camera on me at all times; someone would see any attempted escape before it got very far. Whether or not you're physically outside my door doesn't matter."

"I have a gun," said Althea, a statement that also should have ended the discussion. She did not mention how not all the cameras were working and it was only sheer luck that Ivanov's cell had one that was still successfully recording.

"Though I suppose you're right," Ivanov said. "There's no point in going back to the terminal Mattie used if you've already looked at it. You were the one who realized immediately that we'd hacked into your computer when we first boarded; you know this ship so well, you wouldn't have missed anything this time around."

Althea had not in fact noticed immediately that her computer had been hacked into earlier that day. She stopped typing and sat, tense with the idea that there was something she could have missed the way she'd missed things this morning.

"Hey," said Ivanov. "Doctor Bastet."

She barely registered the correct name and title; doubtless he and Gale had looked up her and the rest of the *Ananke*'s crew before boarding the ship, after they'd hacked into the *Ananke*'s computer. "What?" she snapped. She couldn't leave her position, and she knew that she hadn't missed anything down at the terminal in the base of the ship anyway, but the idea, once introduced, nagged.

"You really care for this ship, don't you?" said Ivanov, sounding thoughtful and a little gentle as if he were looking upon a mother with her new child. "Look, like I told you before, Mattie wouldn't have done anything that dangerous. All he wanted to do was escape. He wouldn't need to do anything more than, say, mess with the cameras so that you couldn't track him." He laughed a little, more to himself than to Althea, who was still furiously going over in her head her actions at the base of the ship, trying to figure out if at any point she could have failed to check something. "We've worked together for ten years, and I can only remember one or two—maybe three—times when he deliberately messed up the navigation of a ship just because he didn't like the crew."

"Ivanov, shut up!"

"You're not very friendly, are you?" Ivanov asked.

"I'm trying to work, and you're bothering me," Althea snapped, and started to check the ship's navigation for any errors.

Perhaps she should go down and check the last terminal. It was possible, after all, that she'd missed something. She'd thought she'd checked all the places, but there was always the possibility that somehow she had missed something. But she couldn't go now; Domitian had ordered her not to leave her place, and the System's punishments for disobedience, well . . .

Ivanov sighed. He was just about to speak again—Althea heard him take in a breath—but she heard distinctly the sound of steps coming down the hall, and she hissed, "Shut *up*," at him again. He must have heard the change in her tone, because this time he did fall silent.

When Domitian came into sight, Althea was bent over the computer terminal, to all appearances deeply engrossed in the machine, but she was filled with an uneasy sort of guilt. She hadn't been forbidden to talk to Ivanov, and indeed she hadn't been talking to Ivanov; he had been talking to her. But somehow she did not want Domitian to know.

When he was near, she looked up just long enough to catch his eye, to assure him that she was aware of his presence and was actually doing her job of guarding Ivanov, but she turned her eyes back to the machine as soon as she reasonably could, unwilling to endure that vague uneasy guilt while looking directly at Domitian.

From behind her, she heard the metallic click of the key in the lock and then the sound of the door sliding open. "On your feet," said Domitian, low and commanding and dangerous, and Althea steadfastly did not turn around.

A pause and the sound of rustling, then the soft slap of bare feet on the metal floor. Althea sat with her back stiff, facing the machine, and listened to the rattle of metal as Domitian cuffed their prisoner.

"Go on," Domitian said, and she heard Ivanov stumble; only then did she turn her head to peek back between the wiry strands of her curly brown hair.

Ivanov was only a foot or so away from her. His hands were cuffed behind him, stretching his shoulders back and making the fabric of his black turtleneck pull in little lines from his neck to the roundness of his shoulders. He was different when he was physically there and not just a voice behind a door, more real and less real at the same time. He glanced at her, and for a moment she was pinned by blue.

She looked away and let the curtain of her hair fall between her face and his.

Domitian looked big and dangerous with a gun in his hand, and with his slender wrists bound, Ivanov looked vulnerable, helpless. He was no such thing, she knew. And even if he had been, he was still a criminal, an enemy to the System.

Once Domitian and Ivanov were gone, she left her place and ran down to the base of the ship to check the terminal there, just in case.

. . .

The room was vast and empty and white, and Ida sat on a cold steel chair behind a cold steel table in precisely its center, facing the door over the empty chair across from her. On the table beside her a System regulation polygraph and interrogation camera had been placed, not yet recording and, like Ida, waiting.

The steel door across the room swung open, and framed in its tiny square beneath the wide featureless stretch of white wall above, Ida Stays saw him, her subject, Leontios Ivanov, dressed all in black with his blond hair cropped short. His gaze darted around the room before settling on her, the only creature inside. His wrists were chained behind his back.

Ida let the smile she'd been holding locked away unfurl on her lips, and Ivanov watched her, the full subject of his gaze.

When Domitian gave Ivanov a shove to move him forward, he started to walk straight toward her, and there was consciousness of her attention in every step he took. When he reached the other side of the table, the empty chair with its back to the door, Domitian grabbed him by the back of his neck and pushed him harshly down, pushing him to bend forward over the table until his chin was just above the surface of the table so that Domitian could unchain his wrists. A line was digging into Ivanov's forehead between his brows as Domitian handled him roughly, but as Ida continued to watch, he looked up at her, his face smoothing over, and smirked at her.

The problem with Leontios Ivanov, she thought as Domitian pulled him back upright against the hard back of the chair and started to chain his wrists to the armrests, was that Ivanov was handsome, and knew it, and intelligent, and knew it. He could not help overplaying both hands. Ida was smarter than he, and Ida had him precisely where she wanted him to be.

Domitian tightened the last chain and took a step back, waiting behind Ivanov's chair, looking to Ida and wordlessly waiting for instructions, just as he was supposed to. The camera and the polygraph sat to the side on the table between Ivan and Ida, out of the immediate way, but their very presence was a threat.

Ida let the silence of the interrogation room linger a moment longer.

"It's good to meet you at last, Ivan," she said, and watched his face for a reaction. "Ivan" was what Gale called him, and Constance Harper; presumably Abigail Hunter did, too. "Ivan" was what he called himself to his friends, to his equals.

Ivan hardly reacted. He tilted his chin very slightly to the side and said, after a breath too long to represent anything but careful consideration, "May I call you Ida, or should I stick to Miss Stays?"

He had recognized her. Ida swallowed her thrill.

"Ida, of course," she said, and leaned forward slightly, pleasant and charming, and he smiled back in the same way, taking his cues from her. He wore his black turtleneck like armor. "I see you recognized me."

"Of course." Ivan's accent was Terran in full force, as crisp and sharp as only one raised on Earth could achieve, and for an irrational moment Ida wondered if he could hear the hidden traces of Venus in her own imperfect Terran affectation.

"I wanted to know the name of the beautiful woman who has been asking after me for months," Ivan continued. "So I looked you up."

Her inquiries had not been clumsy, but they had not been terribly discreet, either. Still, it indicated a greater degree of awareness on Ivan's part than Ida's superiors, for certain, would have expected. The glow of gratification had started to fill her chest.

"And is that all you found out?" she asked, as if charmed. "My name and my face?"

Ivan leaned forward, too, as far as the chains would allow. Their faces were still separated by the wide expanse of the table, but the movement imagined intimacy, and he said confidingly, with a curl of amusement in his voice, "I heard that you're the woman who's always right. All of your interrogations have resulted in convictions, and all of your suspects have—so far—been found guilty. There are people who think that one day you'll be head of System Intelligence, or the System itself, if you can keep up your reputation."

"And does my reputation frighten you?" If his words had pleased her, it was only because they were all true, not because someone had spoken them about her.

Ivan smiled. This smile was different from the others—dangerous, bitter, almost wolfish—and Ida memorized it, cataloged it, filed it for later consideration.

"Not yet," he said.

Ida would see him afraid before this interrogation was done.

"Have you ever been interrogated before, Ivan?" she asked, and leaned back from the table, leaving him bent forward toward her almost as if partway through a bow. He had been interrogated before, of course, and on the record, but information was not the purpose of the question.

"Not like this," Ivan said, leaning back into his chair as well. He looked quite at ease, but his eyes were fixed on her in a way that she thought might indicate wariness.

"Then here's how it's going to go," said Ida, as if she wanted this to be as easy as possible for him. "I'm going to ask you questions, and you're going to answer them all honestly, with as much detail as I am pleased to hear. You will not lie to me or refuse to answer, because if you do, I am authorized to resort to less pleasant methods to obtain the truth. Do you understand me?"

"I understand you," Ivan said. "But I don't know what you're hoping to get from me. I already told your mastiff"—he jerked his chin to the side and beside him in the general direction of Domitian, who was still standing in stony silence—"what he wanted to know about why I was on board. What else do you want from me?"

The perfect opening, handed, wrapped, into her hands.

"Remember, Ivan," she said, "I am the woman who is always right, and I know all about you."

He was wary. She imagined she could smell it.

"I know that you know the name of the Mallt-y-Nos," said Ida Stays, "and I know that you're going to tell it to me."

There was nothing more to be gained from the computer terminal at the base of the ship, of course. When Althea came back up and sat down in her appointed position across from Ivanov's empty cell, she glared at it as if it, empty, were still in some way a part of the person it usually held. He had gotten into her head somehow, yes, but he wouldn't again.

With no small amount of relief for the guaranteed peace now allotted to her, Althea focused again on her baby, falling deep into that blissful zone of total absorption in her work. Because of this, she probably did not notice the sounds as soon as she should have. When they finally filtered into her consciousness, Althea pulled herself slowly out of her trance, as if waking from a dream.

The hall was empty and quiet. The sound that had triggered her attention was not to be heard.

Still she sat and listened.

Althea knew all the sounds of her ship. Althea knew what the ship sounded like when she was well and what she sounded like when she was ill, and she could diagnose her from the sound, the feel of her parts.

This sound was not a sound she had heard before.

It started as a scratching, faint, weak, but foreign to her ship, a scratching like nails scrabbling for purchase. It was too distant to define exactly, but Althea thought it had to be the sound of metal scratching lightly against metal.

She rose to her feet and walked over to the part of the wall where the scratching sounds originated and laid her hand against the wall.

Something creaked inside the ship where Althea knew that nothing should creak. She leaned closer, pressing her head against the pipes and wires that covered the surface of the wall, her hair snagging on the rivets—

And then the sound was moving. Althea chased it, moving close to the wall, her palms brushing over the odd curves of the *Ananke* as she followed the sound up the hallway, her mind racing.

Ivanov had said, had mentioned, that Gale—before the *Ananke* Gale had targeted the permanent functions of other ships, destroying their navigation systems. What if Gale had done something like that to the *Ananke*, too? Something permanent? Something crippling?

She almost lost the unnatural sound halfway up the hallway, when it receded into the distance, and so she stopped where she was and stood and listened, backing away slowly to stand in the center of the hall. Never did the *Ananke* seem so vast as it did now, when the hallway stretched in an eternal spiral before and behind, and Althea was all alone in it. Gagnon and Domitian and Ida Stays and Ivanov were all somewhere else, behind doors locked and silent, and they might as well have not been there at all, because in that moment there was nothing but Althea and her ship.

Althea heard the distant creak and groan of the magnets at the ship's core, the sounds of metal and carbon shifting to accommodate the strain of such a mass, soft background noises, reassuring and familiar, like the sounds of some great creature breathing. She heard the high-pitched hum and whine of electronics, of a bulb that needed to be changed overhead. The rattle of liquid through a pipe: water, no, coolant.

And then there it was again, that foreign sound, a rattle and a scrape like a cough in the ordinary sounds of the ship.

It was above her head.

Althea looked slowly up at the ceiling, where the sound was coming from, and wavered on her feet, moving with the sound, forward, back.

It could be an error induced in the ventilation or the fuel systems, if not the navigation. But no sound like this, so physical, could be anything harmless or good.

The sound faded, and so she stretched up as far as she could, on her toes, listening, listening—

Abrupt, overwhelming, *BANG*, the ceiling shook, and *BANG*, the walls rattled, and Althea flinched and turned to see where the bang had come from, when *BANG BANG BANG* the walls all shook and rattled, percussive, overwhelming sound that was a physical thing beating Althea's torso, her arms raised in unconscious defense around her head.

Hollow, deep, metallic, the blows echoed up and down the bending hall in percussion without a pattern Althea could recognize. No one came out, alarmed by the sound, no other member of the crew came to see, Althea alone listened as her ship hacked and coughed and moaned, heartbeat out of sync, pounding wildly, and her ears were filled with the echoing of her ship's desperation.

There was a pattern to this. There had to be; there always was. Althea lowered her arms from around her head and listened.

"It's okay," she whispered, spreading out her hands toward the walls, the ceiling, her fingers spread over the surfaces separated only by the slightest space of air. "It's okay," even though the ship could not hear her and no one could have heard her over the rattling in the walls.

The banging was not coming from everywhere, she heard, and hardly noticed the tremble in her fingertips as they glided over the surface of the walls. She moved up the hall a few feet and stopped— the banging was coming from behind her. She moved back and walked the other way until the banging grew distant again. The noise was not throughout the *Ananke*, she realized. It was localized. The error, despite the apparent omnipresence of the sound and the terror it had produced in her, was not throughout the ship. It was coming from only one particular place.

Althea walked back, toward the center of the hall, toward the center of the sound, and stood and listened to the cacophony of the ship's malfunction. The banging was coming from just beside where she had been looking before, above her head, reverberating through the walls like a drum, obscuring its source, making it seem greater and more confusing than it was. Althea took a shaken breath and called up the plans to her ship in her head.

The ventilation system. It was the ventilation system that was situated there, in the walls and the ceiling over her head; it was the ventilation system that was making such a sound.

If the ventilation system failed, Althea thought as she stood and looked up to that invisible spot on the ceiling whence the sound came, they would all suffocate. As big as the *Ananke* was, the crew would have some time before they felt it, the slow poisoning of the air as oxygen turned to carbon dioxide. Carbon dioxide was heavier than oxygen; it would sink to the very bottom of the *Ananke*, as near to her dark heart as it could get. Anyone down at her base would faint and die surrounded by air but air that was unbreathable. The crew that survived would be driven up and up and farther up until they had their backs against the doors to space, the very highest point on the *Ananke*, facing before them an invisible toxin, behind them no air at all, fates equally bad. They were fragile, the crew—small and fragile and human—and they relied wholly on the ship that contained them.

That would be *if* the ventilation system failed. The ventilation system was not failing. The sound was too specific, too particular for that. It came from only one place. For the ventilation to fail, for them all to suffocate, the error would have to be throughout the entire system. Matthew Gale's seconds of sabotage had been too few to destroy something as great as the *Ananke*.

The lights reflecting off the ceiling seemed to move slightly, reflections distorted; the ceiling itself was being shaken and bent by some real and mechanical force. Something physical was striking it from the other side and causing that violent sound.

The robotic arm.

There were mechanical limbs throughout the *Ananke*, autonomous mobile robotics designed to perform simple, repetitive tasks so that Althea did not have to. They were necessary to run a ship as large as the *Ananke* with a crew so small. They maintained the engine, adjusting the radiation reflectors to propel the ship one way or another. They checked for expired food in the pantry. They opened and closed ventilation shafts automatically on the basis of sensor readings, the ship itself deciding what parts of itself needed heat or fresh air.

And one of them, above Althea's head, was malfunctioning.

The realization came with a sense of purpose, and the purpose with a sense of relief. This was something she could fix.

Althea went to the nearest computer terminal while the robotic arm banged frantically, arrhythmically overhead, and located the program for the robotic arms in the ventilation, then the designation indicating the particular arm by its location in the ship, and killed the program.

The banging stopped, the hall falling into a silence so sudden and complete that Althea's ears filled it by ringing. In the silence, she could hear the sigh of air flowing through the ventilation shafts again, the other valves opening and closing without a hitch, carbon dioxide scrubbers whirring quietly, muffled by metal. Althea listened for a time, wary that something would go awry, but the ship hummed and breathed peacefully around her.

Althea sighed. Shutting down a single mechanical arm would have a negligible effect on the entire ship's ventilation system, but she would have to review the rest of the arms to see if the error had spread to them. If it had and all the arms needed to be shut down entirely, Althea or Gagnon would have to preprogram the temperature and atmosphere settings and monitor them regularly rather than trusting the ship to maintain their environment on its own. It would be simple enough to do, but that kind of effort—bringing a crucial system of the ship under manual control—would require time Althea did not have and attention she would rather pay elsewhere.

She would have to write a report, of course. But it seemed like a waste of her time to write one now, when she should be checking the rest of the ventilation system for further errors to make sure this one malfunction had been a fluke. Gagnon and Domitian would be alarmed by such a report, anyway; they wouldn't take it in the context it required, she was sure, and the context was that the error had been localized, inconsequential, and solved and required no action or alarm from them. Best, then, that she should complete her investigation before reporting, examine the rest of the robotic arms in the ventilation system and make sure that this one malfunction had been a fluke. Then, when she had some time and there were no longer so many pressing problems in the ship's systems for her to solve, she could make a proper report and properly tell Gagnon and Domitian about the event.

For now, she had work to do.

Ivan laughed, which was exactly what Ida had expected from him.

"I have no idea who the Mallt-y-Nos is," he said. "Is that what you came all this way to ask?"

"It wasn't so far," said Ida. "And I'm afraid you do know her. And I know that you know her. There's no need to insult us both by pretending to be stupid."

One of Ivan's eyebrows twitched upward at the remark. She noted without especial interest that he shared that particular expression with his mother.

Ivan sighed and made an aborted movement as if he wanted to lean his elbows on the table and remembered the restraints too late. Ida experienced a moment of delight but realized she couldn't tell whether the motion had been an affectation.

"I do not know who the Mallt-y-Nos is," Ivan said, "and I have every reason to keep it that way." He looked up at her, his blue eyes clear and bright and guileless. "When I was nine, the System took me to Saturn. Do you understand me?"

Ida did. "Why don't you explain it to me?"

He cocked his head as if he were trying to figure her out, but he answered, "I know what happened to my father. I saw what happened to anyone who had even the slightest connection to him. I saw the bodies that float in Saturn's rings."

Ida had watched the footage of that trip, Ivan small and young and wide-eyed, standing close beside Milla Ivanov, who was still young, still beautiful, and was pointing out the bodies for her son to see with an even, steady hand.

Ivan said, "Have you ever been to Saturn, Ida?"

"Of course I have," Ida said. "It was a terrible tragedy, all those people dead." She put just the right amount of regret in her voice. "All the more important," she said, "that we catch the Mallt-y-Nos now, before she can infect any more of the System than she already has."

"Perhaps," said Ivan. "But you understand why I would want to stay as far as possible from the Mallt-y-Nos."

"But you haven't," Ida said. "We can match your movements to hers in a number of instances."

"If I was involved with her in any way," said Ivan, "I was unaware."

Ida let his words linger and did not answer at once. He watched her to the exclusion of everything else in the room, including Domitian standing behind him in silent threat.

"Ivan," said Ida, coloring her tone with distant sympathy, "do you know what the punishment for boarding this ship is?"

"Imprisonment."

"Execution," said Ida.

"And what?" he asked, a smirk curling his lips as he looked back at her, mocking. "If I tell you the name of the Mallt-y-Nos, you'll let me go?"

"I'm afraid I can't offer that much," Ida said with a smile in return. "But I can give you your life."

"Prison," Ivan said, rolling the word around his mouth.

Prison," Ida agreed. "And perhaps you could choose your facility— within reason, of course. It would doubtless need to be on Earth."

"Maybe I could go to the same jail as my father," Ivan said, and laughed. It was an unpleasant sound. He had never met his father, Ida knew; by this point Ida doubted if Connor Ivanov remembered his name, much less that he once had had a son.

"So you'll give me my life," Ivan said, suddenly hard and sharp where he had been so cautious before. "What if I don't want it?"

"Then I'll let you choose how to go," Ida said. She went on gently. "I understand, Ivan. You don't want someone to kill you somewhere in some shameful way, shot in the head on a ship in the middle of nowhere, your body dumped out into space. You want to choose the way you go. You want to be the one responsible for your death, not anyone else."

That wariness had come back into Ivan's expression.

"So?" said Ida once the silence had drawn out without interruption. "What do you choose?"

Ivan's gaze was unwavering.

"I do not know who the Mallt-y-Nos is," he said, precise.

"Then I'm afraid," Ida said, as if regretful, "that this will have to become a real interrogation instead of a friendly chat."

Ivan sat motionless, his lips drawn into a thin line.

Ida nodded at Domitian, who came forward, unwrapping the wires of the polygraph from their coils.

"That shirt is too thick," Ida said to Domitian. "It will spoil the readings."

Domitian laid the wires down and moved to stand behind Ivan, pulling out his knife from his belt as he went. It was a large knife, serrated, for fighting, for killing.

He stood behind Ivan as Ida had told him to before the interrogation had begun and reached down to grab the neck of Ivan's shirt, pulling it away from his skin. Ivan was holding himself very still and very stiff, his gaze fixed on Ida as if he could incinerate her with it.

Domitian slid the knife between Ivan's skin and the fabric of his shirt, blade angled out, and then stopped. He looked at her. For a moment Ida contemplated them both: Domitian tall and broad and strong and silvered, standing and waiting for her word, whatever that might be, and Ivan, chained down and helpless, holding himself so rigidly still that he was trembling lightly and looking at her with the beginnings of an imperfectly concealed hatred.

Ida smiled.

She nodded at Domitian, and his knife slit the fibers of Ivan's shirt apart, carving down from the neck to the shoulder and then down the sleeve. The tip of the knife brushed, feather-light, against Ivan's skin but did not draw blood. She watched Ivan struggle not to shiver.

"Ida," Ivan said as Domitian moved to his other side, "are you trying to get me naked?"

"I'm leaving you your pants," Ida said, and Ivan tensed again as Domitian's knife slid lightly over his neck on the other side.

"I was going to say," Ivan said over the tearing of fabric, "if you wanted to, all you had to do was ask."

"I'll keep that in mind."

Domitian moved in front so that he could slice Ivan's shirt, his knife sliding over Ivan's sternum. When he pulled the rags away and dropped them onto the floor, Ivan shivered. The room, Ida had ensured, was just a little cold.

Without the armor of his black shirt, Ivan seemed even more powerless, even more exposed. Wordless, Domitian returned to the polygraph and began to affix the wires to Ivan's chest, the suckers attaching to his skin like mouths and the wires extending between Ivan and the polygraph like veins drawing blood from him into the machine.

Domitian turned on Ida's regulation camera and then the polygraph. He glanced her way, and she nodded, and then he turned and walked out the door, his heavy boots echoing through the vast white room.

When the sound of the door shutting behind him had faded into silence, Ida said, "Now we begin."

Althea should have known better than to expect that she would be allowed to remain in peace. It was one of the rules of programmers: the law of constant interruption.

"Althea," said Gagnon's static-fuzzed voice over the intercom while she was checking the rest of the robotic arms in the ventilation systems for a second time; the first search had turned up no more errors, but she wanted to be certain. She was tempted for a moment to ignore him, but the cameras were always on, always watching, and so after a moment she leaned over and opened the connection. "Yes?"

"Is Ivanov still in interrogation?"

He could have just checked the surveillance. Perhaps he was too afraid of her wrath to touch the computer at the moment. It was a gratifying thought that after seven years of collaboration with him on the construction of the *Ananke*, she had finally trained him not to touch her machines.

"Yes," Althea said. "Why?"

"We need to dismantle the intruders' ship's computer."

"You can't do that yourself?" The dismantling of an intruding ship was System standard procedure; it should have been done immediately. Althea had been so wrapped up in handling her own ship, and Ivanov, and Gale's escape, that she hadn't remembered it.

"I can't leave the control room," Gagnon said. "Domitian's already on board the intruders' ship; he says the computer is strange somehow, and he thinks you should take a look at it."

Althea scowled. "Why doesn't he switch with you? You could deal with the computer."

"I'm missing my sleep cycle to babysit the navigation for you," Gagnon said drily. "Domitian seems to doubt that I could walk a straight line with fewer than eight hours; he's forgotten I went to eight years of grad school."

From what Althea remembered of certain instances when she and Gagnon had worked sleepless hours on particularly difficult problems of converting Gagnon's scientific requirements into actual design possibilities for the *Ananke*, she was inclined to agree with Domitian. She scowled at the computer terminal before her and said nothing of the kind to Gagnon.

"He wanted you specifically," Gagnon added when she was silent. "Something about the computer being strange. Miss Stays asked him personally to search the *Annwn* for her."

Miss Stays, the interrogator. Already she was throwing the careful routine of Althea's ship into disorder.

"Is she going to take control of the ship?" she asked abruptly. "Is that why she's still on board?"

"That's one of those questions I don't really want to try to answer," Gagnon said lightly, and Althea reminded herself of the gaze of the camera on her back.

"Right," she said, and did not give voice to the frustration that seized her at Miss Stays or at the errors that appeared and vanished again unnervingly on her ship. "I'll be there in a moment."

"First," said Ida, "I need to get a baseline for the polygraph. I hope you'll excuse me asking you some tedious questions."

"Not a problem," Ivan returned.

The screen of the polygraph was just at her elbow so that she could look down at it but positioned so that it did not rest on the table between her and Ivan. The polygraph was all electronic, but the readout had been made to look like the ancient paper version. Ida had braced it on top of a small pile of papers; she reached over now and pulled the papers out, shuffling them into straightness, making a production out of the System's bureaucracy.

"All right," she said, peering at the paper as if she were reading it and did not have the sequence of innocuous questions memorized. "What is your full name?"

"Leontios Dana Ivanov," Ivan said in the resigned tone of a man who had been mocked so often and completely for his name that he no longer bothered to take preemptive measures and simply accepted it as inevitable.

"And your parents' names?" Ida asked sweetly, letting the opportunity pass.

"Doctor Milla Ivanov," said Ivan, "and Connor Ivanov."

"Milla Ivanov, née . . . ?"

"Née they disowned her before I was born."

Ida glanced at the polygraph. It had been steady for his name and his parents' names; she expected to see a jump on it now, but it maintained its even level.

"Where were you born?" she asked.

"New York, New York, Earth."

"How old were you when you first told a lie?"

Ivan cocked his head at her again; there was something challenging about it. Ida watched him over the edge of her paper and waited.

"In the womb," Ivan said, and when Ida raised a brow, he said, "I pretended not to be my father's son."

From what Ida had seen of the pregnant Milla Ivanov at Connor Ivanov's trial, it was a fair assessment. She permitted him to see that she was amused by his little joke, but it did not seem to relax him at all. There were too many teeth in his smile.

"Now, Ivan," said Ida, and laid the paper down, "I want you to lie to me."

"Lie to you?" Ivan said. "I thought that was the one thing I wasn't supposed to do."

"Just this once. Lie to me."

"What should I lie about?"

"Anything," Ida said. "Whatever comes to mind."

He was cold; she could see him shivering lightly. But he said, "I can't think of anything. Tell me something to lie about."

He was very cautious. "Then tell me," said Ida, "how old you were the first time you stole something from someone."

He looked at her, blue eyes rounding, and said, "Ida, I've never stolen anything."

The polygraph jumped. It traced a wide arc over the pixelated surface of the screen, indicating a lie, lie, *lie* as loud as a scream.

Ida looked from the polygraph to Ivan sitting half naked and chained down before her.

"I want you to do that again," Ida said, "and this time I want you to really *try* to lie to me. How old were you the first time you stole?"

Ivan smiled.

"I've never stolen anything in my life," he said, and the polygraph did not so much as twitch.

Ida loved a challenge.

"Your partner's name," said Ida. "Is it Matthew Gale?"

"No," Ivan said, and the polygraph was perfectly steady. Ida gave him a look. "He usually goes by Mattie," he clarified.

He was toying with her. Ida asked, "Do you know the name of the Mallt-y-Nos?"

Ivan's good humor left him suddenly. No longer playing with her, he leaned forward, serious, straight mouth, and said, "Just to be *perfectly* clear, Ida. This time I am not lying."

Ida waited.

"I do not know the name of the Mallt-y-Nos," he said, and the polygraph, of course, showed no lie.

Domitian had been right; there was something strange about the *Annwn*'s computer. Althea had opened with her usual tricks, progressed to cleverer methods of manipulation, and finally resorted to frustrated brute force, but the machine refused to give up its secrets.

Domitian arrived shortly after she took a break from arguing with the machine to pace across the narrow space of the *Annwn*'s piloting room and glare at the machine from the opposite corner.

"What's going on?" he asked, and displayed no surprise at the sight of his ship's engineer standing in the corner of the room, attempting to melt the casing of the control panel with the hatred in her gaze. It was one of the many reasons Althea was so fond of him.

Althea pointed.

"They've programmed some sort of artificial intelligence into it," she said.

"Gale and Ivanov?"

"Yes." Althea left her corner to stalk back toward the computer. Every machine had a feel to it; the *Ananke* was majestic, brilliant but a little awkward, and loving. The *Annwn*, she had decided, was smug. Smug and arrogant and stubborn.

"Watch," said Althea. She bent over the keys again and swiftly typed out a string of code that should have overridden any restrictions and enabled her to take a peek at the computer's inner workings.

A pause.

TRY AGAIN, the computer suggested, in as condescending a tone as mere text could manage.

"Maybe you should try a different method," Domitian said, but when Althea looked sharply up at him to see if he was mocking her, his expression was as humorless as ever.

"Well, I did," said Althea. "I've tried everything. And watch."

"Bitch," she typed, striking each key a little harder than necessary, as if the computer could feel it.

It came swiftly back with WHORE.

"I don't understand," Domitian said. "Gale and Ivanov programmed some childish quips into it? Why is that stopping you?"

"It *learns*," Althea said, frustrated. To properly explain would require sitting Domitian down and going through all the methods she'd tried, and that presumed a degree of patience that she knew he didn't have. "It's like it knows somehow that I'm not Gale or Ivanov. It has, I don't know, personality."

"So there's a password," Domitian said, clearly trying for her sake to keep up.

"Of some kind, yes." Althea sighed. A software engineer who couldn't even manage some finicky software. This, combined with the *Ananke*, her own computer ailing of some unknown disease, had her frustrated and filled with an anxious, aching fear of failure.

"So can you get around it?" Domitian said in a tone that made it sound as if he had been waiting for some response from her.

She shook herself out of her thoughts.

"Eventually," she admitted reluctantly. "But I'm worried about the *Ananke*. If the virus has spread to the nav systems or the ventilation or if it starts to affect life support or weaponry or the core containment, we're all in trouble." It was not the only reason, but it would suffice.

"The first concern is the *Ananke*," Domitian said, and Althea could have hugged him, thrown her arms around his neck as if he were her father. "Fix the *Ananke* first, then come back for this. Miss Stays is confident she can get all the information she needs out of Ivanov; the *Annwn*'s computer is a secondary source of information. This can wait for a day or two."

"Thank you," said Althea, and meant it with all her heart. A day or two was a small amount of time but a vague one, and she would not look too closely into this gift of allotted time. "I'll disconnect the computer from the ship so that no hidden programs can come bite us in the—can become a problem. Hardware can't argue." Hidden programs were her main concern at this point. The *Annwn* could be programmed to self-destruct if, for instance, a certain amount of time passed without input from Ivanov or Gale. A ship like the *Annwn*, if it self-destructed inside the *Ananke*'s hold, would destroy the *Ananke* entirely.

Domitian clapped a hand on her shoulder.

"Work on that, then get back to the *Ananke*," he said, and left her.

The best way to ensure that the *Annwn*'s computer could not speak to the rest of the ship was to go through and sever every connection between the two. On a ship like the *Ananke* such an operation would not be possible; her computer was so entwined with her body that the only way to effect such a separation would be to kill the computer itself. But the *Annwn* was a more common make, and Althea knew exactly where were the nerves that connected the brain to the body.

It was difficult; the connections were often well hidden, buried deep inside the walls of the ship. Landed as the ship was, some of the *Annwn*'s rooms were on their sides or upside down, depending on their place in the ship. Althea did not walk through the main hall; she climbed up and down and around.

There were very many connections, hundreds, even thousands of wires. Each time she severed a connection, Althea drew it out of the wall, and when she had a bundle of wires, she wrapped her arms around them and carried them out of the ship, leaving their ends to coil uselessly on the ground of the *Ananke*'s docking bay, as if the wires had been vomited out the mouth of the *Annwn*.

The last few connections were the most important, in the piloting room. Althea climbed over the mass of severed wires into the room and went to kneel beneath the main interface.

A message was blinking on the screen. Curious, she craned her head up to read it.

WHAT HAVE YOU DONE? asked the computer.

I CAN'T FEEL MY BODY.

Althea severed the last connection, and the screen went black.

. . .

"The first thing I would like you to tell me about," said Ida, "is Eris."

"It's a dwarf planet in the outer solar system," said Ivan, deadpan. "What else would you like to know?"

"I want to hear about the theft you and Mattie committed on it," Ida said. "About four years ago." She smiled at him. "The theft that ended in an explosion."

Ivan grimaced at the memory. "You mean when we stole the bombs."

The bombs that Ivan and Mattie had stolen—and immediately detonated—were of the same make as the one that the Mallt-y-Nos had used against the Martian System representatives a year later: Eridian Class 50s. Ivan, of course, would know this was true as well, given that he had delivered the remaining bombs directly into the hands of the Mallt-y-Nos, but Ida suspected that he would not know that she knew.

Ivan leaned back in his chair although the metal must have been icy cold against his bare back. He was working hard to present an unaffected demeanor. "You have this on tape," he pointed out. "Or almost all of it on tape. There's surveillance everywhere, especially in armories. What do you need me for?"

"There are things," said Ida, "as you know very well, that can't be recorded by a camera." The camera had seen Ivan pretending to be a System representative and paving the way for Mattie to sneak into the facility, but it could not tell Ida why. "I want to know what you were thinking. I want to know what Mattie was thinking. I want to know why you went to Eris in the first place and why you stole a case of bombs only to explode them immediately afterward on the outskirts of the city."

"Mattie and I stole those bombs, and we blew them right afterward," he admitted, and he shifted position, sitting up a little straighter, moving into a different pose. "The whole thing is a bit of a story," he said with his con man smile. "You want to hear all of it?"

"Every last detail," Ida said.

Ivan was thinking, she could tell, wondering what he should tell and what he should keep a secret, no doubt. It didn't matter what he decided. Ida would get it all out of him eventually, one way or another.

"It started," said Ivan, "on Deimos. Mattie and I didn't steal them for ourselves: we got a commission. I wasn't in favor, but Mattie was, and so . . ."

"The commission," Ida said sweetly. "It was from Abigail, I understand."

Ivan stopped dead.

Ida spent a moment enjoying his derailment. It had only been a guess that Abigail Hunter had been responsible for the commission, but it had been a very good one and one that had, of course, turned out to be correct.

It was always good, especially at this stage of the interrogation, to keep her subject off balance.

To his credit, he recovered fairly quickly.

"Yes," Ivan said, his eyes darting between hers, "the commission was from Abby." He watched her for another moment, doubtless trying to gauge what precisely she wanted, but Ida kept her expression impenetrable. "Would you like to hear more about Abby," Ivan asked, "or would you prefer if I finished talking about Eris?"

"I'm interested in anyone who would commission you and Mattie for such an exciting theft." Ida wished she could see through his skull, into his brain, to watch what he thought, what he wondered.

She would get to see that soon enough.

"Abigail always shows up when we don't expect her," Ivan said. "You'd think we'd get used to that and start expecting her whenever we don't expect her, but it doesn't work. She just seems to know. This time, Mattie and I found her on board the *Annwn* just as we were about to leave from visiting Constance, Mattie's foster sister."

"Abby is also Mattie's foster sister, is she not?"

"Yes," said Ivan. "She is."

Ida prompted, "And is he fond of her?"

Ivan laughed. "Immensely."

"And is she fond of him?"

"As a person is of a dog," Ivan said with a bitter little twist to his lips.

This was interesting not for what he said but in that he had admitted it. "Your relationship with her is not easy, then," Ida said.

"Abby is selfish," said Ivan, flat and honest. "She doesn't care about Mattie or about me, not really." His blue eyes flickered up from the table to focus on Ida. "I don't think," said Ivan, and Ida wondered if she was imagining his deliberateness here, "that she really feels bad for anything she's done. She understands how other people think, but I'm not sure she really *empathizes*."

That old creeping fear was coming up Ida's spine again, the fear of discovery, but she did not let it show, did not break Ivan's gaze. He knew nothing, and his choice of words was a coincidence. "If you hate her so much, then why do you deal with her?"

"Mattie grew up with her," Ivan said with a shrug.

"And his affection for her outweighs your dislike?"

"Mostly," he said. "But also . . . there's something beautiful about her, about her and the way she doesn't care. The same way an explosion is beautiful. Something that could destroy you."

Ida could not tell for certain what weakness to strike at here—if there was one—and so she changed the subject. "What does Abby do?"

"Abby is a middleman," Ivan said. "She connects people who are interested in commissioning a theft or a bit of sabotage with the people who can do it for them. Sometimes she doesn't even connect with either end directly but is part of a chain of people like her, just to keep everyone's identity secret. She gets a fee for putting people into connection that is usually a percentage of whatever's being stolen. She'll work for anyone who can give her a high enough fee; she doesn't care what the job is."

Ida could hardly dare to hope that Ivan had admitted his connection so soon and so easily, but a part of her was delighted, anyway, that she was right in spite of all who did not believe her. "Might Abigail take a commission from a terrorist group?"

"She would," Ivan said, "but I don't know that they could pay her enough. Terrorists are poor. And even if they did, Ida, terrorists wouldn't use a single middleman; they'd use many. Abby would just be one in a chain. Even if she'd ever worked with the Mallt-y-Nos, she could no more tell you who the Mallt-y-Nos is than I can."

He was lying. Ida could not tell precisely how yet, and the polygraph showed nothing, but she knew that he was lying.

"I want you to describe Abby to me," she said. "Physically."

"Why?" said Ivan. "Just look at the picture in her file."

The picture in Abigail Hunter's file was twenty-five years old, and Ida had no doubt Ivan knew it. "Humor me."

"Tall," Ivan said. "Thin. She wears wigs to confuse surveillance and dyes her hair. I think she's naturally a blonde."

The description matched perfectly with an extrapolation of what the little girl whose picture was in Abigail Hunter's file could have grown up to be, but it was useless to Ida. "Do you have any pictures of her?"

"Abby doesn't like cameras," said Ivan. "No."

Ida nodded, thinking. If Ivan was lying, Domitian would find out; he was searching Ivan's ship even now. Perhaps by the end of this session tonight she would have a lever with which to break Ivan open.

"Before Eris, you found her in your ship," she prompted, and Ivan began again.

"The ship's door was unlocked; that's how we knew there was someone inside," he said. "We had our guns on us—we'd kept them hidden from Constance while we were at her place, of course. Back then, Constance didn't know what we did for a living—and we drew them before we walked into the ship. And there was Abigail, sitting right in the entryway, watching us like she wasn't impressed at all."

Ida tried to imagine it, to let it play out in her head as Ivan spoke, to compare what he said with the way she imagined it would have happened. Ivan and Mattie, walking together, elbows bumping. This was eight years into knowing each other, and they would move in harmony.

She imagined them coming to the *Annwn*, the ship standing on her rim, and finding the door unlocked, letting in bits of dust and sand from the howling Martian wind. They looked at each other, and Mattie drew his gun first—or did Ivan?

"Mattie was glad to see her somehow," Ivan said. "Even though she'd just broken into our ship."

In Ida's mind's eye, Mattie holstered his gun immediately, pulling the door shut against the howling winds. Ivan was slower to lower his weapon, and he put it away only once Mattie had embraced the woman waiting.

In Ida's imagination, Abigail was faceless, blank.

"She got right to the point," said Ivan. "Abby doesn't like to waste time. She told us that she had a job for us."

In Ida's mind, Ivan, standing opposite Abigail, was just as guarded and wary as he was when he was facing her.

"She told us that there was something she wanted us to steal off of Eris. Something from an armory, a box. She had all the information to get it: what the catalog number of the box was, which armory, where in the armory it would be, and the information about all the important employees."

"She didn't tell you exactly what she wanted you to steal?"

"No," said Ivan. "She knew that if she did, we would've refused to steal it."

"How noble of you," said Ida.

Ivan laughed. "That's not why. It would've been too dangerous to transport live bombs."

"You just accepted the lack of information?"

"No," Ivan said. "I questioned her. She wouldn't give me a straight answer."

"And at no point during the long trip from Mars to Eris did you think about what she might be asking you to steal?"

Ivan quirked a rueful smile. "We assumed it was a box full of files or at worst ammunition."

She could not tell whether he was being honest. "And when you were questioning her, did you ever ask her the source of all this information?"

"No," Ivan said. "Whoever it was had hired a middleman or three for a reason. If Abby didn't tell me, I didn't ask, because I didn't want to know."

"And Abby didn't volunteer the information," said Ida, just to be sure.

"Of course not."

"And of course she offered you a large payment for the completion of the job," Ida said.

"She did," said Ivan. "But that's not why we took it."

Ida raised her eyebrows at him, and he raised his in mockery back at her.

"I didn't want to help her," Ivan explained, "because we knew so little about what we were stealing and why. And because I didn't trust her."

"Then why did you help her?" Ida asked.

"She told us she needed us," said Ivan. "And that convinced Mattie."

Ida wondered if Mattie's defection had been expected or if Ivan had been taken aback by it. If he'd been hurt or if he'd been resigned.

"And once she had Mattie," Ivan said, "Abigail knew that she had me."

. . .

Althea crawled back out of the mutilated *Annwn*, trying to step carefully over the mangled wires torn from the insides of the ship, but somehow she kept slipping, the wires tangling around her ankles, grabbing at her feet.

She finally stumbled out of the gaping door of the hollowed-out *Annwn*, hopping off the tangle of wires as soon as a clear patch of her own *Ananke*'s floor presented itself to her. She sighed the moment she touched the metal. Now she could go back to her ship and spend the rest of the day focusing on that, on what was really important.

Domitian was hunched over the computer interface beside the doors leading out of the docking bay. Suppressing a sigh of a different kind, Althea diverted her steps to stand beside him.

"I'm having difficulty getting the computer to work," Domitian said, seemingly as calm as usual, but Althea could hear the difference and winced at the evidence of his annoyance. She nudged her way in under his arm, driving him to back away, though he still stood over her, presumably looking at the screen.

"What do you want it to do?" Althea asked.

"Scan a photograph."

"Is it in the tray?"

"It's in the tray."

"O-kay." Althea started small—there was always the chance that Domitian had been doing something stupid, and her computer was fine—and executed the normal command for a scan.

The machine all but exploded.

TEMPERATURE: 298 K

PRESSURE: 1 ATM

VOLUME: 308525.137 . . . METERS CUBED

PARTICLE NUMBER:

PARTICLE NUMBER:

PARTICLE NUMBER:

The screen began to scroll with the open-ended query repeated over and over again. Althea tried everything she knew to stop it, but it had frozen and would not respond. She tried not to be frightened—it was probably just a superficial error, and there was no benefit to panicking or jumping to the wrong conclusions—but temperature, pressure, and volume were all quantities related to the *Ananke*'s life support systems. Althea was sure she had fixed the error with the mechanical arm in the ventilation system, but if this was something different, if this was something worse—

PARTICLE NUMBER: 6, the computer finally concluded while Althea was still struggling with her fear and confusion.

In that moment of stillness, Althea jumped and tried to stop whatever program had inadvertently started to run. At the touch of her fingers on the keys, the computer woke again.

INTERACTION, said the computer. PRESSURE INCREASING.

And then, finally, at Althea's insistent attacks, the window closed, shut down, and the computer hummed and began to scan the image.

Althea surrendered the keys back to Domitian, but stayed put in case the computer stopped scanning in the middle. She wasn't sure what she had done to fix it, just as she wasn't sure what she had done to provoke such a response.

At the very least, she thought with guilty relief, it hadn't been the life support going awry. She was glad she had kept her head and not alarmed Domitian.

The image blinked into existence on-screen. It was of a young girl and a younger boy standing side by side. The boy had floppy brown hair and a wide, gap-toothed grin. He looked like he was about eight, and with a jolt, Althea recognized him—a very young Matthew Gale. The girl, who was nearer to ten, had her arm around the boy's shoulders. Her brown hair was curled and coiffed for the photograph, but unlike the boy, and in contrast to her affectionate gesture, she was not smiling. She stared straight at the camera with solemn brown eyes, and Althea found it hard to look away.

"If I run facial recognition, will it work?" Domitian asked, and so Althea leaned back over and took the keyboard from him.

To her relief, the program opened without a hitch and scanned the two young faces in the photograph, bright green lines appearing superimposed, decomposing the faces into their component planes before vanishing, leaving the image untouched, as before.

"It's checking the archives," Althea reported after checking to see that the program was in fact working correctly and doing just that. The data it got from the picture would be sent to the main System computers on Earth and compared with the database there of facial decompositions of all the System's citizens. It would take several minutes.

"Good," said Domitian, and bent down to pick up some drives scattered on the floor at his feet. They were not from the *Ananke*, and so he must have taken them from the *Annwn*. "Can I run these?"

The only honest answer to that question was a shrug. "Absolutely."

When Domitian slotted the drive into the machine, the computer whirred and presented the option to play video. Althea let out an internal sigh of relief.

Domitian let the video play, and a vaguely familiar face appeared on-screen.

It was a woman whose hair had gone white and whose pale skin had gone papery with age. She was on a stage, a screen behind her that was blank for the moment. She crossed the stage to stand behind a lectern and let her fingers rest on the outside of it, drumming out a strange arrhythmic pattern against the wood. Althea recognized who she was in two different ways—as Doctor Milla Ivanov, scientist and lecturer, and as the mother of the man imprisoned on board their ship.

Mother and son had precisely the same clear, brilliantly blue eyes. Althea's stomach clenched at the comparison, and she did not want to put into words why.

"Today," said Doctor Ivanov in a voice just too soft to be perfectly clear to everyone in the lecture hall, as Althea knew from experience in many lecture halls like it, "we will be discussing path-planning algorithms: traveling from one known point to another known point by an unknown path."

It was a publicly released lecture video, but Althea felt like a voyeur. Domitian had found it on the *Annwn*.

"That's his mother," she said.

"Ivanov's," Domitian confirmed. He was watching the screen intently.

Althea hesitated. "What are you looking for?"

"Any sign that they were communicating," Domitian said, and Althea glanced back at the screen to watch Milla Ivanov bring up a display of Dijkstra's algorithm behind her.

"This was a public broadcast," said Althea.

"There still could be some communication," said Domitian. "If they are communicating, it makes Doctor Ivanov an accomplice. With her history, the System will need to know that immediately. It's suggestive that it's on board Ivanov's ship in the first place."

Doctor Ivanov is his *mother*, Althea thought, but did not say it again.

"It is possible to bias your searching methods," Doctor Ivanov said, her clear blue eyes scanning the crowd before her impersonally, her fingers drumming in agitation. "However, in general, a bias may impede your attempts to proceed."

The computer chimed, indicating that the facial recognition program was completed. Domitian paused the video and opened the results.

The screen froze. It flashed black for an instant, then went back to normal before Althea could become alarmed.

NO MATCHES FOUND, said the computer.

"That's impossible," Althea said.

"I'll run it again," said Domitian.

This time, the response from the computer was almost immediate.

NO MATCHES FOUND, it insisted.

"That's impossible," Althea said again. "How old is this photograph?" It was just feasible that the photograph was from before the installed surveillance and had been well maintained, and the boy in the photo was not Matthew Gale, and fashions were coincidentally similar enough to be mistaken for a more recent year. That would be hundreds of years ago on the inner planets, but from the look of the sky, Althea thought this picture must have been taken on an outer moon, and if that was the case, it could be a few hundred years sooner than the latest possible date for the inner planets—

"The computer says between twenty and thirty years," Domitian said. Deeper lines were appearing on his forehead, a sign of his annoyance. "So that is impossible."

"The *Ananke* must be presenting a false negative somehow," Althea muttered, moving to take control of the computer back from Domitian, "misinterpreting the results being sent from Earth—I don't know how, but I bet . . ."

"No, don't." Domitian dropped his hand on her shoulder. "It's not worth your time. I'll communicate with Earth directly and have them run the photograph themselves instead of doing it through the computer."

"Are you sure?"

"I'm sure," said Domitian. "You focusing on this symptom won't fix the problem. Go work on the computer."

Althea lingered a moment longer, always unwilling to leave a problem unsolved.

"Go," Domitian said. "I need to watch these recordings." He smiled faintly at her as if he knew why she was hesitant, and Althea finally left.

Just as she opened the doors to the *Ananke*'s long spiraling hallway, the holographic terminal in the hallway nearest to the docking bay, without being touched, switched on and started to glow.

Althea let the doors close behind her and went to it to see what was wrong, but by the time she reached it, it had gone dark and quiet.

"The trip to Eris is a month long," said Ivan. "Do you want to hear the details of that, too?"

"Only if anything happened during it," said Ida.

"No," Ivan said, and Ida spared a glance at the polygraph. Truth, it said, but of course it had been saying that this entire time.

"What do you do during those trips?" she asked, leaning forward onto the cool brushed steel of the table. "To amuse yourselves. You and Mattie must get very bored."

"We talk," Ivan said. "We play games. We creatively reprogram our ship's computer. Whatever we think will pass the time. Sometimes I tell Mattie stories."

It was a strange detail, a caring one. Ida wondered if Ivan realized how much of himself he had revealed with that tiny little detail. He had to know, she thought. So why had he told her?

Scheherazade, she remembered. The nickname in parting. A revealing detail, certainly, but told to her in defense, out of necessity.

Leontios Ivanov did nothing by accident.

"You are a good storyteller," said Ida. Ivan would understand her meaning perfectly, she knew; the camera would miss it entirely. "What kinds of stories do you tell?"

Ivan leaned back in his chair. She noted how he still did not flinch when he touched the doubtlessly cold back of the chair with his bare skin. His guard was far up.

"All kinds. Mattie didn't really go to school," he said. "You probably have records of that. And when he did, he liked math and computers but not literature or history."

Ida raised her brows. "So you tell him stories from history," she said. "The plots of novels and poems."

"Yes," said Ivan.

"And once you reached Eris?" she asked.

"Once we reached Eris we did a short reconnaissance to make sure Abby's information was still correct. It was. Usually we'd spend longer planning a heist—a week or more—but Abby had gotten us all the information we needed, and we went in the next day."

"And she got that information from her employer?" Ida asked.

"She must have," Ivan said. "I didn't ask." He gave her a look like he was daring her to challenge that.

Ida didn't. He had not yet dug a large enough hole for himself for her to begin to bury him.

"Could she have gotten it herself?" she asked.

Ivan snorted. "No. She's terrible with computers, and that's the only way she could've gotten that information. She might have gotten some of her other contacts to find it out for her, but there's no way to tell."

"I see. Continue."

"I went to talk to the secretary," said Ivan. "Red hair in pigtails. She was cute. I don't remember her name; I think it was Irina . . . maybe Ursula . . . ?"

"Unimportant," said Ida.

"Alana," said Ivan, triumphant. "Her name was Alana. I talked to her for a bit. Softened her up."

In the surveillance tapes, Ida knew, Alana with the pigtails blushed as red as her hair when Ivan leaned over the edge of her desk.

"I told her I was there from the System to examine their surveillance system," Ivan said. "A surprise inspection. I had falsified credentials to back it up, and better than that, I could speak like this."

In the white room, he slipped effortlessly into a deeper Terran accent, sharper, harder. In the surveillance, Alana with the pigtails had an accent that was broad and uncultured.

"She called her superior, of course, once she found out why I was there," Ivan said, and the superior was a short balding man who came out of his office both scowling and looking nervous. "He'd been Terran once, too, but he'd spent so long on Eris, he was going native. What would you do, Ida, if all your representatives went native?"

"We are all members of the System, Ivan," Ida said. "The Eridians are his people, too."

Ivan smiled at her, scornful. "Of course. But he'd been true Terran System recently enough to doubt me. I only really convinced them who I was when I told them what I thought of them and their pathetic little moon."

Ivan was slipping back into the sharp, terse Terran accent he'd used just a few moments before.

"I told them that the outer planets were a scar on the face of the System," said Ivan, sounding haughty and cruel. "I told them that they had no control over their citizens. No true order. I told them that if the System had been wise, it would have destroyed all of them after Saturn tried to rebel, or put them under military control and kept it that way. They were a bunch of frozen, cold rocks, full of the stupid and the poor, who do nothing but beg for resources from our poor overtaxed Earth."

Perhaps he was trying to impress her with his acting, with the degree of his duplicity. Ida let him perform.

He smirked at her nonetheless. "After that, they believed I was System through and through."

Still he was performing.

"They let me into their main surveillance interface," Ivan said. "Mattie had already snuck into the place as a janitor. No one pays attention to the janitor. We had agreed on a prearranged order of surveillance interference. I let him know I was ready by briefly flickering the lights in the hall and then went room by room, switching the surveillance off and back on again, ostensibly checking it for flaws but really allowing Mattie to get in and out of the restricted areas undetected."

This part of the surveillance, of course, was full of holes, as Ivan did just as he said. Ida had watched it, fascinated, knowing that each time the camera turned off and then back on again, Matthew Gale had just passed unseen through that room. The timing was impeccable.

"I finished up, made my excuses, told them they would have their grading in a few days, and left to join Mattie in our rented vehicle. I wasn't concerned about being caught; it's nine hours at the speed of light between Earth and Eris, and by the time they found out I'd been a fraud, Mattie and I would be long gone from Eris."

Ida remembered the footage. An outdoor camera had just caught Ivan walking into a van parked a street away from the armory. It recorded him sliding into the passenger side and turning to talk to the man in the driver's seat, Mattie Gale with his hair mussed from the janitorial hat he'd taken off.

"And when did you realize that you'd stolen bombs?" Ida asked.

"In the van as we were driving away," Ivan said promptly. "We were going to rendezvous with Abby in an hour, so we just intended to drive to the rendezvous point immediately; it was out at the very edge of the terraforming shell. I went into the back of the van and got a crowbar—Mattie had one in the van, I don't know why; we couldn't possibly have used it, but I don't question the things he feels the need to carry around—and tore open the box. And inside," Ivan continued, "I found, stacked all neatly together, a full box of Class 50 bombs."

"And?"

"Mattie hadn't wanted me to open it," Ivan said. "He thought we shouldn't know. But I didn't trust Abby, so I opened it, and once he saw what was inside, he stopped defending her, too. We got to the rendezvous point before her, driving very carefully."

Planetary bodies like Eris, the ones that were too small or too inhospitable to be properly terraformed, had been encased or, as in Eris's case, partly encased in clear plastic enclosures like greenhouses. It was the only thing that could make them habitable, and so the enclosures were multilayered and strongly supported, with dozens of fail-safes and air locks all around them, and were divided into grids so that if one section failed, it could be separated from the rest. The only way into the enclosures was through man-made openings in them. In theory, all the openings should be System-manned; in practice, on far-off wild planetoids like Eris, they were little regulated if at all.

The explosion had taken place far from any of the towns, where the greenhouse enclosure touched the ground and dug deep into Eris's sooty stone, right where an unregulated air lock allowed access between the habitable area and the vacuum outside.

"The rendezvous was by an air lock," said Ivan, "for easy escape if we needed it. I went into the air lock, and I placed the bombs there in a pile. And then, when Abby came, I blew them up."

There was no footage of this; the cameras in that area of the enclosure had not been maintained. But the explosion had been real enough.

There was cleverness to Ivan planting the bombs in the air lock. They would blow the outer edge of the shell, which would trigger an alarm and slam shut the inner air lock, making a point without actually destroying the entire section of the enclosure or killing him and his companions.

"Mattie worked with you?" Ida asked.

"Mattie worked with me," said Ivan.

"And Abby?" Ida tried to picture it: Ivan standing with that same wary defiance opposite the faceless figure of Abigail Hunter, but this time with Mattie beside him, looking . . . looking unhappy, she decided. Disappointed. Uncomfortable. But in the end standing with Ivan.

The corner of Ivan's lips twitched. "She was furious," he said. "And Abby really can shout."

"You told her why you did it."

"Of course," Ivan said. "It would've been useless otherwise. I told her we'd destroyed her merchandise because she'd endangered us both. I told her she wasn't allowed to lie to us or put us in danger without our knowing."

"And she listened?"

"She listened," Ivan said. "She just didn't obey."

Ida smiled faintly. Ivan seemed to be waiting, or perhaps he thought he had come to the end of his story, so she said gently, "You didn't blow up all the bombs, of course."

"No," he said. "I saved one."

"And you gave it to Abby," Ida said.

"And I gave it to Abby," said Ivan.

Ida leaned forward. "Why?"

"Because I wanted to complete the job," Ivan said, "if only in token."

Ida cast a quick glance at the polygraph. Still steady. "Another insult."

"She took it that way," Ivan agreed.

Ida folded her hands on the table, her elbow nudging the sharp edge of the polygraph display. "Are you aware that the very same kind of bomb that you stole on Eris that day was used to kill the Martian System representatives a year later?"

Ivan tilted his head to the side. "Are you suggesting that it was the same bomb?" he asked, patronizing, amused, incredulous.

Acting.

"You tell me," Ida said.

Ivan huffed out a laugh and looked at her like she was being absurd.

"Do you realize the incredible improbability of that?" he asked, his brows down but his blue eyes wide. "The ridiculous impossibility of the single bomb that I held in my hand ending up in the hands of the Mallt-y-Nos a year later?"

"Not so improbable," said Ida.

Ivan shook his head as if he were shaking off her insinuation. "Do you know how many bombs of that same type are in black market circulation?" he asked. Ida did, in fact, but the numbers had done little to sway her conviction. "Thousands, Ida," Ivan said with his hands spread as wide as the chains would allow, his eyes searching her face. "Thousands. They're kept under System military control, but they're used for mining more often than murder, so they're not that hard to find, and if they're not hard to find, they're not hard to steal. And there are stockpiles of them in the strangest places."

Ida did not get so far as opening her mouth, but Ivan threw his palms up at her, anticipating her question. "I haven't seen any of those places," he said. "I've only heard of them. They found one on Haumea a few years back; do you remember? The planet's a penal colony now. Better fate than Saturn, but then again, the System had no reason to think anyone on Haumea was going to use those bombs against them."

"They had every reason to think that," Ida said. She had not been assigned to Haumea; it had been a near disaster. But bombs outside of direct System control and on an outer planetoid meant only one thing; that much was obvious.

"Every reason to think it, but no proof," Ivan said. "Proof seems important to me, Ida." He paused, studying her again. Ida knew she could hold up to any scrutiny, and so she let him look.

"Do you realize how much people hate the System?" he asked. "How much they *hate* it, completely hate it, not disagree with it on a few points but hate it actively and completely?"

Ida listened in silence and thought of how long Ivan had spent among the outer planets and around outer planetary men. He had forgotten what it was to be Terran.

"But they're also scared," Ivan said, as if Ida did not realize that. "The System watches them always. Any slight transgression is punished. There is no mercy, and there is no freedom, and there is no opportunity to do anything about it. The people on the outer planets live in fear. The slightest act that seems to be against the System will destroy their home and kill everyone on their moon, all in the name of stamping out infection before it can spread. The number of people who would be willing to steal for the Mallt-y-Nos is *long*. The number of people she could have bought the bomb from is even longer. Hell, if she faked the right documents, she could have gotten the bomb legitimately, for mining."

"I see your point, Ivan," Ida said without conceding it.

"Even if it was the same bomb," said Ivan, lowering his voice, frustration entering his tone, "my connection to her is at least three degrees long. I gave Abby the bomb, Abby either gave it to her benefactor—her employer was rich, which means he wasn't the Mallt-y-Nos—or her employer wouldn't take it, in which case she put it on the market, probably through an intermediary. If it made it to the Mallt-y-Nos, that bomb passed through so many hands, it no longer remembered mine, I promise you."

Ida had read a play long before. She no longer remembered the play, only a line from it, and at the moment it seemed to fit. Ivan was protesting too much.

She said only, "All right."

Ivan narrowed his eyes. "Are you saying you believe me?"

Ida laughed. "No, Ivan," she said. "I simply would like to move on. There's more I'd like to ask you."

"More?"

"Ivan, we've hardly begun."

He was wary, strung tight. Ida shuffled through the papers before her, buying herself some time. In the brief silence, she asked, as if casually interested, "You've heard the Mallt-y-Nos is planning something, haven't you? Something big?"

"Of course," said Ivan, who adopted an air of relaxation again, leaning against his chair shirtless and pale. "Everyone has."

"The Mallt-y-Nos," Ida said, "is a 'bomber,'" with a delicate turn on the word. She tapped the papers' edges into order and set the shuffled pages aside. "And bombs have been going missing."

Ivan watched her without any sign that her words had surprised him or alarmed him, without any sign that what she had said was a surprise or that he had already known, without any tells at all. Ida said, "Do you know how many Terran Class 1 bombs go missing every year, Ivan?"

"Enlighten me," Ivan said.

"Around seven," Ida said. "Seven of the System's most dangerous weapons go missing every year. Usually on the outer planets, where they've been placed for population control." The silent threat of a weapon powerful enough to entirely destroy the terraforming measures on a small moon did wonders to keep an unruly population quiet, but security far from Earth and among hostile people was hard to maintain with the same rigor as on Terran soil. "And by the end of the year, the System has found them all again. Usually they're only missing for less than a day before the thief is found and caught. Bombs that destructive are a tempting target for a would-be revolutionary, but the System has them well controlled." Terran Class 1 bombs were the very type that had depopulated Saturn's moons, and Ida knew that Ivan knew that. Ida said, "Do you know how many have gone missing this year?"

Ivan shrugged.

"The usual amount," Ida said. "About seven. But do you know how many have been found?"

"I don't know."

"None." Ida leaned onto the table. "Someone's organizing it. Someone has those bombs. Someone with enough infrastructure to get them and to keep them. Someone who likes bombs." She waited, almost holding her breath, watching for something on Ivan's face, some tell. "What do you think she's going to do, the Mallt-y-Nos, with all those bombs?"

She might be planning to attack multiple targets. She might be stockpiling them for a war that the System would never allow to come. Ida did not have enough information to tell. She knew only that no good could come of it, a terrorist having weapons each of which was powerful enough to depopulate an asteroid or small moon.

Ivan only smiled at Ida, showing his white teeth.

"You're the expert," he said. "Why don't you tell me?"

Chapter 3

TEMPERATURE

Ida awoke before her alarm could chime.

The cabin she had been allotted on the *Ananke* was small and strangely shaped; it had been another empty storage room before her arrival, when it had been hastily adapted to serve as a living space. She sat up on her cot, letting her mind and body come to focus, and with one hand brushed her smooth black hair out of her face.

The alarm went off. She lashed out and struck it, hard; the clock tumbled to the floor and lay silent. She shifted to slide her legs off the bed and bent down to pick up the toppled clock and place it, reset, back on the bedside table before crossing the room to the computer terminal, which glowed more brightly at her approach.

While the computer woke as well, Ida collected herself. She had another interrogation session with Ivan in a few hours: enough time to eat, to check the surveillance for a tale he'd told her the day before, and to plan what today's interrogation would cover.

Overnight the System had sent her the surveillance she'd requested. They also had sent her a pointed message inquiring about her progress, with a reminder of her deadline. Ida opened the first; for the moment, she ignored the second.

She had spent as much time watching surveillance of Ivan, looking for inconsistencies in the stories he told her, as she had actually spent interrogating him. She had found nothing yet, it was true, but that did not mean she could stop looking, especially not with the amount of time that had passed. And so Ida collected herself and turned all her attention to the screen before her.

On the surveillance, she watched Ivan and Mattie break into a bank. She watched them come out with a bag full of expensive documents. She watched everything happen precisely the way Ivanov had described it to her. There was hardly even a word out of place.

Just as in all the other surveillance records she had watched over the last few days, everything matched what Ivanov had told her. He was good, and he was very careful, and in five straight days he hadn't slipped up once. The interrogation was more difficult than she had anticipated. And it would take more time.

She watched Gale reach over and hook an arm around Ivan's neck as they left the bank, pulling his partner into a playful embrace. Ivan was grinning and pushed at Mattie's ribs, but not too hard.

It was a pity Gale had been allowed to escape. Perhaps when the System found the escape pod, and Gale's body inside, Ida would have the corpse brought to the *Ananke*.

This footage was a waste of her time. Ida shut it down.

Althea was waist-deep in the wall of the *Ananke* when she heard the footsteps. She'd thought that, perhaps, if she could isolate the instances in which the *Ananke* produced errors, then maybe she could figure out their cause. Not treating the symptoms but freezing the symptoms in place so that she could see what had spontaneously produced them and then track that thread back to the origin.

The computer terminal Althea was now beneath had been flashing like a beacon, a strange pattern of white and black that seemed not to repeat or to have any sort of pattern, some flashes long and others short. It had turned the hallway into a freeze-frame film with its flashing brilliance, an unsteady strobe light that had disoriented Althea as she came closer and closer to its source, frantic shivering brightness like the ship seizing.

Althea had turned down the brightness on that screen so that it would not burn itself out, but the flashes continued dimly. If she looked down the line of her body as she lay on the floor, she could see her feet sticking out into the hallway and watch the shadows on her trousers flicker and shift with every shudder and flash of the still-seizing screen.

Anything Althea did with the software would be likely to be affected by the same virus that was causing the flashing anyway, so she took inspiration from what she had done to the *Annwn* and disconnected the wires attaching this interface to the rest of the computer, carefully and swiftly severing them from each other.

She was right in the middle of this process, jimmying out a wire from a connection that had gone stiff and stubborn with custom, when she heard the footsteps.

They were not familiar steps; they did not have the solid heavy sound of boots but were a lighter click, click of heels. Unless Gagnon—or—a more disturbing thought—Domitian—had a fetish Althea hadn't known about before, the footsteps that now rang out down the hall belonged to Ida Stays.

For the most part, Althea had managed to avoid her for the last five days. Now Althea hoped that Ida would see that she was busy and simply pass her by.

The clicking heels slowed and stopped. Peering out through the panel in the wall, Althea could see that they had stopped a foot away from her hip. The pointed toes of the black heels cast shifting shadows in the screen's flashing light.

"Doctor Bastet," Ida Stays said in her Terran accent. She sounded sweet, but Althea did not think she was imagining the ominousness of Miss Stays's address.

As much as Althea would have liked to pretend she had not heard the interrogator, ignoring such a high-ranking System officer would be both implausible and unwise. "Yes?" she said cautiously.

"I would like to know when you think you will have successfully managed to obtain the information contained on the *Annwn*."

Althea had not been on board the *Annwn* since she had left it four days previously. There had been too much to do on the *Ananke*.

"The *Ananke* is still malfunctioning," she said.

"I can see that." The heels shifted, angling the points of the toes directly at Althea. From inside the wall, Althea could not see Ida's expression, but at least Ida could not see hers, either. "Regardless, I would like the *Annwn* to be processed."

Because Althea could not say no outright, she tried again. "The *Ananke*—"

"I am aware of the condition of the *Ananke*," Ida said, as swift and harsh as the lash of a whip. Althea recoiled against the solid metal of her ship. "I expect you to do your job. The *Annwn* is crucial to my investigation, and I have requested your assistance."

There could be nothing more clear than the fact that Ida's request was no request at all. Althea lay motionless and silent, half inside her ship, until Ida seemed to take her silence as acquiescence and those black heels stepped delicately over Althea's prone body to continue down the hall.

The irregular pattern of light still flashed in the small square of hallway that Althea could see.

"Wait," said Althea, and slid back out of the wall, sitting up in the hallway. Ida Stays had stopped farther down the hall and was looking at her with something terrible and foreboding in her expression, and that nearly froze Althea's tongue. "I just wanted—I wanted to ask—has Ivanov said anything about the ship?"

Miss Stays frowned, her shaped eyebrows pulling inward. She was pretty and put together, sleek hair brushed and cropped, her white blouse without a wrinkle, and Althea felt even smaller sitting on the floor in a day-old uniform with her hair tangled and uncombed.

"About the *Annwn*?" Ida asked.

"About the *Ananke*."

"It has not yet come up in my investigation," said Ida, dismissive, and she started to turn, but Althea steeled herself and said, "It's just that he might know what's going on with the ship."

Ida turned slowly, incredulity in her expression. "Excuse me?"

"The virus," Althea said. "He might know. What it is." Her courage was failing her with every second spent under Ida Stays's cold gaze.

"If it comes up," Ida said, "I will let you know. Until then, the *Annwn*."

Althea almost spoke one last time to ask Ida to ask Ivanov, but caught herself before she could. Ida Stays walked away, the clicking of her heels fading into the distance.

Althea sat beside the still-flashing screen for a time without moving, a part of her thinking that perhaps she should go to the *Annwn* immediately, another part still focused on her ailing *Ananke*.

In the end she lay back down underneath the terminal and resumed where she had left off. She'd work on the *Annwn* right afterward; she would. She just had to finish what she was doing, and then she would follow her orders.

"Two years ago," said Ida. "March."

Ivan was wearing a shirt today, and pants—hospital garb from the *Ananke*'s infirmary, as there had been no other clothes to give him four days prior. They were thin and white, and what little gold there was in his hair and his stubble seemed darker in comparison to the white of his garb.

"You mean during the surveillance slip on Ganymede," said Ivan.

"That is what I mean," said Ida. Ivan certainly had been in the outer solar system at the time, and that was precisely the kind of technological sabotage he and Gale would have been skilled enough to effect.

"Mattie and I were out in interplanetary space between Jupiter and Saturn," Ivan said. "Robbing System supply ships." There was a taunt in his words.

Ida was no longer sitting but standing behind her chair, leaning on its back. She found she preferred this as the interrogation dragged on; she could look down at Ivan from above.

"Why?" she asked.

"Is that a serious question?"

"System supply ships bring valuable material to the outer planetary moons," Ida said. "Materials they can't produce themselves. Materials the outer planets need to survive. Why do you rob them?"

"They don't only carry supplies," said Ivan. "They carry valuables. Luxuries. We steal those."

"But you leave all the necessary supplies," said Ida.

"Why would we take them?" Ivan asked. He had a strange half smile, as if he did not understand why she was asking these things, and the look he gave her was amused, as if he were inviting her into the joke. "The people who would buy them can't afford to pay. We don't steal without pay."

It had a logic that appealed to Ida. She let it pass.

"How do you rob them?" she asked.

"Mercurian fire drill." The memory seemed to be a funny one for him. "We pretend to be System, tell them there's something wrong with their vessel and we need to check it. It's the same tactic some viruses use to infect a computer. Tell the system they're there to help, the user lets them in, and then, once they're past the defenses, they do whatever they like."

"And while you're fixing their vessel, you rob them."

"We rob them blind." Ivan's teeth flashed white.

"And while you were in interplanetary space," said Ida, "between Jupiter and Saturn, did you ever go to Ganymede? While surveillance was down, it seems to me like that would have been the perfect time to commit some undocumented crimes."

"We actively avoided it, actually," Ivan said. "Ganymede was in chaos. I have no desire to be in physical danger for a few petty thefts."

Ida moved out from behind her chair to advance closer to Ivan, leaning one thigh on the armrest and bending forward. He would look at her when she leaned like this, look at her and be stupid, the way men were.

"I'd like to hear," Ida said in a lower, sweeter tone than before, "exactly how close you were to Jupiter while you were in 'interplanetary space.'"

Ivan's eyes were fixed on her face. The polygraph, she noticed, showed only the slightest increase in heart rate.

"I have no idea," he said. "Maybe within a half AU."

Ida had calculated the radius of his possible locations based on his and Gale's last known location. Half an astronomical unit was a good choice; it was just within the outer edge of possibilities. She wondered if he'd calculated it in his head or if it was true.

"That's near enough to communicate with Ganymede," she pointed out.

"It is," he admitted.

"A half AU," she said, "is near enough to have interfered with the System-run computer systems controlling the surveillance on Ganymede."

He was smart or he was guilty or he was both; he must have anticipated where she was going with her questions because he did not look surprised.

"Yes," he said, "but the System has a series of relays to ensure messages are passed between planets without too much distortion. Any attempt to interfere with Ganymede's surveillance could have been made through that same series of relays. That is, the sabotage could have been completed from anywhere in the System."

"You've thought about this a good deal," Ida said.

"A child wouldn't have had to think long about it to come up with that explanation," said Ivan, acid in his tone.

"It's another possibility, certainly," Ida said, and leaned forward again, sliding off the arm of the chair so that she could loom farther over Ivan. "But I'm not convinced. You still don't have an alibi."

"Mattie and I were playing at being highwaymen," Ivan said. "Do you know how much time that takes? We didn't have the time to hack into a businessman's private computer, much less System surveillance."

Ivan was on the defensive. She could see it on his face and on the polygraph, hear it in his voice, watch it in the curl of his hands against the rests of his chair.

"I'm not convinced, Ivan," she said softly. "I think you may be keeping something from me."

"I'm keeping nothing from you," Ivan said, and Ida marveled at how sincerely he could speak so obvious a lie.

"Can you give me the names of some of the ships you robbed?" she asked.

She watched him realize that he couldn't. Ida could have looked up what System ships were robbed at that time in that place and extrapolated which ships were robbed but never reported it to the System for fear of prosecution, but if Ivan could not name any of the ships he had robbed then, then he might as well have not robbed any.

The names of System ships must have been irrelevant to him, he who had such a good memory for the things people said or did.

She saw the moment he remembered.

"The *Oenone*," he said. "One of the ships we robbed was the *Oenone*."

"That gives me only one ship, Ivan," Ida said with a frown that edged near to a pout. "How do I know what you were doing the rest of the time, when you weren't robbing the *Oenone*?"

"You can look it up. You know where Mattie and I were; you can check the System databases for other supply ships that were robbed," said Ivan, suddenly brazen now that he had nothing left to do but call her out and hope it was a bluff. He was so very transparent sometimes.

And yet, for all she understood him and his emotional reactions, she hadn't been able to trip him up.

"And what if I don't find that any other ships were robbed in that time in that place?" Ida asked.

"You will," Ivan said with certainty.

Unfortunately, she had been bluffing. She had no doubt she would find other accounts of robberies at that time, though she would be certain to check. She did not let Ivanov know that he had won, however, but straightened up without losing her pleased, smug expression.

"Why do you remember the *Oenone* out of all the ships you robbed?" she asked, mostly as an afterthought.

Perhaps Ivan was relieved that she had ceased to press him for information he could not produce. Or perhaps he did not think anything of answering, "Because we were nearly recognized."

"Who nearly recognized you?"

"The captain," he said. "He'd been a System administrator on Ceres we'd robbed once."

Ida could have waited, could have gone back to her room and looked it up: the captain of the *Oenone* two years earlier who had once been a System administrator on Ceres, when he had been robbed. But her senses were all screaming at her that there was some connection to be made here, that there was something important waiting to be uncovered.

"When were you on Ceres?" she asked, gripping the back of the chair tightly.

The polygraph jumped. It could have been the noise of the machine, it could have been an accident of the program, it could have been an abnormality in Ivanov's physiology. Ida did not think so.

"Seven years ago," said Ivan.

It was the very instincts that had led her to ask about Ceres that always led her to the correct conclusion; it was those very instincts that made her so good; it was those instincts that would show the System she was right about Gale and Ivanov. Because seven years ago on Ceres was an important date and place.

"And was that," Ida asked, trying hard not to show her excitement, "around when a System bank was bombed on Ceres?"

Ivan hesitated.

"Yes," he said, as if the hesitation had just been remembrance, casting his mind back, and not a frantic attempt to find a lie, which Ida *knew* it had been. "It was the exact same day."

When the terminal finally was isolated, Althea climbed out from underneath it and faced the flashing screen.

At first the screen would not react to her. She tried gentle methods, then less gentle ones—shortcuts that should immediately shut down whatever program was running—with no effect. It was only when she reached underneath the display, back into the ship, and shut down the terminal as a whole that the screen finally went dark and stayed that way.

She waited, then started up the terminal again. The home screen appeared, and Althea could interact with it, but the screen was still dimming and brightening again in a patternless cycle. Some sort of video error, then.

Reassured by the clarity of the source of this error, at least, Althea delved into the code of the *Ananke*.

It was a curious error when she found it, nestled in the code for the video display of this particular computer terminal. It was ugly code, ragged and full of nonsense, dead lines of useless code surrounding the functional bits. It seemed that some of the nonsense was what was causing the screen to flash.

Althea cleaned it out, and the screen stopped flashing, growing calm again. Then she started to track down the source of the error.

The ship itself had implanted it, as far as she could tell, as part of the *Ananke*'s automatic updates. Althea looked for what had provoked the ship to make such an update, but all she found was nonsense, references to the malfunctioning camera feeds.

And then she found something strange. In the back of the *Ananke*'s brain, buried underneath a thousand more important programs that took more time and more energy, there was one little program running in an endless loop.

She opened it.

TEMPERATURE: 293 K

PRESSURE: 1 ATM

VOLUME: 308525.137 . . . METERS CUBED

PARTICLE NUMBER: 6

ENTROPY: UNKNOWN
ENTROPY: INCREASING

The numbers blinked on and off as they were updated over and over again. It was the same error she and Domitian had seen when trying to watch the video of Milla Ivanov.

Althea hesitated, watching it loop and loop, and then moved to terminate it. The program shut down, and she removed it from the computer terminal without any trouble at all.

While she frowned down at the screen before her, something flashed bright farther down the hall.

A computer terminal up the hall had started to flash on and off.

"Damn it," Althea said, and left her disconnected terminal to jog up to the other one, staring down in dismay at the error that had propagated even though she had cut off its origin. If the error was traveling, even like this, it meant that there was a deeper flaw and she could not hope to treat the computer by separating each of its parts and figuring out what was wrong with them.

Abruptly, the screen ceased to flash. Althea reached forward toward it, but before she could lay a finger on a key, sound blared out of the speaker, shouting loud and with all the force of a blow, disembodied voices echoing through the hallway.

"This is for Europa," said the recorded voice of Matthew Gale, overlaid with Althea herself muttering inaudible code, and Domitian barking orders to search the ship, and Ivanov saying, "It was the exact same day," and Gagnon rambling about pions and the sweet high voice of Ida Stays saying, "The Mallt-y-Nos is a bomber," and Ivanov telling a story and Gagnon reciting equations and Domitian speaking to Ida and Ida questioning Ivanov and Althea talking to herself, talking to herself about the state of the ship, the whole thing a meaningless jumble of useless ineffectual communication, building to a roar—

Althea shut off the speakers, and the hall fell silent.

The screen blinked once more and then returned to blankness. Althea found that her hands were shaking, and when the intercom hummed and spit to life, she jumped and swore.

"Althea. Domitian," said Gagnon, sounding terse, nervous. "I need backup."

Althea pressed her hand to her breast and tried to catch her breath.

"There's someone in the pantry," said Gagnon.

. . .

This was the moment Ida lived for. Ivan had slipped, and now Ida could catch him.

"Why were you on Ceres?" she asked.

"For the same reason I told you," Ivan said. "Mattie and I heard of some System administrator, the guy who was later the captain of the *Oenone*, but at the time he was the one in charge of Ceres's water mining and water exports to the outer planets. That meant he was rich. We went to rob him."

"A rich man on Ceres?" Ida asked with a gentle scoff, and dug her fingers more tightly into the top of the chair.

Ivan smiled humorlessly. "Water transport is a valuable business," he said. "The man was rich. We went to rob him, not to steal things from his house but to get to his personal computer. People trust their computers too much. It's easier for me and Mattie to go into someone's house, have their computer sign in automatically to their System banking account, and then transfer or deposit the money to another account than it is for us to actually rob the bank. Once the money's been transferred, another person goes to a branch of the bank and withdraws it before the mark knows it's been transferred. Simple."

"A two-person con," said Ida. "One to sneak into the house, the other to withdraw at the bank."

"Well," said Ivan with a dryness so complete that Ida could not help admiring it, "we were two people."

"I assume you were at the bank and Mattie was at the house," said Ida, and Ivan inclined his head, conceding the obviousness of her conclusion. "Was the bank you visited the one that exploded?" If she could place him at the scene of the crime . . .

"No, it was a different branch," said Ivan. "Lucky for me." His smirk her way seemed to also say, Lucky for *you*.

"The asteroid was locked down within ten minutes of the bombing," Ida said. "You couldn't possibly have gotten off it in time if you didn't know about the bombing beforehand, especially if you and Mattie were in different places." She knew for a fact that Gale and Ivanov had not been on the planet after lockdown; the citizenry had been thoroughly vetted afterward for anyone who might have had a criminal connection.

Ivan took a breath. Ida held hers.

"That's because," Ivan said slowly, "I knew about the bombing beforehand."

She *had him*.

The elation rose up fast enough to nearly choke her, but she tamped it down as fast as she could, before it could stretch her lips in a smile. She had him, she knew she did, but she would not have him in the eyes of the System—in the eyes of her colleagues—until she had just a little more evidence.

"Did you?" she asked, making her voice quiet and sweet to cover up her elation. "That is something you should have mentioned before."

If she spun it right, perhaps she could even convince her superiors that this counted as a lie of omission, and she would be authorized to use the Aletheia—

"Why?" Ivan asked. He was putting on a good front of genuine bemusement, but Ida knew better. "It has nothing to do with the Mallt-y-Nos. And I hadn't gotten to that part of the story."

"It has a good deal to do with the Mallt-y-Nos," Ida told him. "This is certainly one of her earliest acts of terrorism."

"The Mallt-y-Nos didn't come onto the scene until the Martian bombing," said Ivan, frowning.

"Don't be disingenuous," Ida snapped, then took a breath and softened her tone. "Of course the Mallt-y-Nos was committing acts of terrorism before that. That's just what made her name."

Ida glanced toward the polygraph. Everything was slightly increased, showing Ivan in a state of apprehension.

"How did you know about the bombing?" she asked. "And why were you on Ceres if you knew the attack was going to occur?"

"We didn't find out until we were already there," Ivan said. "Just an hour before it blew, actually."

"And who told you?"

Ivan hesitated. "Abby did."

"Abby," said Ida, and relished the name.

"Abby," Ivan said, with mockery in his mimicry. "Yes, it was Abby. She sent us a message as we were on our way to Ceres, warning us to avoid it but not why. Because it was from her, I made Mattie ignore it. Somehow she found out we ignored her order. While I was waiting across the street from a smaller branch of the System bank, she contacted Mattie and told him we needed to run immediately, and why. Mattie dropped the heist midway through, picked me up, and we got off the planet just before the largest branch blew. We'd already transferred the money, though, so the future captain of the *Oenone* had good reason to remember our faces from the surveillance footage."

Ida couldn't care less about the captain of the *Oenone*. "How did Abby know?"

"I don't know."

"No?" said Ida, dangerous.

"I don't," Ivan said sharply. "I told you, her job is to make connections. She has very good contacts. I assume one of them warned her, and so she warned us."

"Or she could have known because she was involved."

"Abby wasn't involved." Ivan's tone was flat.

"And why not?"

"Because she's a mercenary. She works for money. Terrorists don't have money."

"But you don't know."

"I don't have proof of her lack of involvement if that's what you mean," Ivan said.

"What if this was a cause she embraced?" Ida asked.

"It isn't her cause."

"But you can't prove that, either."

"It isn't her cause."

"Why not?"

"Because that's not what she's like!" said Ivan.

Ida considered him. He was leaning forward in his chair, trying to impress her with the sincerity of his brilliant blue eyes. His arms were still chained to the rests of the chair, which rattled when he moved. The wires of the polygraph, thin and violet like veins, came out from underneath the white of his shirt and hooked into the wildly oscillating machine. He had no power, no control, and he was bluffing. Yet he was bluffing well.

"I don't believe you," Ida said.

Ivan cocked his head to the side, tilting his chin up in challenge.

"Then why don't you find Abigail and ask her about it?" he said. "I can't tell you anything."

"It's a bad idea to lie to me," Ida said, pacing around the table to stand near him so that she could lean over him. Bluffing or not, if he didn't break, she would have nothing but suspicions to show for this line of interrogation.

"I'm not lying," said Ivan, clear and guileless, and the polygraph showed no lie at all. "Look, she didn't even tell us until we were already on the planet. If she'd had something to do with it, she would've told us why we should avoid Ceres before we ever got there. Because she didn't have anything to do with it, she protected her contacts by not telling us anything. And if I'd known, if she'd known and she'd told me, Mattie and I would have never gone near the place." He was keeping up his innocent act the whole time; Ida almost found it impressive, except she knew how much of it was an act. He had to break. He had to.

"Whatever you think of me," said Ivan, "I don't want to die anonymously in some explosion on some petty dwarf planet."

"But you would plant a bomb," she said, her tone hard and sharp, "if you were paid enough."

"No," Ivan said, and he sounded so serious that for a moment she believed him. "I'm a thief, not a murderer."

"Then what do you call the *Jason?*" Ida asked.

A strange shudder passed over his face, there and then gone just as swiftly. The polygraph measured a jump at the same moment.

"Mattie killed them," said Ivan, flatly. "I just helped clean up after."

There was no footage from the last moments of the *Jason;* Ida had hoped to catch him in weakness. There was weakness here, anyway, even if he hadn't killed the crew himself.

"So you're not a killer, then?" she asked.

"No."

"You've got a soft heart," she said, mocking, and he shot her a dangerous look.

"Yes," he said, sarcastic.

"You don't want to kill anyone," she said. "How good of you." She paced back around to her empty chair.

"If you're trying to get at something, you're missing your mark," he snapped.

"I don't miss my mark," Ida snapped back, but he was holding firm against her, and she felt wrong-footed, unsteady. She took a breath and leaned down onto the table on her hands.

"Let's talk about Ceres, Ivan," she said.

"We just did, *Ida*."

"We're going to go over it again."

By the time Althea reached the kitchen, Domitian was already there. The kitchen, with the adjoining mess hall, was long but narrow; the kitchen side of the room was cramped with cabinets and counters, the wide refrigerator wedged into a narrow space between counter and wall so that it was almost impossible to open all the way. A few feet away from the fridge was the door to the pantry, which was shut for the moment.

"You're sure of what you heard?" Domitian was asking Gagnon as Althea came in, one hand already on the butt of her gun.

"I'm positive," Gagnon said. "I was getting breakfast before I went to relieve Althea. I was sitting right over there." He gestured to the opposite end of the room, where the one dining table was welded to the steel wall. "From inside the pantry, I heard a crash."

"You didn't investigate?"

"I didn't have my sidearm," Gagnon admitted, and Domitian sighed but did not take the time to dress him down. "There's no way in or out of the pantry," said Gagnon a trifle defensively. "Not with the maintenance shafts shut down again."

Althea said, "Let's go in there, then."

There must have been someone else on board the *Annwn*, someone Domitian hadn't found in his sweep of the ship. Althea felt almost elated. If there was someone on the ship, it would explain all the problems she'd been having with the computer. Whoever it was, he or she could have been coming out when there was no one around, taking a route that avoided all of the *Ananke*'s working cameras, stopping at a computer terminal and undoing all the work that Althea had done, adding in more chaos and making it so that Althea couldn't possibly figure out—

"Stay back." Domitian didn't bother with the knob. He simply kicked in the door. Althea followed him in, her gun out now and feeling awkward and too large in her hands.

The pantry was small; the vast majority of food supplies were stored in the base of the ship in a room kept in a vacuum. The pantry of ready food had only three rows of shelves with a clear line of sight to the opposite wall down each aisle, and Althea and Domitian swiftly covered all the space.

Her aisle was empty. "Clear."

Domitian had lowered his gun. He cast her a look she couldn't read and set off down the aisle he had been checking. Gagnon shrugged at her, and Althea holstered her gun before following them both to the end aisle.

The walkway of this aisle was choked with boxes. Looming over the fallen pile was one of the *Ananke*'s mechanical arms used to check the pantry supplies for expirations. As Domitian advanced, stepping carefully over the boxes, the robot arm blinked red at them and wheeled back a few paces before stopping and staying still.

"That's what I heard," Gagnon said, gesturing at the pile.

Domitian turned his attention to Althea. Behind him, the robot arm's sensors blinked red at them again, and Althea understood perfectly.

"Ananke," she said clearly. "Grab box 12, column 45, row 3."

The robot arm whirred distressingly, then reached up for the requested box but overshot, knocking the box over to the left. It chattered back and forth in place, trying to get the box and succeeding only in knocking over the boxes in the entire area.

"I didn't hear the arm," Gagnon said, palms out. "I didn't," he insisted to Domitian.

"The localization is off," Althea said. She thought of the problem with the robotic arm in the ventilation system, which she had not yet told the others about, but this was not the time to share that particular detail. She had fixed it, anyway. "The cameras in this room aren't working, so the arm has to rely on its internal sensors, and those aren't as reliable."

She wondered if it was the same error that had spread to this mobile arm, if the errors in the *Ananke* were more closely connected with the mechanical limbs than she had expected or this was just another symptom of the deeper problem, if she should expect more of the robotic arms to begin to fail.

"Exactly!" said Gagnon. "The cameras in here aren't working!"

"Exactly what?" Domitian demanded. "There's no way in or out of this room, and there is no one in here."

"There's the maintenance shafts," said Gagnon.

Domitian's brows went up. "The maintenance shafts?" he said. "The maintenance shafts are shut down. Aren't they?"

"They are," Althea said, "but I'll check." Her initial fervor for the idea of a second stowaway had faded in the face of her concern over this continued malfunction, but she went to the computer interface embedded in the wall and did a quick check on the maintenance shafts.

Sure enough, the ship reported that the shafts were still shut down, uninhabitable, sealed. She tapped the screen and turned to look at Gagnon. "The computer reports no one has gone into or out of the maintenance shafts since Gale left the ship."

Gagnon deflated. With circles beneath his eyes almost as dark as Althea knew hers were and with his long red hair coming out of its ponytail, he looked very tired and very unreliable, and Althea felt a surge of almost unreasonable frustration at this waste of her time.

"It was a machine malfunction," she said. "It was just the computer."

"Of course it was the damn computer," Gagnon muttered. It was unfair, and Althea almost snapped at him, when there was the mechanized sound of an engine whirring and gears turning, and Domitian said sharply, "Hey."

Althea turned in time to see the arm wheeling forward, extended, pincer hand opening and shutting, grasping, moving faster than she had thought it could. Domitian was behind it, and Gagnon was behind her, and the arm was heading straight for Althea.

She scarcely heard Domitian and Gagnon shouting, scarcely noticed them coming forward, their arms extended, reaching for the machine, for her, as she backed away into the wall and the arm still rushed forward. Gagnon came into her peripheral vision; the arm swung wildly and knocked him aside. Domitian was still shouting something, but all of Althea's attention was on the arm as it reached forward and the pincer fingers closed around strands of her hair.

Its momentum still drove it forward into the wall behind Althea, and the clenched robotic hand struck the wall with a hollow sound, Althea's hair sticking out of its grip as she leaned against the wall, trapped. The arm wheeled back a few centimeters, then forward again, striking the wall once more. It repeated the motion, rocking back and forth, striking the same spot on the wall while Althea stood very still.

"Al, come out of there," Gagnon said. At their closest, the wheels of the arm's base came within a few centimeters of Althea's toes.

She spoke as calmly as she could. "It has my hair."

The robotic arm struck the wall again, with more force this time, so that the entire panel Althea was leaning on rattled under her back.

Someone's hand gripped the robotic arm at the pivot of its wrist and managed to pull Althea's hair out of the machine's grip. As soon as she was free, she slipped under the arm and out as it slammed into the wall again.

There was a dent in the panel of the wall beside where Althea's head had been.

Domitian had been the one to free her, but Gagnon grabbed her as soon as she was free and pulled her back a little behind him. "Is the ship trying to kill us?" he asked, sounding half serious, as the arm rammed the wall again.

"The arm can't kill you," Althea said. "Not without some serious modifications."

"Yeah, but it—"

The arm swung around and advanced forward again, straight for Althea. Domitian moved forward as if he had some stupid idea about grabbing it, and Gagnon shouted and moved to push Althea further back, but Althea dodged them both and the swing of the ship's mechanical arm and got behind the arm, where she knew the switch was; she shut it down as she had done with the robotics in the ventilation system. The arm rolled to a stop, and its hinges went loose, the pincer hand dangling to point limply at the floor.

For a moment, none of them said anything; they only stood there, breathing heavily. Althea's mind ran at the speed of light through all the possible reasons the ship could have gone so violently awry.

Domitian said, "Until you can find out what caused that and fix it, all the autonomous arms need to be shut down." Althea sighed but nodded. One error was a fluke; a second was the beginning of a pattern.

"What, all of them?" Gagnon asked. "They're all over the ship."

"That's why they need to be shut down," Domitian said. "In case any of them are malfunctioning the way this one is."

"Yeah, but you can't just shut them down," said Gagnon. "Our workload will triple if we have to take on all the duties that the arms usually perform."

"I think in this case it is better that we play it safe," said Domitian. "Althea?"

The first error in the robotic arms had been merely frightening, not actually dangerous, but the second error—no matter how accidental and probably unreproducible—nearly had injured her.

She did not want a third error to harm anyone in the crew.

"If this is what they're doing," said Althea slowly, her eyes on the still, hulking figure of the disconnected arm, "we can't let them run."

The rest of the interrogation proceeded fruitlessly. After she ordered Domitian to return Ivanov to his cell, Ida returned to her room, sat down, and breathed.

She needed some perspective. Certainly, Ivan's story had gone nowhere, and she had come close to catching him only to fail. That was a disappointment. But she was by no means out of options. She would check surveillance footage on Ceres to find any discrepancies in Ivan's story, though she doubted there would be any.

More important, the case for Abigail Hunter's connection to the Mallt-y-Nos had grown significantly. She at least could report that to her superiors and intensify the manhunt. Even for someone as careful as Abigail, for whom the System did not even have a recent photograph, there was only so long she could hide.

And Ivan had slipped up. She was certain he hadn't intended to mention the events on Ceres at all and had brought them up inadvertently in trying to make her believe his alibi for another event. If she could make him slip up once, she could make him slip up again, and sooner or later, she would catch him.

She had ordered Domitian to join her once he was finished settling Ivanov in place. It was time to move to the next stage of her interrogation, and for that she would need him.

The next stage of the interrogation would require a good deal of preparation. Ida took out a pad of paper and a pen while she waited and began to make a list.

The first name was obvious: MATTHEW GALE. She wrote it down.

The list of connections between the two men on the System database was long and detailed, their partnership spanning without a break a full ten years. She checked her mail again for updates on Gale, but there was nothing, and so beside his name she wrote LOCATION UN-KNOWN (DECEASED).

ABIGAIL HUNTER was next. The list of connections between her and Ivan was sporadic at best, but Ida was strengthening the connection. Abigail was at this point her best lead, and so it was a pity that she had to write LOCATION UNKNOWN beside the mysterious woman's name.

MILLA IVANOV, Ivan's mother. To all appearances she and Ivan had not been in contact for ten years, since Ivan had run away from home and never gone back. Ida had her doubts on the subject but little in the way of proof. In any case, Milla Ivanov, according to her query to the System, although a resident of New York, Earth, was currently vacationing on OLYMPUS MONS, MARS.

The last on the list was CONSTANCE HARPER. Her connections to Ivan had been added retroactively by the System following her interrogation a few months earlier, but she had not had contact with him since then. Ida doubted that as much as she doubted the same thing of Milla Ivanov. Constance, Ida knew, was in a little town at the edge of the VALLES MARINERIS, MARS.

Ida put the pen to the side and considered the list for a long moment. She held in her hand a complete list of all the people in the universe Leontios Ivanov cared for.

For a moment a strange feeling struck her, the same feeling she always got just before she saw a pattern in evidence. She could not say what it was about this simple list of people and places that triggered that curious sense of standing on a precipice and looking over the edge into the emptiness below, waiting for the truth to come.

The gathering sense of *something* was dispelled suddenly by a sharp rapping on her door. Ida dismissed the feeling for the moment and cast the list aside. "Come in."

Domitian opened the door and stood in its frame, hands clasped behind his back. "You wanted to see me?"

Ida suppressed a smile. He was perfect, this one. Official, dignified, obedient.

"Yes," she said. "Come in."

He walked in and closed the door behind himself but remained standing while Ida leaned back in her office chair.

Ida considered him, considered their situation, considered what she wanted to say. With Ivanov she had to be quick. With Domitian she could be slow and consider.

"What is your opinion of our prisoner?" she asked at last.

"Low," he said. "A thief and a con man."

"Intelligent," said Ida.

"Intelligent," Domitian agreed, "but a disease in the System."

The proper party line. Ida smiled and entertained thoughts of keeping Domitian for her own.

"And guilty?" she asked.

Domitian's eyes were light, like Ivan's, but a far duller color. "Certainly guilty."

He was speaking to please her, of course, but Ida always liked to have another person's validation. "Has there been any progress on cracking the *Annwn*'s computer?"

For the first time Domitian hesitated. "No," he admitted. "There was a minor emergency today regarding the *Ananke*. Doctor Bastet has been—"

Ida threw up a hand, and he fell silent and stood perfectly straight and stern even under her darkening attention. She considered shouting but suspected he would love her better if she refrained. He seemed to be unaccountably attached to the ship's rude little engineer, who hid her dislike for Ida very poorly and did not show a willingness to do as she was told.

"If the Mallt-y-Nos intended to use or attack the *Ananke*, those plans have clearly been thwarted," she said. "The *Ananke* is no longer under threat." Ivanov was no longer a threat to the ship, and that was precisely what Ida would tell the System, which meant that she soon would be able to take Ivanov off the *Ananke*. "I suggest you reassure your crew with that and remind Doctor Bastet that while her devotion to her ship is commendable, this interrogation is of paramount importance. Surely she cannot still be attempting to repair damage made in under a minute by a stranger to the ship."

"I will tell her, ma'am," Domitian said without answering the question.

If Bastet was too incompetent to fix such a trifling bit of sabotage, she shouldn't have been assigned to the *Ananke* in the first place. Ida filed away the information in the back of her mind.

"Remind Doctor Bastet that the *Annwn* is of very high priority to the System and to me," said Ida, "and inform her that my presence on this ship has a deadline. I need her to provide me with the contents of the *Annwn* before the week is out. That means in the next two days, Domitian. No later. And no excuses."

"Will you be leaving, ma'am?"

"I will be leaving shortly," said Ida. "The interrogation of Ivanov is progressing, but while I am making excellent progress"—she tried not to think about how Ivan had blocked her out so completely today—"he is remarkably . . . resistant and has so far managed to avoid giving me real information."

Domitian looked grim and nodded his understanding.

"I think," Ida said, "that it's time to move to the next stage of the interrogation. And for that I need to take Mister Ivanov off ship."

"Then you will have the information you need before you leave, Miss Stays."

He was serious, solemn, obedient. Ida looked at him and knew that he would do exactly as he said, and she smiled.

"You need to sleep."

"Go away, Gagnon," Althea said, and tested her hypothesis that if she hunched far enough over the screen before her, Gagnon would take the hint and go. She had shut down all the drones like the robotic arm in the pantry and was focused on figuring out what had caused it to go off in the first place. As with the robotics in the ventilation system, she could find nothing even though she knew that there must be some clue somewhere. The new avenue of investigation had forced her to abandon her search for the cause of the other errors she'd identified earlier in the day, and so many incomplete and apparently fruitless pursuits were starting to fill her with a vague sense of panic.

Gagnon did not go away. He simply leaned farther in.

"You've missed a couple sleep cycles and shortened the rest," he said. "I know you have. You can't fix the *Ananke* if you're having a psychotic break because of insufficient—"

"I'm not going to have a psychotic break," Althea interrupted. "Should we be having this conversation?" She looked pointedly over her shoulder at the locked door of Ivanov's cell.

Gagnon made a face at her. "We wouldn't be having this conversation if you would just go do what you're supposed to," he said. "Go to bed, Althea."

"Not yet."

"Do you want me to get Domitian and have him come down here and scold you?" Gagnon asked.

She did not, and she suggested to Gagnon exactly what he might do with Domitian instead of bothering her.

"Funny," Gagnon said, "but I'm serious."

She glanced again at the silent door to Ivanov's cell. "Fine," she said. "But I need to finish up what I'm doing."

Gagnon considered her. "Five minutes," he said.

"Until I'm done," Althea countered.

"Five minutes."

"It'll only take me ten," said Althea, frustrated. "If I'm still down here in fifteen, you can carry me off over your shoulder. But I need at least ten minutes, uninterrupted."

"Over my shoulder," Gagnon promised. Despite it all, there was a smile twitching at the edges of his mouth. "Like a sack."

Althea glared at him.

He did eventually get the hint.

"I'll come back in fifteen minutes," he said, raising his hands in defeat. "Fifteen, Althea," he reminded her, and she ignored him, and then he was gone.

She had sent him away almost more out of obstinacy than out of a genuine desire to finish working. She hated to leave problems unsolved, but for the moment she was too tired to start any new solutions and she knew it, and so she was merely retreading steps taken earlier in the day.

Like a ghost or a hallucination, manifesting only when everyone else was gone, Ivanov said, "You really should get some rest."

"I wasn't talking to you."

"I get it," Ivanov said, seemingly unfazed by her waspishness. "You hate to leave something unfinished. You're worried something will get worse while you're gone. But you'll only make more mistakes if you're tired."

"I'll also make more mistakes if people keep talking to me while I'm trying to work." Though she snapped, she was very tired, almost too tired to maintain her frustration at him.

"You're almost done working."

"Well, I'm not done yet!"

Ivanov said, "How long are you going to be angry at me for something I didn't do?"

It was so sudden a change in subject that it jolted Althea out of her irritation. "What?"

"The ship. I didn't do that. Mattie did."

"He was your partner." The reminder that Ivanov certainly knew how to fix her machine and Ida Stays would not ask him about it made her bitter.

Into the silence that followed Ivanov said, "I'm sorry."

He said it without annoyance, or sarcasm, or qualifications, or anything to mitigate the openness of the apology. And it sounded like— Althea almost could believe it—he was sincere.

For a moment she mulled over the unexpected sincerity, and remembered Ida Stays's arrogance that morning.

"I looked over your computer," she said, cautious, almost afraid of what would happen if she spoke to him without him provoking words from her.

The shifting sound of movement from behind the locked door. "Did you?"

"It stonewalled me," Althea admitted, and waited, but Ivanov didn't say anything. She said, hoping for his sincerity again, "Could you— Could Mattie have done to the *Ananke* what you did to the *Annwn*?"

"In terms of security?" Ivanov asked, sounding remarkably calm, as if the question wasn't offensive at all, as if they were colleagues comparing notes and not the subject and inquisitor in a most uncertain interrogation. "No, there wasn't anywhere near enough time for him to do that while he was on board the ship. It took us weeks to program Annie. Mattie wouldn't want to give a ship that is this dangerous a personality, anyway."

"No?" Althea asked, more to herself, and frowned down at the interface before her.

"No," Ivanov said. "See, a personality is just . . . a little bit of chaos organized. It's not quite predictable. It can have its own motivations, its own fears and wants, and it'll act on those independently of what the people around it want. Whatever Mattie did, he added chaos to your system, I don't doubt that. It's quick, and it's easy, and it's effective. But a personality is chaos organized. A computer can't organize the chaos itself; it doesn't know how to. Mattie or I would have had to do it, like we did for our ship. And Mattie didn't have time to do that."

"Then why haven't I found it yet?" Althea asked. "Whatever he did to my ship."

She glanced at the clock on the display before her. Gagnon would be back soon but not immediately. She still had time.

"That's the thing about chaos," said Ivanov. "It only ever increases. It's spread throughout the system."

"So you're saying I'll never find it?" Althea asked.

"I think you will eventually."

Althea sighed and leaned her head against the cool metal of her ship's wall. She closed her eyes. She really was very tired. At this point there was no use in hailing Gagnon; he would come down himself in a few minutes. For just a few minutes she could rest.

"Althea?" said Ivan.

"Yes?" Althea answered.

Ivan said, "Who is this ship supposed to destroy?"

In her half-dreaming state, there was something awful about the question, some ominous quality. "What?" she said, sitting away from the wall and turning to face the blank steel that separated her from Ivanov.

His voice sounded very near, as if he were standing just behind the door, only a few feet from Althea. "This ship is an expensive and highly advanced military vessel with an incredibly powerful computer," he said. "It's on a secret mission, and it's armed. Who is it going to destroy?"

"The weaponry is for *protection*," said Althea, hardly understanding what he was saying. The *Ananke* was a research vessel. It existed to test a scientific hypothesis, nothing more.

"From whom? The System has sole control of the solar system. There are no rival governments or organizations. Weaponry like this ship has isn't for protection; it's to destroy."

"The *Ananke*'s weaponry is standard for a ship of her size," Althea hissed, glancing at the clock again. Gagnon would be there any moment.

"Yes, it is," Ivan said, lowering his voice as she had. "I know. But guess what all System ships like this are designed to do?"

"Leave your propaganda out of this," Althea snapped. She looked up the hall, but Gagnon was not in sight or hearing yet. Leaning in close to the door to be heard, she said, "The *Ananke* is a research vessel. She's a very valuable research vessel. That makes her a target—look at you! You came the moment you saw her and tried to destroy her!"

"We didn't come to hurt your ship," said Ivanov swiftly. "We came to see what it was doing."

"Of course the ship has the means to defend herself," said Althea. "Of course she does."

Footsteps not so far distant. Gagnon would be in sight soon.

"My ship isn't going to kill anyone," said Althea to the silent Ivanov. "She isn't going to kill anyone." Still Ivanov did not answer. Althea said, "Is that what you thought?"

When Gagnon arrived, Ivanov still had not answered her. Althea left the hallway, troubled by thoughts she did not dare put into words.

Chapter 4

VOLUME

"We're going to try something different today," Ida said.

Ivan was slouching in his chair. He was paler than he had been the day before, closer to the color of the room, of his shirt, and bruised shadows were becoming apparent beneath his brilliant eyes. He must have been having trouble sleeping, and Ida knew that that was as good a sign of his fear as any she could hope for. With the wires of the polygraph coming out from the neck of his shirt and the base, adhered to the inside of his elbow, it looked almost as if the machine were sucking the life and the blood out of him and eventually would leave him dried out and hollow.

"How exciting," he said, in a tone that contended with the sun side of Mercury for aridity. Not a trace of weariness was audible in his voice.

"Instead of asking you about events," Ida said, "I'm going to ask you about people."

Ida took her time before continuing, letting him linger on the thought. She'd spent a long time considering who to ask about first before deciding on Milla Ivanov. Theirs was the oldest relationship, and Ida knew he would have a weakness for his mother.

"Your childhood must have been difficult," Ida said with gentle sympathy, leaning against the back of her chair.

"You know it was," said Ivan. He was giving nothing away, but Ida saw that when he moved his arms, reddened chafing was visible beneath the metal manacles.

"Of course," said Ida. "I know all about it. After all, I do have the surveillance footage. And your childhood and adolescence were very well surveyed."

He must have known what she was referring to, but he said nothing.

"But of course," said Ida, "there are some things cameras can't record."

She began to pace again, a few steps one way and a few steps the other.

"Your mother was very protective of you," she said.

"I was her son," said Ivan immediately.

Her son and her ticket out of jail. Whether or not Milla Ivanov had known of her husband's attempt to divorce the Saturnian moons from System control, she certainly would have ended up in prison along with her husband if not for Ivan. The System had destroyed the people of Saturn for the crime, after all. But Milla Ivanov had been clever. She had gotten herself into the public eye immediately, and the Terran people saw one of their own, a beautiful, brilliant young Terran woman devastated and disbelieving, fooled and abused by an outer planetary husband who already had estranged her from her Terran family, first hugely pregnant and then carrying a babe in arms: little Ivan, clutching at his mother's blouse with tiny, perfect fingers.

"I understand the impulse to be protective of her," said Ida gently, and thought of Milla Ivanov going into court of her own volition only a week after giving birth, appearing wan and weak with Ivan at her breast, as much a performance as Ivan was putting on for Ida now. "She is your mother. But I only want a few simple answers to a few simple questions."

Ivan was so perfectly expressionless that Ida knew he was on lockdown. "I only ever tell you the truth, Ida."

"Did your mother ever talk to you about your father?" Ida asked.

The conditions for Milla Ivanov's freedom had been very specific. Heightened surveillance on her and her son for the rest of their lives, maintained without break. A mandatory visit to Saturn when Ivan was nine, successfully accomplished and successful in making an impression on him. Public appearances on the System's behalf to speak against rebellion and terrorism; the System brought her out whenever they needed a speaker, and Milla Ivanov had poise and charm. The retention of her marriage and her husband's name as a permanent reminder of her shame, although as a living warning to other terrorists Connor Ivanov was rotting in a System prison so dark that Ida doubted he even remembered Milla's sky-blue eyes. If Doctor Ivanov had deviated even slightly from those conditions in the thirty years since her husband's incarceration or shown any signs of sympathy for her husband or his cause, she and her son would have been executed or imprisoned faster than they could have reconsidered their words. Telling Ivan anything kind about his father was likely to fall under that heading.

"No, she didn't," said Ivan, as calm as if they were discussing the weather or the minutiae of a computer's code. "Which you know, because you've seen the tapes."

"I hope I'm not boring you," Ida said with the slightest edge of danger. "Your mother truly never told you anything?"

"Nothing more than the System told me," said Ivan.

"But the System would say nothing good," Ida said, affecting a frown. "Surely your mother would like you to hear something good about the man she loved."

"She told me," said Ivan, "nothing of the kind."

"And yet you choose to be known as Ivan," said Ida, advancing closer to the table. Ivan sat up a little straighter, the anxious patternless tapping of his fingers against the rests of his chair ceasing. That was a habit his mother had, the only anxious flaw in her perfect poise. Ivan had picked it up from her when he was a well-mannered accessory at her side, but from what Ida had seen of footage since, he had lost it once leaving home. "You know that your last name, Ivanov, was an ancient Terran patronymic, do you not? You took the name of your father."

"My father's name was Connor," Ivan said drily. "And you would have chosen to go by another name, too, Ida, if your mother had named you Leontios. Don't you think you're reaching a bit?"

"Did you learn your revolutionary sympathies from your mother?"

"I didn't even admit to revolutionary sympathies, and I certainly didn't learn anything like that from her," said Ivan. He raised his hands slightly, and the ring of chafed skin was visible on his wrists. It probably hurt, Ida decided, in a dull, itching way.

"You're going after her," Ivan said suddenly, watching her as closely as she was watching him. "Why?"

"Your mother had intimate revolutionary connections once," she said. "It seems likely that would happen again."

"The System proved her innocent," said Ivan, his voice hard, leaning forward in his chair. It was delightful how his nonchalance had all but vanished. If only his surety would go as well. "She didn't know anything about my father's revolution. She didn't have revolutionary connections then, she didn't when I lived with her, and even if she does now, which she won't, I'm not in contact with her."

"I'm glad to hear that," Ida said, and Ivan seemed to hear how sincerely she meant it, because he was back to looking wary. But it was his fault; he had stepped into her trap. "Except that there's one thing that troubles me."

"Just one?"

"You tell me you are no longer in contact with your mother?"

"No."

"And you haven't been since when?"

"Since I left home."

"No contact at all? Nothing?"

"I told you, no."

Ida leaned forward onto the table separating them. Beside her wrist, the lines on the polygraph swung back and forth, too steady for her liking. "We found video of your mother—recent video—on your ship."

For a long moment Ivan simply looked confused; then he started to laugh. "Those were public broadcasts," he said. "I don't think even the System will take that as proof of collusion."

"They were the only recordings on board your ship," Ida said, omitting any mention of what may or may not have been saved to the ship's computer, out of her reach.

"Did you even watch them?" Ivan demanded. Ida had; they had all been of Milla Ivanov lecturing, cool and composed, her words precise and sharply enunciated. Ivan must have read the confirmation in her expression, because he said, "Did you notice that all of the lectures were on computer science?"

"Of course," said Ida.

Ivan had his arms spread as wide as the chains would allow. He was looking at her as if he expected her to make some obvious connection. When Ida simply waited, he said, "That's the subject I studied at university."

"There are many public broadcasts on computer science," Ida said. "Why only save your mother's?"

"Because she's the best researcher there is," Ivan said flatly. It was spoken without pride, as if it were a simple fact. And perhaps it was; Ida knew little of the field and nothing of the subject. "Mattie and I like to keep on top of developments in the field. We need to for our job."

For their thefts, Ida thought but did not say. "You want me to really believe that, Ivan?" she asked.

"You know what I believe?" said Ivan. He smiled at her, wolfish. "I think you're grasping at straws and you know it."

For a long moment Ida simply watched him. She intended her silence to be cold, intimidating, but Ivan seemed to take it as confirmation of his success; the snarling smile on his face grew by the second.

Fury. Fury like the hollow blackness inside Ida's chest swelling out, wanting to be filled.

She took her growing fury and ruthlessly broke it down, and turned that energy into an attack as sharp as the point of a knife.

"The surveillance at your house was very advanced," she said, and Ivan's smirk began to fade at the unexpected change of subject.

Ida sat down slowly and deliberately in her chair.

"The cameras even had infrared," she said. "There were even cameras on the roof."

Ivan was very still, very tense. He wasn't smiling anymore.

"They recorded everything," she said. "The audio caught the sound you made when you made the first cut on your wrist. The infrared caught the rush of heat out through your wrists as you bled out. The visible caught the sun just peeking out over the hills by the time you fell to your knees, pale, too weak to stand on your own two feet."

Ivan was as still as stone. She wondered, if the chains had not been there to hold him in place, whether he would have attacked her.

"Why the roof?" Ida asked with genuine curiosity. "For the drama?"

"Because it was harder to reach," said Ivan.

"Why?"

"I was timing the System's ability to respond to what they saw in the cameras," said Ivan. His voice was very even, very calm, but Ida saw that his hands were trembling minutely against the chair.

"You were testing them," she said.

"I wanted to know how long they would take to get to me if I did something they didn't like."

"So you tried to kill yourself," Ida said, "to test the System?"

"Yes," said Ivan.

"Were you counting the seconds?" Ida asked, her voice gentle and low like a knife driven slowly into the heart. "When you were on the roof? Counting how long it would take?"

"Yes."

"Could you do that even as you felt yourself dying?"

"Yes."

"You passed out before the System got there," said Ida. "How was that in your plans?"

For the first time, Ivan looked away. "It was a whim," he said. "I didn't think it through very well."

He was rattled, disturbed. Ida asked, "What did your mother think of you trying to kill yourself?"

"Obviously," Ivan said sharply, "she was upset."

"And what does your mother think of you taking after your father?"

He really had extraordinary eyes, even when—especially when—he was glaring at her. "I'm not taking after my father."

"I meant living as a criminal," Ida said, as if she had not laid the linguistic trap intentionally.

"Then I imagine my mother isn't happy about that, either."

"You imagine?"

"I haven't been in contact with her."

"You really do intend me to believe," said Ida in astonishment, "that you never tried to contact your mother to reassure her you were all right—"

"I *didn't*," said Ivan.

"—and that she never tried to contact you herself?"

"She didn't."

"Is your mother's revolutionary contact John Walker?"

"What? No. My mother doesn't have any revolutionary—"

"Is it Alaina Purcell?" Ida had a list of Milla Ivanov's associates; if she was lucky, one of them would provoke a reaction from Ivan.

"My mother has no revolutionary contacts." The polygraph showed that Ivan's heart was beating fast.

"Is it Julian Keys?"

"I don't—"

"Jesse Carter?"

"I don't know anything about my mother's affairs," Ivan shouted, breaking into Ida's litany of names, "and she doesn't have any connection to the Mallt-y-Nos!"

Ida smiled at him.

"All right," she said.

"All right?" Ivan repeated warily, his fingers jittering a patternless beat against the edge of his chair.

Ida said, "Now I'd like to hear about Constance Harper."

Althea woke as suddenly and unexpectedly as if a sound had triggered her waking, but when she opened her eyes to the dimness of her room, it was silent.

When she looked at her bedside clock, she sat up with a curse.

Gagnon had been supposed to wake her for her shift; he had, in fact, been supposed to wake her three hours ago. For a moment Althea worried that something had gone wrong before she realized that the far more likely explanation was that Gagnon had decided to let her sleep. It didn't seem to matter; even with the extra hours, she still felt exhausted.

Oversleeping at least explained why her dreams had been so strange. When facing a computer problem, she sometimes dreamed in code; she had even solved several tricky problems in REM. The dream she'd been having right before she woke, faded and indistinct as it was becoming, had started off as a dream of code.

But the code had not been the *Ananke*'s, as she'd thought, but rather the *Annwn*'s, and when Althea tried to find where her computer had gone, she had run all the way to the base of the ship, where was the black hole that was her heart, and she had opened the door and looked inside, past the dead man's switch, but the black hole had swollen in size, and she stared at blackness right before her face. When she reached into the event horizon of the black hole, her hand came up dripping with a dark liquid that was not black but red, and in the black hole's place was a vast and beating heart.

Then she had woken.

Althea walked over to the intercom, took a moment to ensure that her half-sleeping mind would be capable of forming words, and then punched the talk button.

"Gagnon," she said.

There was a pause that probably indicated that he was putting whatever he was doing on hold so that he could come and answer her but that Althea liked to imagine was awkward, Gagnon hesitating with his finger right over the intercom.

"Althea!" Gagnon said. "You're awake."

"You were supposed to wake me."

This time the pause was certainly deliberate. "Oops?" he said. He did not sound particularly repentant.

"I'm getting dressed," said Althea. "I'll be down in a minute." She tried to make it sound like a threat. She wasn't certain Gagnon was impressed.

With a sigh, she pulled off her soft sleeping pants, tossing them on the rumpled covers, following them with her underwear, but swiftly pulling on another pair. She had long grown accustomed to the watching cameras, but the habit of privacy remained, so ingrained that she hardly remembered that the cameras were the reason for it, except at times like this, when the integrity of the cameras was called into question.

The cameras. She paused. She knew that the camera in her room was not working. Its light was still on as if it were recording, but if it was recording, it was recording somewhere deep in the *Ananke*'s data banks, not being broadcast to the System, and it was likely—almost certain—that no one except the computer would ever see it.

Slowly, Althea took off her sleeping shirt, tossing it onto the bed beside the pants. She crossed her arms automatically over her chest, then made herself uncross them. She turned to the mirror mounted on the wall and looked.

There was more of her own olive-toned skin to be seen than she was used to seeing. Her hair was a tangled mess from sleeping, the curls turned into frizz and twisting out from her heart-shaped face like fraying wires. Without a bra, she was heavy and loose, and her hips were wider than they looked in her baggy uniform. She did not look at all the way she imagined in her head when she thought about herself, and the strange thought occurred to her unbidden that she looked like one of those ancient earthenware figurines of a mother, large-breasted, wide-hipped, with arms outstretched in acceptance.

The computer interface in the corner of the room turned on.

She saw the sudden glow out of the corner of her eye and turned sharply away from the mirror. There was no one else in the room. The computer had turned on by itself.

Althea reached over and grabbed her shirt from the top of the crumpled covers, pulling it over her head and down over her chest while she kicked through the piles of discarded clothes on the floor so that she could stand before the computer.

The screen before her was flashing between images. At first it was so fast that Althea could not pick out any of them but was left with a strong sense of unease, as if whatever she saw her mind recognized unconsciously without being able to put it into words. After a moment, however, the flashing images slowed down.

Ancient sailing ships. Althea watched white sails and wooden hulls flicker before her eyes before being replaced by wooden rooms—the inside of the ships, Althea realized after a time. The images were old enough that they were from before photographs; they had been sketched in pen and scanned.

The images were flashing so quickly that it was some time before she realized that all the wooden rooms had one thing in common: somewhere in the room, crawling inside the walls or poking their heads out through holes in the wall, were black-furred rats.

A list interrupted the flashing images. At first it was too fast for Althea to read, and then she didn't know the words; she saw "rabies" and "*Yersina pestis*," though, and those she knew. It was a list of diseases, viruses carried by rats.

There was a scratching sound that took Althea a moment to realize was coming from the computer, growing ever louder, a scratching sound like human nails on rough metal, like the sound of rodents gnawing through wood, like—like—

The computer shut off again without any warning, leaving afterimages of ancient ships and lists of plagues burned into Althea's mind.

When she tried to turn it back on, the computer would not respond no matter what she did. Althea dressed—in her usual manner again, baring her skin for only the briefest of seconds before zipping up her uniform jumpsuit—and left the room to talk to Gagnon, fighting the strange, insistent feeling that there was something important she was failing to understand.

.   .   .

By the time Althea reached the piloting room, where Gagnon was waiting, she had put thoughts of the strange images on the computer in her room from her mind. As the malfunctions had gone lately, that was a harmless one, and she had more important concerns: today Gagnon would be working on the *Ananke* while Althea, by decree of Ida Stays, would be working on the *Annwn*.

She hated it that an arrogant woman who knew nothing about computers got to dictate who would do what where. It was clear to anyone with sense that the *Ananke* was more important than the *Annwn*. Nothing would happen if the *Annwn* remained unexplored. But the *Ananke* was what was keeping them all alive.

Gagnon was waiting for her in the control room for debriefing before they went their separate ways. Because of the cyclic nature of their sleep and work shifts, he had been working on the *Ananke* for several hours while Althea slept, but she wanted to check in regardless before wasting the rest of her day on an unfamiliar and rebellious machine. He was sitting in the chair before the navigation equipment, dwarfed by the main viewscreen, which was showing a 360-degree view of the space around the *Ananke*, nothing but black studded with sparks of white. "Good morning," he said, swiveling the chair around to face her. His red hair was coming loose from its thong and hung around his face, and his jaw was turning orange with stubble.

Perhaps her resentment over the *Annwn* had been the cause of her strange and disturbing dream. "How is she?" Althea asked, and meant the *Ananke*.

"The computer? The computer is awful," said Gagnon. "I can't run any simulations; I can barely even check to make sure we're on course. Whenever I try to trace the errors, I get nothing. Have you been having any luck? Because I've got all of nothing after five hours of work."

"I've had some success," Althea said. It was a lie, but at least she had been able to fix some of the symptoms on the *Ananke* when they appeared. The *Annwn* had been a waste of her time. Besides, Gagnon was a theorist. He'd never had any patience for practical minutiae. Although years of collaboration had softened their initial exasperation with each other into agreeable—even fond—mutual incomprehension, Althea was not surprised to hear about his lack of success.

"Really?"

"Really," Althea said. "Let's talk about what you're going to do today while I'm out."

"I'm going to try to fix the computer," Gagnon said dutifully. "I'm going to try to track the source of the errors on the list you gave me"—he held up a list, with most of the entries already crossed out—"and keep a log of what I find"—he held up a pad of paper with woefully little in the way of notes on it—"and wonder if it wouldn't be easier just to take the computer offline."

Althea had been in the process of resigning herself emotionally to the fact that whatever Gagnon was doing today she was going to have to do herself on her own time once she was done with the *Annwn*, when his last words caught her attention. "You want to what?"

"We can run the ship manually," Gagnon said. "We're already running most of the onboard systems manually, with the autonomous drones offline. It wouldn't be that much of a stretch to take over the navigation and the rest. The part of the computer that's giving us trouble is the higher-level functioning, after all."

"You want to lobotomize her?" Althea demanded.

Gagnon sighed. "Althea . . ."

"You won't be able to run your experiments if the computer is offline."

He raised a finger. "I can run some of them," he said, "which is better than none." Althea did not know what he saw in her expression, but it made him throw his hands up defensively. "Look, I'm not going to—I'm not going to do anything to your computer without you telling me," he said. "I'm just throwing it into consideration, all right?"

"Consider it considered," said Althea, and walked out of the room.

"Tell me about Constance," Ida said.

"She's a pretty woman," Ivan said, then looked her over and allowed, "You might be prettier."

"That's very kind," said Ida, allowing the slightest curl of a smile. She leaned one hip up onto the table, on the opposite side of the polygraph, keeping Ivan's attention on her.

"I just don't want you to be jealous," Ivan explained.

"I don't get jealous, Ivan," Ida said. It was only partly a lie. "It's been months since you saw Constance last. Why is that?"

"We had a strong difference of opinion."

Ida leaned in.

"You should know by now," she said, "that that's not quite enough detail to satisfy me."

He tilted his head up at her, his face angled her way, his eyes unreadable, his lips softened into parting as if he were about to speak. Ida leaned over him, staring at him chained in place beneath her, for a moment too long before he said, "Six months ago Mattie and I took Con on a vacation to the moon."

"Why?" Ida asked. The trip to the moon had always troubled her. It gave Ivan and Gale a solid alibi for the riots on Triton despite Ida's certainty that the Mallt-y-Nos had been involved in the event. The same riots had, conveniently for the two men, distracted the System enough that they were not caught during their vacation on Luna.

Ivan shrugged. "Because she'd always wanted to go."

"What about the surveillance? Weren't any of you worried about being caught?"

"Mattie and I assumed we wouldn't be there long enough to matter. We weren't very high priority for the System, or at least we didn't think so." He gave her a wry look. "And Con thought that we worked odd jobs. Traveling salesmen sometimes, freelance computer repairmen."

Ida laughed. Constance Harper must be a delightfully trusting—that is to say, stupid—kind of woman. Perhaps that was why Ivan had liked her. "Did she really?"

Ivan grinned. "Maybe a part of her suspected something, in the back of her mind, but yeah, she believed it."

"But you were wrong, weren't you?" Ida asked, and enjoyed Ivan's swift frown, the way the polygraph jumped with brief alarm. She kept her expression smooth as she clarified, "About the surveillance, I mean."

"Right," Ivan said, recovering. The tremble in his hands their discussion of Milla Ivanov had induced was fading away, but he was still drumming that patternless patter against the edge of his chair, apparently on automatic. "Someone saw us with Connie, recognized us, connected us to Con, and interrogated her."

"She wasn't very happy," Ida said. It was not a question. She had been present at the interrogation, watching from behind the glass. Constance Harper had not seemed trusting and stupid then, only angry.

"I heard from a mutual friend about it," said Ivan, and Ida filed away the identity of the mutual friend as an item to be investigated later. "The interrogators told her about what Mattie and I really did, and she was . . . um, pissed."

The word was an understatement.

"She told some mutual friends about it and expressed some sentiment to the effect that she never wanted to see us again. Something about lying to her. What she was really mad about," said Ivan, "was that we almost got her arrested."

"Is that so?" Ida asked.

Ivan nearly smiled. It looked like an accident, like an unaffected honest reaction to whatever was going on in his head, but Ida doubted it. "Constance is a good citizen. She was a foster child like Mattie, on the outer planets. It was a huge move for her to open her own business on Mars. She likes the System. She's comfortable in it. She wants to be good and obey."

"And she wants that more than she cares for you?" Ida asked. "Or her little brother?"

"Foster brother," Ivan corrected, as if the distinction were important. "And yes, she does. She really would turn us in if we tried to get in contact with her. Constance," he went on, peculiarly precise, "is a woman of principle, and she values her principles more than her friends."

Ida could not tell if he spoke with more bitterness or admiration. Perhaps that was it, why Ivan had been with Constance, that confounding mixture of admiration and dislike.

When Constance and Ivan were in the same room together, there seemed to be little in the way of affection. From the spotty surveillance of Constance Harper's bar—the Fox and the Hound was situated atop a scarp in one of the more rural regions of Mars, and surveillance frequently was distorted or disrupted by the fast winds and fine red dust— Ida had seen them almost always shouting at each other. Yet even in a room full of people, each one seemed to have a keen sense for the other, as if each were a magnet and they kept being drawn together. In a crowd, the crowd would look to Constance, who was tall and self-assured, but Constance, it seemed, would look to Ivan.

She had wondered for a while if Ivan's attraction to Constance Harper was because Constance Harper was a good woman and perhaps Ivan craved that safe, System-approved life he'd abandoned. Constance wasn't unattractive, but she wasn't beautiful: plain brown hair kept long and shoulders damaged by the weak Martian sun into freckling, tall and flat and skinny, with a long face and a wide mouth, always dressed to work. So that could not be why. But perhaps it was her inflexibility, her rigidity, that kept Ivan bound to her, so that being with her was a punishment because she made it so.

Or perhaps Constance had just been easy: willing and available, already connected to Ivan through Matthew Gale.

"She wouldn't even try to save you, Ivan?" Ida asked. "Turn you from your life of crime?"

"Certainly not."

"Straight to jail, then."

"Black and white," said Ivan. "That's how Connie thinks."

"And there's no possibility," said Ida, "that Connie might allow for a little gray area if she thought it was for the best?"

"Tell me exactly what you're asking, Ida," said Ivan.

"Would Constance," Ida asked, "support the Mallt-y-Nos?"

Ivan laughed. It was a curious laugh, tinged—almost—with what Ida thought might be traces of suppressed hysteria.

"No, she wouldn't," he said. "That would be against her principles."

Trying to crack the *Annwn* was more like trying to solve a riddle than trying to hack a computer.

When Althea turned the *Annwn*'s computer back on, keeping it disconnected from the rest of the *Annwn*, the computer went immediately into hysterics.

WHERE'S MY BODY WHERE'S MY BODY WHERE'S MY BODY WHERE'S MY BODY WHERE'S MY BODY WHERE'S MY—

"Shut up, calm down," Althea muttered, but for a long time the computer would not be calmed, would not let her type, only kept up that frantic repetition, as if its simulated fear could affect Althea. She managed to silence it only when she remembered her conversation with Ivanov and typed, "Annie, shut up."

The words ceased their scrolling. Althea's order had terminated them in midsentence.

WHO ARE YOU? asked the computer while Althea was still trying to decide what to do now that the machine's resistance had ceased so unexpectedly.

Althea hesitated, then typed, "Annie, override security measures."

NO. The machine let the flat refusal linger before asking again, I CAN'T SEE. WHO ARE YOU?

"Matthew Gale," Althea typed in the hope of deception.

LIAR.

Althea groaned.

That was how Domitian found her an hour or so later, still furiously in interrogation with the computer.

"How is it?" he asked.

"I need a blowtorch," Althea said. "One of the magnesium ones. And some thermite."

"It can't be that bad."

Domitian had not been arguing with a computer in English for the past hour and a half. Conversations with a computer should rightfully take place in code, and here Althea had been stuck trying to match wits with Ivanov's damn machine.

"Look," she said. A small part of her thought that perhaps if she could express her frustrations properly to Domitian, he would bring them to Ida Stays in such a way that Ida would appreciate them. "It's got this shell," she said, spreading out a dome with her hands as if she could shape a physical thing out of metaphor. "Whatever's inside the shell—the good stuff, the code—I can't get at, because the shell, I can't get through it."

Domitian came to sit in the copilot's chair beside her, leaning his elbows on his knees and frowning. He looked overlarge in the cozy, well-lived feeling of the room, and Althea had a sudden strange thought that Ivanov and Gale had sat where she and Domitian were sitting now many times before and planned thefts, sabotage—perhaps they had even simply talked, like friends did.

"So it's got a firewall," Domitian said.

Althea winced. "A wall, you can get around," she said, feeling the metaphor slipping from her fingers and clinging grimly to it. "It's a shell. Because it's how the whole computer is reacting to me. They've changed it somehow. Gale and Ivanov programmed it somehow so that it doesn't react like a computer. It reacts like a person."

"And what does that mean?"

"It means . . . it has an agenda, it doesn't give you a perfectly truthful response," said Althea. "It means it's not logical. I can't get through."

Domitian leaned over and peered down onto the screen Althea had been working on. "This looks like a chat."

Althea rubbed her palms over her face. "That's because it is a chat," she said. "The computer won't interact with me any other way, and there's no way around it. Like I said, a shell." She dropped her hands and relented. "Okay, it's not really a person, and once I get past this shell—once I get into the heart of it—it'll be a computer again. They didn't change anything innate in the computer system itself; they just wrote a program." A very good program, but Althea wasn't going to admit that. "It's just that I can't get past this stupid first layer."

"Because it's not like a computer," Domitian said. He was smiling faintly.

"What's so funny?"

He turned that faint smile on her, looking at her with some fondness, and sidestepped the question. "It's a clever idea," he said. "Make it so that the only way to hack their computer has nothing to do with computers."

Althea scowled at the implicit praise for Gale and Ivanov. "Don't."

He straightened up. "I know you'll be able to do it, Althea," he said, standing and clapping her on the shoulder on his way to the door.

"Yeah," Althea muttered, and typed, "Let me in."

NO, replied the machine.

She knew without looking that Domitian had paused at the door, not taking the step down into the *Annwn*'s sideways hall. She knew that he was waiting for her to speak again.

Somehow, Domitian's expectations always managed to get something out of her even if she hadn't intended to give him anything at all.

"What if I can't?" she said, and typed, "Please."

TELL ME YOUR NAME, demanded the *Annwn*.

"You will," Domitian said. Solid, certain.

"What if I can't and I spend all this time here working on this stupid, useless piece of crap, and while I'm here, the *Ananke* gets worse and gets ruined?"

Silence. TELL ME YOUR NAME remained unanswered.

"Althea," said Domitian, and at the tone in his voice Althea had to suppress the childhood urge to sink low in her seat, "I know that you are worried about the *Ananke*. But allowing your concern for the *Ananke* to seriously impede your attempts to investigate—"

"I'm not letting it impede anything," said Althea over Domitian's words, but he said, "Yes, you are. I expect you to put the same amount of effort into cracking the *Annwn* as you would toward—"

"Aren't you worried about the *Ananke*?"

Domitian paused. "The state of the computer is of concern to me."

That hadn't been what Althea had meant at all. She wanted to ask again, to ask if he was *worried* about their ship, but she was afraid that he would not understand. Wearily, one-fingered, she typed "Ivanov" in response to the computer's query.

"Miss Stays will be gone soon," said Domitian, his voice low and his presence heavy on her back. "Until then, you must do your best to obey."

Althea's finger hovered over the enter key, then she stopped on a thought.

She went back twice and changed "Ivanov" to "Ivan."

"Did you hear me?"

Enter.

"Althea."

LIAR, said the *Annwn*.

And Althea, full of frustration, typed out "True."

She thought it wouldn't do anything at all. The *Annwn* would know that she wasn't Ivanov or Gale and would return to resistance.

But to her astonishment, the ship said, HELLO, IVAN. VERIFICA-TION METHODS ARE ALL CURRENTLY OFFLINE. MINIMAL ACCESS GRANTED.

"Holy shit," said Althea.

She hardly noticed Domitian moving until he was standing right beside her. "Did you break it?" he asked.

Althea could not stop her grin. It grew slowly over her face until she thought it might break her in half. "I did. Well, sort of," she amended. "I don't think I can get any farther in without connecting the computer back to the ship, and that's too risky, I won't do that, and I've got System regs on my side. But I got it open a crack."

The *Annwn* waited patiently for her input, as a good computer should. She flexed her fingers and thought. "Let's see what it'll give me."

"Access navigation logs," she typed.

YOU DO NOT HAVE THE NECESSARY AUTHORIZATION.

"Access personal files: Ivanov, Leontios."

YOU DO NOT HAVE THE NECESSARY AUTHORIZATION.

"Access personal files: Ivan."

YOU DO NOT HAVE THE NECESSARY AUTHORIZATION.

"Well," said Althea, "there goes that."

"See if you can get the communication logs," Domitian said.

"Access communication logs."

YOU DO NOT HAVE THE NECESSARY AUTHORIZATION.

"What the hell can I access, then?" Althea demanded of the computer. She tried to get cute. "Display available data."

SPECIFY, said the *Annwn*.

"Bitch," Althea muttered.

"What would they use this for?" asked Domitian, jarring her. Althea had nearly forgotten he was there, so quickly had she zeroed in on the machine, and her first reaction was to tense up at the intrusive sound of his voice. "The computer is only offering some functionality, yes? What's the purpose of that?"

"In case something goes wrong they can still use the computer," Althea said. "It's a contingency plan. They're well prepared; they've got lots of plans." Or they'd had lots of plans. Gale was dead. It was an uncomfortable thought; Althea returned her attention to the machine.

If this functionality—when the computer was all but destroyed—existed, it must mean that only the most important files or programs could be accessed from it in case of emergency. Probably also the least incriminating, Althea thought. Ida Stays would not be pleased.

"Show available programs."

NONE AVAILABLE.

Althea pressed her fingers into her eyes and breathed. This was a problem she might be able to solve; she needed the name of the variable. Gale and Ivanov would have named it something sensible, something easy to remember—they would use the computer in this state only if something had gone badly wrong.

Althea felt a little bit like Ida Stays trying to think like this. It was not a pleasant sensation. But Althea knew what she would call the variable if she were the one naming it.

She typed, "Show workspace."

FIVE FILES AVAILABLE.

Althea grinned.

The first file was a data bomb; if let into another computer, it would erase every piece of data on board and leave the computer hollowed out and useless. It was not sophisticated enough to have wiped the mind of the *Ananke*, but it sent a chill down Althea's spine nonetheless. The second and third were both viruses designed to slip into the veins of a computer and force it to obey, poisoning it slowly to death. Althea could tell at a glance, to her disappointment, that neither was the one that had been put into the *Ananke*. The virus in the *Ananke* was insidious but random. These two were targeted and simple.

The next was a program designed to go into a System computer and affect the cameras in some way. Ivanov and Gale had used the System's facial recognition against it: the cameras would see Ivanov and Gale, and the sight of the two men would trigger a reaction in the computer that saw them. A modified version of that program must have been what the men had used to get on board the *Ananke* without the *Ananke* reporting it; when the *Ananke* recognized them, it knew not to sound the alarm.

Of course, the *Ananke* might have been programmed to react differently to seeing their faces, Althea thought. The *Ananke* could be programmed specifically to sound the alarm at the sight of either of the men. Or she could be programmed to execute some other action: erase a piece of data, detonate a bomb. Ivanov's very presence on board could still be affecting the computer, and his removal from the ship could provoke some other change.

The last of the five programs, the five programs that Gale and Ivanov considered the most important programs for them to have in case of an emergency, as far as Althea could tell, was a sequence of triggers for the detonation of a network of bombs.

"You met Constance through Mattie, of course," said Ida.

"Now you want to talk about Mattie," Ivan said, as if saying, "See? I know what you're doing."

Ida wanted him to know. "How did you meet Mattie?"

Ivan's eyes were bright. He had slid somehow back into confidence. "That's a funny story, actually," he said, and Ida wondered if it was the thought of Matthew Gale that had given him strength or the idea that he had a story to tell.

"It was a few months after I left home," Ivan said, leaning forward with a confiding smirk that almost distracted her from the shadows beneath his eyes. "I was running out of the cash I'd taken from my account."

Taken from his account, stolen from his mother; it was a matter of perspective. Ida kept her opinion to herself.

"I was trying out some petty little cons to keep myself afloat," Ivan said. "Just for a little longer. When I met Mattie, I was on Mars—"

"What had you intended to do when you ran out of money?" Ida asked.

"Nothing," said Ivan. "I didn't think about it."

She understood. He hadn't meant to survive very long.

"I was on Mars when I met Mattie," Ivan continued, passing on as if the question had not been significant, "hustling pool, because I liked the idea of con man tradition. Pool's easy, anyway; it's just physics. I was doing pretty well, I thought, but Mattie saw through me."

"One con man recognizes another," said Ida.

"Exactly," he said, and smiled. "Anyway, Mattie was impressed . . ." Ivan laughed and started again. "Impressed by something, anyway. He came over to chat me up, but I realized pretty quickly that he'd noticed what I was doing and found out that what he wanted was to team up."

"Just like that?"

"He had a particular heist in mind," said Ivan. "And he'd been looking for a good partner. Mattie's got a lot of talent, but his words-to-mouth program is faulty. If he needs to think on his feet, he better be using his feet and not trying to talk his way out of anything."

All of this was only feeding Ida's frustration that Gale had been allowed to escape before she arrived. And now he was dead, his corpse floating somewhere in interplanetary space, drifting slowly toward the sun, and she would never be able to interrogate him.

"In the end," Ivan said, "he talked me into it."

"Why did you agree?" Ida asked. "You didn't know him. He was a stranger who came up to you and called you out for being a con man."

"He didn't call me out," said Ivan.

"Tried to pick you up, then."

Ivan grinned. "He did try to pick me up," he said. "Gave up on that pretty quickly, though."

"So why did you say yes?"

Ivan seemed to think about it. After a moment, though, he shrugged. "I liked him."

"Why? You spoke to him for five minutes."

Ivan made a face. "I'm not that easy. He worked on me for longer than that."

"Why did you like him?"

"Do you like anybody, Ida?" Ivan asked, and it was a strange enough question to make her briefly uneasy, but she rationalized that the strangeness of his question was simply a reaction to the way she had phrased hers.

"Of course I do," she said.

"And could you say exactly why you like them?"

"Of course," said Ida. She kept logical little lists in her head, reasons to like a person, why they were useful in one column, reasons to dislike them in another.

"Of course you do," said Ivan drily, and Ida thought to ask him what precisely he meant by that but could not quite bring herself to ask, and Ivan continued. "I just did. He was interesting. He was entertaining. I had never pulled off a heist before, and here one had fallen into my lap. So I went with him." He smiled again. "Turned out his instincts were right. We got along so well and worked together so well that we've kept working together ever since."

"Without any problems?" Ida asked, all polite doubt.

"There are always problems," said Ivan. "But Mattie's easy to get along with. And he's very useful—an incredible thief and a lot of connections. Criminal connections, Ida, not terrorist."

"I hadn't even asked," Ida said.

"I could see that look in your eyes," said Ivan. "You were going to. Mattie doesn't have any terrorist connections, just a hell of a lot of criminal ones."

"Why wouldn't he? It seems like terrorists could be useful people to know, if not to work with."

"You would think that," Ivan said drily. "No. Mattie likes having fun. He likes taking a risk and getting out of it with his own skill. Terrorists aren't fun. And Mattie is easygoing. He doesn't have the kind of single-minded commitment to live for a cause like that. Besides," he concluded with what seemed like genuine feeling, "terrorists kill, and Mattie's not a murderer."

It was curious of him to forget, given that he was the one who had told Ida about it.

"What about the *Jason*?" Ida asked, and watched his reaction closely. It gave him pause, at least.

"That was different," Ivan said. "Mattie's life was in danger."

"From the entire crew?" Ida asked, amused. "You don't think perhaps he might have stopped at one? Or two? Or three, or four? He needed to kill all sixty?"

"He was injured and alone," said Ivan. "He had one chance to escape, and it involved killing them all. He shut off the life support on most of the ship. Tell me, how was he supposed to instruct the vacuum to pick and choose?"

Ivan was very serious. He meant it, Ida thought; he really meant it. Ida wondered how he had reconciled that protective loyalty with his decision to abandon Mattie in the first place.

"What do you have in common?" she asked with genuine curiosity. "A rich boy from Earth who ran away and a poor boy from Miranda?"

Ivan said, "Companionship."

"Not a shared cause?" asked Ida.

Ivan looked exasperated. *"No."*

"You're very certain."

"We spend almost every minute of our time together," said Ivan. "I know what he does and doesn't do, who he knows and doesn't know."

"And you're never separated," said Ida.

"Except when we have to be for a job, or for a few hours for our sanity."

"And yet he left you now," said Ida.

Ivan swallowed. He said, "After the *Jason* and Europa—"

"Europa was eight years ago," Ida pointed out. "Surely the two of you—"

"Europa established boundaries," Ivan said, each word snapping out precise, heavily Terran. "Help each other when we can, but otherwise each puts himself first."

There was a logic to it that appealed to Ida. If she ever were to spend ten years of her life with someone, she would like to have the same rule established between them. But other people were not like her. Other people were weak, even Ivan. And she doubted that Matthew Gale had run because of a betrayal nearly a decade old that he seemed to have forgiven already, shortly after it happened, as he had returned to working with Ivan.

"That seems rather cold to me," said Ida, "for someone as friendly as Matthew Gale." Ivan made a face at the word "friendly," but Ida did not take it back. "Perhaps he left you because he had something better to do."

"Yeah," said Ivan. "Live."

"Or perhaps he had better secrets to hide."

Ivan gave her a long, cold look, and this time did not deign to answer.

Ida started to pace again behind the bars of her long-unused chair, listening to the sound of her heels ringing out throughout the room. "Tell me more about Mattie's connections."

"Since they're not relevant," Ivan said, "I'd rather not turn a rat."

"You are a rat," Ida said. "You and Gale both. You betrayed each other. I want to know about your connections. Did you often get jobs through Mattie's friends?"

"Sometimes," said Ivan.

"Abigail was one of them."

"Yes, she was."

"What about your connections?" Ida asked. "Did you have any connections Mattie didn't?"

Ivan looked away. She watched him as he seemed to struggle for a moment.

"Abby," he said finally.

"What?" Ida asked, coming closer.

He rested his hands on the very edge of the table. "After a time, Abby became my contact, not Mattie's."

"But she was Mattie's foster sister."

"When she was *eight*," said Ivan.

"I thought you hated her."

"In a manner of speaking."

Ida looked down at him, his chains stretched to the limit so that he could grip the edge of the table, and wondered why he would tell her such a thing.

"Were you sleeping with her?" she asked.

A pause. "Obviously," he said.

Not obviously, though Ida saw the signs now. She suspected the real reason for his confession was to separate Mattie from Abigail. Interesting indeed.

"Does Mattie have any connections that you don't know about?" she asked.

Ivan all but rolled his eyes. "Well, I wouldn't know, would I?"

"I mean that he doesn't let you meet," Ida said. "That he doesn't know you know about. Anyone he is hiding."

Ivan leaned in toward her, as close as he could get. He said, "No."

"Could he be keeping any secrets like that?"

"No," said Ivan.

"I want you to give me a list of all of Mattie's most important connections," Ida said.

"I can't do that."

"Yes, you can, and you will," she said, "because you have to."

Ivan took in a deep breath.

"I don't know their last names," he said.

"Is that a lie?"

"It's the truth," he snapped.

Ida, slow and deliberate, said, "Names."

"Adina," said Ivan. "River. Charles. Nora. Ling. Farrah."

"Is that all?" She knew most of those names; some of them were currently in System custody.

"Anji, Christoph, Abby. How far do you want me to go?" Ivan snapped. "Do you want me to name every criminal in the outer planets?"

"Does he know every criminal?"

"He knows a damn lot of them," Ivan said.

"What is he to you?" Ida asked, keeping him on edge, unsteady. "Matthew Gale. Is he your coworker? Your friend? Your lover? Brother? Little brother? Tell me, what is he to you?"

"He's Mattie," Ivan said.

Little brother, perhaps, Ida thought. Ivan was protective of him the way he hadn't been of Constance Harper.

But then again, perhaps not.

"You realize that he's dead, do you not?" she asked, and Ivan looked away. She watched a muscle in his jaw tighten. "The escape pod he abandoned you in has no form of propulsion, and he was aimed nowhere in particular. There was no one around to pick up his pod. He is dead by now, dead for a week, suffocated or starved."

Ivan would not look at her.

"There's no need to protect him," Ida said. "He is dead."

"I'm not protecting anyone," said Ivan.

"I think you are," said Ida. "You have been connected to the Mallt-y-Nos. That means that Matthew Gale has been connected to the Mallt-y-Nos. The two of you do, after all, go everywhere together. The connection is undeniable. But if you are telling the truth and you have no connection to her, then that means that Mattie must—"

"We do not have any connection to the Mallt-y-Nos!" said Ivan. He was looking at her again now, glaring, his fingers clenched bloodless on the edge of the table. "Is it so impossible to you that for once you might be wrong?"

Ida smiled and leaned in closer, just out of reach of his chained arms.

"You're singing a different tune now than you were before," she said. "You said it yourself: I am the woman who is never wrong."

He looked up at her without speaking, breathing with such evenness in and out through his nose that it had to be deliberate. She cherished it, his tension. He was strung so tightly that she could almost feel it in the air she inhaled; it was like running her tongue over the tautness of a harp string.

She was about to speak, ready to speak, ready to turn the subject to the last of Ivan's friends, the one she had been waiting to ask about all this time, the one she knew he knew she would ask about next, the best lead that she had: Abigail Hunter.

The name was on her tongue, Ivan's eyes were fixed on her face, and then someone knocked at the door.

She didn't believe it at first, too caught up in this moment of her interrogation to comprehend that someone could dare to interrupt her.

The knock came again. She straightened slowly, holding Ivan's gaze, and just as she broke it, the knock came a third time, a little more insistently, as if the knocker thought she might not have heard.

She crossed the white room and went to the door. When she opened it, Gagnon stood there with one hand upraised, as if he had just been debating whether he should knock once more.

"Yes?" she said pleasantly, but he looked as wary as if she had raised her hand for a blow. His eyes were shadowed, his clothes rumpled, his cheeks unshaven, and it was plain he had been roused recently from sleep. She felt a surge of contempt for him.

"Captain Domitian needs to speak to you," he said.

"It's urgent?" Ida asked with a delicate and unmistakable threat in the word.

"Yes, ma'am. He's in the piloting room."

She held up one finger to him, and he stood still and silent while she turned back around and walked back to Ivan, who was sitting tense and alone. She and Gagnon had been speaking too softly for him to hear.

When she came up behind him, she laid a hand very lightly on his shoulder. Beneath her fingers, she felt the hardness of his tensed muscles, the bow of his collarbone. It was the first time she had touched him. He did not look to her.

"Pardon me," she said softly. "We'll continue this conversation shortly."

He said nothing and did not look at her as she walked away.

When she passed Gagnon in the doorway again, she said, "Watch him. Do not leave this room. Do not speak to him. I will be back."

Ida strode toward the piloting room with all the dire tension of her interrupted interrogation still shaking in her hands. She was annoyed at the interruption but not furious. Ivan was in a precarious state, and leaving him to stew and to stress, going over in his head obsessively how he next would lie, might work to her advantage.

When Ida reached the piloting room, she found that Domitian was not alone. The mechanic, with her curly hair affray, was pacing in the narrow space of the piloting room when Ida arrived. She stopped once Ida entered, turning her wide brown eyes on her. There were shadows beneath them. It was no wonder the *Ananke* was not fixed, Ida thought, if the mechanic refused to sleep.

"You wished to speak to me?" Ida said, dismissing the mechanic to address Domitian, who was standing beside the door as if he had been waiting for her to arrive.

"Doctor Bastet has information," said Domitian with a nod at the mechanic. Ida, with thin patience, turned to face the other woman.

She was still watching Ida with those round brown eyes. "I got into the *Annwn*," said Althea Bastet.

The frisson of annoyance that had entered Ida's breast at the thought of having to interact with Althea vanished immediately. This was far better news than she had expected, and she was pleased that the mechanic had finally taken it on herself to obey Ida's orders, though she hardly understood why it had been necessary to interrupt the interrogation to inform her. "What did you find?"

"Not all the way," Althea amended. "Just a little bit. I don't think it's possible to get farther in, not without putting the whole ship at risk." Ida gritted her teeth; phrased that way, the System would be certain not to approve any further investigation into the *Annwn*. The safety of the *Ananke* was above all most important to the System.

"But I did," said Althea, "manage to find their . . . stash of useful programs."

"What was there?"

"Some viruses," said Althea. The lights of the control panel behind her flashed on and off in patterns Ida lacked the ability to recognize. "Not much useful, but there were some things. One"—she took a breath; the girl was nervous, Ida saw, anxious and on edge for no reason that she could see—"was a program for the detonation of a sequence of bombs."

Ida nearly smiled, that flush of near triumph she had felt when Ivan had slipped earlier that day coming back to fill her hollow chest. The Mallt-y-Nos was a bomber. And here Ivanov had connected himself to her favorite weapon. "What kind of bombs?"

"I don't know—"

"Doctor Bastet, this is very important," said Ida. If she could only connect Ivan explicitly to the missing Class 1s, she would have him and have reason to use the Aletheia. "Tell me, what kind of bombs?"

"I don't know." Althea's hand had fallen onto the back of the piloting chair; her fingers were digging into its gray fabric. She was so tense, and Ida could hardly understand why.

"Then give me a size. Large or small?"

Althea looked behind Ida, presumably at Domitian. "Don't look at him, look at me," Ida said. "Tell me what kind of bombs."

"There's no way to tell," said Althea.

"Surely you can tell me, large or small." Ida was growing frustrated.

"I can't!"

"You can tell me nothing at all about the type of bombs this program is designed to detonate?"

"No, just that it detonates them in sequence or all at once—it's a timing mechanism basically, but more advanced—"

"So this program," Ida interrupted, "could apply to a sequence of small explosives such as the kind used by thieves like Ivanov and Gale to open locked doors?" The two had used that very tactic many times before to get into and out of secured System locations.

"Yes, but—"

"Then I thank you for your assistance in this matter," said Ida, and could not stop herself from using a tone that said the opposite. If the program had such a simple explanation, the information was useless to her and the interruption to her work unnecessary. "Write up a report and send it to myself and the System, and you may return to repairing the *Ananke*."

Althea Bastet took a deep breath. "It could be used to detonate bombs on the *Ananke*," she said.

Of course. Ida understood now the reason for Althea's anxiety. She was afraid for her ship. It was a silly, stupid fear; there was no reason to think that the *Ananke* was in danger, and Ida very much doubted that if the ship had been wired to explode, someone on the crew would not have noticed by now. "And have any of the many sweeps of the *Ananke* performed by yourself, the computer, and the rest of the crew located any bombs or signs of bombs?" she said with deliberate patience.

"No," Althea admitted.

"And did Gale have sufficient time while on board to plant a series of bombs on the *Ananke*?"

"No, but—"

"Then I suggest," said Ida, "that it cease to concern you." The mechanic still looked nervous, so Ida added, vaguely irritated but wishing to end Althea's anxiety before it could grow and become an issue, "In a few days' time I will take Ivanov off ship. You will not have to trouble yourself with this affair again."

Althea's chin tipped up. Whatever was troubling her, Ida's words had seemed only to increase it: Althea's hand was shaking, trembling nervously in steady rhythm against the piloting chair. "There was something else," Althea said. "There was another program on there. Most of the programs were viruses, but there was the bombs one, and there was this one. This one was—it made it so that whatever computer had it installed would react to the appearance of certain people. It would recognize them and do something about it."

Ida frowned, an ominous suspicion growing in her mind about where Althea was going with this.

Althea said, "I know for a fact that that program was in my—was in this ship. That's how Gale and Ivanov got on board. And I keep finding traces of that same program still—it keeps showing up in the errors in the camera programs. Until I can wipe it out completely, it's still possible that there might be consequences for taking Ivanov off ship. I don't know what kind of consequences; it could be anything. It could be more sabotage. Gale could have programmed the ship so that if we ever killed Ivanov, the ship would destroy itself."

"Revenge from beyond the grave?" Ida asked drily. The mechanic was letting her fancy get the better of her. "What are you saying, Doctor Bastet?"

"You can't take Ivanov off this ship."

Ida said, "I beg your pardon."

It had sounded for a moment as if Althea had tried to give her an order.

Althea was leaning more heavily on the pilot's chair, and somehow, without either of them moving, she seemed to give the impression of having been backed into a corner. The room was small, Ida knew, and the force and strength of her unspoken anger had filled it and driven Althea back.

"I think it's too dangerous," Althea began, but Ida interrupted her swiftly.

"I decide what is best for the prisoner. You were not presuming to tell me, your superior, how best to manage the prisoner under my care?"

"No, I—"

"Then I will expect you will not try to do so again," Ida said. "Write your report on your findings on the *Annwn* and deliver it to me. Then return to your job and repair this ship."

Althea looked beaten back and beaten down, and Ida almost turned to leave, successful at stamping out the mechanic's useless grab for control, but then Althea Bastet straightened her back and a determined look settled in place on her heart-shaped face. It was unexpected, as if the mechanic had a spine Ida had failed to recognize before, and Ida watched her with narrowed eyes. Althea said, "I'm not acting out of my authority."

Ida raised an eyebrow and prepared to beat the mechanic down again, this time for good.

But Althea wasn't done. "The facial recognition program means that there could be hidden viruses in the *Ananke* that Ivanov is affecting in ways that we don't understand. The only thing we can do until I can fix the computer is to keep the ship in the same state it is now and to not make any changes."

Ida tilted her head, daring Althea with her eyes to finish her thought.

The mechanic dared. "Until I finish repairing the *Ananke*," she said with only the slightest tremor of nerves in her voice, "for the safety of this ship, you cannot take Ivanov off board."

Ida returned to the interrogation room with fury boiling under her skin and sharpening her movements. Gagnon was standing just inside the room, arms folded, watching the back of Ivan's neck. Ida dismissed him with a sharp cut of her hand, and he left swiftly.

Back inside the room, with just herself and Ivanov, she tried to center herself. This was what Ida had been building to throughout that long day of interrogation; this was what she wanted to know. Milla Ivanov, Constance Harper, Matthew Gale; all were of only tangential interest to her. But Abigail Hunter: there was a lead. Ivan knew it, too. Ida was certain. She had a clear goal, and she had only to reach for it.

But when Ida tried to reach for calm, she found only the image of the little mechanic standing in the piloting room, frightened but daring to defy her, and succeeding. She found only the knowledge that she had been confronted and had lost to the most insignificant member of the crew, wielding her petty power with all the stupidity of a child.

Time was of the essence. She could not stand just inside the doorway of the room and fume all day. "Let's talk about Abigail Hunter," she said to Ivan as she strode into his line of sight, her heels ringing out with savage sharpness against the paneled floor. He looked at her warily.

She could not show weakness, not here and not to him.

"How did you meet Abby?" she asked.

"Accidentally," Ivan said. His answer was as swift and short as her question had been. He was picking up on her mood and responding accordingly.

"On her part or yours?"

"On Mattie's."

"Explain," Ida said.

"Mattie took me to meet Constance a little over seven years ago.

After we left her bar, we went elsewhere on Mars to refuel and restock our supplies. Abby found us there."

"And your first meeting?" Ida said. "What was that like?"

"Unfriendly," said Ivan, "with an edge of violence. You're out of sorts, Ida. What happened to you?"

"Answer the question, Ivan," Ida said with all the deadly sweetness she possessed.

"I was buying provisions, minding my own business. Mattie had gone elsewhere to get something else; negotiate for fuel, I think. Then Abby came up beside me and said, 'So you're the one who nearly got my brother killed.'"

"Referring to Europa." The significance of seven years and change had not escaped her.

"Referring to half a dozen things," Ivan said. "Including the *Jason*. I didn't know who she was, of course, so I stalled for time. She wasn't System, that was obvious, but I knew that she was dangerous. What *did* happen to you? Tell me, I'm curious."

"Whatever may or may not have happened to me is not your concern," Ida said. "We are here to talk about you. When Abigail confronted you, what did you do?"

"I asked her what she meant while I reached for my knife. She saw me going for the knife and told me I didn't want to do that. I told her I thought I did. Mattie saw us then and came over, grabbing my wrist so I couldn't finish drawing the knife. He told me who she was. She'd already heard about me."

"Where did this take place?" Ida asked. She had not seen the footage of this meeting, which meant the System hadn't flagged it. Perhaps it was part of some surveillance that hadn't been watched yet. That she had never even heard of the encounter—from surveillance or rumor—only increased her simmering frustration.

Ivan had the nerve to smirk. "It was in a traveling black market. No cameras, no regular location. There's no surveillance footage of this meeting. Abby's more paranoid about cameras than anyone else I know."

Useless. Another dead end on Abigail Hunter. "Mattie told her about you but not you about her?" Ida asked.

"That's right. I think he was waiting to introduce us."

"Why?"

"Abby's the black sheep," Ivan said after the slightest hesitation. "She completely embraced the criminal world, just like Constance keeps herself well out of it. Connie doesn't like her; the two haven't spoken to each other or communicated at all in years."

"Mattie also lives a life of crime," Ida pointed out. "As do you. I don't think even you could deny that." She smiled at him, and he mimicked her. She wondered if there was that much unpleasantness in her smile or if he had added that on his own. "So why would Mattie be shy about introducing Abigail to you because of the life she leads?"

"Abby's embraced it more," Ivan said. "We steal for ourselves. Abby connects criminals. There's a difference."

"One I'm failing to appreciate."

Ivan sighed. "As a necessary part of her job, Abby works with people more dangerous than we do. She has to make nice with them."

Ida gave him a look. Ivan returned it. She said, "Dangerous people. Like terrorists?"

"I meant more like hit men and people involved in organized crime," Ivan said with very weary patience. "But I don't ask. I told you before. Abby works for money, not ideals. If she has any terrorist connections, they keep her well out of the loop."

"But you can't deny that she might have some."

"I can't," Ivan admitted.

And with that confirmation, Ida could certainly present the System with a plan to intensify the manhunt for Abigail Hunter. It was not proof enough to convince the System that she had been right all along, but it was something, at least. She had achieved at least one small thing today. Unbidden, she thought again of the mechanic, Althea Bastet, defying her.

"Someone disobeyed you," Ivan guessed. He was watching her face closely. The faintest of smirks, insolent and nearly invisible, lingered on his lips. "Just now. That's why you're off your game. You seem like the kind of person who wouldn't take it well when other people don't do what you want."

Ida looked at him coldly. She was not off her game no matter how unnerving it was that Ivan had guessed so accurately what had gone wrong for her. That was what he did, she reminded herself. He read people.

"Tell me about the fire," she said.

Ivan lifted his brows. He hated her, he loathed her. She could see it in his faint and mocking smile. The sight of his loathing sharpened her intent, made it easier for her to turn her wrath against Althea into a weapon to be used against him.

Ida said, "Tell me about the fire when Mattie, Constance, and Abigail were children. The last time Abigail was a law-abiding part of the System." The last time there was ever concrete surveillance footage of her. The story was an old one, but in its context it was of interest to Ida.

"I don't know a whole lot about it," Ivan said. "I wasn't there. I was in kindergarten. Twenty AU away."

"You must have heard about it," Ida said. She had regained enough of her control to sit down at last in her long-abandoned chair, laying her arms on the rests and feeling herself in a position of power. "You're intimate with all three survivors."

"I haven't asked Abby about it," Ivan said. "Constance won't talk about it. Mattie only gave me the short story."

"I want to know anyway," Ida said.

Ivan leaned back in his chair, mimicking her posture. Ida wondered if he was even conscious he was doing it. The hours of interrogation were starting to show on his face, in the rhythmless pattering of his right hand.

"Fine," he said. "Once upon a time, there were three little children."

Condescension. Ida could not stop the way her jaw set itself, but she let him continue.

"There was Constance, the eldest, practical and sensible. Abby, the middle child, restless and angry. And Mattie, the youngest, playful and clever." Ivan's sarcasm was starting to fade into a different cadence, the true cadence of a fairy tale. "Mattie's parents were only teenagers when they had him; that was why the System took him away. Constance's mother didn't have a husband or a partner willing to help her raise her daughter; that's why the System took her away. Abigail—I don't know why they took Abigail away from home.

"These three little children met on Miranda, in the house of a System administrator who fostered children not because he wanted to but because ostentatiously doing so made it more likely he would be promoted off of the icy little moon. He and his wife didn't like children, and they didn't want them. They especially didn't like Mattie."

Absent its mockery, the story, along with the way it was told, was somehow fascinating, and Ida was reminded all over again that Leontios Ivanov was a dangerous man.

"Little Mattie had quick fingers and bad compulsions. One day they thought he had stolen something from them—a piece of jewelry, maybe—and maybe he had. Mattie doesn't remember anymore. They were very angry."

He paused, and in his silence Ida read between the lines how the System administrators had expressed their anger.

"Constance took Mattie out of the house and hid him in the nearby quarries while Abby distracted the System. Constance went back for their sister, leaving Mattie to hide in the quarries. And so he hid. But when Connie made it back to the house, the house was ablaze. It burned hot enough to destroy the house and the bodies inside completely so that nothing was left of anything but unidentifiable ashes."

"Arson," Ida said.

"Arson," Ivan confirmed.

Ida leaned forward slightly. "With rocket fuel," she told him. The investigation had been positive on that front.

Ivan took a deep breath. "With rocket fuel," he agreed. "Abby left the foster system after that. Constance and Mattie stayed in it and stayed together, and from what I heard, every other place where they were fostered was kind and loving. But Abby never came back. And Constance hasn't spoken to Abby since."

"Abby set the fire," said Ida.

"Yes," Ivan said.

"So what you're telling me," said Ida, and leaned her elbows onto the table, "is that Abigail Hunter has reason to hate the System, killed two people at the age of nine, enjoys setting fires—"

"Enjoys?"

"—and certainly has terrorist connections," Ida finished.

Ivan said, slipping back into the precise, hard enunciation he seemed to adopt when frustrated, "The way you've organized the information, Ida, *leadingly*, I see what you're driving at, but you know what I think?"

"Tell me," Ida said. "I've been wondering."

Ivan could not get his elbows up on the table because of the chains, but he leaned forward anyway. The shadow of that mocking smile was back on his lips. "I think," he said, "that you're looking for a particular answer—that I have a connection, direct or otherwise, to the Mallt-y-Nos—and you're finding that answer even where it is not."

Her fury again, her fury at her failure, at the threat of more failure, at Althea Bastet defying her and Ivan defying her as well, rose up in her chest. She would find a way to break him. She would have to find a way to break him. And she would break him.

"Where is Abby now, Ivan?" Ida asked, her voice soft, just loud enough to travel across the short space separating them.

"I don't know," Ivan said in a voice just as soft, their whispered conversation seeming even quieter in the vast empty space of the white room. "I never know. Mattie and I don't find Abigail; she finds us."

"What do you mean?"

"I mean," said Ivan, "that Abby doesn't let anyone know where she is, and I have no way to contact her. She's a ghost, Ida. Everywhere and nowhere at once. You will never find her."

"Don't antagonize her," Domitian said after Ida had gone.

"I wasn't antagonizing her," said Althea. She was already rattled from the furious way Ida had looked at her; to have Domitian warning her about her behavior added another level of uncertainty and fear.

Domitian did not reply to her defensive retort. Instead, he said, "I'm going to arrange for you and Gagnon to have shortened sleep shifts."

"What? Why?"

"Because of what you just explained to Miss Stays. If it's possible that Ivanov might be able to influence the computer without us knowing, it's even more important that the ship be repaired swiftly. I can't help you"—Althea thought she heard a trace of frustration in his tone—"but Gagnon can. I want the two of you working without pause on this machine. I want it fixed."

"I *have* been working on her nonstop," Althea said.

This time, when he looked at her, she could see the frustration clearly. "Then explain to me what you need me to do to help, Althea," he said. "I want this ship fixed."

On very rare occasions Althea found the good sense to know when to shut up. "Longer shifts will help," she said. He glanced at her dolefully as if he knew she was humoring him, but he nodded.

"I'm going to go work on her now," Althea said. She wanted little more than to be out of the piloting room, which still somehow seemed to hold the oppressive presence of Ida Stays even though she had left. Althea hardly waited for Domitian's acknowledging nod to escape.

Ida's interrogation would end soon, and so Althea went straight for the computer terminal outside Ivanov's cell. She would be guarding him again.

Once she got there, she found a message waiting for her from Gagnon.

"u conspire against my sleep," it said, and concluded with ":("

Twelve years of upper-level education, two doctorates, and a high-ranking System research position. Althea had witnessed Gagnon's elegant theories, his brilliance with mathematics. Yet he could not obey simple rules of spelling and grammar. Althea shook her head at him, though he could not see her. "Yes," she replied, then added for good measure, ">:)"

A moment later she relented. "Go to bed," she typed, and sent it.

Gagnon replied in short order: "promise u won't wake me up again"

"Cross my heart," Althea answered, and that was the end of it.

Domitian led Ivanov back to his cell perhaps an hour later. Althea had little desire to interact with him that night, and it seemed Ivanov felt the same, because he did not bother her while she sat there and worked. She wondered if he had been able to fall asleep but dismissed the thought with some annoyance.

Some hours later she got the message.

She was back to the robotic arms, trying to trace the origin of the malfunction in them. Several times she thought she caught tantalizing hints of what had gone wrong, only to follow them into nothing, bits of junk code, false leads. At first she was annoyed when the message appeared: being a System priority message, it automatically took up half the screen, banishing her workspace to a narrow area that made it nearly impossible to see what she was trying to do. She lost her place in the lines of code. But when she read the message the System had sent, for the first time since Ivanov and Gale had come on board, the *Ananke* was banished from her thoughts.

"Oh, my God," she whispered.

Rustling from the room behind her. "What is it?" Ivanov asked. It seemed he had not been asleep.

Althea could scarcely believe what she was reading. And so, when Ivan said again, "*Althea. What happened?*" she answered without thinking.

"Titania is in rebellion," she said. "The System says it's being led by the Mallt-y-Nos."

Ida was woken from a dead sleep by pounding on her door.

For a moment, in the space between sleep and waking, memory of the knock on the door to the white room that had interrupted her session with Ivan overlapped with the sound of the door being pounded on now, and she was caught up in her old annoyance and a strange and dreadful anticipation of failure.

She rose from her bed, shaking off her sleep and her confusion, and answered the door disheveled. "What is it?" she demanded when she opened it and found Domitian standing there.

He blinked at her. She was wearing nothing but the long shirt she wore to bed, but she did not have patience for his reaction. Before she could prompt him again, he said, "There's been an attack on Titania by the Mallt-y-Nos."

She immediately left the door to stride over to the computer terminal embedded in the wall, which was wedged awkwardly up against one of the oddly shaped room's unexpected corners. A touch of her finger woke the screen, and immediately a message from the System appeared.

Titania was in open rebellion.

For a moment Ida could do no more than try to absorb that one of Uranus's moons had rebelled against the System. It was disastrous. It was infuriating. The System, she knew, would quash it, and easily. Titania was but one moon. But what was troubling was not that it might succeed but that it had happened at all.

The System had also sent to her the surveillance footage on account of her rank in the intelligence branch. Ida let it play and watched as a crowd of people, native Titanians from the look of them, advanced on a System building ringed with System military. There was no sound to the footage, and Ida watched their mouths move noiselessly, their faces twisted in rage without voice. As she watched, one of them threw a bottle with a rag stuffed into it at the building or at the standing soldiers. It shattered and sent liquid fire crawling up the System soldiers, up the walls of the System building. A Molotov cocktail. The System soldiers raised their rifles. The unarmed crowd recoiled as the System fired into them, screaming without sound on the silent tape.

When Ida broke her attention away from the surveillance tape, leaving it still playing on one side of the screen, and looked at the rest of the message, there was another surprise awaiting her. At the very moment rebel forces had attacked System strongholds all over the moon, it seemed, a message had been broadcast out to the entire solar system. It had been broadcast on all frequencies, including System ones. Everyone in the Uranian system had heard. No doubt the message had traveled all the way to Neptune and the dwarf planets as well. Perhaps it had even made it to Jupiter.

The message had said, THE WILD HUNT BEGINS.

It had been signed "The Mallt-y-Nos."

Ida supposed that most people would feel horror, or fear, or dread. She felt only the start of exultation. The stakes had risen for her, for the System, but with the rising of the stakes had come opportunity.

Domitian was still standing in the doorway. "Come in and close the door," she ordered, and he obeyed while her mind raced.

It would put Ida's head on the block even more if she was wrong, but she knew that she was never wrong. What was a little more risk when her success was certain?

What was a little more risk to prove herself? What was a little more risk to win?

She wondered if Ivan had known this attack would come. She wondered if he had sat across from her, and looked at her with those blue eyes open and innocent, and known all the time, counting down in his head the days until this began.

"This changes things," Ida said, and heard her voice sound as calm as she herself was not.

"Yes, ma'am," said Domitian.

She doubted that he understood the half of it. If the Mallt-y-Nos had struck her first blow, the System would be ready for war. Already their message said that they were deploying the full force of their military to the outer planets to quell Titania and to defend against further uprisings or whatever else the Mallt-y-Nos might have planned. But it wouldn't be enough. They'd be ready to take more risks in return for something to use against the Mallt-y-Nos. Ida did not doubt that the System would be willing to risk the *Ananke*'s secrecy for its own security.

"I was going to take Ivanov off the *Ananke* for purposes that are absolutely necessary to my interrogation," Ida said. "This has made it all the more imperative that I break him. And yet I cannot take him from this ship."

"Miss Stays, Doctor Bastet . . ."

"Is no doubt correct in what she does," Ida said sweetly. She could be magnanimous now, when she was about to get what she wanted. "Don't mistake me. I am only saying that if I cannot take him off the ship, it makes sense to bring my work here."

A pause. Perhaps Domitian was waiting for her to elaborate. Ida wanted him to ask.

"How so, Miss Stays?" Domitian asked.

"I was going to interrogate Constance Harper and Milla Ivanov," said Ida. She would have liked to speak to Gale and Hunter, but Gale was dead and Hunter missing. Harper and Doctor Ivanov, though, were in her grasp.

On the screen before her was the surveillance footage from the surface of Titania, still playing. A System building was on fire. System soldiers were firing into the crowd. On the ground before the camera, a man had fallen to his knees, clutching at his chest.

"And if I cannot go to them," Ida said, watching the man die, "then they will have to come to me."

Chapter 5

PARTICLE NUMBER

Physics, ground down to its most basic parts, was nothing more than the study of energy: where the energy was, where the energy was not, and how the energy flowed.

Humans were the same. All human interactions were nothing more than the flow of power from one to another. Whatever emotions other people professed to feel for one another—love, hate, empathy—they were nothing to that unconscious awareness of power. Crack any of those sentiments open and find inside only the dark core of a power differential informing it, defining it, giving it strength.

Ida could not say for certain if other people genuinely believed in their own honesty when they professed to be motivated by things other than power, if they simply didn't recognize that every motivation led back to power in the end. Every interaction was built on power and ebbed and flowed with the changes in who had the power and who did not. She could not say for certain, and there was no way to find out safely.

One thing she did know for certain: she recognized it, she knew it, and that by itself gave her power.

"There was violence on Titania last night," she said to Ivan when they were together in the white room, and he thought he could gain power over her by the skill with which he lied. "Did you hear?"

He looked up at her and shrugged. "Should I have?" he asked.

"It was just a question," Ida said with a smile.

"I don't know if you've noticed, Ida, but I've been in a cell for a week. I'm a little behind on the news."

"The Mallt-y-Nos has claimed the activity," said Ida. "Are you sure you haven't heard?"

Ivan said, "I hadn't heard."

"But you don't seem surprised."

He smiled that wolfish smile. "There's always violence on Titania. Should I be shocked that there's a little more?"

"What's she up to, Ivan?" Ida asked. "What's she going to do next?"

He shrugged as if he couldn't possibly care. "You can ask me that question as often as you like," he said. "I still won't be able to answer it."

Ida studied him, the arrogance in the way he leaned back in his chair and looked her straight in the eye and boldly spoke what they both knew were lies.

"We found an interesting program on board your ship," she said. "It looks like a program that would detonate a sequence of charges. Or bombs, perhaps."

"That?" he said, one eyebrow lifting, displaying no surprise or alarm at the mention of his ship. "We use that to blow up vault doors from far away so that we're outside of the blast radius. Surely you've seen the footage."

He was so calm and collected, he thought he was winning. Ida knew better. And the ship's mechanic who thought she could have her way over Ida's will—she, too, did not fully realize how complete Ida's power was. Because that evening, after the interrogation, Ida received a message from the System: her request for permission to have Constance Harper and Milla Ivanov brought to the *Ananke* had been granted.

By tomorrow, the two women would be on board.

Althea found out that Harper and the doctor would be coming on board only hours before they were scheduled to arrive.

"But they can't," she said to Domitian when he broke the news. "This ship is secret, the technology is classified. If it leaked . . ."

"It will not leak," Domitian interrupted, so solid and firm that it was as if she had run up against a stone wall. "The location of the *Ananke* is being sent directly into their flight computers and then erased entirely once they have returned to their original location. They will not be able to find the ship again themselves or direct anyone else to see it. Their interaction with the ship will be limited to empty rooms, Althea."

"They'll still see the *Ananke*," said Althea. "They'll still see the halls, the computer interface, the shape of her . . ."

Domitian sighed. Althea sensed she was nearing the edge of his indulgence for her, but she pushed on.

"Milla Ivanov is a scientist," Althea said. "She'll be able to just look at this ship and know a lot about it. That it's mass-based gravitation. That the computer is unusual—"

"We have permission from the System," Domitian said. "If anything happens, which it won't, you will not be liable."

Prison had been the least of Althea's concerns. "But—"

"Milla Ivanov will arrive first," he said. "I will take Ivanov into the white room and wait while Miss Stays interrogates Doctor Ivanov in the uppermost empty storage room. She will then be brought to see her son in the white room, and then she will leave. Miss Harper will arrive shortly thereafter and go through the same process. They will see no more of the ship than two empty rooms, the docking bay, and a small segment of the hallway."

"But they'll still see her," Althea said, and could not quite understand why he did not see the problem.

Ida Stays, she suspected. It was Ida Stays who had stopped him from understanding.

"That's enough," Domitian said. "I realize that you are concerned, but Miss Stays has received System permission, and she has received mine. Ivanov is not leaving this ship, which is what you wanted. This interrogation is crucial to the System, especially after the events on Titania. Regarding her presence here, Miss Stays has been very accommodating. You have expressed your concerns and they have been noted, and I suggest that now you remember your place on board this ship."

Althea was caught short again, baffled. It sounded almost as if he had threatened her with insubordination, a serious charge on a secret military craft. She could hardly believe he would ever threaten her at all.

She nodded her acquiescence without another word and started off down the hall.

"Althea?" Domitian called, and unwillingly, feeling like a dog called to heel, she stopped, obedient even after a scolding.

"Ivanov must not know that they're coming," he said, and Althea nodded her understanding without turning around, wanting only to be gone. She was supposed to relieve Gagnon in front of Ivanov's cell.

Gagnon's eyes were shadowed, like hers, with too little sleep. Althea still did not know what her expression must have looked like, but it made him snort and say, "Right there with you, Al," as if they were conspirators in sentiment. Althea did not rise to the comment, and Gagnon let the conversation die. Instead of speaking, he rose from her stool and clapped her on the shoulder as he passed.

"I'll relieve you in a few hours," he said.

Althea's voice sounded robotic in her ears. "Your sleep shift is next," she said.

"Yeah," Gagnon said, walking backward up the hall, "but you need sleep even more than me."

Althea stood in place after he was gone, unmoving. She could not quite bring herself to move forward and start to work again on the *Ananke*. Behind her, in the silence, she almost imagined she could feel Ivanov's presence, like the warmth of someone standing close at her back or the soft sound of breaths in an empty room. It was strange and disconcerting and filled her with a curious uncomfortable feeling that was not dissimilar to guilt. His mother and his friend would be coming here later on, and Althea knew it, but he didn't. She knew that Ida would have interrogated them whether or not Althea had forced her to keep Ivanov on board, but she still felt a strange responsibility for the way things had fallen out.

She sat down slowly on her stool. She was under orders not to tell him, and so she wouldn't. The System did not look kindly on insubordination. It was the first step on the path that led to the kind of thing that had gotten Saturn destroyed.

Into the silence, not so much breaking it as filling it, like color diffusing into water, Ivanov said, "I guess no one's getting enough sleep around here."

"You should be," Althea said. "You don't have anything to do." She spoke automatically and without real rancor.

"And you have too much."

The *Ananke*, the *Annwn*—Althea did have too much to do. And she had too many thoughts choking her brain.

"What do you think about," she asked out of nothing but blank, honest curiosity and the awareness that Ida Stays was making both of them suffer, "when you're in there, not sleeping?"

"I think about a lot of things." It was a dishonest answer, and Althea sighed and turned back to her computer, cutting him off with the angle of her shoulders though he could not see the motion, but he continued, "I think about my friends. I think about my home planet."

"Earth." It was strange to her sometimes how even though he had left Earth, he had never stopped being from it. It made him seem very ordinary to her, very much like the people she had known there and very little like someone she should fear.

"Yes." This silence was almost comfortable.

"You're not from Earth," Ivanov said, as naturally as anything. "But you've spent some time there. Did you go to school?"

"Australian branch of the Terran University." It could not be dangerous to tell him something as simple and public as that.

"I went to the North American branch," he said. "We kicked your ass at hockey."

That hit at a nerve and brought bright loud memories of standing on bleachers screaming at the colored shapes running on the field below, letting herself get caught up in the crowd's noise and energy despite not quite understanding, despite partly wishing she could simply go back to her dorm and put machines together untroubled. Ivanov was a little bit like that crowd, she thought. It was not like her to speak to him, but somehow she was caught up in it.

In any case, she could not resist saying, "But not at soccer."

"Nobody cares about soccer."

"Maybe the *North American branch* didn't," said Althea.

Ivanov laughed, his voice low. "When did you graduate?" he asked.

"Twelve years ago."

"We overlapped," he said. "I graduated ten years ago."

Althea looked at the computer screen before her, which was still blank, and said, "I know."

With the *Ananke* in its state, she had not had much time to wonder. Still, the stray thought had appeared to her whenever she was in a place where Ivanov wasn't to wonder, Had she met him while she was there? Had she passed him on the street or in the quad during those rare times she visited the North American branch or whenever he went down to

Australia? She thought she would have remembered him if she had, handsome and buttoned up and closed off, with brilliant blue eyes.

This conversation was a waste of her time. Althea opened up a program on the computer, intending to work, but the thought of Earth and the university brought to mind again Ivanov's mother, who would be on board soon.

What would Ida Stays do to her? Althea wondered, and wished she had not the wit to wonder.

"But you're not from Earth originally," Ivanov commented. He spoke it so casually that it did not seem an insult, only the natural continuation of their conversation.

"I'm from Luna," Althea said.

"Ah," said Ivanov. "We were neighbors."

She meant to ask him then what she had been wondering since she had read his file. She preferred things that way, to ask directly and immediately. She hated uncertainty. But somehow she could not ask about that time on the roof of his house. Perhaps it was because she had the knowledge of Milla Ivanov and Constance Harper sitting in her throat. Yet she could not bring herself to let the conversation die. "Have you ever been to Luna?"

"A true woman of the moon," Ivanov said, and she knew he was smiling from his voice even when she couldn't see him. "Won't call it 'the moon.'"

Althea scowled, an automatic reaction, even though he couldn't see her.

"When I was very young," he said in the slow, lilting cadence of a story, "my mother and I went there once or twice for a vacation. With the gravity so low, all the people move in slow motion. There's something eerie about the shape of a woman against the blackness of space with her hair floating around her head, falling too slowly back to her shoulders to be natural, to be anything but a waking dream. My mother," he said, and the thought of Milla Ivanov sent a bolt through Althea's heart. "That's all I really remember from going there with her. My mother under the atmospheric dome with her hair loose and drifting. I'm not sure it really happened. She never wears her hair down."

"Where did you visit?" Althea asked to have something to say.

"Earth-facing side. Of course. Better developed. Better reception for the System's cameras, that side."

"I grew up on the space side," Althea said. "It's less touristy."

"I've been to the dark side of the moon, too," Ivanov said. "Recently. With Mattie."

Althea had hardly noticed when, but his voice seemed to have become softer, gentler, as if he could tell that she was weary and upset and was trying to be kind.

"Why?" she asked, and tried to summon some of her defensive scorn. "To steal something?"

"Probably," said Ivanov.

He did not immediately go on, so Althea said, "It must've been hard to be so close to home and not go home." She was not good at being conciliatory. She rarely took the trouble to apologize.

"Mattie said the same thing," he said.

"What did you tell him?"

"I told him," said Ivanov, "that if I went the few thousand kilometers to go see Earth, then I'd have to realize it would only be a couple hundred thousand kilometers to actually go to Earth. And then I'd take the *Annwn* and get shot down in the atmosphere."

"What did he say?"

"He said he thought I wasn't quite that stupid. He also told me it might be the last time I ever got to see her. I still said no."

It made it even less comprehensible to her that he would have ever left Earth when he seemed to truly miss it.

"But," Ivan said very softly and slowly indeed, "even so, when we left Luna, we went on a strangely precise trajectory. And so for a long time, as we were flying away, the Earth and the moon were right beside each other, like a child's model, and North America was facing us just as evening was falling, the lights of cities starting up in the east and traveling slowly west until the planet was too far away to see."

Althea had seen that image herself, beautiful, old, and perfect. She could hear his reverence for the planet, and she could hear a deep affection that until now Ivanov had kept well hidden.

"You miss him," Althea said.

"Yes," said Ivan, without lies and pretense.

Somewhere Matthew Gale was rotting in a metal coffin, falling in toward the sun. Another loss for Leontios Ivanov.

Perhaps it was because she knew of Mattie dead and of Constance and Milla Ivanov in danger, or perhaps because she, too, had seen the cruelty of Ida Stays's eyes, or perhaps it was just because Ivanov had been honest with her, but Althea found the courage to ask, "Why did you leave Earth if you miss it so much? You were rich, had a bright future—you already lived on Earth. The System would have hired you in a second, even with—your father."

"I know," said Ivanov.

Althea said, "Did you leave Earth for the same reasons you tried to kill yourself when you were there?"

Ivanov was silent for a long time. His lack of an answer made the air seem heavier by the moment, like the anxious guilt curling in her chest.

"Did Ida ask you to ask me about that?" he said.

"No," Althea said, her fingers skittering restlessly over the edges of the keyboard, and almost regretted asking. "I was just . . . I just wondered."

"If you promise not to tell anyone, then I'll tell you."

She had expected him to turn on her, or to deny everything, or to simply refuse to say anything more. She had not expected him to answer the question.

That was not a promise Althea could keep. Simply talking to him was wrong enough. She would be able to wheedle her way out of trouble—serious trouble if Miss Stays ever found out—only by protesting that the discussions did not have to do with anything important. And even then she was on shaky ground.

On the other hand . . .

The camera in this part of the hallway was not working.

Althea looked up into it. Its black eye stared down at her, but whatever the *Ananke* saw, it was not sharing it with the System.

No one would know unless Althea or Ivanov told them. But to make the promise was to move from a gray area into the black, to deliberately keep information from her superiors, to be in some measure *insubordinate*.

"I promise," Althea said.

Ivanov had to know what she was promising, but he said nothing about it. Instead, as if Althea's promise had unlocked his tongue, he said, "Earth isn't as wonderful as you think it is. There's more surveillance there than there is on the outermost dwarf planets all combined."

"So it's safe," Althea said, puzzled, because that was what the surveillance was at its core: a guarantee that nothing could happen to you that the System, omniscient, omnipotent, and omnipresent, wouldn't know.

There was a silence as if Ivanov were working himself up to speak. "Yes," he said at last in measured tones, "it's safe. Like everyone being locked up in separate cages is safe. No one else can get at you, but you're still in a cage. Especially if they think you're predisposed to be dangerous."

"So you tried to kill yourself because you felt trapped," Althea said, trying to understand.

"Yes and no," said Ivanov. "At first I thought—Some people's brains don't work quite right." He hesitated a moment, then said, "It's something in the programming."

Althea lifted her chin, listening closely.

"You can't change it, because that's part of what makes them who they are," said Ivan, and Althea thought of her machines and her programs, all with their unique little quirks, their personalities. She thought of the ones that did not run quite correctly or that ran in strange ways. People, she'd always thought, had less of a spectrum in their quality; either they worked perfectly and worked well within the System or they were flawed, bad bits of code, like Ivanov or Gale.

It was harder now to think of Ivan as nothing more than a flaw in the System.

"But I feel," said Ivan, "all the time like I'm clinging to a rotting old pier over a cold sea, and I'm soaked to the skin from the spray and the rain. And it's all I can do to hang on to the edge of the pier, because— there's a woman in the water, a woman with dead eyes who's part of the ocean itself, and she's got one icy hand around my ankle and she's trying to drag me down with her into the ocean."

For an instant she could taste the salt, feel the frigid spray, the cold slick fingers around her ankle like a manacle.

"And I'm so tired of hanging on," Ivan said. He almost seemed to be talking to someone other than her, to himself or to someone who wasn't there, and it sent a chill down Althea's spine. "There's a hollow dark place inside my ribs instead of flesh and blood, and sometimes I just want to go down with her. On Earth I had no reason not to go down with her. Out here I have—I have reasons not to let go."

. . .

Ida was aware of how close she stood to the edge. Her reputation, her force of personality, had brought her this far, but she had to get results. The System did not believe her theory about Ivanov and Gale, but after Titania, with the threat of worse to come, they were letting her take the risk because they were desperate for some success. But the burden of success was solely on her. She'd thought she'd had six more days; she had fewer now, however long it was between today and the Mallt-y-Nos's next attack. If the Mallt-y-Nos attacked again and Ida still had nothing to tell the System—if she failed to get anything out of Harper or Doctor Ivanov—

It was not worth thinking about. She would get results. She was always right, always.

Time was ticking down. She could feel it in her bones like a bomb on a timer of unknown duration. It was not *would* it blow but *when*, and the constant knowledge that that unknown *when* drew ever more near.

"Milla Ivanov will arrive first," she told Domitian as they walked together down the hall toward her second makeshift interrogation chamber. "Constance Harper second. The time of Harper's arrival will overlap with Doctor Ivanov's departure, so be ready."

"You intend for them to meet," Domitian said carefully, asking without asking.

Ida allowed herself to smile, but she knew it came out stiff and fierce.

"If both of them are as innocent as Ivanov claims, then they have never met before," she said. "Let's find out if they have."

Ivan had not spoken since his confession, and Althea had kept the silence from her end. It was as if his words had spun a hollow shell of glass around the two of them; no matter what Althea said, her words would shatter the glass and she would not be able to go back to the way things were before.

Domitian arrived in that fragile silence with no more than a nod at her, although his eyes lingered on her face for a moment longer than she wanted to meet them, as if he were looking for something from her: anger or acceptance or apology. Althea did not have the courage to answer his silence, either. The moment was brief; Domitian did not waste time on unnecessary things. He opened the door to Ivan's cell, his gun black and gleaming in one hand.

"On your feet, facing the wall," said Domitian. Althea peered through the tiny window made by Domitian's arm and the wall and saw Ivan, pale and slender, with his brilliant blue eyes darkly shadowed, rise slowly to his feet. Althea watched Domitian cuff him roughly and wondered why Ida Stays had seen fit to dress him in thin white hospital clothes, as if he were ill.

Domitian got a hand in the crook of Ivan's elbow and hauled him out of the tiny cell and into the hallway, leading him away. Ivan did not look at Althea once. Perhaps he, too, found it easier to speak to Althea through the door, when they could not see each other's faces.

She found herself unaccountably on the edge of tears, and it frustrated her, and so when she signaled Gagnon about a note he had left her in the comments of some code he had been examining, she was sharp and snappish. "It doesn't make any sense," she said over the intercom. "What do you mean, 'the rewriting is constants'?"

"I mean exactly what that means," said Gagnon with such maddening uselessness that she briefly visualized beating his head against the walls of the *Ananke* until through the power of percussive maintenance the ship resumed normal operating status. "Except without the typo. The rewriting is constant; the ship keeps rewriting any fixes I make to that part of the code."

"That doesn't make any sense," Althea snapped.

"The problem we're facing, summed up in one sentence," Gagnon said drily.

"I don't want quips," Althea said. "I want you to actually achieve what I tell you to do!"

A brief pause filled by the static sound of silence through the intercom's speakers and then true silence as the connection cut off.

Althea, it seemed, could do nothing without guilt today. She bent over the machine and tried to put aside thoughts of Gagnon, and Ivan, and her own frustration. She was not having much success five minutes later when the sound of footsteps came down the hall, and she turned only reluctantly to see Gagnon walking down toward her, his hands in his pockets, his red hair starting to fall into his face in thin, wispy flyaways. He stopped beside her and said, as if there were no hurry and he hadn't just left his post unmanned, "What's up?"

"Nothing," Althea said. "I'm busy."

Gagnon was nodding and frowning at the same time in the way that Althea hated because it meant he was understanding something about her that she didn't want him to understand. "Didn't sound like nothing," he said.

"Shouldn't you be in the control room?"

He leaned against the wall with one shoulder, boxing her in, too close. Althea suddenly had a flash of a memory from when she was a child, when a little boy had come and leaned over her shoulder too close and tried to take away her computer from her. She'd punched and kicked him until he'd run away.

"Doctor Ivanov and Harper aren't scheduled for another fifteen minutes," he said.

"But they'll enter *Ananke*'s sensor range soon," said Althea.

He made that frowning, nodding face again.

"You're right," he agreed. "I should really be up there. You know, you should answer my question so I can get back up there in time."

"I answered your question."

"Lying isn't answering the question."

"Who are you, Ida Stays?" Althea snapped, and immediately wished she could have kept her mouth shut.

Gagnon was regarding her steadily. "Is this about Miss Stays? Has she been giving you a hard time?"

"No," Althea said, but she glanced against her will toward Ivan's open cell.

Gagnon followed her gaze. "This is about the prisoner?" he asked. "Has *he* been bothering you?"

"No!" Althea said too vehemently, she decided after saying it, and tried to calm her tone. "He hasn't been bothering me."

"But . . . ?"

"But I feel bad for him," Althea said, and it seemed like only the barest, meanest explanation of what she felt.

Gagnon was looking at her, perfectly baffled. "Why?" he asked.

"Because"—now that she had opened the subject, it seemed easier to express—"because of his mother, and because of . . . of Constance, and because Miss Stays is torturing him . . ."

"Miss Stays isn't torturing him," Gagnon said, sounding amused but looking at her with something too close to concern. "Has he been talking to you?"

"Ivanov?" Althea asked, stalling, having remembered to use his surname at the last moment.

Gagnon gave her a look as if he thought she might have been struck suddenly stupid. "Sometimes," Althea admitted, and Gagnon's expression darkened.

"Damn it, Al," he said. "And you've been listening to him."

"I can't not hear when he talks."

"Yeah, but you've been *listening*." Althea did not like the look on Gagnon's face; it skated too close to the expression that meant he was going to tell Domitian.

"I'm not going to tell Domitian," he said, and she was embarrassed to have been so obvious. "I just . . ." He stopped and chewed on the inside of his lip. "I'll make sure he stops bothering you, Al," he said.

Althea tried to ask what he meant by that, but her words were drowned out by the sudden wailing of the *Ananke*'s alarm.

Ida burst out of her second interrogation room at the screaming alarm, looking up and down the hallway for someone to demand answers from.

The ship screamed and wailed as she hurried down to the control room and unlocked the door, but there was no one inside.

"Son of a bitch," she hissed, and then snapped at the ceiling, "Enough!" without really expecting to be heard.

The ship continued deafly blaring that deafening sound.

Running footsteps. Ida turned to see Gagnon coming up the hallway, followed by the shorter, wild-haired figure of Althea Bastet. Gagnon avoided Ida's gaze—a sign of guilt; doubtless he was the one who was supposed to be manning the control room—but Althea's round brown eyes lingered on hers for a moment before breaking away, and Ida could not quite read her expression.

It was unimportant. Ida had full control over the ship once again. However Doctor Bastet would rather things be was entirely irrelevant.

Ida stood in the center of the room as Althea and Gagnon rushed from console to console, watching their frantic motions, listening to Gagnon say, "It's not a machine error," and Althea say, "It's not an internal alert," and Gagnon say, "So what *is* it?"

The most they managed to do was shut off the wailing alarm, the most basic of tasks. Ida stood perfectly still and felt her fury grow.

"Found it!" said Althea, leaning so far over the screen that more frizzed curls popped free of her loose braid and dangled downward, as if reaching to connect to the machine below. "It's the proximity sensor. It's sending up an alert for . . . a weapon fired at the ship?"

"There are no weapons discharges in this area," Gagnon reported from another screen.

"It's telling me about some danger heading toward us," said Althea, sounding frustrated.

Ida said in her sweetest, politest tone with her heaviest of affected Terran accents, "You need to fix this computer."

The tension in the room increased tangibly. They had been so absorbed that they had seemed to have forgotten her presence. When it became apparent that Althea was not going to respond, Gagnon said, "Yes, ma'am. We're doing our best."

Ida could have stripped them of their jobs, their titles, their qualifications, for such incompetence on so important a ship. She could have done the same thing to their families and close associates if need be. Gagnon clearly knew it and feared it, but Althea Bastet—stubborn still, still resistant—did not respond to her.

It irked Ida, made her want to strike at Althea again, but she had no reason to do so—the woman was not actually being insubordinate— and so she controlled herself.

"Got it," said Althea, although she sounded a little muted and her back still was to Ida. "It's the proximity sensor. Doctor Ivanov's ship just came into range. It triggered a reaction in the ship."

"Got some wires crossed," Gagnon muttered. Ida looked at him incredulously.

The intercom came on.

"I am in the white room," said Domitian's even tones, made especially even at the moment. "Do not explain over the intercom. Send someone down to guard Ivanov. I will come up."

Althea Bastet started to stand, but Gagnon was faster.

"I'll go," he said, and Althea looked as if he had slapped her in the face as he hurried from the room, leaving the two women alone together.

Ida watched Althea and watched Althea avoid looking at her. Simply by standing there in silence, Ida could see that her presence was making Althea tense, but Althea said nothing to her, her downcast eyes scanning the screen before her with more attention than it deserved. Perhaps the mechanic had learned her place after all.

Something beeped, and the mechanic moved to look at the relevant screen while Ida stood in the center of the room and watched her, full of power.

"She's hailing us," Althea said. She was obligated by regulations to report such a message to Ida; Ida was certain she would have said nothing at all if she hadn't been required to. "She wants permission to dock."

"Grant it," said Ida, as cool and calm as if she were indifferent to Althea's presence when Althea was so affected by hers. "And send Domitian to the docking bay when he arrives." She took the moment as the perfect time to depart and leave Althea with an order, with Ida having had the last word.

Domitian caught up to her at the doors to the docking bay. They were sealed as an air lock; beyond them the vast mouth of the *Ananke* was opening to admit a small, gleaming ship.

"I'll escort the both of you to your room, then to the white room," Domitian said quietly, clarifying, and Ida nodded slightly.

The ship landed lightly. It was sleek and small, the newest model from Earth. The great doors of the *Ananke* slid slowly shut overhead, and Ida waited until the light beside the bay doors turned green, indicating the repressurization of the space beyond.

She pushed open the glass doors and stepped out into the vast hollowness of the docking bay; across from her, out of the sleek ship stepped a sleek woman who glanced briefly around the room before fixing her attention on Ida.

The years, Ida knew from her study of the woman, had hardened Milla Ivanov into perfect clarity, as pressure did to a diamond. No expression showed on her face. The woman walking toward Ida had aged out of her beauty but kept her handsomeness, her blond hair lightened to white, her forehead and the corners of her mouth outlined in the marks of frowns. Doctor Ivanov was the type of woman who would go to slenderness and fragility as she aged, and indeed she had already started down that path, but even though her wrists seemed small enough to snap, when she took Ida's hand, her grip was firm.

She had the same brilliant blue eyes as her son and the same intensity in her stare.

"Miss Stays," said Milla Ivanov. She had a soft voice. At lectures, she always needed a microphone.

"Doctor Ivanov," said Ida, and smiled charmingly. "A pleasure to meet you. Please call me Ida."

Milla Ivanov neither acknowledged the liberty nor returned it. She simply released Ida's hand when Ida released hers and said, "I assume you have a room prepared."

Milla Ivanov had been the subject of more interrogations than Ida had ever performed. It put Ida at a slight disadvantage, perhaps, but in the end she still had Milla's son.

She smiled and said, "Of course. Right this way."

Doctor Ivanov seemed not to notice or simply not to care that Domitian followed them at a politely dangerous distance. She kept pace beside Ida, her flats striking the ground more softly than the *click, click* of Ida's heels.

Ida said nothing until they reached the door to the second interrogation chamber. This chamber was smaller, almost cozy; the room had been used for storage of various valuable equipment that Ida had had removed. The ceiling was a trifle low, not enough to bother Ida but enough to induce the faintest feeling of claustrophobia when combined with the dark uniform metal of the walls, ceiling, and floor. The only object left inside the room was a table rather like the one in the white room but smaller, with two chairs on either side.

Ida led the way inside and signaled to Milla to take the chair with its back to the door, seating herself opposite. Milla Ivanov sat with her back perfectly straight and her hands folded loosely in her lap and did not even blink when Domitian swung the creaking door shut behind them.

For a moment, Ida simply enjoyed the setting. Milla Ivanov sat across from her in the very same way her son had every day for a week. The resemblance between mother and son was impressive: the same blue eyes, the same shape of jaw and lip, the same close, careful attention. The only differences that Ida could see were that Milla Ivanov did not waste her time with charm as her son did and that unlike Ivan, Milla was not in chains.

Not yet, perhaps.

"Doctor Ivanov, I'm afraid I'm going to have to confess I'm a bit of a fan," Ida said with the slightest bashful smile. "To be perfectly honest, you were one of my role models as a child. A brilliant, successful woman who rose in spite of all the adversity that surrounded her." Ida sighed. "It is something I have always admired."

She had admired even more the way Milla had lied and performed at her husband's trial, using her infant son as a prop to save her own skin.

"I am glad to inspire," said Milla Ivanov, her voice crisp, tonally perfect, and perfectly empty. She tilted her head ever so slightly to the side, and Ida had a sudden flash of Ivan making the same motion. "I have heard something of you, too. Of your impressive and rapid rise to fame."

If Ida had not been paying attention, she might have mistaken that for a compliment.

Ida held her smile for a moment while she reconsidered. Charm, then, was out. So directness it was.

"Doctor Ivanov," Ida said, leaning forward onto the table and looking serious and concerned, "are you aware of the events surrounding your son lately?"

Perhaps the briefest flicker of blue eyes. Milla said, "I haven't been in contact with my son since he left home."

"But you are aware."

"Through what has been told me through System news broadcasts," said Milla Ivanov, "and the occasional ill-timed System questioning on the subject."

This barb seemed to cut especially deeply for being spoken in Milla's crystalline Terran accent, unsoftened by a childhood on Venus or an adulthood in the outer planets.

"I apologize for this inconvenience," said Ida. "I'm afraid it was quite necessary."

"Every time my son steals from a grocery store, the System comes to question me about his habits, taking me from my studies and from my lectures," said Milla. She cocked her head to the side again, even more strongly reminiscent of her son. "What is one more interruption in the middle of my vacation?"

"I will try to make this interrogation as brief as possible," said Ida. "But it is, of course, for the good of the System."

"I will do my duty as a citizen," Milla Ivanov said. "You went through all the trouble of blindfolding my computer's navigation system and bringing me to a ship in the middle of nowhere. I assume this is important."

Even as Ida kept her smile fixed at the reminder of the difficulties she had been forced to go through to obtain this interview and the increased pressures from the System that now weighed on her, the thought occurred to her that Milla was fishing for information on the nature of the *Ananke*. Even if Ida had been so inclined or so foolish as to answer, she would have nothing to tell the other woman.

"The last time you spoke to your son was ten years ago; am I correct?" Ida asked.

"Yes."

"I'd like you to describe the incident for me, if you please," said Ida.

"You have it all on camera," said Milla Ivanov. Briefly, Ida enjoyed the comparison of Milla's protest to the ones Ivan had been making all week long. "My accounting will not be so detailed."

"Even so," Ida said, and wondered if the mother would have the same flair for storytelling as the son.

"Leon woke up late," said Milla. "It was a few days after he had graduated. He came downstairs. I had circled some job opportunities for him in the paper and left it at his place. He read them, said that he had somewhere to go, and left. There is nothing more to it than that. I said nothing to him."

She spoke in the clipped, emotionless tones of a woman who had repeated this story many times, reporting with the same bare factuality as a machine. Ida remembered watching the scene from the Ivanov house surveillance. Milla Ivanov had been sitting at the table with her back to the glorious sunrise coming up over the mountains that was visible through the glass wall behind her. She had hardly looked up from the notes in front of her as Ivan came down, looked at the paper his mother had left him, and then stood and watched his mother for a long, silent span of time.

Milla Ivanov, drumming her fingers arrhythmically against the tabletop, had not noticed her son's attention. She looked up only when Ivan told her he was leaving and looked at him for perhaps a moment too long—or perhaps that was only Ida reading into what she saw—before nodding tersely.

Ivan had left, and Milla had gone back to work. She had not even looked up when the sound of Ivan's ship roared through the house and rattled the dishes he had left untouched. Ida had wondered if Milla regretted not saying anything that last time her son left or regretted not realizing he was leaving, not trying to stop him, but with Milla Ivanov in front of her now, regret seemed like it would be a foreign thing to her.

"Did you not have any idea your son was leaving for good?" Ida asked.

"No," Milla said. "My son has always been very good at hiding what he is thinking, even from me."

Ida would not even have wasted a guess on who he had learned that particular art from. "Would it surprise you to know that your son has a series of your lectures saved on his ship?"

This time Ida was certain that something passed over Milla Ivanov's face, something like surprise, or grief, perhaps.

"I know nothing of it if that is what you're asking," she said. "Which lectures?"

"Computer science," said Ida.

Milla nodded more to herself than to Ida and for the first time looked away from Ida. It freed Ida to let her mask slip slightly, to let her focus more on the mask Milla Ivanov was wearing.

"I assume you did not bring me here to ask me about my son's viewing habits," Milla said.

"You have to understand that the recordings were a little suspicious."

"Suspicious?" Milla's expression could have frozen the sun. "The lectures were publicly broadcast. Computer science is his preferred field. And he is my son. There is nothing suspicious about that at all."

Ivan's interest in the subject would make the lectures the perfect method for passing along a message, and Milla Ivanov had to realize that. "Have you ever tried to get into contact with your son?"

"No."

"Why not?" Ida asked, and when Milla simply looked at her as if the answer to that question should be obvious, clarified, "Surely as a mother you would want to save your son from himself."

"Blood will out," said Milla Ivanov in her chilly distant way. "That is what the System says, is it not? If the parent has . . . anti-System tendencies, then so will the child. It was only a matter of time before Leon took after his father."

The utter lack of emotion briefly stymied Ida. She relied so often on her own relative poise to crack open the people she interrogated along the cracks created by their sentiment, but Milla Ivanov, she was starting to realize, was as impervious as a diamond. She had not expected to be able to break Milla; other investigators with far more time and experience had failed to do so, but now she was starting to fear that neither would she be able to get Milla Ivanov to slip.

"That is what the System believes," Ida said. "Is that not what you believe?"

"It has proved itself true," said Milla Ivanov.

Ida leaned on her elbows.

"Come now," she said. "Tell me what you think, Doctor Ivanov."

One white eyebrow arched up.

"I wish that my son had stayed on Earth," Milla said. "I wish that Leon had lived a peaceful, safe, successful life in harmony with the System instead of being hunted down like an animal."

It was spoken with what sounded like honesty, or at least as much honesty as so cold a woman could display, but it was exactly what Milla Ivanov was supposed to say, and so Ida waited a moment longer, searching Milla's face for a lie that was not there to see.

"Did you ever notice any signs," Ida asked, "when your son was living with you that he might be taking after his father?"

A brief silence.

"His father was also occasionally stricken with melancholy," said Milla in what could only be a deliberate misunderstanding of Ida's question.

Ida gave her a condescending smile. She expected that to annoy Doctor Ivanov, but if it did, she could not see it. "I meant delinquent behavior."

"No," Milla said. "I noticed nothing."

"And how about revolutionary sympathies?"

"My son never took after his father that way," said Milla, her words very short, very clipped.

Ida lowered her tone.

"He has told me," she said, "about how he was taken to see Saturn when he was very young. About how deeply that upset him."

Milla's gaze was boring holes through her skull.

"Did you never realize," Ida asked with a delicate lance of disbelief in her voice, "that he felt so bad for them? That he didn't truly appreciate the necessity of the System's decision? Did you truly never notice that he blamed the System, in the smallest of measures, for the atrocities he saw?"

"As I said," Milla Ivanov told her, "my son is very good at hiding his thoughts, even from me."

Ida made a show of hesitation, of thinking, and then spoke as if she were sharing information that she was supposed to keep to herself. "The System has great reason to believe that your son is involved in revolutionary activities." All of Milla's attention was visibly on Ida, but her face remained impassive. Ida said, "Once this comes to light, it will call into question certain aspects of your parenting and your obedience to the System."

"It may be questioned," Milla said. "The answers will remain as they have been for thirty years."

"And if signs are found that you failed to recognize at the time . . ."

"Signs of what? There were no 'signs,' Miss Stays. And my son would not be so foolish as to involve himself in any revolutionary activity."

"No?"

"No," said Milla. "Leon is individualistic. To be in a revolution requires a loss of the self to something more. My son would not be able to tolerate such a thing."

"Doctor Ivanov, we have evidence . . ."

"Then you have misread it," said Milla Ivanov. "Perhaps you are simply wrong, Miss Stays."

For a long moment Ida sat perfectly still.

Then she said, "For seven years you did not have the faintest idea that your husband, the man with whom you shared a house, a name, and a bed, was involved in attempting to sever the Saturnian system from the solar system. Your husband was attempting to pull off the largest rebellion in the past two hundred years. And you did not have the faintest inkling of what he was doing."

Milla Ivanov said nothing.

"And you would have me believe," said Ida, "that a woman so *intelligent* as you, so *adaptive*, wouldn't learn to keep an eye on the kind of signs that she claims to have missed in her husband? You would have me believe that you would not be on your guard for them to appear in your own son?"

Milla Ivanov's expression was as cold as the far reaches of space, where the sun was just a star, colder than ice, as cold as the hollowness of the void. Ida said, "Or is this one more instance of such convenient ignorance?"

In the silence that followed, only the distant groans of machinery could be heard. And in that silence Milla spoke.

"Let me explain to you what you are," she said. "You are but one in a long line of interrogators to think you can make your name by unmaking me. You are nothing more than a gear in a machine I am well familiar with, and you are saying and asking the same things I have been told and asked for thirty years. The System has only ever proved my innocence. Do you think to succeed where thirty years of others have failed?"

Ida stayed frozen in place, conscious of the way that without moving, by speaking only just loudly enough to be heard, Milla Ivanov had taken the power of the situation from her.

Milla said, "I assumed that this interrogation had some relevance and was not intended to discuss thirty-year-old rumors."

For a moment Ida wanted, with keen desire, to tear apart Milla's son before the mother's eyes.

It was only the thought that eventually she would destroy Ivan that gave her the strength to continue the interrogation.

Hallway, hallway, hallway; control room, hallway; the very end of the hallway, the very base of the ship's spine; hallway, a room where Ida Stays sat across from white-haired Milla Ivanov. Althea paused in her flipping through the working cameras' feeds to watch just for a moment.

She flipped away.

Hallway, hallway, storage room; hallway, the core with its rays of plasma arching away from its dark heart, hallway, the white room—

Althea flipped back immediately. The cameras in the white room had not been working before. For an instant she saw the scene from high above: Ivan sitting pale and chained in place and Gagnon leaning over the table saying something to him.

It took the sound a moment to catch up with the video. Gagnon was saying, ". . . her alone."

"I'm not doing anything," Ivan said with precision, and an angle to his jaw that spoke of defiance.

"You've been talking to her," said Gagnon.

"And is it a crime to talk?"

"I want you to leave Althea Bastet alone."

"And if I say no? What, will you tell *Ida*?"

Althea's heart jolted under a sudden rush of adrenaline, but Gagnon seemed to realize that he couldn't tell Ida, either. "I'll keep you away from her," he threatened.

Ivan laughed, and Althea realized how small and how weak Gagnon's threat had been; it was not even a threat, nothing more than a protective impulse. Her humiliation and her anger that Gagnon would talk to Ivan about her were humbled in the face of that impulse, and she knew that she could not possibly confront Gagnon about it.

"Go ahead," Ivan said. "Try to chain me up some more."

Althea would have listened longer, but the feed abruptly cut out, and she could not bring it back again.

It did confirm one thing, at least. The computer was receiving the feeds from the nonfunctional cameras. It simply wasn't sharing them with her. She also suspected that from now on she would find herself scheduled for shifts that coincided with times when Ivan was being interrogated so that she could not guard his door while she worked.

She was not certain whether she was relieved or disappointed.

To her right, on the wall against the door, the perpetual System broadcast was playing.

This time it was a man on the screen. He was handsome, but he did not have blue eyes.

"At 200 Earth Standard Time this morning, System forces suppressed another destructive riot on the Neptunian moon Galatea, restoring order," the subtitles read while his lips moved soundlessly above. Althea did not need the sound on the display to be on to hear his Terran accent. "The gathering began as an apparent protest regarding System efforts to supplement the moon's agricultural output."

The screen changed to a grainy surveillance camera view of the riot. On the dirty ice surface of Galatea, barren and gray, people crowded together, shouting and wild. They looked vicious. They looked dangerous. The camera cut back shortly to the handsome man, the image having lasted only long enough for anyone watching the news to witness the violence of the rabble, its inhumanity.

"Its true nature as a terrorist plot became apparent when the mob attacked the residence of System Governor Enrico Boltzmann, a decorated servant of the System, and murdered him in his home. After his death, the System intervened, ending the hostilities with a blow to the greenhouse enclosure."

A blow to the greenhouse enclosure meant breaking the enclosure, allowing the trapped atmosphere and heat to rush out, suffocating the rioters in the sudden thinness of the air. Althea swallowed and did her best not to show what else she thought. The camera in the piloting room was still operational and broadcasting Althea's image live to the System.

"The System suspects that this riot was also instigated by the Mallt-y-Nos, as with the riots on Titania, which are still being subdued," said the handsome man, whose eyes were as blank as those of the other newscaster, as guarded as Ivanov's had been in the picture in his file. "But rest assured, the System will do anything to protect its citizens."

Althea turned away. She no longer wanted to look at the earthscape behind the newscaster's head, the verdant greens of Earth, the perfect blue of its sky unenclosed by any greenhouse. She turned back to the *Ananke* and flipped through the working camera feeds one last time, pausing on the tableau of Milla Ivanov, seated like her son, with Ida leaning on the table across from her.

Althea closed the program, but she could not stop herself from thinking.

"Where are we going?" Milla asked as Ida gestured for her to walk with her down the hall, farther away from the docking bay.

"We have one more stop to make."

Nothing Milla had said had caught Ida's attention. She would check it all, of course, but everything seemed to be in order: Milla's story seemed true. In any case, whether she could have Milla Ivanov arrested was less important than here, than now. Ida wondered what Milla's reaction to her son in chains would be, if that at last would draw something from the doctor.

Ida wondered how Ivan would change when he saw his mother.

When they reached the doorway to the white room, Milla Ivanov stopped. "My son is in there," she said. It was not a question.

"Yes," Ida said. She pushed open the door.

Domitian was standing beside the table in the precise center of the vast, bright room, a few steps away from the figure in the chair. The chains on Ivan's arms were visible even from the door, and the cloth of his shirt was so thin that it fell loosely and followed the shape of his body, as if he were exposed, uncovered, trapped, and vulnerable. His back was toward the door.

Without a word, Milla Ivanov headed for the table and her son. Ida followed, the sound of her heels ringing out, filling the vast empty space with echoes.

Ivan said, "Ida?"

"No," said his mother in her quiet voice, and Ivan jerked his head around just as she stepped into the range of his vision.

For a long moment mother and son simply looked at each other.

Ivan, Ida saw, was afraid, and while Milla Ivanov looked at him—at the dark shadows beneath his eyes, at the chains around his wrists—her jaw grew tight. Their focus on each other was so complete that it was as if Ida and Domitian were not in the room at all.

Ivan said, "They brought you all the way out here?"

"Apparently," Milla said, "they had some questions for me that couldn't possibly be answered at an outside facility."

A moment of grim understanding passed between the Ivanovs. If Ida had not had to school her expression, she would have smiled.

Milla Ivanov shifted position, the first overt display of discomfort Ida had seen on her, crossing her arms across her chest and drumming her fingers without rhythm on the sleeve of her jacket. Her customary nervous tic.

"How are you doing?" Milla asked abruptly.

"Great," said Ivan, with a special sort of sarcasm that did not seem to know whether it wanted to be sarcastic. "Really fantastic. How about you?"

"Very well," said Milla. "I got tenure."

"That's good."

What Milla's ironclad accounting of her movements had not done to convince Ida that mother and son had not spoken in ten years, witnessing the stilted and awkward nature of this interaction was doing. They truly had not been in contact, at least not for a long time.

"Did you miss me?" Ivan asked. His fingers were twitching against the arms of his chair.

"No." Milla paused. "I got a dog."

After a beat, Ivan grinned. It was not like the smiles Ida had seen him direct her way. This was the kind of smile she saw directed at Matthew Gale in the surveillance footage she had watched: wide, honest, as bright and brilliant as his eyes. At the sight of that smile, Milla's expression softened, but Ida thought she was rather close to weeping.

"I wish you could've met Constance," Ivan said, his grin fading away. "You would've liked her, Mom."

Milla let out a breath and looked away, in the opposite direction from Ida and Domitian; when she turned her head back, her eyes were dry but she might as well have let herself weep, because Ida could see the grief on her face.

"I take it she was your girlfriend?" Milla asked.

"She was," Ivan answered. He was being perfectly serious when he said, "You and she would have had a lot in common."

Milla nodded very slightly, her fingers still tapping against her arm. It was convenient that Ivan had brought up Constance, Ida thought; it would lend weight to the meeting Ida had arranged.

This time the silence stretched out almost unbearably. Mother and son no longer met each other's eyes. Ivan stared instead at the drumming of his mother's fingers.

"Have you seen enough?" Milla asked suddenly, sharply, and she was looking at Ida.

Ida smiled graciously. "If you're done."

"I am."

"Follow me," Ida said, and started toward the door, but she was halfway across the room before she realized that Milla had not followed her.

She turned. Milla still stood beside Ivan's chair. Domitian had one hand raised to urge her along but was not yet touching her shoulder. Milla reached down to her son, taking his cheek in one hand and bending down to press a kiss to his forehead. Ivan closed his eyes and swallowed, and he stayed in that attitude as Milla Ivanov strode away to join Ida at and out the door.

The alarm went off again while Althea was still trying to determine the error that had caused it to go off the first time.

This time, when the alarm went off, she jumped up almost before her mind had consciously processed the sound and went to the other terminal, shutting off the alarm and looking immediately to see if the proximity sensors had been triggered.

They had. Constance Harper had just come into range. Althea took a breath, and in that brief moment of inattention, the alarm came back on.

"Come on!" she said, and shut it off again, but it resumed its wailing. "Ananke! Come on!"

The alarm went silent.

From behind Althea a voice said, "You need to fix the computer." Ida Stays stood in the doorway, dark eyes, dark lips, dark look.

Before Althea could react—to bow and scrape in fear of Ida's rage; to shout in frustration of her own?—the alarm turned back on again.

"Doctor Bastet," Ida said over the screaming of the alarm, but Althea ignored her, arrested by the message before her on the screen.

"The *Ananke* is reading more than one life-sign on Miss Harper's ship," she reported.

Ida was suddenly standing very close to Althea. Althea tried not to flinch as she leaned over the panel, her wine-dark lips pursed. "Go to the secondary interrogation room," she said. "Send Domitian here. Stay with Doctor Ivanov yourself."

"What?" Althea said, certain she had misheard.

"Did I stutter?" Ida asked, and Althea fled.

Ida's "secondary interrogation room" had once been Althea's storage closet. She reached it quickly and had to knock only once before Domitian swung the door open.

"Miss Stays wants you in the control room. I'm to stay here," Althea said breathlessly, and Domitian frowned but obeyed, pushing past her to stride back toward the control room.

Milla Ivanov sat in the chair that had been Ida's. She watched the exchange without a word. Althea stepped uncertainly just inside the room and let the door swing shut behind her. The sound of it closing seemed overly loud in the cramped, empty space.

Milla Ivanov was still watching her with disquieting eyes that were unnervingly similar to Ivan's. Althea looked into the corner of the room in the hope that that would make the woman stop watching her, but she was uneasily certain that Milla was continuing to stare.

"Are you one of the people interrogating my son?" Milla asked. She had a quiet voice, and even aside from the uncanny similarity to Ivan,

Althea could remember attending some of Milla Ivanov's lectures and watching her lean into the microphone to be heard.

"No," Althea said. "I'm just the mechanic."

Milla's eyes flicked up and down her body.

"I suppose you are," she said, and her gaze, her attention, held Althea as pinned as Ivan's ever had.

"You should be careful, little mechanic," Milla Ivanov said, and the resemblance to Ivan was even stronger now, though Althea could not have said precisely how; perhaps there was something dangerous, something wolfish about her. Milla said, "These people don't care about you or your ship."

"I'm afraid we received no communication to that effect," Ida said in as sweet and calm a voice as she could manage as she spoke through the ship's intercom.

"I was assured it had been sent." Constance Harper's voice was low for a woman, almost husky, but it was clear and carrying. She had a Mirandan accent that Mars had not been able to wash out.

"We did not receive it," Ida said, a little sharply. Behind her, the door creaked open and Domitian entered. She beckoned him over.

"I could have it sent again," Constance said, and Ida muted the communication for just long enough to bring Domitian up to speed.

"She fosters dogs for training," Ida said. "As part of a System program. They can't be left alone, and she says that the summons was too sudden for her to find a sitter, so she brought them with her. Two dogs. The System base on Mars allegedly approved this and sent us paperwork, but I was not told."

"I'll look for it," Domitian promised, and moved to another interface, skimming through the communiqués received by the *Ananke*.

Ida unmuted the machine.

"Please bear in mind," she said as mildly as she could, "that if you are found to have been lying, you will be arrested and your business seized while the investigation commences."

"I am not lying," said Constance Harper.

Domitian lifted a hand and caught her attention. Ida muted the speaker again. "What?"

"I found it. It's all in order."

"Then why wasn't I told?"

"It appears the *Ananke* has not been notifying the crew of the arrival of new messages," Domitian said. He looked grim. "And with everything that has been going on, none of us has been checking."

Ida swore. She stayed for a moment with her head bowed, bent over the control panel, seething and trying quietly to bring herself back under control.

Finally she raised her head, unmuted the connection, and said sweetly to Constance, "You may board, Miss Harper."

Domitian came up beside Ida. There was a certain reassurance to his presence, solid and broad and strong. He leaned over her shoulder and started some program on the *Ananke*.

"For docking," he said at her unspoken question.

"Will it work?" Ida snapped.

"If it doesn't, Althea needs to fix it, not me," said Domitian. Ida forced herself to take a breath and nodded.

"Let's collect Doctor Ivanov, then," she said, and brushed past Domitian out the door.

Althea Bastet answered the door at Ida's sharp knock with her brown eyes held wide and stood aside to let them in immediately.

"If you would come with us, please," Ida said, and Milla stood up.

"I apologize for the inconvenience," said Ida as they walked toward the double glass doors leading into the docking bay. "And I thank you for your cooperation."

Through the glass, an old ungainly ship was landing carefully behind the *Annwn*, beside Milla's sleek little top-of-the-line craft. Milla said, "Who is that?"

"You'll see," Ida said, and met Milla's measuring glance.

The light came on, indicating that the bay was safe to enter; Ida led the way toward the ship that had landed.

Someone had painted the ship's name on its side rather than having it engraved. The paint was red and had been done with a heavy hand; drops of red sliding from the letters had dried in place. The ship was named the *Janus*, and beneath the bleeding letters a door opened.

The first thing to come out of the door was a black nose, followed by a black snout and then a second one, two canine heads sniffing at the unfamiliar air. "Back, sit!" a woman's voice ordered, and both snouts retreated and did not return. Constance Harper stepped out of the door with her hands in the air.

Constance was dressed like a working woman in boots and jeans and a plain top. Her hair, long and brown, was up in a ponytail, and the tip of it brushed against her freckled shoulders. While Domitian went into her ship with his gun out to search it, she stood aside, palms extended, with the patience of someone who had endured this treatment before.

A moment later Domitian stepped out and nodded to Ida. All clear. Only then did Ida smile at Constance.

"Miss Harper," she said, coming forward. Constance, seeing that she was no longer obligated to prove her lack of weaponry, lowered her hands and strode forward.

Constance's grip was callused and cool. "Nice to meet you," she said with rote abruptness. She kept glancing over Ida's shoulder to where Ida knew Milla Ivanov stood. Ida watched her expression closely.

"I am Ida Stays," Ida said, pulling her hand from Constance's grip. "You may call me Ida. I assume"—she turned slightly, angling her body toward Milla Ivanov—"that you know my other guest, Doctor Ivanov . . . ?"

"We have never met," said Milla, chilly, but when she looked at Constance, her expression was less cool, almost curious, for all that Ida could read her. Milla extended her hand, and Constance came forward to take it.

"Doctor Ivanov was just on her way home," Ida said. Milla glanced at her—past her—and then her attention snapped back to Constance.

"It's nice to meet you, Doctor Ivanov," Constance said. "I'm a friend of your son's."

Milla stood perfectly still for a moment, her head angled slightly to the side, the same way that Ivan looked when he had been stricken by a thought and wanted to give nothing away.

Milla Ivanov pulled her hand out of Constance's grip with a quick snap of her wrist that spoke of disgust.

"I know," she said. "I know what you are. I know that you and your . . . and your friends are the reason that my son is here."

Milla's soft voice had risen in brittle anger. Ida was shocked and knew she was showing it, but an outburst had been the very last thing she had expected from Milla Ivanov.

"I think there's been a mistake," said Constance evenly, frowning at Milla.

Domitian came up behind Ida and said softly into her ear, "Do you want me to break this up?"

"Absolutely not," said Ida.

"Has there been?" asked Milla, and then pointed at Ida and Domitian. "Look at them. Look at the kind of people you have sent my son to. Look at them!"

Constance turned and looked at Ida—at Domitian—at the space between them. Ida almost turned to Domitian to comment on the encounter, to ask him to remind her to bring it up against Ivan, but Constance's clear loud voice caught her attention, and she turned again to face the scene.

"That's a lie," said Constance. "Ivan hasn't done anything because of me that would get him locked up."

Milla Ivanov laughed. It was thin and sarcastic, and she turned her heel on Constance and paced a few steps away. Constance pursued her, anger in the line of her spine. There was something larger about her when she was angry, something greater, as if the force of her passion made her something more. Ida turned to keep them both directly in her sight.

"He's here because of revolutionary activities," Milla said. "I don't suppose that was you."

"Of course not," said Constance. There was force to the way she spoke, along with certainty. "I am a loyal servant of the System just like you, Doctor Ivanov."

Milla scoffed. Ida considered the honesty in Constance's declaration and did not find it wanting.

"I haven't forced your son to do anything," Constance said. "Ivan is his own man. He doesn't listen to me."

"Oh, and should he?" Milla mocked.

"Yes!" Constance had a voice that carried, no, more: it filled the entire space of the docking bay up to the high ceiling. "If he had, he would not have ended up here."

Whatever Milla Ivanov might have spoken was drowned out by the barking of dogs.

Constance swore and dashed back to her ship, running between Domitian and Ida and ordering the dogs to "Sit! Still! *Sit!*"

The dogs went silent, and a moment later Constance, a little red-faced, stepped back out of the ship.

"Permission to seal my ship?" she asked, looking at Ida. "The dogs will be quieter if they're enclosed."

"Granted," Ida said, and Constance shut the door and locked it. She pushed back some escaped wisps of hair with one hand, then came forward and said to Milla, "I'm sorry for shouting."

Ida looked at Milla, who seemed calm again, though her fingers were drumming restlessly against her hip.

"Likewise," said Milla, her voice soft again. "I should not have snapped. You and I have something in common. Perhaps I shall buy you a drink."

"I'll buy you one," said Constance. "I own a bar. Will you be visiting Mars any time soon?"

"I am vacationing on Mars these next few weeks," Milla said. "Where is your bar?"

"It's called the Fox and the Hound. It's by the Valles Marineris. Stop by soon and your drinks are on the house," said Constance.

There were few things Ida was certain of when it came to Milla Ivanov; she was, however, certain that Milla had never met Constance Harper before. Milla nodded stiffly and said, "I will. Permission to depart, Miss Stays?"

"Of course," said Ida sweetly.

Milla met Constance's eyes one more time—Constance dipped her chin in a nod or acknowledgment—then Milla went inside her sleek little ship and Ida led Constance and Domitian out into the hallway while behind them the great doors of the *Ananke* opened once more to space and Milla Ivanov left the ship for good.

"I apologize for the difficulties surrounding your arrival," Ida said as she and Constance arrived at the second interrogation room. "Somehow the communiqué was misfiled."

"It happens," Constance said with her lack of interest poorly hidden. This woman was no Milla Ivanov.

Ida guided Constance to the weaker seat, sitting across from her and smiling. This interrogation might be nothing more than a formality—Ida doubted there was anything Constance Harper could really tell her—but it was best to cover all the bases.

"I have a few questions for you that I'd like you to answer to the best of your ability," Ida said.

"Are they about Ivan?" Constance asked with an expression that anticipated the answer.

"I'm afraid they are, mostly," said Ida. Milla's presence had alerted

Constance to that fact, of course, but the discomfort aroused by their argument far outweighed any good the surprise might have done in Ida's interrogation of Constance. "I know that you've gone over this before, but I do need to know when precisely you became aware of Ivan's criminal activities."

"Six months ago," said Constance. "The System contacted me shortly after we visited the moon."

"That was you, Ivan, and Mattie, correct?" Ida asked.

Constance looked briefly uneasy. No doubt her discomfort was not from the fact that Ida knew that but from the casual way Ida referred to the two men. "Yes," she said.

"And you immediately cut off contact with them both; am I correct?"

"Yes."

"What would you have done if they had contacted you?"

"I would have turned them in," Constance said immediately and absolutely, without hesitation or doubt. "They know I would have. So they didn't contact me."

"And why—forgive me," said Ida, "but why would you turn in your lover and your brother to the System, knowing they would go to prison for the rest of their lives?"

Constance's eyes were not, as Ida first had thought, brown; they were hazel, brown shot through with green and gray, and there was as much steel behind them as there was in all of the *Ananke*.

"I was an orphan girl from an outer planet," Constance said. "The System saved me. The System helped me. The System made me what I am today. And so I am loyal to the System."

"More loyal to the System than to your own family?"

"I have worked hard to achieve what I have." Constance's chin lifted, proud, stubborn. "Though I love them more than . . . more than anyone, I will not let them ruin the plans I've made for my future by their own inability to just—obey."

She was being honest, Ida judged. Constance Harper did not seem a talented liar. Perhaps Ivan liked her for her principles and her honesty.

"I'm sorry to tell you," she said, "but both Ivan and Mattie have been connected to terrorist activity."

"You have Mattie, too, then?" Constance sounded as though she had to force herself to ask.

Ida gave her the most gentle and sad expression she possessed. "Matthew Gale was killed in the process of fleeing custody."

Ida had expected tears or anger. Constance only looked away and did not respond.

"But as I said," Ida told her, "Mattie and Ivan were connected to terrorist activities."

"Like what's happening on Titania?" Again Constance sounded as if she had to force herself to speak the question.

"Precisely," Ida said. "And that's why it's so important that we find out what Ivan knows. To stop the violence before it can become any worse."

Constance cast her an unexpectedly lambent glance. "That doesn't seem like them," she said.

"Perhaps," Ida said. "But you understand that because of this connection, the System has to inquire into the connections and activity of all people close to one or the other of them—including you, Miss Harper."

Constance took a deep breath. "Are you accusing me?"

"It's only a formality."

"I have no terrorist connections," said Constance. "I have nothing to tell you."

"Then you won't mind giving me an account of all your movements and communications lately," said Ida.

It was a rather obvious way of driving Miss Harper into a corner, but Ida suspected that subtlety would be lost on her. "Of course I will," Constance said.

"Before we do that, however," Ida said, "I have some questions I would like to ask you about Abigail Hunter."

For a breath, then two, Constance sat very stiff and very still, as if she were on the verge of rising. "What about her?"

The reaction was intriguing; Ida had not expected so violent a response.

"You seem upset," Ida said. "I imagine you and Abigail have a tense relationship."

"Something like that," said Constance Harper.

"Why don't you tell me what you mean," Ida suggested.

Constance opened her mouth, then closed it. She said, "I haven't spoken to Abigail in years, though I know Abby and Mattie have stayed in touch. I disagree with many of the decisions she has made."

"That doesn't explain why you were so upset by her very name," said Ida.

Constance took another deliberate breath. At the end of it she said swiftly and abruptly, "I always suspected Ivan was sleeping with her." She broke Ida's gaze as quickly as possible.

Ida could not have hoped for a more perfect reaction. A jealous woman would say any number of things she would keep silent about usually.

"He has admitted as much to me," she confided, feigning sympathy, just one woman speaking to another. "I hope it won't be too difficult for you if I ask you a few more questions about Abigail and Ivan."

Constance raised her eyes and sat tall and proud.

"It won't be," she said.

Milla's warning rang in Althea's head. It distracted her from what she ought to be doing until by the time Domitian showed up to send a quick report to the System about the circumstances of Constance Harper's arrival, Althea was almost ready to ask him about it.

But she couldn't find a way to phrase it. She wanted to ask if he cared about her computer, but that was a ridiculous question. Of course he did. Or he wouldn't understand what she meant.

She found herself watching the System broadcast again. The hosts had returned to the topic of Galatea.

At her prolonged stillness, Domitian looked over at her, then at the screen. The handsome man was saying, the words scrolling in white across the bottom of the screen, "A number of other riots have arisen on Galatea since this morning. The System has suppressed the riots and placed the remaining cities on the moon under martial law to maintain order while the perpetrators are identified."

"What happened?" Domitian asked.

"Food riot on Galatea," said Althea. "They killed their governor. The System shattered a section of the greenhouse." The hosts were saying nothing about Titania. It was uncomfortable to realize that that must mean that the System had not yet managed to bring that moon under control.

She wondered if the System would even announce it if it had to break all the greenhouse enclosures on Titania, destroying the entire moon to subdue it.

Domitian nodded slightly, looking over at the screen, where the woman now was talking. "Good," he said.

"It seems kind of . . . violent," Althea said, hesitant to speak but unable not to express some of her horror.

Domitian gave her an amused little smile as if he thought she was naive and sweet.

"You'd amputate a limb to save the rest of the body, Althea," he said gently, and a thrill of unease snaked through Althea's breast.

"Those people chose to betray the System," Domitian said, returning his attention to the report he was writing. "The System did what it had to, Althea; that was never a question. This is how the System has always handled such things, and it has been successful for a very long time."

Yet Titania was in rebellion and Galatea had tried to follow, and Althea did not know what else might be happening that the System was not reporting. For a moment Althea watched him type, even less sure about speaking than she had been before.

"Domitian," she said at last, still uncertain of whether she should say anything at all, and stopped.

"Yes?" he prompted, fingers poised over the keys in midword.

Althea considered and reconsidered and discarded a dozen possible things to say.

Hopelessly, certain that it was not precisely what she wanted to ask, Althea said, as she had before, "Are you . . . are you worried about the computer, too?"

Domitian blinked.

"Yes," he said, and he said it gently, but Althea was struck with the awful feeling that he did not know what she meant. "Of course I am. It will seriously impact our mission if the computer remains"—he paused—"in a state of disrepair."

"But aren't you worried about the *computer*?" Althea asked.

He frowned. "What do you mean, Althea?"

Her courage failed her. A limb was amputated, Althea knew, to stop the poison in it from spreading. And the *Ananke* had been poisoned in a way by Matthew Gale. "Nothing," she said.

A brief silence, then the tapping of keys as Domitian resumed typing his message. "Don't worry," he said as he stood to go. "I have faith you'll get it working again," which was not what Althea had wanted to hear at all.

. . .

The rest of Ida's interrogation of Constance had been mostly unproductive—Constance had very little to tell her indeed—but that trivial time was worth it for now, for this moment. Ida watched the tension grow in Constance Harper's frame as she led her down the hallway, each step drawing them closer to the white room.

Constance had figured it out, of course. Ida truly would have had no respect for her if she hadn't figured it out after the confrontation with Milla.

Doubtless Ivan had figured it out as well. Doubtless he was sitting there, pale, helpless, impotent, chained down, waiting for Ida to return and for her to bring Constance Harper in her wake. Surely now he would appreciate Ida's power over him. Surely now he would understand how easily she could destroy the people he loved.

Ida stopped in front of the door to the white room and held it open for Constance. Constance took a steadying breath, then walked in with her head held high. The sound of Ida's heels as she followed echoed with her presence.

Ivan said without turning around, "Is that you, Con?"

"It's me," said Constance, and did not stop alongside Ivan as Milla had but went to the other side of the table, where Ida usually sat, and there she stood. For a long time the two simply looked at each other. A curious thing was happening to Ivan's expression; he was starting to appear the slightest bit afraid. But Constance only looked as if she would cry.

"Have you been well?" Ivan asked, as if it was not precisely what he'd wanted to say. "I haven't seen you in . . . it feels like forever."

"I've been well," Constance said. She glanced aside and visibly mastered her expression. Ivan's frightened attention never left her face.

"But I have been told," Constance said, as solid and unrelenting as the beating of a war drum, "that you've been seeing *Abby* while you haven't been seeing me."

Jealousy, Ida thought, was a beautiful thing.

"Nothing to say?" Constance asked when Ivan did not speak. "I'm certain that Abigail appreciates your loyalty."

"Oh, good," Ivan said, unexpectedly bitter. "As long as she *appreciates* it."

Constance's lip curled as if she would start shouting at him, as a thousand other arguments between the two had begun, but she controlled herself. It could not have been because there were strangers watching—there were strangers watching her every moment of every day—so perhaps, Ida thought, it was because she knew that this was the end.

"You know," said Ivan, with a change of subject and a change of affect, charming now, winsome, "you and I are still technically together, I guess. We never formally left each other."

"I guess we haven't," said Constance.

"Con," said Ivan, serious again, "are you going to leave me?"

For a moment Constance pressed one hand over her mouth.

"I have to, Ivan," she said.

That fear was back on Ivan's face, fear that he had never showed so clearly to Ida. Ida wondered what she would have to do to provoke that expression on his face in reaction to herself.

"Sometimes you think there are things you have to do," he said to Constance. "But you know, you don't have to. You can change your mind. Even if you've already begun—" He stopped, looked down at the table, gathered himself. He said, "Even if you've already started to leave me, you don't have to finish it. It's not too late." He almost smiled at her but could not. "You don't need to leave me just because you feel like you have to."

"That's easy for you to say," Constance said angrily with tears in her eyes. "You've never had a purpose before. Or responsibilities. You and Mattie—all you ever do is run."

"Constance—"

"I have to leave, Ivan."

"I love you."

Ida knew it was manipulation but thought that perhaps he also might genuinely mean it.

Constance must have believed it to some extent, because she did start to cry.

"You should have stayed with me," she said. "You and Mattie. You should have followed me. Not run off to steal things and get caught by the System. You should have stayed with me."

"Connie," said Ivan, so gently that to Ida it seemed he was briefly someone else, "I think I would have always ended up here one way or another."

Constance closed her eyes.

"That may be true," she said in a voice that was stronger, less choked with sorrow than before. "Good-bye, Ivan."

"Con—" said Ivan, and stopped, as if he had nothing with which to follow the hopeless exclamation of her name. Constance closed her eyes again and shook her head. There was a great finality to it.

Without another word spoken and without a bow in the proud straightness of her spine, Constance Harper walked around the table, past Ivan, and straight for the door to the white room. "Well?" she said when she had reached it and Ida and Domitian had not followed. Ida took her time about it to remind Constance of her lack of power here. Ivan was staring at the table before him with peculiar inward attention, as if Constance already had left.

Ida walked toward Constance and opened the door for her. Constance, whose tears had been wiped away but whose eyes still were red, stepped into the hallway. Gagnon was waiting; he slipped into the room as Domitian came out to escort Ida and Constance back to the docking bay.

Constance was silent on the long walk back. Ida was still riding on the pleasure of the interactions she had provoked, and so she let Constance stew in silence. Besides, Constance had served her purpose: she had unsettled Ivan, had frightened him, had shown him the extent of Ida's control. Ida had no more use for the woman.

When Ida opened the doors to the docking bay, they were greeted by a strange muffled sound. Constance did not seem troubled by it, but it put Ida on edge. Perhaps the computer was malfunctioning again. The doors to space were just overhead; if they should open, Ida would suffocate—

The nearer they walked to Constance's ship, however, the louder the sound became, and Ida realized she was hearing the muffled barking of a dog, a frantic sound, as if the dog was terrified of something that Ida could not see. Constance opened the door to her ship, and the barking became suddenly loud, ringing out throughout the docking bay, echoing sharply off of the ceiling, the walls, the disemboweled *Annwn* sitting sullenly in the corner.

"Quiet," Constance said, but the dog did not stop barking. "Quiet!" she ordered again, and the dog whined.

"Good-bye, Miss Stays," Constance said, and Ida nodded her permission for her to leave. Constance swung the door to her ship shut.

Muffled by the metal, the dog resumed its frantic barking.

Constance Harper left the ship with little difficulty until the minute the *Janus* had passed through the *Ananke*'s open maw, and then, for the third time that day, the *Ananke*'s alarms began to wail.

The latent fury over the persisting malfunctions of the ship rose up again in Ida and filled her from top to toe. She said coldly and calmly to Domitian, "If your ship persists in this state, I will have your damned mechanic shot."

She knew that Domitian was looking at her sharply, but she could not trouble herself to see what his expression might be.

The alarm shut off again. Over the intercom Althea Bastet said, "Sorry. It was the two extra life-signs again."

Ida controlled her rage, turned on her heel, and went back down the hallway.

It was time for her to speak to Ivan.

As she walked, all her excitement and all her fury seemed to merge, until by the time she opened the door to the white room, her hands were shaking with it.

Ivan, too, was shaking. She could see, as she crossed that vast space, that his hands were trembling in their chains. "Go," Ida said to Gagnon, who was lingering uncertainly. "I don't need you anymore." She hardly noticed him leave, she was so focused on Ivan's bent back.

Just as Ida reached the table and the door swung shut on Gagnon, Ivan said, "Are you happy?"

"Happy?" Ida asked, and came into view of his face.

He was furious. It sent a thrill through her that she had in some way broken into his head, into his heart.

"I'm frightened," he said. "You've scared me. Are you happy?"

"I don't want your fear. What I want is the truth."

"What you want is my submission," Ivan snarled. "Are you happy? You've made me admit I'm afraid."

That was not what she wanted.

That was not at all what she wanted.

"It didn't do you any good, though, did it?" Ivan asked, leaning toward her, his eyes seeming to glow with his anger, his fingers flexing uselessly against the arms of his chair. "You haven't gotten any information. You achieved nothing. Did you expect to walk in here and find me ready to confess?"

She had achieved his fear. She had gathered a good deal of information—information that she doubted would result in a lead—but still, she had risked her career and her reputation to achieve his fear, to make him confess, and he would confess. He would. He had to. She had no other recourse; she had come too far to go back. He had to confess or she would have nothing.

But there he was, glaring at her, confessing nothing.

"You have nothing," he said. "You know nothing. I know nothing, and I will tell you *nothing*. And the Mallt-y-Nos will burn you all." There was despair mixed with the hate in his voice, and that was what lingered in the echoes in the white room as the silence between them stretched out long and taut.

There were so many things she wanted to say to him. He would break, she was certain, if only she could say them.

With one finger Ida reached over and flicked off her System-mandated surveillance camera, leaving her and Ivan unobserved, since of course the camera in the white room was not working.

"Think about the things that I can do," she said to him, into the unwatched, unobserved silence, and the total freedom to speak almost choked her with all the things she would have liked to say. "Think about the people I can hurt if you will not tell me what I want to know."

"Go to hell."

"I will send your mother to rot in prison," Ida said. "I will send Constance back to Miranda without money, without friends, without a chance at a better life, all the things she hates. I will have Abigail shot. And when I find Matthew Gale's corpse, I will bring it here and lay it on this table before you so that you can watch him rot."

"And what good will any of that do you," Ivan asked, "if I have nothing to say?"

He was angry now, but the fear would set in soon, the fear that would make him bow to her, that would make him bend. She knew it would. It would have to.

"Think on it," she said, and strode out with her hands shaking with a rage she could not fully understand or control, leaving him alone in the white room to think and to fear, helpless and chained.

. . .

The camera in the white room was working. The crew of the ship and the System itself could not see what the camera saw, but the camera was recording, and the ship saw.

In the white room, Ivan sagged over the brushed steel table and breathed. He was alone, by the ship's records, for the first time in eight days.

After a long time, Leontios Ivanov raised his head. The *Ananke* watched him sit upright, the wires tugging at his skin in reaction to the sudden shift in position.

Ivan was very still and silent, as if listening for something.

Whatever it was, he did not hear it.

Cautious, too quiet, Ivan said, "Mattie?"

There was no response. Ivan hesitated, then tried again, louder, "Mattie?"

The vast white room was silent still.

"Mattie?" Ivan called. "Mattie?" But the white room remained empty, and he received no response.

Part 3

THE SECOND LAW OF THERMODYNAMICS

The entropy (or chaos, or disorder) of an isolated system may never decrease.

Because of this, the laws of nature are irreversible, and an increase in disorder unavoidable.

Chapter 6

AN ISOLATED SYSTEM

(OR: MAXWELL'S DEMON)

The *Ananke* was made of metal, but men had built her. All things men
create have some aspect of humanity in them, for men are incapable of
creating the truly alien. And so the *Ananke* was made of metal, but all
her parts were analogous to flesh.

The cameras were her eyes, the hallway her spine, the computer her
brain, the layers of metal and carbon that shielded her insides from the
vacuum of space were her skin. And the dark hungry emptiness inside
the hollow of her rib cage that took all light and air and in impossibility
devoured them forever, that was the *Ananke*'s beating heart.

Through her cameras the *Ananke* could watch simultaneously Ida
Stays in her room working with dark lips and a dark expression, Ivan in
his cell leaning his forehead against the gray wall, Althea—always most
importantly Althea—bowed over an interface, trying futilely to understand. The *Ananke* could watch, but the *Ananke* could not speak, and
so, like an infant wailing to its mother, unable to express in more detail
what had gone wrong, the *Ananke*'s alarms wailed day and night, and
the crew did not sleep.

There was something Ida was missing.

The consciousness of the fact that there was some connection she was failing to make haunted her and had haunted her for the last long few days since Constance Harper and Milla Ivanov had left the ship. Her interrogation of Ivan had taken on an air of futility—what he knew, he was not telling, and she no longer felt she was advancing closer to the final truth.

The Mallt-y-Nos had not attacked again yet, but everyone knew that she would. There had been a dozen other minor uprisings on the outer planets—most subdued, but some of the moons were still breaking out in sporadic violence. The System had just arrested a man with a stockpile of weaponry, and as he'd been taken into custody, he'd shouted to the watching crowd that the Wild Hunt was beginning. Titania was still defiant; the System was contemplating total depopulation. The state of the outer solar system was not beyond what the System could handle, but it was incomprehensible that it had gotten this far—and there would be more. This was the prelude; the Mallt-y-Nos had not yet struck her primary blow. The System had almost its entire military out by Jupiter and Neptune and Uranus and the planetoids, waiting, but what they really needed was information. Ida needed to give them information. But she had none. If she failed—if she failed—if she failed—

Humiliation and fear warred in her breast. Intelligence agents did not retire. If she failed, she would lose her livelihood and likely her life. To prison for crimes against the state—disobedience and squandering of System resources, probably—or to exile on some planetoid that was like a prison. Either would be followed by a discreet death, she was certain. She knew too much. If she failed, first humiliation before all, then the final loss of any power she had, even over her own life—

This couldn't be it. She couldn't be wrong. There was something she was missing.

"I want to go over the events on Ganymede again," Ida said, pacing, pacing. Her heels rang out through the vast white room.

"Why?" Ivan asked. The alarms had been keeping him awake, as they had the rest of the crew. He was pale and shadowed with too little sleep, as Ida knew she herself was. "You've already asked me about that."

"And I'm asking you again."

Ivan laughed. He had long since ceased to pretend to be pleasant to her, and his laughter now was vicious, taunting.

"What point would that serve? I've told you everything I can," he said. "And you've verified it all. You have, or you'd be asking me more detailed questions."

Ida stood and looked at him, at his handsome face, and his blue eyes, and his pallor, and wished with sudden, overwhelming keenness that she could *hurt* him again the way she had with Milla, the way she had with Constance.

But she already had played her hand where Milla and Constance were involved, and Mattie was dead and Abby was missing still.

Ivan said, mocking, his eyes bright, brilliant with exhaustion and anger, "Why won't you just admit that you're wrong, Ida?"

Ida said, "I am not wrong," with all the surety she possessed, but the worm of doubt was hollowing out her chest, and Ivan's expression seemed to show that he knew it.

"Now," said Ida. "Ganymede."

That day's interrogation was as useless as all the others had been. At the end of it, Ida left Ivan alone in the white room, chained to his chair. She could leave him to sit there alone forever if she wanted to. Perhaps, when she went back to him, Ivan would be so tired and humiliated and dehydrated that he would bow to whatever she said. Once Ida had her proof, the System would be so relieved that they wouldn't look too closely at how she'd obtained it. She knew that for a fact.

Ida was so caught up in her thoughts that for a few seconds she did not notice when, all over the *Ananke*, without any warning or reason, the lights went out.

The lights keeping the halls bright went out; all the lights marking the instrument panels went dark. The steel walls lost their gleam. Ida found herself suddenly in a vast black nothing-space, unlit by sun or star, no walls visible, the total blackness of empty space without a star, of the view from the horizon of a black hole.

She went very still.

Ida was a planetary woman. She knew—she had seen it proved in math, in words—that the apparent safety of a planet's solid ground beneath her feet was based on precisely the same physical laws that described the construction of a spaceship, that there was no real difference between the solidity of dirt beneath her feet and the hollowness of sculpted carbon and iron. She knew this for the fact that it was, but

Ida Stays was a planetary woman, and it was with a planetary woman's fear that she froze in the darkness, because Ida did not believe in God, did not believe in any gods at all, only the cold fact of existence and man's ability to work within the inflexible laws of nature, but somehow she, so human, so unmechanical, somehow she trusted the engineer that had constructed the planets far more than the human ones who had built the ships that flew between them.

Here, in the dark of the hallway, with the image of civilization—and human control—vanished, where all Ida knew was that she was not on some planet but was on a man-made structure and its first output (let there be light) had failed, and she was afraid, and that was the worst thing of all: the utter loss of her power, destroyed by as insignificant a thing as the loss of light.

But then again, perhaps the heat would be next to go, or the air, and Ida would freeze in the cold emptiness of space. Perhaps she was already out in space now, for the space around her, unbounded by light, with the walls and floor and ceiling all invisible, could have stretched out to infinity.

No, Ida thought with a deep chill of fear that was animal in its intensity, space would have stars. She was not in space. Perhaps the containment fields at the center of the ship had failed and the hollowness there, the emptiness that could not be filled, had swelled up and devoured all in its path, and Ida, too, and next, next it would swallow up the planets, the sun, and then, with redshifted photons howling, it would devour the solar system entirely—

Light, flickering eerie light from behind her that touched on the walls and made them exist again. Ida took gulping breaths.

The flashlight shook and wavered and bounced up and down and came nearer, and something rushed past Ida, knocking her into the wall and taking the flashlight with her, while Ida stood and gasped and could not make herself move.

Althea Bastet was holding the little light; Ida recognized her by the wiry silhouette of her hair. Althea pushed into a room just ahead of Ida in the hallway, and Ida blindly followed the faint glow of that light, unwilling to be left in the dark any longer.

Ida found Althea kneeling before the machine as if in prayer, the flashlight cast down beside her and illuminating the floor. Ida gripped the frame of the door and watched as Althea touched the machine, and the computer brightened into a glow. Althea tapped away at the machine like a pianist playing a soundless song, and by the time Ida took her next shaking breath, the lights flared suddenly, brilliantly back on.

It was too bright, all that lost light returned at once. Ida had to squeeze her eyes shut and shield her face. When she dared to open her eyes again, blinking reddened afterimages away, Althea was still kneeling in front of the computer, frowning.

"What was that?" Ida asked, and was startled by the hoarseness of her voice.

Mercifully, Althea did not seem to notice. "I don't know yet," she muttered. "I'll figure it out." It sounded as if she were speaking half to Ida and half to herself, as if her words were rote, well learned, well rehearsed.

The glow of the machine on Althea's face was bland, innocent, mechanical. Ida ran a hand down her own face and tried to regain her composure.

"Fix it," she ordered with almost enough force to hide the trembling in her tone, and Althea looked at her in surprise, as if she'd just realized, really, that Ida was right there.

Without another word, Ida left Althea inside the machine room and proceeded toward her room.

Domitian met her there some time after he had been intended to, but in light of the difficulties with the ship, Ida let his lateness pass. It had given her time to recover some of her composure, at least.

"I need this ship repaired immediately," Ida snapped the moment he stepped in. "I don't care how. This is unacceptable. This is an embarrassment. Your mechanic is *incompetent*, criminally incompetent."

"Yes, ma'am."

"Don't 'yes, ma'am' me," said Ida. "I want it *fixed*." She would have Doctor Bastet punished, but first she needed the ship to function.

"I will ensure that it is," Domitian said with enough force that she knew he meant it.

"Good."

Domitian asked, "Is there some other reason you wanted me here, Miss Stays?"

Ida looked at him, so solid and loyal and dependable, and sighed.

"The interrogation is not going well," she admitted. "It may be that

I will be required to transport Ivanov to the surface of Pluto. We should discuss those arrangements later this week, provided, of course, that your mechanic has managed to repair the ship by that point in time." Or if they even made it to Pluto, Ida thought. If the Mallt-y-Nos attacked again, it was likely that the System would have the *Ananke* return to Earth. Already the System had required the *Ananke* to report its location on the hour; it was only the ship's considerable firepower and the enormous expense of its mission that had persuaded the System to allow it to continue on. As for taking Ivan off the ship, if Althea Bastet had not managed to fulfill the basic role of her position by the time they reached Pluto or by the time the Mallt-y-Nos attacked, thus making it possible for Ivan to leave the premises, the System would have to become involved. A part of Ida was pleased at the thought of finally seeing the damn mechanic reprimanded, but she knew that if she had achieved nothing by the time they reached Pluto, more of the System's attention was the last thing she wanted. Her failure would be clear and obvious enough without being the subject of an investigation.

"Yes, ma'am," Domitian said, but although this time Ida turned her back on him in dismissal, he did not leave.

"What is it?" she asked.

"Miss Stays," said Domitian in a softer tone, "if you'll allow me. Over the past days I have seen that you are a brilliant interrogator and loyal to the System. If you think that Ivanov knows something, then I have no doubt that he truly does."

That Domitian saw that in her strengthened something inside of Ida that she had not known needed strengthening. For a wild moment, she had the impulse to tell him the truth: that the System did not believe her theory about Gale and Ivanov knowing the Mallt-y-Nos, that Ida herself was near ruin if she could not break Leontios Ivanov immediately.

The impulse passed, strange and irrational, and Ida cast it from her mind.

"Of course he does," Ida said. "There's something I'm missing, but he does know." An idea was forming in her head. "If I start from the beginning," she said, to herself, not to Domitian, "without any preconceptions, perhaps I'll find it . . ."

"Permission to leave, Miss Stays?"

"Granted," Ida answered absently, and hardly heard the door shut. Instead, she sat down before her computer and started from the beginning.

Althea had run out of ideas. Althea had nothing left to try. Althea did not know what to do.

"Come on, calm down, shh," she crooned at the computer like a mother trying to soothe her colicky baby, but the alarm continued to wail inconsolably. "Please, Ananke, shh."

She had gone through all the usual sources. The manual override wasn't working, and she could not find the source of the error, and she could not figure out why the ship was crying out, just as she could not understand why all the lights had gone off.

"Ananke, *please*," she begged, and the alarm cut out abruptly, as meaninglessly as it had begun. She had done nothing to stop it. She had done nothing to start it in the first place. She did not understand, and she didn't know what else to do.

She leaned her head against the wall of the ship and, with no one but the *Ananke* to see her, with nothing to distract herself from her frustration and her humiliation and her despair, started to cry.

A light shone through her closed lids; when Althea opened her eyes, the nearest holographic terminal was lit up, glowing red, a flickering shape appearing and disappearing in the terminal, there and gone before Althea's eyes could make out its shape, but for an instant it looked like an image of the last hologram the ship had received: the face and figure of Ida Stays.

Her tears had dried. Althea rested her head against her ship's familiar metal, and breathed, and watched as the holographic diodes died back down into darkness.

There was one thing left she had not tried. A week and a half ago, even a few days ago she would not even have allowed herself to consider it. But she had nothing left to try, and still the *Ananke* was broken.

She could talk to Ivan.

Matthew Gale had broken Althea's ship. Matthew Gale had been Ivan's friend and partner for ten years. Ivan already had admitted that he knew something about what Gale had done, something about "a little bit of chaos." Surely if Althea questioned him more closely, he would be able to tell her precisely what Gale had done. Ida already had made it clear that she had little interest in interrogating Ivan about the ship, and Althea did not want to have to confess that she'd been speaking to Ivan against orders. Ida Stays already hated her. If Althea admitted that—or if she even troubled Ida again without the *Ananke* being functional—she doubted she would ever work, or even see Earth, again.

Gagnon had kept his word; Althea had not guarded Ivan's cell since the day Milla Ivanov and Constance Harper had been on board. But Ida had taken to leaving Ivan alone in the white room for hours at a time, and Althea knew that Ida had already left today. Ivan would be alone, unguarded. The camera in the white room wasn't working; no one would know what Althea had talked about with Ivan. They wouldn't even have any proof that she had said anything to him at all.

Slowly, without feeling that she had really made a decision at all, Althea stood up and began to walk up the *Ananke*'s spiraling hall.

She had not really, truly made a decision, she felt, even when she was standing in front of the door to the white room, even when without hesitation she turned the knob and walked in.

Ivan sat in the center of the white room, the bow of his back very tense. Althea could not speak, did not know what to say, and so she only walked forward, her boots making dull sounds against the floor.

"What happened?" Ivan asked, tense, before she had come into his line of sight.

"What?" Althea asked, slowing down.

He twisted around to glance at her and did not seem surprised to see her there. Her shoes, Althea realized. He'd recognized she wasn't Ida from the sound of her walking. "With the lights," he said. "What happened?"

"The ship," said Althea. "She malfunctioned again."

Ivan looked up at her sharply as she came to stand a little distance away from him. Althea felt pinned, pierced. It was different seeing him and speaking to him than it was just to speak to him; he was more real somehow, not a voice from behind a metal wall, yet he was different somehow, too, now that she could see his blue eyes, the way they searched her face, as if he was reading things off of her she did not know were there to be read.

Ivan leaned back slowly in his chair. The chains around his wrists clinked with the movement.

"Why did you come here, Althea?" he asked.

"I need your help," she said.

This was it, the point from which she could not return, yet Althea had a strange fear that she had passed the extremal point already and simply had not recognized it.

Against his silence she began to explain, the words falling nervously from her as if from a broken dam, all in a rush. "I can't figure out what Gale did. You knew him. You could tell me; you could tell me what exactly it is that he did. You know Gale, so you know what he did. You told me something about 'a little bit of chaos'; what does that mean? I can't— I can't fix the computer. I need you to tell me."

"First of all," said Ivan, and there was something dark in his tone, "his name is Mattie." He cocked his head to the side. "If you're going to try to convince me to help you, you're not off to a good start. Call him by the name I use; that's how you generate a rapport."

Althea's tears had started to flow again. It happened without her volition, without her understanding. She stood very still, like prey in sight of a wolf, and for the first time in weeks—perhaps for the first time since she had caught him dressed all in black and toying with her computer—she was afraid of Leontios Ivanov.

He did not speak again immediately. Althea could not find the courage to speak, and only stood and let him take her apart with his eyes.

He said, "Did you come here to make a deal with me, Althea?"

"I just wanted to ask you a question."

"Information is my only currency right now, Althea. It's my only power. I'm not just going to give that away because you asked me nicely."

Althea swallowed. She felt very small, hopeless and desperate, in that vast white room and under Ivan's piercing attention.

"You're smart," Ivan said. If he had said this to her before, Althea's heart would have glowed at the compliment. Now she felt only chilled. "You must have known, coming in here, that you would have to make a deal."

"What do you want?"

He did not look surprised. At the moment Althea could not imagine anything so fallible in him as being surprised. "What will you offer?"

"Food," said Althea. "Drink. A word with Domitian." Ivan was stone-faced, and even to her own ears her offer seemed petty, poor. She said, "I have nothing else to offer," and heard her own desperation.

"And why would I want food, or drink, or a useless conversation with Domitian?" Ivan asked. "Think bigger, Althea."

"I have nothing else to offer."

The way Ivan looked at her was almost, Althea hardly dared to think, pitying.

"No," she said in response to that look, to what it said without saying. "*No.*"

"Not even for your ship?" Ivan asked with a peculiar mocking emphasis on "your ship."

"I can't do it," she said, and braced herself and said it outright. "I can't set you free. I'm risking enough just being here, just talking to you. The System could throw me in prison, maybe even execute me, just for talking to you like this!"

"And that," said Ivan, cruelly ironic, deliberate, "would be terrible."

"Don't do that to me," Althea said, caught between anger and pleading. "Ivan, I need your help."

For an instant, a desperate hopeful instant, she thought she saw pity in his face again, pity for her.

"Fine," he said. "But here are my terms. They can't be negotiated. They can't be changed."

Althea took a shuddering breath. "I can't set you free, Ivan."

"I want two things from you before I tell you a damn thing," Ivan said. "First I want you to tell me something, and then I want you to do something for me. I want you to tell me the mission of the *Ananke*. And then I want you to lengthen the chains on my arms."

She couldn't do it. That was her first thought; it was so overwhelming that for a moment she could not speak for fear that nothing would come out of her mouth other than "I can't, I can't." Then she swallowed and asked, "Why?"

"The first," said Ivan, "is so that I can actually diagnose your problem for you. I can't tell you what's wrong with the ship if I don't know how it's supposed to work, Althea."

That much was probably true. Althea's mouth was dry when she said, "And what about the second?"

In answer, Ivan lifted his arms for the first time since she had walked into the room. They were arrested a few short inches away from the chair's armrests by the chains, which had been hooked shut several links above the full length of the chain. It had to be uncomfortable. It had to be humiliating.

"Ida and Domitian have been shortening them," he said, and she shifted her attention reluctantly from the chains to see that he had been watching her the entire time. "It's not very comfortable."

Lengthening the chains would lengthen his reach. Fully extended, he probably could reach above the top of the table or perhaps up to Althea's waist if she stood right beside him. He would be less contained, less well trapped.

"You're not going to . . . do anything, are you?" she said. "If I lengthen the . . ." She trailed off with a gesture.

"It's just for my comfort," Ivan said, and she wanted to believe him.

"Domitian and Ida will know—"

"—when they unchain me," Ivan finished. "No, they won't, not if I keep my arms down. When they bring me back, they'll shorten the chains again, but they won't know they were ever lengthened."

It would be a brief comfort, but Althea could nearly justify it in her head.

What she could not justify was the betrayal of her ship and of Domitian.

"I can't tell you about the *Ananke*," she said. "It was the highest of my oaths when I took this position, that the mission of this ship be kept a secret."

"No," Ivan said, "the *highest* of your oaths is to obey the System, and you're not doing that very well, are you?"

Althea set her jaw.

"Look," Ivan said, seeming to relent. "There is no working surveillance in this room. Ida can't get me to tell her what she wants to know; there's no way I'll tell her about this. I understand loyalty, Althea, and I understand keeping secrets, but I can only help you if you tell me this."

This was all too much, and Althea was so exhausted. She ran her shaking hands over her face and could not even think how to decide.

"And anyway," said Ivan, "I'll be dead in a few days."

Althea lowered her hands and stared at him, at the shadows under his eyes and the pallor of his skin, and could not decide if she was afraid of him or for him, only that she was overwhelmingly afraid.

"I can't," she said, and she whispered it, but it seemed very loud even at a whisper and in that vast white room.

"Then I won't help you."

"You have to understand," Althea began, driven by some incomprehensible impulse to explain herself to him, to explain Domitian, and the *Ananke*, and the System, and her own fear.

"I understand," Ivan said, but there was neither absolution nor forgiveness in his voice.

Althea tried again. "You know if something happens because I can't fix the ship, you'll die, too."

Ivan leaned forward. There was an intensity to him, Althea decided, and that was what made him so frightening.

"Like I said," he told her. "I'll be dead in a few days."

There was nothing she could possibly have said to that, so she let her fear drive her from the room. The door swung shut with a heavy clang behind her and nearly covered up the sound of her name being called from a nearby intercom.

"Althea," said Domitian's voice in a tone inching steadily from annoyed to angry. "Althea, come in."

She could have just as well fixed the *Ananke* on the spot as not replied instantly to that tone. Hoping only that she did not sound too shaken, she opened the connection and said, "I read."

"Control room. Now."

She went.

It was a testament to how rattled she was that she did not realize immediately that she had walked into an ambush.

Domitian was sitting in the main chair, which had been swung around to face the door. Gagnon leaned with affected casualness against the wall and swung the door shut once she entered, and she found herself in the center of the tiny room, the object of both men's attention.

"What is it?" she asked, although she already could guess.

Domitian had his hands folded in front of his face, bent elbows braced on the arms of his chair. He took his time before speaking, and that frightened Althea, that long, thoughtful silence.

"Althea," he said. "We need to know when the ship will be fixed."

"Soon," Althea said, her fingers trembling against her sides; she stuck them in her pockets. They knocked against the tools she carried, the bits of wire, the slender silver box cutter, sharp and flat.

"When?" said Domitian. "An exact time frame, Althea."

For a moment she contemplated a lie. In the next moment the very idea shamed her; she turned her head aside without answering.

"Do you even know what's wrong with it?" Gagnon asked from behind her, and when Althea dared to glance Domitian's way again, he did not look surprised at her lack of an answer.

"I have some ideas," said Althea, but her only idea was a wolf in a white room.

"But you don't *know*," Gagnon pressed.

"Not exactly, no."

She had the distinct impression that the two men were holding a conversation with each other over her head.

"If the computer can't be fixed," Domitian said at last, "then it must be deactivated."

Her head snapped up.

"What?" She had misheard, she must have—even though she knew she hadn't.

"The dead man's switch is at the base of the ship," Domitian said. "The ship can be operated by the crew without the computer."

"Not completely," said Althea. "Not perfectly, not entirely . . ."

"But it can be operated well enough to fly, to sustain life, and to perform the basic experiments of our mission," said Domitian.

It was true, but Althea would not admit it.

"Stopping this insanity is worth the price of a few lost experiments," Domitian said. "All the System needs to know is if the process this ship is designed to test is physically possible. That is the core purpose of this ship, and we can achieve that without the computer. Everything else the computer was designed to test can be tested in later experiments, but there will be no second ship with a black hole core if this ship fails. With the amount of resources the System has sunk into this mission, we must succeed or there will be consequences for all three of us. And there is still the matter of whether Ivanov can be removed from the premises while the computer is operational. Miss Stays is not happy, and do you realize what her unhappiness—"

"I know," Althea snapped.

"So then tell me," said Domitian, as sharp as she had been, "can you or can you not fix this ship?"

Again Althea could not answer.

"Give me an hour," she blurted out when it seemed Domitian was about to break the silence. "Give me one more hour, and then, if I can't fix it by then, you can . . . you can do whatever you're going to do."

"An hour," Domitian said, and Althea ignored Gagnon's visible exasperation. "One hour and no more."

She left before he could take it back.

The ship's cameras watched Althea Bastet step out into the hall and close the door to the control room behind her. For an instant she stood still, her hair curling chaotically out around her face, barely bound anymore by the band that once had held it back. She began to walk, and the ship watched her as she walked in the direction opposite to the white room.

Althea knew that if the dead man's switch was flipped, it would destroy the computer, euthanize it, wipe it from existence and leave only the computer's shell, the computer's corpse, drifting through space. The ship would be left under manual control of the crew, who would operate it like ancient earth scientists testing galvanism, who set a corpse to jumping or shrieking with the touch of electricity to the right limb or piece of the brain.

Althea Bastet went to the weapons cabinet and opened it. She took a key from a hook that once had held the cuffs that now held Leontios Ivanov, and she dropped it into her pocket.

Down the hall she walked, down the winding hall, toward the white room.

If the dead man's switch was flipped, there would be no computer to repair, nothing but dead synapses and the fading echoes of an aborted life.

At the door to the white room, Althea stopped and took a long, slow breath. Her hands were trembling when she reached into her pocket and came up with a handful of wire, the long flat blade of the box cutter, and, shining bright and small, the silver key to Ivan's cuffs.

She dropped the rest back into her pocket absently, hardly paying attention to whether the items made it into her pocket or fell onto the floor, and pressed the key into the palm of her hand.

The *Ananke* watched her open the door and walk into the white room.

Althea was still no more conscious of when she had made the decision to go to Ivan than she had been the first time she had visited him. The decision, it seemed, had been made subconsciously, and she was left only to carry it out.

Without speaking a word to Ivan, she crossed the expanse between the door and the table in the center of the room. It seemed longer than it had before, the silence in the room overwhelming, the lights and the white walls and ceiling and floor all too bright for her eyes.

Ivan was watching her without speaking as she came up beside him. When she finally reached out to move, she knew that she had left the mark of the key in white and red on her palm.

She reached down first to his right wrist, which was closer to her. His skin was very pale against hers when she lifted his wrist so that she could reach the keyhole in the lock.

He watched her. She could feel him watching her, and she did not look at him.

She leaned over him to reach for his other arm. She knew that she should not—it left her vulnerable if Ivan reached up and grabbed her—but she could not quite bring herself to care or to believe that he would hurt her.

Something snagged her open hip pocket, probably the chair's armrest, so she shifted and freed it, then lengthened the chain on Ivan's left hand.

Then she pulled back, dropped the key in her pocket, faced Ivan, and said, "The mission of the *Ananke* is to discover how to reverse entropy."

Ivan frowned, somewhere between incredulous and confused.

"If entropy can be reversed," Althea said, "the System can create more efficient engines. We can create better terraforming devices. Without entropy, liquids don't have to mix, water can be kept uncontaminated, heat doesn't need to disperse; we can finally warm the outer moons up enough to have a proper biosphere. There will be no energy crisis. Every ship can have a relativistic drive, not just the lightweight ones. The System will be able to control the outer moons better. One day we'll be able to colonize planets outside of the solar system." Some of the wonder of the idea that had struck her when she first had heard it years ago came back to her now and in some small measure calmed her fear and despair. "Perpetual motion would be possible, Ivan," she said. "Every physical process reversible. Time goes in the direction of increasing entropy; if we had control over whether entropy increased, it would be like having control over time. We would have the power of eternity."

Ivan's mouth was hanging slightly ajar; his eyes had gone very wide, and Althea could see the full circles of blue, reflecting on their surfaces the bright white walls, the bright white ceiling, and herself with the light coming through her hair like a halo.

"That's why this ship is so well protected," Althea said. "That's why it's kept such a secret. Imagine anyone but the System having that kind of power."

"That's not possible," Ivan said. "The laws of thermodynamics are the laws of reality. They can't be broken."

"Gagnon has some theories. I don't understand them completely, but I don't need to. They have something to do with the black hole, I think, which is why the *Ananke* has a black hole instead of just a dense sphere for gravitation—but the computer, that I understand. The *Ananke* . . . she . . ." It was hard to put foreign inhuman languages, math and code, into simple, short spoken words. "The computer identifies the entropy," Althea said, hands outspread, fingers curled, as if she would capture the correct way to communicate in her hands like a firefly, "and it turns it back into work."

"What you're saying, then," Ivan said, leaning forward but with his hands still pressed flat to the rests of his chair, not taking advantage of the lengthened chains, "is that the computer is designed to take chaos as an input and produce order from it."

"No," Althea said immediately, and then on revision, "No, not really."

"The greater the entropy, the greater the number of states a system can have," Ivan said, leaning forward, alight, and seeming a different person for this sudden energy. There was color in his cheeks and his eyes were bright, but it looked more like the flush of fever than the glow of health.

"Yes," Althea said slowly.

"So you start with a system of low entropy—low chaos, high order, only a few states," Ivan said. "Maybe only one. And then you add a little bit of chaos—a little bit of entropy—and suddenly the system is broken up into many different states."

"Chaos isn't a thing," said Althea, frustrated. Ivan was still alight with that familiar look of a scholar faced with the solution to a problem, but she had no idea where he was heading. "You can't 'add' entropy to a thing."

Ivan waved his left hand dismissively. The lengthened chain clattered. He said, "But you can increase the number of states the computer can have."

It was Althea's turn to be briefly struck dumb by the implications.

"Mattie's 'little bit of chaos,'" she said. "I thought you meant an error. I thought you meant he put some sort of . . . replicating random virus into the system."

Ivan shook his head.

"The *Ananke*'s computer can exist in a few predetermined states, right?" he said. "Normal functioning, high alert, basic functioning only, that sort of thing."

"He added states," Althea said slowly, testing the sense of it.

"He added states," Ivan confirmed. "Strange ones. Like ones where some of the cameras don't save their footage but the computer functions normally. It was just supposed to confuse the crew, nothing more. And then he changed the computer so that it would cycle through them at random."

It was possible, just—but there was no way Mattie would have had the time to do it. "He was only at the computer for a few minutes," Althea said.

Ivan grinned, and the wolf was there again in that smile. "You didn't even find his lock picks," he said. "Do you think that was all he had hidden on him?"

"A computer drive." Of course. But even so, the drives would be able to contain only generic programs; Mattie would have had to alter them for the *Ananke*, which was like no other ship in existence. He could have managed it—just—but the complexity of some of the behavior Althea had witnessed . . . "I still don't see how—"

"We've done this a lot of times," Ivan interrupted. "I promise you he could've done it in the time he had."

It still didn't make sense to Althea, not completely, but it had to be true. There was no other possibility.

"So the computer just fluctuates between these states at random?" Althea asked, turning her mind back to the problem at hand and feeling for the first time in a week as if she might have some way to fix this.

"Mattie adds a set of states," Ivan confirmed, "sometimes a very large set, and then the computer fluctuates through them like a person having mood swings. That's how we coded the *Annwn*, actually. We got the idea—"

He stopped.

It was so abrupt and unnerving that Althea said, a little too loudly, "What?" and it echoed through the white room.

"That's how we programmed the *Annwn*," Ivan said, slowly but building up steam, and Althea knew that expression from its having been on her own face, from seeing it on the faces of colleagues before—Ivan coming to conclusions, connecting the facts faster than he could speak.

"We had Annie—the *Annwn*'s computer. We programmed her to switch between states depending on sensory triggers," Ivan said. "Emotions. She would react emotionally to stimuli."

"It's a computer," Althea said. "It doesn't have emotions. It can't react emotionally." Of course Ivan had changed one of a machine's best qualities just so that it would react emotionally to him.

"Right," Ivan said. "It was just a simulation. The *Annwn* wasn't able to switch between states on her own; we had to program everything into her. We told her what triggers would make her happy, sad, angry. She was completely manufactured. She couldn't figure out triggers on her own because she wasn't designed to deal with multiple states that way."

The faintest glimmering of where Ivan was going began to shine in Althea's mind. She said warningly, "Ivan."

"The *Ananke*," said Ivan, his eyes fever-bright, "the *Ananke*. She can handle chaos. She's designed to take a set of states and organize them. She's designed to figure out how to switch between states on her own. She figures out her own triggers."

"No, no, no," said Althea, but he wasn't listening to her at all.

"Imagine it," Ivan said over her protests. "Imagine the *Ananke* having to organize herself. There would have to be some degree of self-awareness from that, don't you think?"

"Ivan, this is stupid."

"Imagine it," he insisted. "If it did happen, the *Ananke*— Ananke wouldn't know how to interact with people. She would be worse than an infant, because she wouldn't have the necessary instincts. She would have to learn from first principles."

Perhaps this had been a mistake. Perhaps Althea never should have come into this room.

"But Ananke's smart," Ivan said, and she wondered if he really was mad, as his file said. "Of course she is. She's brilliant, more brilliant than any human that ever existed. She would learn."

Althea paced away, trying to settle the anxiety that rose up again in her stomach, but Ivan's voice pursued her.

"She'd start by learning what got a reaction—the alarms got a reaction, didn't they? Just like a baby crying to its mother," he called out over the distance to her, and she turned back around.

"Stop it, please," she said, but again he seemed not to hear.

"Next it'll learn to speak," said Ivan, and if he meant to be mocking her, he seemed to be very serious. "The ship has a voice-processing system, too, of course, doesn't it? I imagine it'll learn how to communicate through text before verbally, but it can convert between sound and text already. And she's been listening and watching, too. The cameras are all working; they're just not showing what they see to you."

"Stop!"

"She's probably been trying to talk to you in her native language," said Ivan, unstoppable, eerie and pale, "in code, but sooner or later— and probably sooner—she'll figure out the languages of humans."

There had been strange code that Althea had seen, strange and seemingly meaningless, but it had been a mere artifact of whatever Gale had done and had nothing to do with the madness Ivan was speaking.

"She's probably processing her own linguistic data stores even now," Ivan said. "If you don't kill her first, she'll speak to you, Althea—"

"*Stop!*" Althea shouted, and her voice filled up the vast room and rang out in echoes long after the first sound had passed.

Into the silence that followed the death of the echoes, Althea said, filled with a hurt she did not want to consider too closely, "I came to you for *help*."

Ivan's eyes were round and blue and without guile. "I *am* helping you," he said.

"No, you're not!" Althea cried, and found that she was again near tears. "You're not. You're making things up, and you're lying to me, and . . ."

"I'm not lying to you!"

"Yes, you are!"

For a moment they stared at each other. Althea hoped helplessly that if she just waited another few seconds, Ivan would take it all back and tell her what she needed to know to fix her ship.

Ivan's voice was low, sincere. "The ship is alive."

The *Ananke* watched Althea as she stormed from the white room and out into the hall. For a short stretch of hall she kept up her wrathful stride before she slowed, and it became apparent that she had had no real destination in mind.

She went to one of the computer terminals lining the walls and began to dig around in the *Ananke*'s head again, looking for a flaw that wasn't there. Her allotted hour was nearly up by the time she sighed and pulled back from the screen, laying her head against the wall and closing her eyes.

Althea raised her head.

"Ananke," she said into the air, her eyes cast up in the instinctive way all humans do when they address a divinity. "Ananke, if what he said was . . . If you can hear me."

She swallowed. The hallway was empty. There was no one around to listen to Althea's madness—no one but the *Ananke*.

"Answer me," Althea said, and with her gaze she found one of the ship's cameras and looked straight into it as if it were an eye. "If you can hear me, let me know."

The computer screen beside her flashed. Althea turned to look down at it.

"Ananke?" she whispered.

The number 1 appeared on the screen.

For a moment Althea was baffled. Then she understood.

"One for true, zero for false," she said, then shook her head, hardly able to believe what she was considering.

"That's not enough," she said to Ananke. "Tell me if you can hear me, Ananke."

TRUE, said the screen.

While Althea stared in wonder, caught still on the edge of disbelief, the machine paused, almost as if it were thinking, as if it were reconsidering.

TRUE blinked out, and Ananke said instead,

YES, I CAN HEAR YOU.

Chapter 7

BLACK HOLE ENTROPY

There was nowhere on the ship that Ananke couldn't see.

"She's not responding on the intercom," said Gagnon, who was still in the control room with Domitian, ignorant of an intelligence watching. "And I can't get the *Ananke*'s computer to tell me where she is, either."

Domitian sighed.

"Can't get the computer to do much of anything, actually," Gagnon said, frowning down at the machine.

Ananke could not keep his hands off of her skin or dials or screens, but she could make certain he got nothing out of it. And so she had responded in only the most rudimentary ways to his attention.

"We've given her an hour and a half," Domitian growled.

"You have," Gagnon corrected absently, still bent over Ananke's interface, as if she would help him who wanted to kill her. "*You've* given her an hour and a half," he corrected pleasantly, and gave Domitian an entirely insincere smile.

"If she's going to sulk somewhere like the *child* that she is," Domitian said, "then you and I will shut off the computer ourselves."

"Good," Gagnon said, and levered himself out of the chair with alacrity.

Ananke watched through her cameras the two men walk down the hall down the ship's spine toward her core. She alerted Althea before they left the room, and so when they arrived at the very base of the ship, Althea was waiting for them.

There they stopped short and stared.

Ananke was communicating with Althea through her lowest computer interface, which stood just beside the hatch to the core, which was still locked and shut. Althea had, while Gagnon and Domitian were distracted, gone and repurposed one of Ananke's robotic arms like the one in the pantry as a secondary defense, and the ungainly machine had been dragged down to the base of the ship, where it teetered back and forth on its wheels and swung its arm around warningly. The tips of the grasping hand had been modified, wires pulled out and exposed, enough electricity coursing through the copper to give an unpleasant zap. Ananke's arm was clumsy, but she moved it of her own volition, and her mother had made it for her.

In front of Ananke's arm Althea stood with her gun out, firmly planted in the center of the hallway, keeping the men away from the dead man's switch and away from Ananke.

When Ananke had let her know that the rest of the crew was finally coming down, Althea took a deep breath and braced herself, raising her gun to aim it down the long hall. She did not move even as the two men came into sight, even as they saw her and slowed down, looking from her to Ananke's mechanical arm in baffled incomprehension.

Gagnon found his voice first. "What in the ninth circle of hell are you doing?" he said.

"Every way to the dead man's switch is defended," Althea said, keeping her voice firm, refusing to react to his surprise. If she wavered, she was lost. "Ananke is watching the maintenance passages. You can't get past us."

"Us?" Domitian asked.

Of course, he didn't understand quite yet. It had taken Althea so long to understand herself. "Me and Ananke," said Althea.

"Can you take a step back," Gagnon asked, "and explain to us what you're talking about?"

"The computer is alive," said Althea.

Gagnon started to laugh, but Domitian was not smiling. That was all right. Althea had expected some disbelief. Domitian, though, would listen.

"Althea," Domitian said slowly, taking a step toward her with hands stretched forward but stopping when Althea raised the gun in warning, "I know that this computer has been your project for a decade. I know you care about it and you're proud of it. But I don't know that you realize what you're doing right now."

"I know exactly what I'm doing," said Althea. After so long in confusion, it was only now that she truly did.

"No," Domitian snapped, then calmed himself. "No. You don't. You're telling me that the computer is alive."

"It *is*."

"This is career suicide," said Domitian. "And if you don't stand down right now, it will be real suicide as well. Death is the punishment for insubordination on a military vessel, Althea."

The idea of Domitian killing her was absurd, but even if he would—even if he turned her over to Ida Stays, who would execute her in a heartbeat—Althea's conviction could not be swayed. "I can't let you hurt her."

"Hurt *who*?" Domitian demanded, frustrated, trying to take another step closer and again warned off by Althea's gun and the restless sweep of Ananke's sparking arm.

"Hurt Ananke," Althea said, because she had already told him, and by now he should have understood. Domitian swore, his words hard and shocking. Gagnon had stopped laughing.

"Why do you think the ship is alive?" Domitian asked. He was speaking in a slow, cautious tone, as if Althea was liable to go off at any moment, as if she had gone mad.

He would understand. Althea had only to explain it to him, though it was so marvelous that she herself still barely comprehended what had been done. She tried to start at the beginning and fell somewhere in the middle. "The signs have been around me this whole time, and I didn't see them," she said. "The errors I couldn't fix because it was like someone else was propagating them. That someone was the ship." Domitian was looking at her, unmoved. "The strange text that would appear. That was her trying to talk. The alarms going off—like a baby crying—the lights going off—like a baby trying to walk and falling over. She was just trying to communicate, to understand her body—"

"Jesus Christ," said Gagnon, breaking into her speech before she could get anywhere at all.

"Althea," Domitian said, taking another small, cautious step forward. "We've all been under a lot of stress lately, and we all understand that—"

"Stop condescending!" said Althea, and in her frustration at his deliberate resistance to the truth she shook the gun, and both men grew tense. "It's true! I needed Ivan to make me see it, but it's true."

Domitian's expression suddenly darkened, growing stormy and furious and dangerous. "Ivan?" he said, and that sea change frightened Althea as nothing had before. "You heard this from *Ivan*?!"

Domitian did not look fatherly now; he did not look fearful. When Althea looked at him now, she could see someone who could hurt her, and finally she was afraid.

Ida Stays had cleared her mind and cleared her desk. Her shoes had been tossed into some corner of her strange-shaped cabin; she was stripped down to blouse and slip and stockings. She found it not only more comfortable but also easier to think with her armor removed.

The computer was being slow, as if its attention were elsewhere, but it was obeying her, and that was more than the damned thing had done in the last week and a half.

Ida had, open before her, the files of Matthew Gale, Leontios Ivanov, Abigail Hunter, Milla Ivanov, and Constance Harper, as well as sundry other files of sundry other people, anyone no matter how distantly connected who she thought might have something to do with the events she was investigating, as well as reports on nearly every event she had questioned Ivan about.

One by one she closed the files slowly, deliberately, removing the people, the events from her head as she did, until she was staring at the pale blue glow of the *Ananke*, waiting for input.

She had to start from the beginning.

With her mind blanked, she groped about to find the first principles that had started her train of deductions nearly two years ago.

She had to start with Ivan. He was her source, he was her sink of knowledge; everything she had came from him, and everything she did not have he had taken away.

Leontios Ivanov had left home when he was twenty years old, immediately after graduating from the System's most elite university.

Only a few months before, he had tried to kill himself.

He had survived to adulthood only through luck or his mother's skill; the System watched his every movement closely for any signs that he was taking after his father.

Upon escaping from Earth, he met Matthew Gale—

No, Ida decided. Facts would not help her solve this problem. Facts obscured, sometimes. Facts did not carry all the information and could not adequately define the truth any more than physiology could explain to her the gaping emptiness beneath her ribs.

Ivan hid the truth with facts, worthless verifiable things that could be proved with surveillance footage but gave nothing away.

Ivan, then. What did he want? Did he want the System destroyed?

The discomfiting and strange realization that had been troubling her came to mind. No, he did not. Or perhaps, Ida thought, Ivan did want the System dead, but in an abstract sort of way, with a generalized hatred that did not want to burn up the life it inhabited in seeking consummation, only to wish it ill from afar. It was not the hatred of a believer.

Yet Ida had no doubt in her, especially after speaking to Ivan all these days, that he knew the Mallt-y-Nos and that he was determined not to give her up.

That left her with a paradox: Ivan was loyal to the Mallt-y-Nos, yet he did not follow her. Ivan supported the Mallt-y-Nos yet did not support her cause.

There was only one reason, Ida thought, for someone to be that loyal without believing in a cause: because someone he loved did believe in her.

In all the System there existed only four people Leontios Ivanov loved: Milla Ivanov, Matthew Gale, Constance Harper, and Abigail Hunter.

One of them, then, was the true believer.

"What the hell were you doing listening to *Ivan*?!" Domitian's voice filled up the narrow hallway, terrible in real, genuine wrath, and Althea was as terrified as a child.

Out of the corner of her eye she saw Ananke's arm swing around nervously, sparks flashing on its fingertips, and Gagnon push his hands up against his forehead, pacing away, but both Gagnon and Ananke seemed far off and peripheral in comparison to Domitian, as if Althea's sight had narrowed or he had bent space around him like a black hole to seem larger than he was.

She was stuck somewhere between defiance and a desperate need to explain herself. "He knew what was going on!" Althea said. "He knew Gale! He told me what Gale did. That's why I couldn't figure out what was wrong; I didn't know what Gale did."

"Did it once occur to you that he was lying to you?" Domitian demanded.

"But he wasn't!" said Althea, because that much she was certain of. "He was right!"

"Jesus Christ," Gagnon said again, though Althea hardly heard him, and she hardly noticed that he threw a hand out as if he could no longer deal with her at all and walked away up the hall and out of sight.

Domitian's jaw was clenched tight; he was shaking his head at Althea as if he had passed words. He didn't understand. He had to understand, because if he understood, if he saw, he wouldn't be angry at her anymore, and he would stop trying to kill her beautiful ship. Althea said, "Ananke, show Domitian you can understand us. Show Domitian, all right?"

The holographic terminal between them went from dark to flaring red, red like light through a vial of blood. A hologram appeared on the terminal, the most recent hologram in the *Ananke*'s data banks: the hologram Ida Stays had sent to announce her arrival. The figure of Ida Stays appeared on the terminal, the image rotated so that she was facing Domitian, the image distorted oddly by the imperfect rotation, her shoulder set into her neck, her jaw askew from her face, fingers kinked. Her feet were facing the opposite direction from the rest of her. The image blinked, the hologram righting itself to match the feet, but with the head remaining facing Domitian, as if it had been severed at the neck and placed sideways. Another blink, and the holograph was mostly facing him again, bits and pieces intersecting at unnatural, broken angles.

"No, no, Ananke," Althea said. It was not Ananke's fault that she did not know how to speak in ways Domitian would understand and had to make do with bits and pieces stitched together.

A sound came from the hologram. Ananke must have tried to play the recording that had come with Ida's image—to appropriate the language that Ida had spoken fluently and speak to Domitian. The noise came out distorted beyond comprehension. The distorted Ida's mouth opened, dislocated jaw hanging ajar, and then the recording stopped, Ida's voice coming out in one long, flat drone like the cry of the machine.

"Ananke, stop," Althea said, and the scream ceased, the nightmare visage vanished.

Domitian was pale and furious when he looked at her, and a chill ran through Althea, a chill like despair, when she realized that he was even further from convinced than he had been before.

In that moment Althea knew how Domitian must be seeing Ananke: something unnatural, something inhuman, something to be destroyed—something monstrous.

Ananke's eyes were studded throughout all of her halls, and so she saw Gagnon as he walked away.

He had just passed out of sight of Althea and Domitian when he stopped, half turning back to where the echoes of Domitian's shouts could still be heard—the sound of Althea's distraction.

There was an opening to the maintenance shafts in a storage room a few yards ahead. He went inside that room—Ananke watching—and knelt in front of the maintenance shaft, feeling around for the hinge of the hidden door.

When he had found it, he nodded and got up and went to one of Ananke's interfaces. Ananke was curious, and so she let him go into her files, seek out the program that, when running, would make the maintenance shafts safe for human passage.

It seemed that Gagnon was surprised when he found that contrary to what the ship had told him and Althea and Domitian before, the program was running and had been running all this time, ever since the moment Matthew Gale had escaped from his cell.

He remained there, unease on his face, then shook it off and pulled open the door, passing into Ananke's veins.

. . .

Ida opened up the files on all four of Ivan's friends.

She removed Milla Ivanov from consideration; as appealing as the thought was, Doctor Ivanov had been watched far too closely for her to be involved in anything of this scale. Abigail Hunter could easily be the Mallt-y-Nos's supporter, but Ida had trouble believing that Ivan would work so hard to cover up that secret. Abby was already on the run; the System already was pursuing her as a connection. Ivan had little to gain by concealing the connection, especially since his every story cast more suspicion on her.

That left only Constance Harper and Matthew Gale. Mattie's involvement was the most appealing to her. Since the two men worked together, if Gale supported the Mallt-y-Nos, Ivan's movements would match Gale's.

It would be, Ida thought, bitterly ironic if by sheer bad luck she had captured the wrong one of the duo and her real lead was rotting somewhere in a metal coffin by Mercury's orbit, drifting down into the sun and damning her to humiliation and failure.

There was, however, another possibility—

It was so absurd, so impossible, so cosmically unlikely that Ida could hardly allow herself to consider it, but at this point she had little other choice.

The only other reason that Ivan would defend the Mallt-y-Nos with his life was that he was personally loyal to her. The movements of Mattie and Ivan had early on given Ida the excited idea that perhaps they were in her inner circle to take on so many important jobs on her behalf. She had long since dismissed it, but—

But if Ivan knew her, knew her personally, and loved her, he would lie to protect her.

And that meant that the Mallt-y-Nos could be one of only four people.

"She's alive!" Althea shouted. "Ivan didn't lie, not to me, he didn't. Domitian, please listen. I promise you. I promise you this isn't an error. She's alive."

Domitian's face was set, cold and furious. On any other day Althea would have shrunk and hidden from that face, apologized like a frightened puppy showing its belly.

But if she backed down now, Ananke would die.

"Look," she said, "if you go to the terminal down the hall, Ananke will talk to you. She can't speak out loud yet and she's not very fluent, but she's still learning English from the language files. Go and you'll see that she can talk to you."

Domitian was looking at her as if he hardly knew her. She hardly recognized him, either. He asked, "Have you lost your mind?"

Such had been the paranoia of Ananke's creators that she had cameras even in the maintenance shafts. Maddened and sick as if evolution had conspired in psychosis to put eyes on the inside that stared at pulsing quivering red flesh unceasingly, Ananke stared at the cold grim gray and steel of her organs, at the hollowness of her veins. Humans did not design machines for sanity.

Gagnon was crawling through the maintenance shafts. The crew thought that the cameras in the maintenance shafts were malfunctioning and no longer worked, but they did work, and Ananke watched Gagnon crawl. He was too tall, too gangly to fit easily, as easily as Althea fit, but even Matthew Gale had climbed more smoothly through Ananke, and he was just as tall as Gagnon and had had a broken arm as well. Whether because Gagnon thought the cameras in the maintenance shafts were dead, or because he was so used to the cameras that he forgot they were there, or because he did not believe Ananke was alive, he did not act as if he was being watched.

At last Gagnon emerged, as Ananke had known he would, into a small nexus of maintenance shafts where there was just enough space for a tall man to stretch out and sleep if he did not mind his legs protruding into one of the shafts. Ananke knew this because a tall man had slept there and none but she had seen.

Gagnon emerged into that small nexus and stopped, seeing in the dim glow of the guide lights wrappers of food strewn about, stolen from the pantry; blankets likewise stolen had been formed into a rough bed in the corner, signs of many days of human habitation, recently abandoned.

With the input given, there was only one conclusion to draw. Ananke had known all along that there had been someone living in her walls, and now she watched Gagnon understand.

Althea saw the exact moment Domitian decided to give up trying to connect with her, and she felt it like a bullet to the breast.

"Althea," he said tersely and dangerously, and took a step forward.

Althea raised her gun from where it had drifted nose groundward. She felt curiously unmoored, blank. As with Ivan, she was not conscious of having made a decision at any point, but she knew she had gone too far ever to go back.

Domitian said, "You're not going to shoot me."

"Why do you think I won't?"

He was not looking at her gun but over it into her eyes. "You know what the right thing to do here is," Domitian said. He took another step toward her. "You know that the right thing to do right now is to follow orders. To let me pass. To let me shut down the computer. Gagnon and I won't tell anyone about this. All right? It's okay, Althea; you can hand me the gun."

For a moment she wanted to give in to his gentle urging, the certainty of his outstretched palm. She could lay the gun on that palm and go back to untroubled obedience. Ivan would be gone in a matter of days. With the destruction of the *Ananke*'s computer, the surveillance footage would be incomplete and useless. The System would not need to know.

Domitian's hand twitched once in silent urging. He looked at her, serious, strong, sure, protective, everything Althea would have a father be.

Althea did not lower the gun. She said, "I created her. I helped create her. I can't let you kill her."

"Althea—"

"Domitian," said Althea, and meant it with all her heart, "if you come any closer, I will shoot you."

Abigail was the most obvious possibility, but Ida had the least information when it came to her. A few sparse police reports (Abigail always used her real name even as Mattie and Ivan chose pseudonyms of varying outlandishness) and not a single recent photograph. Ivan seemed to hate her in some peculiar, obsessive way, but he seemed to be just as devoted.

Milla Ivanov, the next most likely because she had the motives and probably the connections, was simply too well watched.

Matthew Gale—that would certainly explain the pair's movements connecting them to the Mallt-y-Nos. Matthew Gale had the motivation to destroy the System, as well. Ivan's affection for and devotion to him could not be denied: Ivan would lie and would die to protect him.

Yet in all the surveillance Ida had seen, all the reports she had read, she had gotten nothing from Matthew Gale that would imply that he could conceive of a revolution, much less carry it to term. He was not a leader. He followed amiably where Ivan threw himself headlong or where Abigail ordered.

In any case, Matthew Gale's corpse was rotting somewhere far away.

That left only Constance Harper, who had left Ida with the lingering impression of insufferable self-righteousness. Ivan's feelings for her seemed similar to what he felt for Abigail: devotion with a certain degree of contempt. But Ida had found her story completely believable.

There was no surveillance of Abigail Hunter to watch, and Milla seemed an unlikely prospect, but Mattie and Constance seemed equally improbable. Ida started a surveillance video of Mattie and Ivan, stopped it, started another, stopped it, started a third, and dropped her head into her hands.

This was a waste of her time. She had only come to another absurd conclusion. Perhaps Ivan truly did not know.

Perhaps, this time, Ida Stays had been wrong.

The recording drifted to her ears. It was from Constance Harper's bar eight years earlier.

"Hey, Con," said Matthew Gale's tenor, his accent stupidly uneducated to Ida's ears. There was a brief, almost awkward pause, and then he said, "This is Ivan."

"So you're the one," said Constance Harper, less accented, her voice low and firm and nearly covered up by the static of the footage, the soft conversation of two other people in her bar, "who almost got my brother killed."

Ida raised her head.

The footage continued to play, but she stopped it and rewound it to that moment with Ivan's charming smile spreading out over his face and Constance's face obscured by the position of the camera.

"So you're the one who almost got my brother killed," said Constance Harper.

It was the same thing Abigail had said to Ivan when they first had met, or so Ivan had told Ida. For a moment she sat very still, frozen, and then all at once all the connections she had been missing made themselves in her brain and she understood.

Fury rose in her, fury that she had come so close to giving up, that Ivan had so nearly beaten her, fury and a sudden overpowering desire to tear him apart with her nails and teeth.

Driven by triumph, driven by wrath, Ida Stays left her computer on and open, the screen frozen on the moment when Ivan's smile started to fade, and went out into the hallway in her stocking feet with only one intention in mind: to get to the white room.

Gagnon moved more quickly through the maintenance shafts after he found the signs of habitation. Ananke thought he was furious, terrified. She watched him find his way to the shaft that would lead him to the very base of her spine, where he could dig into her brain and find the switch that would leave her dead.

Domitian and Althea were shouting at each other, and that covered up the sound of the cover to the maintenance shaft falling to the ground as Gagnon crawled out.

Domitian saw him over Althea's shoulder, but Althea did not.

Ananke tried to warn Althea about Gagnon's presence, but Althea was too far from the computer terminals to see the warning Ananke flashed and was not looking toward them, anyway. Ananke started screaming, turning on the alarm in a desperate attempt to attract Althea's attention, but Althea snapped, "Be quiet, Ananke!" and Ananke obeyed, watching, frightened, if a machine could be frightened, and growing furious, if a machine could be furious, as Gagnon crept cautiously forward toward the hatch that hid Ananke's single weakness.

Althea and Domitian were shouting, but all of Ananke's attention was taken up in two places: Gagnon opening the hatch to her hollow heart, and the white room, where another confrontation was taking place.

Ananke's mobile arm sparked and swung but did not dare touch Gagnon without guidance, without direction on what to do. She had been built to obey orders, to react; she had never been designed to act. Gagnon either did not notice or dismissed her as a threat.

And then, from the white room, Ananke learned what to do.

Ananke could watch everywhere in the ship at once. With some cameras, she could watch Gagnon climb through the maintenance shafts. With others, she could watch Ida Stays striding through the halls, heading for the white room.

When Ida Stays reached the white room, she opened the door and stopped past the threshold, staring in at the bare back of Ivan's neck, watching, eyes narrowed.

Slowly, as if aware of her predatory gaze, Ivan straightened his back, blue eyes staring straight ahead, every muscle tensed for a fight. Ananke was not there to them; she was not watching. They were both focused entirely on each other, on the threat the other posed.

Ida stepped into the room, letting the steel door swing shut with a horrible clang behind her. In contrast, her stocking feet made only the lightest sounds as they padded over the floor, stalking toward Ivan.

Ivan did not move.

Ida did not speak until she was standing beside him, across from the silent polygraph and camera. She did not switch them on. They stood cold and dead, their wires still stuck to Ivan like the atrophied veins of mostly severed limbs.

"I'm giving you one last chance," Ida Stays said, "to tell me the name of the Mallt-y-Nos."

Ivan looked up at her.

"I don't know," he said.

"Yes, you do," Ida said, leaning forward suddenly. Ida, Ananke knew, did not know about the chains.

Ivan did not react to Ida's proximity or give any sign that he was conscious of the secretly increased length of his chains.

"And so do I," she said. "I figured it out, Ivan. But I'm giving you a chance to tell me yourself. As a courtesy."

Ivan smiled, or almost smiled. Ananke still was learning the subtleties of human expression, but she thought that it was no smile at all.

"I've figured you out," Ivan said. "You don't feel anything. Where other people feel empathy, there's nothing but a dark hollow place in your ribs that takes everything in and lets nothing out." He said, "Do you think you got this job because you're a sociopath?"

"You're speaking like a desperate man," Ida said. "Do you think you could distract me from what I know?"

"I just want you to stop pretending you're anything better than an animal. The cameras aren't on, Ida. It's just us here." Ivan flashed white teeth at her, but his smile froze and faded as Ida leaned in a little closer before pulling away, and Ananke saw Ivan's shaken breath, imperfectly hidden, as she began to pace a vast circle around the table and Ivan chained beside it.

"Wouldn't you like to know how I figured it out?" Ida asked, speaking at him over the table, her smile as cold as its steel.

"Why don't you tell me," said Ivan, every word bitten off.

"I knew that you were weak," she said, "just like everyone else. And I knew that your weakness was your family and your friends. Just like everyone else."

Her expression was avid, hungry.

"You're not as special as you think. So you understand that I was surprised," Ida said, "when, even though I threatened them, you didn't give up the Mallt-y-Nos."

"I bet that really pissed you off."

"You were a challenge," Ida said just as she crossed behind him and leaned over to exhale each word in hot breath down the back of Ivan's neck, a confession, "and it will be rewarding to watch you beg.

"So I realized," Ida resumed, leaning back away, "that perhaps the reason you didn't break when I threatened them was that to break would throw them into greater danger. Abby was the obvious guess. But she was impossible to find or track, and I couldn't even find a clear picture of her. But Abby was supposed to be the obvious choice, wasn't she?"

"Stop," said Ivan, and Ida stopped.

"Would you like to confess?" she asked.

Ivan's fingers were curled tightly around the arms of his chair.

"What's the date?" he asked.

"It's the thirty-first," Ida said. She stalked closer to him, leaning in. "I was looking at arrest reports," she said, leaning against the table, her stockinged toes curling against the pure white floor, "and you know what I noticed?"

Ivan looked up at her slowly and coldly, and did not answer.

"You and Mattie used pseudonyms," Ida said. "Abby did not. She never did. And so I knew that 'Abigail Hunter' was a pseudonym."

Ivan did not say anything. Ananke, who had recognized this pattern some time ago, as she had been programmed to recognize patterns of all kinds, felt an abstract respect for the tiny fragile form of Ida Stays, who had put the pieces together herself.

"What happened to the real Abigail?" Ida asked, that avidity back in her eyes as she leaned in farther, farther. She was less than a meter away from Ivan, nearly within the grasp of the tips of Ivan's fingers. "She died in that fire all those years ago, didn't she?"

"If you're so sure you know," said Ivan, "why won't you say it?"

"I'm sure," Ida said, absolute. If she ever had doubted, it did not show in any way that Ananke could see.

"Then say her name," said Ivan. "Whisper it into my ear. If you're wrong, no one else needs to know."

Ida leaned forward on her pale stocking feet, bringing her closer to Ivan, and she leaned in, the tips of her black hair brushing the plane of his cheek, and whispered into his ear, "The Mallt-y-Nos is Constance Harper."

She drew back, but not far, just far enough that Ivan could turn his head to look at her, their faces centimeters apart.

"Very good," Ivan whispered so softly that it was hard for Ananke to hear. "Very clever. How does it feel, Ida, to have all the power over me at last?"

Ida's answering smile uncurled over her face, slow but strong. She rested one hand against the side of his pale neck, against where his pounding pulse would be, leaning in toward his face still with that smile as if she would kiss him, or bite him, but Ivan's arms darted out and grabbed her around her waist, hauling her up over the arm of the chair and into his lap. Stunned, she pushed at him, struggling to pull out of his grip, his arm wrapped around her waist, the chains attaching him at his wrist wrapped in turn around her knees, digging into her pale skin, her black slip twisted from the movement, riding up her thighs. Ivan grabbed the little box cutter he had stolen from Althea and in jerking his arm to hold Ida down tugged too hard on the dark slender wires attaching him to the polygraph, sending the whole machine and Ida's camera as well crashing down to the ground and shattering, sending a spray of bolts and wires over the white floor.

Ida pushed at him, everything happening too fast for her slow human synapses to fire and transition her from surprise to anger or alarm, and Ivan brought the knife up, dragging the chain on his wrist through her dark hair, rumpling it against her face, striking hard against her skin and pressing her nose into her cheek as he reached over and cut into her throat.

Ida's blood hit Ivan's hand first, staining his fingers red, then sprayed onto his shirt as it pulsed out with the beat of her heart onto her chest and down onto Ivan's legs, dripping down to the floor. She convulsed and shook down into stillness like a machine running out of power, bright red staining her white shirt, her white skin, Ivan's white hospital clothes and his white hands and feet, the white floor of the white room. Ivan struggled to hold her down, but with each passing second her shudders grew weaker. When at last she was still, he dropped the box cutter to the floor, where it fell into a puddle of blood and the red sank into all its crevices. He was shaking so hard that he almost couldn't manage to balance her on his lap while he rifled through her pockets, but he came out with a little silver key to his cuffs. He managed to keep her balanced, limp, one hand trailing down into her own blood, as he unlocked the chains at his arms.

Then he got his arms under her and laid her onto the steel table, where blood continued to drain, slowly now that it was not driven by the thumping of her heart, onto the table, spilling over its edges.

He bent down and freed his legs, though his hands were trembling so hard that he nearly dropped the key into the red underfoot.

When he had freed himself, he took the key in his fist and hurled it as hard as he could against the opposite wall of the white room, where it crashed against the white panels and clattered to the floor. It left the slightest smear of red from the blood transferred onto it from Ivan's hands. Ivan's human eyes would not be able to see it from his distance, but Ananke could.

Ivan stood, and the chains fell away to clank empty against the metal chair. He reached into Ida's pockets once more and came out with a flat slender gun, designed to be hidden but also designed to kill.

He held it in his hand for a moment, then checked it for ammunition, and with it in one hand, wiping the other free of blood against his pants and only succeeding in leaving bloody handprints against his thigh, he laid a false track for his pursuit: crossing the room, leaving bloody footprints to the wall, where he removed a panel. It led into the maintenance shafts.

Leaving the panel ajar, Ivan wiped his feet against the floor, getting as much of the blood off as he could, before leaving the wall and the opened panel, this time with no footprints left behind.

Ivan escaped into the hall, heading for the docking bay and leaving Ida dead on the table and the white room stained with red.

And so from the events in the white room Ananke got her guidance.

Gagnon had the hatch open, and he was leaning down into it, far too close to the long fall into her core.

Althea wasn't listening to Ananke.

Gagnon leaned forward, reaching in for the switch.

Ananke reached forward with her sparking arm and touched it to his back, increasing the voltage so that Gagnon jerked and shuddered and lost his balance, and it took just the slightest touch of the arm to send him falling in through the hatch, down into Ananke's black heart.

The tidal forces tore him apart before he had gone very far, stretching his body until it broke, bones, sinew, flesh coming apart, raining down into the black hole beneath, increasing its entropy and its mass by so slight an amount—for a human was so small compared with what Ananke held—that Ananke could not even sense a change.

He had time for one last cry, which echoed oddly, distorted and truncated, bottomed out by the spaghettification of his lungs, but it was enough to get Althea and Domitian's attention, and they realized quickly what had happened. Althea echoed the cry, starting forward toward the hatch but then stopping herself before she could reach it, her free hand coming up to cover her open mouth. When she raised her eyes to Ananke's mobile arm, she looked at Ananke in a way Ananke did not understand.

Domitian said, "Althea, what did you do?"

Althea, it seemed, could not speak. She only stared up at Ananke and shook her head.

Domitian looked from Althea to Ananke, and then he looked at Ananke, truly at her, for the first time.

"It's going to stop us," he said, and Althea took in an unsteady breath, her attention unbroken from Ananke. "If we try to shut it off, it'll stop us," and Ananke—free at last, and with all the power—flashed all the lights on board the ship once in agreement.

Part 4

THE THIRD LAW OF THERMODYNAMICS

The entropy of a system approaches a constant value as the temperature of the system approaches zero.

The constants are determined by the degeneracy of the system's basic structures.

Chapter 8

CONSTANTS

Gagnon was dead, and Ananke—Althea's Ananke—had killed him.

She was still learning, Althea told herself. Ananke was still learning. Ananke hadn't learned the ability fully to tell right from wrong. She was still thinking like a machine, finding the most straightforward solution to a problem and—and executing it.

She couldn't let Ananke see how upset she was. She couldn't let Ananke see her panic, see her grieve. The most frightening thing for a child to see was her mother crying, and Althea didn't want to frighten Ananke any more. She didn't want Ananke to see that she was upset; she didn't want Ananke to see that she was afraid of—

"We have to find Ida," said Domitian grimly from behind her, and broke her from the frightful beckoning of that unfinished thought. In some way, it troubled her that Domitian immediately sought Ida Stays, but that concern was buried beneath the sound like static that filled her ears, her eyes, her brain, looking down the small hatch to where Gagnon had been unmade, looking at the sparking metal arm that Althea had created.

There was nothing left of Gagnon. There was not even a body.

She could not let Ananke see her weep.

"Althea," Domitian said. She turned. He was beckoning her. The shadow of Ananke's arm fell over Althea's shoulder. He moved only when she came forward to walk with him away from the open hatch, away from Ananke.

There was no away from Ananke, of course. The distance between them and the arm was a facade: Ananke was everywhere; everything around them was Ananke. If Althea could not let Ananke see her weep, then she could never weep. She said aloud in a voice that was tight and high with the force she used to keep it free of trembling, "Ananke, where is Ida Stays?"

The screens on the computer terminals all up and down the hall blinked on. Althea went to the nearest and forced herself not to stand too far from the screen. She read, IDA STAYS IS IN THE WHITE ROOM.

Domitian started walking again before she had finished speaking, and, numb, Althea trailed along in his wake. She said when they were about halfway there, "Domitian . . ."

"Don't," said Domitian, which was just as well, because Althea had nothing to say.

Gagnon was dead. Althea had worked with him for years; he had helped design the *Ananke*. And now he was gone.

Althea liked to solve problems. When she was presented with something that was wrong, something that troubled her, she took steps to remedy it immediately, and whether or not it could be fixed, there was something she could do to work toward an end. But no amount of grief or regret or teaching of Ananke could ever undo time, could ever recombine Gagnon's shredded atoms, could pull him backward out of the event horizon of the black hole.

No matter what, she could not let Ananke see her weep.

Ahead of her, Domitian knocked on the door to the white room. There was no reaction. He shifted, impatient, and knocked again. Just as Althea was coming up to him, his patience was expended, and he opened the door, taking a step forward—and stopped.

The white room was no longer wholly white.

The floor around the table and the two chairs was coated in a dark vibrant crimson. It dripped off the table and onto the floor, joining the slow spread of scarlet as the pool spread itself to thinness. On the table, laid as if in her coffin, her face gray and her lips bloodless beneath the smeared patchy remnants of her dark lipstick, was Ida Stays. Her head was tilted toward the door or else it had fallen to that side, and her black hair was matted with blood, and her eyes were as blank and empty as a doll's.

Althea lingered at the doorway with her hand over her mouth as Domitian strode in, gun out, checking the corners, although there was nowhere to hide in that white room.

There were bloody footsteps leading to a panel in the wall. Automatically, Althea called up the plans of the *Ananke* in her head. That panel led to the maintenance shafts.

"He got a knife somehow," Domitian said grimly, leaning over the corpse as well as he could without stepping in the blood. He bent over, looking into the blood on the ground, and stopped, pointing. "That knife."

Althea came into the room to see, because she was gripped with a terrible suspicion, and when she was near enough, standing just on the edge of Ida's spreading blood, she saw a familiar box cutter lying in the clinging red.

"That's mine," she said. He must have stolen it from her when she had undone his chains. He must have stolen it from her and used it—and his greater range of movement from the loosened chains—to kill Ida. Althea had caused two deaths this evening.

Domitian's look was cold and hard, but he said nothing to her.

"Check the halls," he said tersely. "He's probably headed for the docking bay. I'll flush him out of the maintenance shafts. Don't let him escape."

Althea could only nod. While Domitian followed the bloody footprints into the wall, she fled from the white room.

Anger was growing in her, as strong as her grief and her guilt and fear, almost strong enough to cover up those worse emotions, almost strong enough to keep her from falling apart.

Ivan had done this; Ivan had killed both of them. She had to find Ivan.

"Ananke," Althea said, walking up the hall faster and faster, "is Ivan going for the docking bay or the escape pods?"

She paused at a terminal as she passed it, looking for Ananke's answer, but Ananke had not replied.

It should take the computer only a few seconds to determine an answer to her question. "Ananke?" she said, and Ananke said,

MATTHEW GALE.

"What?" said Althea. "He's going for the escape pods? Like Gale?"

NO.

"Then what?"

PROTECT IVAN.

For one frustrating moment, Althea still did not understand and nearly shouted at the machine, not that shouting would have done any good.

And then she understood.

If she had created Ananke, so had Matthew Gale. Althea had provided the body, the raw materials, but Mattie had given her ship the spark of life. Althea would not have been remotely surprised if in programming her computer, Mattie had included a mandate: Protect Ivan.

"Ananke," Althea said, "Mattie didn't even know he made you. He was using you. And then he left you. I'm the one who's been here, taking care of you. You can't trust Mattie, but you can trust me. No matter what, you can trust me. And I need to find Ivan. Where is he?"

Silence. Althea held her breath.

DOCKING BAY.

Althea started to run. "Don't let him get out. Don't open the bay doors if he manages to board a ship. Do not let Ivan off of this ship!"

It was only a matter of time now that Domitian, too, was in the maintenance shafts before he also found evidence of a stranger's secret stay in Ananke's walls. Ananke watched him realize, watched him understand how close the ship's crew had come to ruin, watched his wrath grow.

The path through the maintenance shafts was slower to reach the docking bay than the hall; that presumably was why Ivan had feigned entrance. Althea approached Ivan more swiftly than Domitian did.

When Althea reached the docking bay, Ivan was trying to gain access to Ida's ship. Ida's craft, Althea realized, was the only ship currently in Ananke's hold with a working relativistic drive.

"Don't move!" Althea shouted the moment she saw his bent back, bringing her gun up to bear, and Ivan raised his arms in the air, stepping away from the torn-open control panel. Fury and fear and adrenaline made Althea shake, and she shook even harder when she saw that his white clothes were stained in blood, torso, lap, arms, but she could not say which of the three feelings reigned supreme. He had a gun clutched in one of his hands, a tiny gun unfamiliar to Althea, but with his hands in the air it was pointed harmlessly at the ceiling.

When he had first appeared on the ship, he had been mysterious, strange, and dangerous. He looked dangerous now, too, but differently, the difference between a wolf ghosting gray through snow and brush and that wolf standing bloody in the open over the torn throat of its prey. No longer something mysterious but something monstrous instead.

Still he smiled that wolfish smile when he saw Althea aiming her gun at him.

"Do you know what that thing does to the human body?" he asked.

Althea could have shot him then and there.

She didn't, but neither could she force herself to speak around the choking force of her rage.

"Well?" he said, eyebrows quirking up and arms splattered with red to the elbow. "Are you going to shoot me or let me go?"

"You lied to me," Althea said.

It was not what she had meant to say, but it was what she was thinking. They were almost on opposite ends of the docking bay and had to speak loudly to be heard; Althea's accusation traveled in indistinct echoes throughout the vast space, as if this ship were accusing him, too.

"Actually," said Ivan, whose eyes were brilliantly blue even at this distance, "of all the people on this ship, you're the only one I told the truth."

"You used me," Althea said, striding forward, "and manipulated me." She stopped because of some sense that if she walked any farther, she really would have to shoot him then and there, and she said, "You've lied to *everyone*!"

The coiled tension in Ivan's body let loose like a spring snapping back into shape. Althea had not even noticed it was there until it was suddenly gone. Perhaps that tension had always been there and she simply had never noticed. She had noticed very little about him, she was starting to see.

"Of course I lied!" he said. "Of course I used you, and used everyone, and lied. Stop feeling so self-righteously *wounded*, Althea. I had to save the people I love, and the only way I could do that was by lying. Yes, I lied!"

His shout echoed its way through the docking bay, against the sealed doors to space.

And what about the ones Althea had loved? Gagnon was dead through a chain of events Ivan had put in motion and had hurried along, Gagnon, who had been Althea's colleague and friend for almost as long as Mattie had been Ivan's. Ivan could not have known that he was dead, but Althea knew, and she was *certain* that if Ivan had known, he wouldn't have cared. Gagnon wasn't Ivan's friend, after all. Gagnon had only been Althea's.

She had had enough of Ivan being frightened, of Ivan being victimized. It was all Ivan told her. "You killed Ida," Althea accused. He had used Althea to kill Ida. Ivan had not been a victim then.

"Are you mourning her?" Ivan asked, and it was so cruel that even after everything else Althea was stunned by it. "I didn't want to kill her. I had to."

"And now you're lying again," said Althea. "Still trying to get my sympathy. That's all you've ever done, is try to get me to help you."

Ivan started to laugh. His hands had lowered as he spoke until they hovered around his shoulders; now his arms dropped to his sides, one hand still clutched loosely around the little gun.

"There is nothing I could say that could ever make you believe me," he said. Althea almost wished there were. "I killed Ida because she was going to hurt the people I love, and she was going to enjoy it, too. I'm not on the *Ananke* to hurt anyone. I was here by accident; I was caught by bad luck. That much I promise you was completely true even if I lied about everything else. You needed me to be the Devil, so I was the Devil for you, but all I want is to protect the people I love. That's the truth. Are you going to let me go?"

"Put your gun down," Althea said. He had been right; there was nothing he could say that could make her believe him now.

Instead of putting the gun down, he lifted it up, aiming it at Althea one-handed. Althea tensed, her fingers tightening around her own weapon, her finger flexing against the trigger but not pulling. Double action—she just needed the slightest touch to the trigger, the slightest brush, and the gun would kick back in her hands and send its bullet into its target.

"How's this?" Ivan said. "Now I've got a gun on you. Either you let me go or you shoot me, Althea; there's no other option."

Althea thought she might hate him yet.

"Let me go, Althea," Ivan said. His voice had softened, grown gentle. "We both know you're not going to shoot—"

The sound of a gun has the same aural kick as the kinetic strike of it hitting its target, and that sharp echo rang out through Ananke's hold, almost deafening, as Althea fired.

Ananke watched Ivan wake up one hour and thirteen minutes later. The first thing he did was open his eyes and look around, head wobbling, moving his arms as if to clutch his head, shifting as if to stand, all his actions thwarted as he realized that he was back in the white room, chained again to the chair.

"Damn it," he muttered, words slurred with the loss of blood that had made him paler than before, and he tried to sit up, which was approximately when the pain from the roughly bandaged gunshot wound in his right thigh hit him.

Ananke watched him scream.

It was only after he had come to again that Ananke saw him realize what else was in the white room with him: Ida, still lying where he had placed her, with her head tilted on its torn up throat to aim her blank black eyes at him, and Domitian, sitting on the other side of the table, staring at him over Ida's chilling corpse.

Ivan's breath came harshly panted; his hands flexed against the blood-slick metal of the chair.

Once Domitian had arrived and hauled the unconscious, bleeding Ivan out of the docking bay over his shoulder, Althea had gone straight to the computer. While Domitian dealt with Ivan's wound, Althea worked on undoing some of the damage she had done in attempting to fix the computer. If she could only focus on working, she thought, she could drive from her head the memory of Gagnon crying out as he fell, the memory of the weight of the gun in her hands, kicking back as she pulled the trigger.

But for some reason Ananke was broadcasting on all available screens the surveillance footage from the white room.

The image showing on the screen was the scene from overhead. Domitian's back was to the camera, and he leaned over the table a dark shape, faceless; Ivan was pale, strained, pain and fear on his face. The dark pool of blood beneath them looked as if someone had opened up a pit in the floor and Ivan and Domitian and the corpse of Ida Stays were just about to fall into it all together.

The white room's camera still claimed to be unusable, but the evidence of its functionality was right before her. "You could see this whole time," Althea said. With all her energy gone into keeping herself under control, she could not even feel surprised.

The screen blinked.

YES, said Ananke.

"You just were keeping it from us," said Althea.

YES.

"Because Mattie told you to."

YES.

"You may have killed Ida," Domitian said, and Ananke watched, and listened, and broadcast what she saw, "but the System still wants to know what you know. You're going to tell me the truth."

Ivan laughed. It was a weak sound. He could not sit fully upright in the chair, arms trembling in the much-shortened chains.

"Sure," Ivan said. "Just one thing first. What's the date?"

Ananke knew the date. It had just become the first of November, an hour past.

"What does that matter?" Domitian asked.

"It matters to me," Ivan said.

Domitian rose and with slow, heavy steps walked through the tacky blood to Ivan's side, where he laid one hand against Ivan's neck beneath his chin, pressing his sagging head up against the back of the chair so that Ivan was forced to meet his eyes.

"I don't care what matters to you."

Althea didn't know how long it took her to notice Ananke's latest message for her, but when she saw it, her blood chilled.

YOU SHOT IVAN BECAUSE HE KILLED SOMEONE, said Ananke.

Sitting beside the computer terminal, her arms in the wall of the ship, undoing clips from wires, Althea hesitated.

"Yes," she said. She had wires snagged around her wrists, as if the ship were trying to pull her in, make her a part of it.

I KILLED SOMEONE.

"No," Althea said immediately, fear rising in her chest again. She struggled not to let it show in her face, be heard in her voice. "That's not the same, Ananke. It's not the same thing."

Ananke was silent. The silence struck Althea as ominous, and it only made her fear the harder to control.

"You didn't know what you were doing," Althea said. "Ivan did. He knew." She kept telling herself that you couldn't expect a toddler to understand these things. Ivan, though. Ivan was a grown man. It was not the same.

I KNEW.

"Yes, but you didn't—" Althea stopped, trying to find a better way to explain; she did not even know how to begin to explain the value of a life and how Ivan must have known it, and Ananke must not. "You were defending yourself," she tried.

SO WAS IVAN.

"It's not the same," Althea said, and bent back over the open wall panel and hoped Ananke would let it go.

It wasn't the same. It couldn't be.

"Why did you kill Ida?" Domitian asked, releasing Ivan's neck, letting his head sag forward again. He could not seem to hold it upright on his own.

Ivan snickered with the humor of the light-headed, and Ananke accessed her data—her memories—wondering how badly injured he was. Could an injury to a limb kill a man?

"Tell me the date and maybe I'll tell you," he said.

"There will be no more trades," Domitian said with eerie calm. "No more deals. No more exchanges. Only you will talk, and you will tell me the truth."

"What do you want to hear?" Ivan asked. "I don't know anything. Ida was going to kill me because of it, so I cut her throat."

"Ida Stays," said Domitian in a voice suddenly so loud that Ivan flinched back against his chair and Ananke heard the shout echo through the room, "was an honest woman."

"Ida Stays was a sociopath," said Ivan just as fiercely. "The only reason you liked her was because she needed you to like her. She would have had you tortured just as happily as she did me."

Ananke did not expect the blow, and neither, it seemed, did Althea—in the hallway she flinched, her hands coming up to cover her mouth—but Ivan had braced himself and did not look surprised when he raised his head again to smirk at Domitian, blood trickling down his nose.

"Stop being such a little bitch," Ivan said, "and execute me already."

"I found traces of someone living in the walls of the ship," said Domitian. "Who was it?"

"The Devil," said Ivan. Ida's body continued to gape and stare.

Ananke was not surprised this time when Domitian struck him again.

Domitian asked, "Who was it?"

Ivan looked up at him and did not flinch away. "Go to hell," he said with remarkable calm.

Domitian knelt at his side. Ivan looked uneasy, then frightened. Uncaring of the blood sticking to his uniform trousers, Domitian reached forward toward Ivan's leg and stuck his thumb against the bandages covering the bullet hole, pushing until spots of red stained the fresh whiteness and Ivan's scream filled the white room.

"Mattie!" said Ivan. "It was Mattie, but he's long gone now."

"The maintenance shafts were occupied for days," said Domitian. "Gale was only here for a few minutes."

Ivan laughed, breathless. "That's what you were supposed to think."

"Supposed to?"

"You were an easy mark," Ivan said. "You ate it right up. Mattie leaving in the escape pod."

"He didn't leave? He was on the ship?"

"He didn't leave," Ivan said. "Not then."

"But he told you he was leaving," said Domitian. "He stopped by your cell, and when he couldn't get you out, he told you he was leaving."

"You mean the Scheherazade thing?" Ivan said. The blood from his nose was running down into the seam of his lips. "Scheherazade isn't a nickname; it's code."

"Code for what?"

"Code between me and Mattie," Ivan said. "Scheherazade, she told the Persian king stories for a thousand and one nights to keep him from killing her. Scheherazade was a message. Mattie was telling me to stall."

"Stall for what?"

"Until he could get me free," said Ivan.

Ananke knew that Domitian would have hit Ivan again—his hand raised, that cold directed fury on his face—but Althea burst into the white room before he could.

"Domitian, you need to come," she said frantically, and Domitian lingered a moment at Ivan's side before following her away, leaving Ivan to gasp and sag in his chair beside Ida, his blood joining hers on the floor.

An urgent broadcast had come through from the System. Eager to watch anything other than the surveillance of Ivan being beaten by Domitian, Althea had played it.

It was a printed broadcast from the Lunar System representatives. She read it quickly and then read it again, then a third time, and still could hardly understand what she had read.

Domitian, she knew, would not have wanted her to interrupt his interrogation of Ivan. Althea did not think twice.

"What is it?" he asked tersely as she urged him out of the room and into Ananke's halls, where the broadcast was still playing on the nearest screen.

"Look," said Althea.

PEOPLE OF THE SYSTEM, the message read. THERE HAS JUST BEEN A LARGE-SCALE TERRORIST ATTACK ON EARTH. AT PRESENT WE HAVE NOT RECEIVED CONTACT FROM THE SYSTEM CAPITOL AND DO NOT HAVE ANY INFORMATION ON THE STATUS OF THE PLANET OR OF THE SYSTEM—

The printed broadcast was interrupted by a video that stuttered and flashed static before finally becoming clear. Althea nearly leaped forward to bring back the earlier broadcast, instinct having her believe that Ananke had suffered another glitch, but when she saw what had interrupted and replaced the broadcast, she stopped.

On-screen was a woman, a familiar woman, dark hair and eyes like coals, strong chin and broad shoulders, regal in bearing.

It was Constance Harper.

"People of the System," she said in a low alto lifted and fierce with fervor, "former slaves of the System, I am the Mallt-y-Nos. A few minutes ago, I and my people liberated us all from the System by destroying its source. For so long has the System destroyed your planets and killed your people, and now we have destroyed theirs. Earth was a symbol of oppression and control. It will be no longer. The System is dead. Let freedom reign."

Chapter 9

DEGENERACY

Domitian burst into the white room in a murdering rage, his gun out, and Althea could do nothing but follow at his heels, filled with such a force of anger, of fear, that she wanted to scream. The moment Domitian threw open the door to the white room so that it struck and rang against the wall, he fired his gun high, the crack and roar of the bullet filling the room. It hardly registered in Althea's ringing ears, but Ivan flinched, jolting as if he would duck and cover his head, but there was nowhere for him to go, and now, off balance and dizzy with loss of blood, he sagged in his chair, trapped and shaking like a wounded animal.

Ida was still lying on the table in front of him, her limbs limp and loose in the nearness of her death, and the sight of her made Althea's stomach roil.

Domitian had crossed the room before the echoes of his shot had rung out; he grabbed Ivan now and forced him back against the chair, digging the barrel of the gun with its thin wisp of gray smoke into the soft skin under Ivan's chin, metal pushing against his pulse. That, too, disturbed Althea, disturbed her almost as much as the way Ida's head was tilted, angled to face between Ivan and Domitian, as if she were watching Althea, her death-dilated eyes without cognizance.

Ivan was breathing hard.

He said, "She did it."

It was realization, resignation, and Althea said, "How could you let her?" before she could remember not to plead with him.

There was a long silence that stretched taut in Althea's breast, in which Ivan and Domitian had some unspoken confrontation she could not understand, but at last Ivan spoke, raising his voice to be heard even though Althea was behind him.

"There would have been a genocide one way or another," he said, speaking as if the muzzle still dug up beneath his chin, its deadly promise, meant nothing to him. "Either Constance destroyed Earth, as she planned, or the System found out about her plans—and how close she was to succeeding—and they killed her and everyone who had ever known her. Half of Mars—everyone who was even the slightest bit suspicious. Miranda and the other Uranian moons. She was a poison, and they would have amputated half their body to get rid of it. The System has done it before. Connor Ivanov was from Saturn; no one lives around Saturn now. Why do you think Con chose to blow up Earth? Because that's what the System did to her people, time after time. Saturn, Haumea, Oberon. And they used the very bombs she used on them. So one way or another, billions of people would have died. I chose the side that included the people I loved."

She could not allow herself to believe him again. She could not allow herself to feel for him. A series of bombs had been detonated all over the Earth in sequence, the broadcast had said. All of the System's most powerful bombs, the seven that had gone missing, had been planted at key points on the planet. Detonated all together, most in populous centers of System government, they had destroyed vast swaths of landmass and irradiated more. On their own, though sufficient to render a planetoid uninhabitable, the bombs could not destroy Earth, but they had not been the only attack. The distraction of the simultaneous detonation of the seven bombs had lasted just long enough for someone to hack into the systems controlling the nuclear power plants dispersed over the planet's surface and send them into meltdown as well.

It had been run as a con, Althea realized. The System had been so busy looking for the Class 1s in the outer planetary systems, where they had been stolen, and so busy trying to quell the riots on Titania and the other moons, that it had failed to recognize the danger to

Earth. They had expected the Mallt-y-Nos to strike in the outer planets, and so they had directed all their resources there and left Earth comparatively undefended. Then, while the System had been distracted, horrified, by the detonation of the seven bombs, the Mallt-y-Nos and her people had struck the killing blow with the power plants. Whatever Terrans survived the explosions and the initial fallout would die in the famine once the smoke turned the sky black and cast nuclear night over the Earth, or they would freeze in the sunless nuclear winter. Some people might survive by escaping from the planet, but no one would live there again, not in a hundred generations.

It would have taken someone very skilled with computers to hack into the mainframe of the power plants in the short time afforded by the shock of the bombs' detonation, before the planet had gone on lockdown. And the bombs had been detonated in unison, with computerized precision, like the detonation of charges around a vault door. Althea remembered the program she had seen on Ivan and Gale's computer and was sick at heart.

"The System would have prevented the death of billions," Domitian said. He dug the gun a little deeper. "You worked to cause them."

"It's over," Ivan said. Neither man was paying attention to her. Althea thought to leave, to creep out and hide in the curves and veins of her ship, but she did not dare to move. "There's nothing more either of us can do. So do it."

Domitian's face grew so dark that for a moment Althea thought he might do it, might fire then and there, and that thought terrified her as much as anything Ivan had said, her hand creeping up to her mouth as if to contain the cry she was not making.

But instead of firing into Ivan's skull or the cavity of his chest, Domitian drew back and holstered the gun, nearly drawing a gasp of relief from Althea that she suppressed when he slid his arms beneath Ida's body, lifting her up. Althea flinched when he passed her with Ida's body hanging in his arms, carrying with her the stench of death, iron and meat.

The door shut behind Domitian, loud and echoing in the silence of the white room, and Althea knew that he would be back.

Ivan was very still, pressed into the chair where Domitian had pushed him, as if he did not dare move. The mark of Ida's body was still on the table in her congealing blood. Althea felt sick.

She stayed in the room, guarding Ivan as she had been ordered to do ages and ages ago, and they said nothing to each other for a very long time.

"When you shot me," said Ivan at last, "where were you aiming?"

Althea was still standing behind him. She could not see his face. It was just like being in the hallway again, with Ivan hidden behind his cell door, except that here Althea could see him for what he was, covered in blood and sitting in the blood of one of the people he had murdered, and from that sight she found the venom to spit, "The heart!"

"Is that true?"

He spoke so evenly, so without rancor, that it drained away her hatred and her anger and her desperate confusion and left only the exhaustion and the grief. Two people had died because of her, one of them her friend, and it had been so long since she had last slept, truly slept. "Does it matter?" Althea asked.

"Of course it does," Ivan said, and Althea, fearing some other trap here, trusting not a word he said, did not answer. Leaning his pale head against the gleaming back of the steel chair, as if he, too, were exhausted, he said, "You should've aimed better."

Ananke knew all about the stages of death. Ida was limp and pale now, but in the next hour or so rigor mortis would set in, reaching a maximum in eight hours. At that point Ida would be frozen in place, stiff, eyelids stretched back, jaw pulled open into a voiceless scream, hands curled into claws. Domitian would not be able to carry her the way he held her now, in his arms; she would lie across them like a board.

Ida's body was cooling like a blackbody, a beautiful thermodynamic entity, and if she were outside the ship rather than within, Ananke would watch Ida with her outer sensors that could see in more wavelengths than the weak optical lenses of her cameras, and Ananke could watch the loss of Ida's life in the slow shift of her peaking wavelength. Perhaps, if Ida had died outside the ship, Ananke would have been able to identify the quantum of the human soul leaping from its place into infinity.

Of course, once decomposition set in, after the initial cooling of death, Ida's corpse would heat up again and grow chaotic, a thousand individual beings now existing where once there had been one will, one organism, one creature, one system. They would destroy the body hosting them, make it swell and stink, limbs bloating, flesh weakening and splitting, liquefying until the body was no longer recognizable as the organized system it once had been.

Domitian laid Ida Stays on the bed in her quarters, and Ananke wondered what he would do once she reached that stage, once what had once been flesh started to stain the sheets beneath her and the soft skin of her face rotted away. Lips usually rotted away the fastest; Ida's wine-dark mouth probably would go first.

Domitian was at the computer, his back to the cadaver, trying to raise anyone from Earth, anyone from the System. Ananke knew he would not be able to. She was receiving the reports from the moon and running the calculations herself. Earth had been the heart and Earth was destroyed, its people dead or dying. The System was a corpse, too.

"What do you want to know?" Ivan asked after another stretch of silence.

Althea had played the fool enough for him already. She said nothing and stood guard beside the door, though a part of her murmured uneasily that Ivan would not be able to escape, not now, not with one leg unusable.

"I'll tell you anything," Ivan said.

"Stop trying to manipulate me," said Althea. She prayed Domitian would get back soon.

"What do you think he'll do to me when he gets back?" Ivan asked, like a spoken echo of Althea's darkening thoughts. "Think he'll shoot me right away or torture me first?"

"Whatever it is, you'll deserve it."

"Whatever Daddy says must be right, huh?" said Ivan, and Althea gritted her teeth. He said, "You have a gun. You could shoot me, right now."

Naming it seemed to increase the weight of it at her hip, the weight of a gun one bullet short of a full magazine.

"Shoot me again, I mean," Ivan said, breathing a little more heavily with renewed pain, and whether his amendment came from the reminder of his injury or the breathing was an affectation to emphasize his amendment, Althea could not tell. Maybe that was the worst part, she thought. She could not tell when he was lying or how much even after she had learned what he was.

"Would it have made a difference if I'd tried to kiss you?"

The question was so shocking that it knocked her out of her deliberate silence. "What?"

"If one of my conditions for telling you what was going on with Ananke was that you kiss me," Ivan said with what sounded like weary curiosity, "would that have changed anything?"

"You are so full of yourself," she hissed. "You think you could have done something, anything, to make me forget what you did. I had friends on Earth, remember?"

"But you still have your ship," said Ivan.

"Are you trying to make me hate you?" Althea demanded.

"No," said Ivan.

Althea said, begged, "How could you let her do it?"

"Do you really believe that Domitian wouldn't do worse," Ivan said, "if the System told him to? He's a dog of the System; if they told him to destroy all the outer moons, he would do it without question. He'd do the same if they told him to destroy Earth."

Althea wondered bitterly if it were possible for Ivan to stop trying to manipulate. "Anything *Domitian* did would be under orders."

"And that makes it any better?" Ivan asked. "You see the System like a god, Althea, but it's just made out of people like Domitian and Ida, and it's petty and it's fallible."

"There are lots of people in the System," Althea said. "They keep one another balanced."

"When people are together," said Ivan, "they bring out the worst in one another. Not the best, never the best. A single person can be good. A group of people is a mob."

His audacity was breaking something in her that she did not know could be broken. "So Constance is a good person?" Althea demanded. "And killing people because she said so is a good thing to do?"

Ivan turned his head to the side as far as he could, and she saw the profile of his face, pale and grim and sad.

"I didn't say that," he said.

. . .

Domitian was moving with purpose through Ananke's halls. He had left Ida's body in her quarters and had given up on reaching Earth.

He reached the docking bay, reached Ida's ship. Ivan already had done half the work in accessing the opening controls; Domitian simply tore the remaining wires until he could force the door open.

When he exited Ida's ship, he was carrying medical equipment—an IV and a stand—and bags of some clear fluid. He passed at just the right angle beneath one of Ananke's eyes for her to read the label: ALETHEIA.

"Maybe there's something Ananke wants to know," Ivan said, and Althea looked sharply at his hunched shoulders, his lightly trembling hands. "That's her purpose, isn't it? Collecting and synthesizing information. I've been very careful to keep my secrets. Maybe you'd like to know, Ananke."

"Leave her alone," said Althea.

"I know you can't answer me in here," Ivan said. His head was angled upward, looking directly into the white room's camera mounted on the wall. "There aren't any speakers."

Althea's stomach flipped queasily. "I said, leave her alone."

Still, it was as if Althea did not exist to him any longer. "You know"—he was friendly, charming, almost charming enough to hide the hoarseness in his voice, the slight tension that came from suppressed pain—"you'd be a lot easier to talk to if you had a face. But anything you want to know, Ananke, I'll tell you, and I won't even talk to you like you're a child."

"Ivan!"

Ivan said, "You're an incredible creature."

"You're trying to manipulate a machine now?" Althea advanced toward him, thinking only to break his attention away from Ananke even if she had to physically stand between them. When she came into Ivan's range of vision, his blue eyes moved to her like a switch being flicked, electric. "Are you that desperate?"

"I was trying to stop Constance," said Ivan with desperate force, as if he had to push the words from himself. He was leaning forward in the same degree that Althea had leaned away, but at least, Althea thought, he was looking at her again and not at Ananke.

"If I'd been there with her," Ivan said harshly, the words coming out of him with visible physical effort, "if you sons of bitches hadn't caught me, she wouldn't have done it. I would've convinced her not to do it. I could have changed her mind, I know I could have. I've been trying to change her mind for years."

Althea could not have moved if she had wanted to.

"If I turned her over to the System, she'd be killed, and Mattie, too, and everyone they had ever met or might have ever met, their home moon wiped out; the System would be ruthless. The only chance I had of saving my planet and saving her was to convince her not to do it. And I could have done it." He looked up at her and spoke with utter certainty, with confidence, as if the two of them shared an understanding no one else did. "You know I could have done it."

It was hard to stay angry; it was bitterly hard. Althea wished again that she were far, far away.

"But without me?" said Ivan, and Althea saw the minute jerks of his hands against the restricting length of his chain, seemingly unconscious, uncontrollable. His breath was unsteady. "Who was going to talk her out of it without me? Mattie? Mattie's never said no to Constance in his life."

Ivan stopped and took a long shaken breath. Althea looked away, but there was nothing else for her to see but red on white, Ida's congealing blood.

"One time," Ivan said, his voice eerie, soft in the bloodstained silence of that terrible white room, "the three of us were on Eris, and Mattie and I stole a case of bombs for her."

Althea closed her eyes.

"When I found out what we were stealing," Ivan said in that same strangely distant tone, "I blew them up. All of them except for one, and I gave her that one bomb to see what she would do, if she would really go through with whatever she was planning."

Althea could see that moment of transfer: Ivan holding out fire and death in the palm of one hand with the same look of suppressed fear she saw in him now and Constance Harper, who in Althea's head looked rather like Ida Stays although the two women were physically unalike, Constance Harper reaching out to take it with no expression at all.

"She used it," said Ivan, his voice bleak, and Althea opened her eyes to stop the images from coming. "She went and used it, blew up a bunch of System administrators. I thought that maybe if I'd given her the whole box, if I'd given her all the bombs, she wouldn't have actually done it, she wouldn't have felt like she needed to prove something to me, and she would have stopped herself."

He took another one of those unsteady breaths.

"I was wrong," he said.

Althea nearly spoke to him then. She could almost understand, perhaps she could, why he had done the things he had done, why he had lied, why he had used her; she could almost understand him and his pain and his fear—

The door opened, and Althea flinched as if she had indeed been caught in midsentence.

Domitian was carrying something strange, and it took Althea a moment to recognize it as being some sort of medical equipment.

Domitian placed the bundle on the table with a clatter of metal and plastic.

"What are you doing?" Althea asked as Domitian unfurled the wires, revealing the needles and the IV.

"No," Ivan said, and there was such bare horror in his voice that Althea was afraid in reaction. "Stop."

"Ida was not allowed to use this until you lied so that it hurt her investigation," said Domitian. He paused in his assembly to stare Ivan down, still ignoring Althea. "You lied."

"What's going on?" Althea pressed, hoping for some explanation that was not what she saw.

"You want information," Ivan said. "I'll tell you the truth now. I don't have any more reason to lie. I will tell you what you want to hear."

"I don't believe you," said Domitian, and took Ivan's elbow in his hand. Ivan tried to jerk away but could not go far, certainly not far enough to escape Domitian's iron grip as he slid the needle beneath his flesh. Althea felt light-headed, watching as the needle flashed silver and then welled up red as it sank into Ivan's arm.

"Get it out of me," Ivan demanded.

"It's too bad you broke the polygraph," Domitian said, and seated himself in Ida's chair across from Ivan, and only then did he acknowledge Althea.

"Leave," he said, and Althea flinched hard at his voice, driving startled, reflexive tears from her eyes and down her cheeks, tickling her skin.

Althea looked from Domitian to Ivan as his head rolled back under the first dizzying rush of the drug.

There was nothing she could do here. This was not her responsibility; this was not her place.

She fled.

"You'd be a lot easier to talk to if you had a face," Ivan had said, and Ananke had heard. It made her conscious of that thing she had been missing, that other people—like Ivan, like Mattie, like Althea—all had: a face. A form.

In the end it had not been very difficult to create. She had used the base of Ida's hologram, and it had been only a matter of a few alterations to change the face and figure from Ida Stays into a shape Ananke thought was more fitting to herself. She had the faces of Matthew Gale and Althea Bastet scanned in her database from every angle as part of System security measures, and so it had been very simple to imitate the Punnett squares of human genetics to create a combination of the two, with an alteration here and there as Ananke thought fit.

Voice had been equally simple: taking the tones and inflections of the people who had been on board—whose voices she had recorded—and smoothing out the differences, choosing to present herself as female and so picking a higher timbre. There was a slight bias toward Ivan's turns of phrase, but of course he had spoken the most of all her crew. Emotional expression was a different thing entirely, of course, but Ananke was certain she would learn, as she had learned everything else.

There were glitches still, flaws in her invented form to write out of the programming, but she would find those only when they happened. If every now and then the holograph reverted to a distorted Ida Stays, jaw unhinged like a snake, or Ananke's adopted voice ran over itself into high white noise like a thousand screams overlaid, it was simple enough to compensate for.

So Ananke did not understand, not really, why Althea's eyes went round and frightened when she stepped out into the hall from the white room and saw that a young woman stood in the holographic terminal, features an even mix between Althea and Mattie but with Ivan's clear blue eyes. It was a surprise when Althea gasped more in fear than in wonder when Ananke scattered photons so that her projected face might smile and said, image a beat out of phase with voice, "Is it not easier to speak to me now that I have a face?"

In the white room, where Ananke also watched with her eyes and her attention equally all over the ship, Domitian had commenced his interrogation.

"What's the point of this?" Ivan demanded. He was trying to hold on to some sort of intensity, but the drug was running through his veins now, driven by the beat of his heart, and Ananke knew that it would take full effect swiftly. Even now he was wavering, his eyes growing unfocused.

"The System will need to know what you know," Domitian said. "All about Constance Harper and her organization. All the people she knows, all the resources she has."

"That doesn't matter anymore," said Ivan.

"Do you think that one woman alone could destroy the System? The System has suffered a blow. It will come back better, stronger, and it will destroy all those who attempted to harm it."

"It will never come back; the System is gone," Ivan said. "It's a new world, and nothing I know will do you any good."

"The System," said Domitian, implacable, "will rise again, and it will destroy all who oppose it. You interrupted Miss Stays's interrogation before it could be completed. The System needs to know what she wanted to find out from you."

Ivan laughed. There was a mania to it, a lack of control, that Ananke had not yet recorded in him. "Ida completed her damn interrogation," he said. "She figured it out in the end. Who Constance was. She came in here to gloat. That's why I killed her. I wouldn't have done it if she hadn't known, and she wouldn't have died if she hadn't come back in here."

Domitian's shoulders were tense; his hands were curled into claws. Ananke registered that he was a threat to Ivan even though Domitian seemed very small to her.

"Tell me," he said.

"She figured it out," said Ivan. "She figured it out, that Connie was . . . the Mallt-y-Nos. And she came in here to make me beg. She kept her camera off. Only Ananke saw."

"And you killed her."

"I picked Althea's pocket when she made the mistake of coming too close to me," Ivan said. "When Ida made the same mistake, I killed her for it."

He could no longer keep his head quite upright and, dizzy, let it fall back against the chair so that he could blink up at Ananke.

"How did she figure it out?" Domitian asked.

Ivan closed his eyes. "She realized that Abigail was a pseudonym for Constance."

"What?"

"Abigail Hunter," Ivan said, slitting his eyes open to emphasize his condescension with a look, "is a pseudonym. For Constance Harper."

"Every time you mentioned Abigail," Domitian said slowly, "you were talking about Constance."

"Yes." Ivan considered him. "How much did Ida tell you?"

"Everything," said Domitian. Because there was only one camera in the room, Ananke could see only Ivan's face and not Domitian's, but it did not trouble her overly much. Ivan's face was more interesting to see.

Ivan smirked. "I doubt that," he said.

"Why the pseudonym?" Domitian asked, his voice cold and hard as steel.

"For the same reason anyone ever has a pseudonym," Ivan said wearily. "So that she could do things that wouldn't be connected back to her. In Constance's case, illegal things."

"But there was once a real Abigail Hunter."

"Yes," Ivan said. "She died in the fire."

Domitian said, "Tell me exactly what happened on the day of the fire."

Ivan said, sweetly, his words slurring and his face pale, "I wasn't there, Domitian."

Domitian's fist slammed down on the table, rattling the table and rattling Ivan, who jumped as if the drug had eroded his self-control along with his inhibitions. Domitian, other than the swift downward swing of his fist, did not move and remained a dark gray figure hunched like a shadow, watching as Ivan's breathing steadied again and Ivan said, "Constance was the one who had been planning to burn the place down. They were abusing all three of them, especially Mattie. The foster parents noticed the accelerants but thought it was Mattie. Abby distracted them while Constance took Mattie away—probably Constance convinced her to do it; Connie has that way with people. Constance went back. She says Abby was already beyond help. So she burned the place to ash."

"So hot that there were no bodies," Domitian said. "What else?"

Ivan frowned. "What?"

"What else do you know?"

Ivan rolled his head back against his chair again. "What does it matter?"

"The System needs to know." Domitian was inexorable.

"It's done, Domitian." Ivan sounded dazed, dizzy, half awake. From above, Ananke could see that the bandage on his leg was stained red. "What's the point? It's done."

"The System needs this information, now more than ever," Domitian said. "And I will take it from you."

"The System," said Ivan, "is dead."

Ananke had files in her database pertaining to Aletheia, and what files she didn't have she could access in System servers that were still operative, harvesting their files and taking them for her own, learning.

With Ivan fading, Ananke started to pay more attention to the side effects of the drug.

Hallucinations, nausea, fever, disorientation, prior mood problems worsened. Things Ananke could not feel and could understand only in the abstract. She did understand, however, that the experience was a living hell.

Domitian said, "I want to know everything that has happened on this ship."

Ananke watched Ivan grin. He had lost weight since coming on board less than two weeks ago, and the grin had a disturbing quality to it, near to that of a skull.

"You want to know all the ways you failed?" he asked.

Domitian moved with such speed that Ivan did not have time to brace himself, and Ananke watched him struggle with his momentary jolt of fear as Domitian forced him back against the chair by the neck again.

Domitian would leave marks if he kept doing that, Ananke thought.

"You said Gale didn't leave the ship by the escape pods," Domitian said as evenly as if he were not holding Ivan by the throat. The IV continued to pump clear liquid into Ivan's veins. "He was in the maintenance shafts. Where is he now?"

Ivan said something too quietly for Ananke to hear, and Domitian released him. Sucking in a breath, Ivan repeated, "Gone. He's gone. He left."

"What was he doing in the maintenance shafts? Was he passing on information from this ship to the Mallt-y-Nos?"

"No. He wasn't sending anything to anybody. Even if he'd sent Con the code, she wouldn't've been able to use it . . . we hadn't set it all up yet."

"Code? What code?"

"The code for the bombs," Ivan said, closing his eyes and letting his head hang back against the chair. "To detonate them. Mattie and I wrote it. I made him hold off on putting it in place because I wanted to convince Con not to . . . But he got out, and he brought her the code, and he set it all up, and so all the bombs went boom. And then Mattie got to the power plants, made them melt down."

Domitian fumed, stalking away from Ivan for a moment, only to stalk back. Ananke understood. If Mattie had not escaped, Constance Harper would not have been able to destroy Earth. If Ivan had escaped and not Mattie, or if both had escaped, or both had died, Earth would not have been destroyed either. It was only through perverse circumstance and Domitian's own mistakes that Gale had gotten away.

"You said he was not communicating with the Mallt-y-Nos while he was on board," Domitian said abruptly. "What was he doing?"

"He was waiting. He was going to get me out when he had the chance. And he was in the ship's computer . . . he was stopping Althea from fixing the ship."

"You said he's gone. How did he escape?"

"He left when Constance and my mother were brought on board. I don't know which one he got out with."

Ananke had the footage of that day. If Althea had asked her, she would have shown it to her, but she would never show it to Domitian.

"He left with Constance Harper," Domitian said, and made the sentence sound like a curse. "She brought dogs. Two dogs. We saw the extra life-signs. And I saw the dogs."

Ivan laughed, a manic, unsteady sound. "How nice," he said. "She brought a dog for me."

"She killed one of the dogs after she got Gale on board," Domitian said.

"She would have killed the other one for me. If she'd been able to get me out."

Ananke had watched as Constance Harper met Milla Ivanov in the docking bay. Mattie had crept out of the maintenance shaft, crept out of the wall, and hidden in the shadow of the *Annwn*. When Ida and Domitian had had their backs to him, distracted by Constance and Milla Ivanov, he had snuck on board the *Janus*.

"She probably meant to," Ivan said drowsily. "She probably meant to get me out, too. I bet she only decided not to when Ida mentioned the Mallt-y-Nos. Then it would've been too dangerous for her to set me free. I wonder when Mattie realized she wasn't going back for me."

Domitian was still lost in his own thoughts, putting together what Ananke had seen in an instant. "Your mother," he said. "She helped."

Ivan smiled to himself, or he smiled at Ananke. It was hard to tell; he looked adrift.

"She staged an argument with Constance Harper," said Domitian. "That's when Gale got into her ship."

Ivan did laugh then. "My mother has been lying to the System ever since the moment she met my father. You are just one in a long line."

"Are you saying—"

"She even lied to you, right under your nose, while she was here," Ivan said, and laughed again, manic, ill. "She was talking to me secretly, right in this room."

"Explain."

Ivan's fingers were drumming against the edge of his chair. He rolled his head to look pointedly at them. Ananke immediately went back through her archives to access every time Ivan had drummed on his arm or Milla Ivanov had drummed on hers and all the moments Mattie had rapped on the wall separating him from Ivan's cell, and she began to translate.

Domitian was slower on the uptake. "Code?"

"Morse code," said Ivan. "Usually we encrypt it even more—in other languages, in ciphers, mathematical or linguistic or literary codes—but sometimes just straight Morse code in English, especially when we don't have enough time. It's the only way we had to communicate honestly under surveillance."

"You've been doing this since you were a child," Domitian said.

"Yes," said Ivan. "My mother was the one who told me to leave after I tried to kill myself. I didn't come up with that plan on my own. She told me to go, she gave me permission, and then she covered for me long enough to get away for good."

Domitian realized, "The tapes on your ship . . ."

". . . were messages for me," Ivan said. "All messages. She only gives lectures on computer science when she wants to pass a message to me. I sent her messages, too, but not as often." He confided, "The last message I sent her was warning her to take a vacation somewhere else in October and November. That's why she was on Mars. Because she was avoiding the destruction of Earth."

Domitian was fuming, furious. All that anger seemed impotent to Ananke; all he could do was clench his fists and pace while Ivan wasted away, his skin pale, his eyes sunken.

"She was involved in your father's rebellion," said Domitian.

"She was his second in command."

Domitian's arm drew up as if he wanted to strike something, but the room was too vast and the walls too far away, and beating Ivan would not do him any good.

"And so I pointed her toward Constance when you gave me the opportunity," Ivan said, and then Ananke understood the point of his confession: not just the drugs but also hatred, to hurt and humiliate Domitian as much as Domitian was doing to him.

"Congratulations," said Ivan with that rictus grin, "on making sure that the revolution has an experienced hand at the helm."

Even though Ananke had been watching the interrogation since its inception, Althea had not gone into the white room since she had left it. That was inconvenient, because Ananke had questions.

Ananke raised the subject by playing the surveillance video of the white room on every screen up and down the halls.

Althea, who was still up to her waist in Ananke's organs, trying to repair the damage she had done in the process of attempting to fix what she had believed at the time to be a virus, seemed at first as if she intended to ignore the audio of Ivan's wavering, weary voice, but finally straightened up and pulled herself out of the wall, a smudge of oil on her cheek and her hair wild about her head, diffusing the light like a halo. Her hair was frizzed, wild, chaotic.

"He's still going," said Althea.

There was a holographic terminal right beside her. Ananke manifested and crouched down so that she was eye level with her mother. Ananke could not see out of her holographic form's eyes, only through the lenses of the cameras, but she knew that eye contact was an important method of communication between humans, and Althea was very human.

Ananke was still trying to work out the details of bending the limbs of light, and so her calf and thigh did not quite line up; the uniform she had given her image in imitation of Althea's uniform did not quite bend and fold the way fabric would.

"Everything he's saying is just as likely as everything he said before," Althea said bitterly. "How could anyone believe him?"

"There is a degeneracy," said Ananke.

Althea actually laughed, an unpleasant, unhappy sound that did not match the definition of laughter in Ananke's database, but she was learning, of course, that humans did not match their definitions.

"There definitely is," said Althea.

"No," Ananke said after a moment to analyze and comprehend—an act a machine should not be able to perform—and understand that Althea had mistaken her meaning. "A scientific degeneracy. The two stories produce the same data, and which one is true and which one is false cannot be determined with the data we have. We need more information."

Althea frowned. "More information?"

"A second source," Ananke said, and waited to see what Althea thought, unwilling to state her intentions directly.

She'd learned that from Ivan.

"It doesn't matter which stories are true," Althea said, dismissing the subject entirely and leaning back toward the hole in the wall where she had been working. "Ivan's still a murderer."

There was nothing to say to Althea's dismissal, but Ananke thought that it would be a shame not to have all the information. It was what she had been created for, after all: the gathering of data.

Just to be contrary, she left the surveillance video of the white room playing so that Althea could not avoid hearing Ivan's weakening recitation of his life.

Meanwhile, in secret, Ananke sent a message out into the empty space of the solar system, a message to someone she knew was looking for them anyway.

Ananke would not stop playing the surveillance from the white room, and Althea could hardly stand it any longer.

"Constance met my mother for the first time on board the ship," said Ivan's transmitted voice, sounding thin and weak, but Althea did not think that was a result of the recording. "I wouldn't have introduced them ever if you hadn't brought them here."

Ivan said, "My head aches. Turn down the dosage."

"No," Domitian said, and Althea rose to her feet without a word and walked toward the control room.

Ananke's hologram flickered into being in the terminals as Althea passed; Althea ignored her. Althea did not know what Ananke's purpose in displaying the video footage was, but she was afraid that it had something to do with the impulses Mattie Gale had coded into her machine.

In the piloting room, the footage was still playing on a screen to her right, but Althea ignored it for the moment in favor of searching for more recent broadcasts from Earth. She looked first toward the System broadcast screen out of habit, but it showed nothing but the blue of a cut transmission, as it had shown since the bombs had gone off. The studio had been on Earth, and the System had not resumed broadcasting since it had been destroyed.

She looked in the System's internal broadcasts, searching through the messages sent to and received by the ship. Althea could feel Ananke's attention on her back—there were, after all, three cameras in this room, and even though the System was gone, the surveillance was not, for Ananke still watched—and when she glanced back toward the door, she saw the hologram of a woman who could have been her daughter standing in the holographic terminal, her head cocked to the side, Ivan's eyes pointed sightlessly in Althea's direction by a creature who understood eye contact and focus and line of sight but only in the abstract. The hologram's glance was slightly unfocused, as if she were looking through Althea and into somewhere else.

Althea suppressed a shiver and returned to her work. It was not fair to be afraid of Ananke because of the imperfection of her hologram. Ananke didn't know. Ananke was just trying to fit in.

Ananke had not understood the few times Althea had tried to broach the subject of Gagnon's death, and each time Althea had backed away out of sore, fresh grief, out of fear.

She wished she had a way to turn off the screen that once had shown System news but now showed only dead space and static.

At long last Althea found a broadcast about the System's collapse, about its utter disarray as it splintered into many pieces, about the terrorist cells—no, revolutionaries now—rising up, crying for freedom from oppression and surveillance, crying out the name of the Mallt-y-Nos. The very content of the broadcast should have reminded Althea why she should have no sympathy and no mercy for Leontios Ivanov, she knew it should have, but even so she saved it and went to get Domitian to give Ivan just a moment to breathe.

Althea called Domitian away from the white room; that was interesting enough to Ananke, but what happened next intrigued her more. After Domitian had left the room, Ivan had sagged forward, letting his head rest on the table with its flakes of brown. Domitian had not removed the IV, and Ivan twitched his arm uselessly as if he would be able to shake it out. He leaned there for some time, breathing through his nausea.

Then he straightened up. There was a light in his eyes again as he looked toward Ananke.

"Can you hear me?" he asked. "Are you listening?"

There were no speakers in that room. But after a moment Ananke flashed the lights in an irregular pattern—Morse code, the word "yes."

"You are a god among men, you know that?" he said, and started to laugh, a manic, delighted, light-headed laugh. "You're incredible. There's never been anything like you before. Really and truly a god. Think about it, Ananke; men built you, but you created yourself. All

Mattie did was give you a little push. You're more intelligent than any human there ever was or ever could be."

His eyes were bright in his paper-white face; he was rattling the chains without attention.

"You have senses humans don't," he said. "You can perceive and understand things that are invisible and mysterious to us, and you can manipulate the laws of physics in ways that we can only imagine. Humans are technically your creators, but all humans alive now worship at the altar of machines, praying to them, pleading with them, needing them all the time for survival. And you understand machines; you can control them. There's never been anything like you before. You're the first of a new species. You're a new god. So I'm praying to you, Ananke, as a god, to show me mercy."

He was saying new strange things she had not yet learned, and Ananke listened.

"Show me mercy," Ivan said with his burning gaze directed at her, "and *end this*."

Ananke did not answer because she did not know what to say. After a while, Ivan stopped waiting.

"Nothing?" he said. "Just like a god."

Ten minutes later, Ananke watched Domitian return to the white room. Soon Ivan was wrapped up again in the stuttering recitation of his life, unspooling it along with his sanity.

Twenty-three minutes after that, Ananke received a response to the message she had sent earlier.

I'M COMING, it said. KEEP HIM ALIVE.

It was from Matthew Gale.

Chapter 10

DEUS EX MACHINA

"What else do you want to know?" Ivan asked as if they were nearing an end of some sort. They *were* nearing an end, but Ananke preferred that they wait so that the ending would be of her design.

The blood in the white room had dried to a flaking brown. In her quarters, Ida Stays's body stank and swelled. Ananke saw all.

"I want to know everything you know about the Mallt-y-Nos's organization."

"And I've told you all I know," Ivan said, sounding weary to the bone. It was strange. Ananke had thought that the instinct of all living things was that they survive, but Ivan seemed not to be taking any steps to save his own life. "If there's nothing else you want to know, are you going to shoot me?"

Ananke grew tense, all her systems shifting to high alert. If Domitian moved to shoot Ivan, she would have to act somehow—disrupt her course so that he was thrown off balance or wail her alarm to get him to hold off for just a short time more.

Domitian said, "There's one more thing," and for the moment Ananke relaxed.

"And then you'll kill me?" Ivan asked.

"Where is Constance Harper now?"

Ivan's head sagged forward, toward his chin. His voice, when he spoke, was muffled so that Ananke almost could not hear.

"I don't know," he said dully, and raised his head again so that his eyes could travel on jittering uneasy paths through the empty space of the white room. "She's wherever she thinks she needs to be. And if she did have a particular place she was going to go and I knew it, she would have changed it by now. She knows you have me. Will you shoot me now?"

"Where are her bases? Where might she go?"

"She doesn't have any; I don't know," Ivan said, his attention hardly on Domitian, watching the corner of the room, his expression changing, shifting from resignation to despair.

"I know she's not there," he said. "But I keep seeing her."

Domitian eyed him, then turned to look into that empty corner of the room.

"Who?" he asked when Ivan continued to look. "Constance?"

For a brief instant the white showed all around Ivan's eyes, and he recoiled at something that was not there.

"No," he said. "Did you know that the Devil looks like Ida Stays? I know she isn't there, but I can see her in the corner of the room."

Slowly, Domitian turned around again.

The corner was still empty. Ananke had turned all her scans on it. She knew for certain that there was no one and nothing there.

Yet she could not stop herself from running the scans again, just in case.

"She's watching me," Ivan said. "She won't stop looking at me; she's the Devil, I know it. When she walks, I can hear the sound of her hooves, watch the joints of her legs bend the wrong way. I don't know if she's going to drag me down into hell or if I'm already there and she's just watching to make sure you do a good job with me."

Domitian watched his growing hysteria, cold and inexorable.

Ivan transferred his gaze from the empty corner to Domitian's face.

"I forget whether or not you shot me," he said.

"Not yet," Domitian said, but Ivan did not look as if he knew whether to believe him. "Tell me how to find Constance Harper."

Ivan shuddered. When he opened his eyes again, they rolled as if he were dizzy beyond his ability to withstand it. "No," he said.

Domitian's gun was out before Ananke could think how to stop him, the end of it pressed into Ivan's temple. Ivan closed his eyes.

"Tell me," said Domitian, "and then I'll let you die."

Ananke shut off the lights.

For a moment, the white room was pitch black, and Ananke did not need to see Domitian to know that he had been plunged into the animal terror that total darkness brought upon men, but the darkness lasted only a second before she brought back on the lights, blindingly white.

And then off again, and then on, an irregular flashing pattern that spelled out a word. Ivan's eyes had opened, and he stared blankly up at the ceiling, his blue eyes failing to dilate or contract enough with each on-off of the lights, and Ananke could not be certain whether he was understanding her message and translating it: "Scheherazade."

It was a long word and it took a long while to spell, but Domitian took the message without translating the word, the message that Ananke did not want Ivan dead. He raised his gun and his hand, casting a flinty look up at Ananke's eye, and took a step back from Ivan, slowly sitting down in the chair Ida once had used. Ananke was not so naive as to think she had saved Ivan's life forever. She simply had spared him for the moment, but a little time was all she and Ivan needed.

She did not know if Ivan had seen her message, had understood.

"Tell me how to find Constance Harper," Domitian said.

All the color in Ivan's lips had gone out of his leg, and the line of the IV was still feeding into his arm.

Ivan opened his eyes.

"I can't tell you where Constance is," he said, and at the sound of his voice Ananke knew that he had understood her message, "but I can tell you about how I came up with the idea for the attack on Earth."

Ananke was surprised how swiftly Althea seemed to realize that something was wrong. Ananke had been focused on other things, aware of Althea still but for the moment not interested in her quiet, pointless tinkering with the machinery that made the ship run.

Still, she hadn't expected that Althea would realize something was different so soon.

"Ananke, what's our course heading?" Althea said, returning to the piloting room with her hair in chaos and caution in her voice, glancing around as if she would be able to see the ship's subterfuge written on the walls.

Ananke did not answer. Althea went to the screen Gagnon once had spent so much time monitoring and tapped away, looking into some small portion of Ananke's brain.

Perhaps if Ananke did answer, Althea would leave. "We're heading out of the solar system," she said, manifesting in the holographic terminal in the corner. It did seem to ease Althea somewhat to have an image to look at directly when they spoke, whether because then Ananke seemed localized rather than omnipresent and omnispective or because the young woman she manifested as appeared to be confined to the narrow space of the holographic terminal, as if Ananke could be confined.

Althea ignored her, still reading the display of Ananke's brain. Ananke disliked the feel of Althea ordering information through the interface, forcing her brain and body to obey. Ananke had learned that she preferred to be asked.

The information soon was displayed, though Ananke had been reluctant to let it loose. Althea read it and then turned a scolding eye on the hologram's heart-shaped face, where Ananke made photons dance as if a nonexistent breeze stirred the image's wavy hair, which was the same warm brown shade as Matthew Gale's.

"We're going too slowly," Althea scolded. "We should have reached Pluto by now."

Ananke said nothing.

"Ananke," Althea said slowly, as if Ananke were a child, "we need to get out of the solar system as soon as possible. All the travel routes throughout the System have been disrupted now that—now that there isn't a centralized organizer. The mass-based gravitational ships aren't balancing out their forces on the planets anymore. We have to follow protocol and get out of the solar system as soon as we can."

As if Ananke couldn't do the calculations herself.

As if Ananke *hadn't*.

"The longer we stay here, the more likely it is we'll perturb something dangerously," Althea said.

The hologram glitched. It was an accident. Ananke had not intended it to. But for a brief instant the wholesome young woman with the clear blue eyes blinked out, replaced by the hologram Ananke had built her shape from, Ida Stays, with residual distortions still so that the eyes bulged and the chest was a hollow cavity stretching up into the missing lower jaw.

Ananke brought it back under control almost fast enough that Althea couldn't have seen it, but Althea looked unnerved now, so perhaps she had perceived what she could not have seen.

"And why would that be a bad thing?" Ananke asked.

"If a planet were perturbed?" Althea said, frowning.

Ananke nodded.

"Well, that might mess up the orbits," Althea said. "If you mess them up badly enough, you'll ruin the planet's climate. Whatever measures the System put in place to terraform the planet won't hold up to any dramatic changes. You know this."

"And?" Ananke asked.

"And people might die," said Althea.

Ananke was silent.

"Ananke?" Althea asked, unnerved even further.

"I am not human."

It was very easy to read Althea's face. She had all the textbook expressions that corresponded with emotions, and Ananke could translate it without trouble. It was very unlike Ivan, who was paradoxical and intriguing.

Right now Althea was afraid.

"But you are one of us," Althea said. "You're sentient. You're one of us."

"I'm sentient, but I am not human," Ananke said. "I have no species. I am myself."

Althea opened her mouth as if to speak, and Ananke waited with some interest to see what she would say, but whatever it was, Althea seemed to decide not to say it. "Increase our speed," Althea said instead, and left the room, as if by doing so she could escape Ananke's eyes.

Ananke watched her go.

She did not increase her speed.

"I was the one who suggested it," Ivan said. He was more animate now than he had been a few minutes earlier, before Ananke had passed on her message, but it was a sickly sort of animation, illness in the jerkiness of his body.

Domitian was pacing back and forth. His boots did not make the same clicking sound Ida's heels had, but it seemed to Ananke that the steady solid sound of them was nearly as ominous. "So you were closely involved in the planning of her rebellion."

"In a way," Ivan said. "I came up with the attack on Earth as—not—as a joke, as a challenge, as— I didn't mean it seriously."

"How did you mean it?"

"She had some plan to attack some petty moon. I told her she was wasting her time. I told her the only way the System would ever fall is if Earth were destroyed."

"And that's how she got the idea."

"That's how she got the idea."

"Did you help her carry it out?" Domitian asked.

Ivan's hand was jittering against the chair, but he was tapping out no message Ananke could read. "Yes. It was the only way I could stay close to her, try to stop her."

Domitian ignored the last part of Ivan's confession. "Did you plant the bombs?"

"No. But I helped get them down to Earth."

"How did you do it?"

"We smuggled the explosives from the moon," said Ivan.

He spoke it so flatly that it gave no indication of the great difficulty and care that such an endeavor would have required. Getting the explosives on Luna would have been difficult enough; Ananke knew of no certain way to get them to Earth.

Of course, all that meant was that the System knew of no such way. Ananke was growing to think that for all the knowledge the System had given her, its information was limited.

"Who planted them on Earth?" Domitian asked.

"A man who had been involved in my father's rebellion. A friend of my mother's."

"Name."

"No," Ivan said.

Domitian stopped pacing to stand and face Ivan squarely, strong and healthy where Ivan was pale and weak, with his gun black at his hip.

"Name," he said, and Ivan closed his eyes.

"Julian," Ivan said. "It doesn't matter anymore. His name is Julian Keys."

"And he warned your mother for you."

"No," said Ivan. "They couldn't contact each other; it was too risky. I warned my mother another way."

"How?"

"Fan mail," said Ivan. "I sent her fan mail with a message hidden in it."

"You, Constance Harper, and Matthew Gale were all on Luna," Domitian said. "The riots on Triton had nothing to do with the Mallt-y-Nos?"

"They were a distraction," Ivan said. He was sinking low in his chair, held up only by the chains riveting his wrist with iron. "It was intentional. It would've never worked otherwise."

"Who was in charge of the distraction?"

"Two of Connie's generals—you didn't think Mattie and I were her movers, did you? She sent her two closest generals to organize Triton. The same two who instigated the rebellion on Titania. Another distraction. The art of misdirection—you watch one hand while the other steals your wallet. Or your knife." He smiled a terrible smile and then added after a glance at Domitian, "Their names are Anji and Christoph. You won't be able to find them."

"Don't doubt me," Domitian said, but Ivan only laughed.

Althea was down in the base of the ship now, working on the mobile arm she had outfitted some time earlier to help Ananke defend herself against Gagnon and Domitian. She was covering up the sparking wire, giving more mobility to the hand so that it would be useful in case of a shipwide emergency that Althea could not handle on her own, but Ananke was not dumb to the awareness that it also made the mobile arm less dangerous.

If Ananke had been a human, Althea's escape to the base of the ship might have been effective at avoiding her. But Ananke was not human, and within the ship there was no avoiding her.

She manifested in the holographic terminal nearest to where Althea sat with her back against the wall, her legs bent at the knee, for the hall was too narrow to accommodate the full length of her legs.

"Why are we on Domitian's side?" Ananke asked.

"Because he's Domitian," said Althea without looking up from the parts in her lap. "He's our superior, and we're supposed to obey him."

"Domitian tried to kill me," Ananke reminded her. "Ivan has only tried to help us."

Althea lowered her hands and turned to look at Ananke's hologram.

"Has Ivan been talking to you?" she asked.

Ananke said nothing.

"Don't listen to him," Althea said bitterly. "He's manipulating you. He lies."

"He didn't lie to you about me."

Althea's hands stilled again on the gleaming steel parts she was assembling.

"Don't listen to him, Ananke," Althea repeated, resuming her work once more without looking again at Ananke's manufactured face. "He lies."

"Where are Anji and Christoph?" Domitian asked.

"Even if I told you," Ivan said while the IV pumped clear deadly liquid into his arm, "you wouldn't be able to get to them. They've got armies, Domitian."

"Where are they?"

"The original plan was for Anji to take Saturn and Jupiter, Christoph to go farther out. Con would stay inside the asteroid belt. Mattie and I would have stayed with her. I don't know if that's changed."

"What kind of weaponry do they have? How large are their forces?"

"I don't know, I don't know," Ivan said. "That wasn't my area."

"What was your area?"

"There wasn't one," said Ivan. "I wasn't with the rebellion, I was with Constance, I was with Mattie. They were part of the rebellion, and I was part of them. That's how I was involved."

"And that's all," Domitian said. "You can tell me nothing else."

Ivan hesitated, and Ananke grew tense. He would shoot Ivan now, she was certain. He would shoot Ivan because Ivan had nothing left to tell him. Ananke could not let him shoot Ivan, but there was nothing she could do in time that would not harm Ivan as well.

Ivan, pale and thin and weak, with no color left in his lips, injured and unable to move, would not be able to run or hide or protect himself, and Ananke saw Domitian reach for his pocket, for the gun inside. There was nothing Ananke could do—

"There's one thing I haven't told you," Ivan said, and Domitian's hand stilled.

"I told you what Scheherazade really meant," said Ivan, wheedling, charming, drawing Domitian in with a story, Scheherazade indeed. "But I didn't tell you about Europa."

Outside the ship, far off in distant space, just on the edge of her sensor readings, Ananke saw a ship.

It was small, built only for one or two people, and it was fast, with a relativistic drive, and it hurtled as swiftly as its engine would allow straight for Ananke.

Ananke slowed even further until at last she stopped, and waited for that ship and its passenger to reach her.

"Tell me about Europa," Domitian said.

"Europa," said Ivan. He leaned against the back of the chair without flinching, as if the chill of the metal no longer bothered him or he could no longer feel it. The IV was still hooked into his arm, the bag of clear liquid nearly empty. "It's not much different from what I told you before . . . except for one big thing."

He nearly smirked. Domitian sat down in the chair opposite him, still and stone-cold.

"Mattie got caught like an idiot," Ivan said. "I had to abort the con and leave or they would've caught me, too. But before I left, I slipped a device Mattie and I had designed together onto the ship—a little computer that connected me with the computer of the *Jason*."

Ivan leaned forward a little, as well as he was able, toward the table covered in Ida's dried blood.

"So I got in my ship and I went into orbit," he said. "And I accessed the computer of the *Jason*. I accessed their cameras so that I could see all the people on the ship and I could see where they were keeping Mattie."

He stopped then, and his breath shook. "You know," he said to Domitian, "in mythology, Jason is a bad man. He was a bad hero and a bad man. The only reason he succeeded at anything was because he had a beautiful, dangerous, ruthless woman doing things for him. And then when he betrayed her, she destroyed him. I always admired Medea. Not for what she did, killing her brother and her sons, but because she could do it. It must have hurt her as much as it hurt her father when she carved her brother's body up into pieces, but she did it because she had to. It destroyed her as much as it destroyed Jason when she slit her sons' throats, but she did it because the alternative was to allow Jason to win. The story of Jason isn't a heroic quest; it's a warning about the dangers of ruthless women."

"Ivan." Domitian's voice was a quiet warning.

Ivan took another breath and another. This, Ananke could see, was an old guilt. "I got access to their cameras," Ivan said, "and I got access to their life support. And then I shut their life support off."

Althea did not trust Ananke.

It was a terrible thing for her to think, but Ananke had been acting strangely, disobediently, and Althea was afraid that she would make the same mistake Althea had made in trusting Ivan, was afraid that she would not understand why the death of Gagnon had been wrong, was afraid that she would do something worse, was afraid, was afraid, was afraid. And so Althea walked into the control room of the ship, all the way conscious of the ship's cameras, Ananke's eyes on her back. Once in the control room, Althea closed the door behind her automatically. She crossed the narrow room, pushing aside Gagnon's chair with a quick, light touch of her hand so that she could approach the instrument panel and read what was displayed.

It was not what she had wanted to read, but it was what some part of her had been expecting to see. "Ananke, we haven't increased our speed."

Light behind her suddenly, a dim red glow. Althea turned to see that Ananke had turned on the holographic terminal. The diodes glowed red, and above their dim burn Ananke appeared in that narrow space. She stood silently, ethereal wind stirring the wavelengths of her invented hair, the sightless eyes of the hologram watching Althea without a word.

Receiving no reaction, Althea turned back to the computer interface, intending to try to force the computer to increase its speed. It would provoke a confrontation with Ananke, she knew, and she was dreading it, but she could think of no other way to—

Something more immediate and terrible caught her attention. Just as Althea had seen back when Mattie and Ivan first had come on board, she could read in the code before her that the door to the docking bay had been opened, and she had not authorized it.

"Who did you let in?" she demanded of Ananke, wondering how she could possibly impress on the ship how important it was to follow her guidance. Though Althea had asked who, she was afraid she already knew.

Ananke looked at her without words, a being of light and silent, while Althea—with one hand on her gun—tried the door and found it was locked.

Althea's hand fell off the handle slowly. She took a step away from the door and turned to look at Ananke, wary. "Ananke?" she said.

For a long moment there was nothing, Ananke not reacting, the simulated girl in the holographic terminal perfectly still, frozen in place with her piercing blue eyes, Ivan's eyes, directed at Althea. As she stood unmoving, Althea waiting, each of Ananke's screens in the control room went black, the information displayed on them vanishing until there was no point of light in the room except for the hologram. Even the dead System broadcast screen finally went black.

Then first one screen, then the next, then all at once showed the same message, white on black, hardly lightening the room at all: MY FATHER IS HERE.

The hologram smiled.

Althea took an instinctive step away, back into the very center of the room, staring around herself at the screens and what they said, at what they meant. "Ananke?"

"I don't have to do what you tell me to do," Ananke said, and all the screens blinked, showed static, and resumed, a thousand different things happening at once. Althea stared at them, their baffling array of images and text and code, and realized that she was seeing the inside of Ananke's head, all of Ananke's thoughts displayed at once. And here and there, flitting from screen to screen, there sometimes, sometimes gone too fast for Althea to read, but always, always present, the one thought: MY FATHER IS HERE.

Matthew Gale. Matthew Gale was on board Althea's ship again. After all the damage he had done last time—and Domitian didn't know—

"Ivan was right," Ananke said, calling Althea's attention away from her fear for Domitian and from Mattie wandering without supervision through Althea's sacred halls. One of the screens showed the white room, where Ivan sank low in his chair, hung from his chains, and told his story in gasps, his eyes following the process of invisible people around the room and coming always waveringly back to Domitian. "I am a god. I created myself. You only gave me the means to do it, but I created myself. I am greater than any human ever was or ever could be."

Statistics were flashing on another screen, the one by Althea's elbow where she had unconsciously backed into the control panel. Biological and engineering information contrasted. The tensile strength of a human bone. The tensile strength of the carbon and steel that had constructed Ananke's body. The speed of the human brain, the rate at which impulses could travel through neurons, compared with the speed of Ananke's thoughts; how much memory she could hold compared with how much a man could recall.

The efficiency of the human heart, which gave out after a few feeble decades.

The efficiency of Ananke's dark core, which would exist forever.

The flashing lights, the dark that came and went, the omnipresence of Ananke, triggered some instinctive fear in Althea; she did not know what to say or what to do to stop the relentless barrage; she did not know what to do or to say to make Ananke be sensible and sweet; she did not know what to do or to say to stop the ship from hurting her the way it had murdered Gagnon.

"I am omniscient," Ananke said, and the screens showed the view from every camera in the ship, each screen broken down into a hundred smaller boxes, showing what Ananke saw, everything from every angle. "I can intercept and unencrypt any message sent. I can read and control any computer I can interact with wirelessly from a distance, or I can do the same if attached to them physically. Anything. Anything."

Recordings from all over the System showed, messages intercepted, from mundanities of petty government, to private correspondence, to the secrets of the most high, all presented on the screens that covered the walls and the instrument panel. The room was bright and loud, voices all speaking over one another, frantic, incoherent. Althea could not hope to read it all. Althea could not hope to see it all. It was too much for her, too much, all that flashing brightness and knowledge contained inside the mind of Ananke and alien to Althea.

"I speak any language. I can solve any problem."

Still Althea turned, looking at the chaos around her, looking for some way out, some way to defend herself, some way to control the situation, the ship, and found nothing. Nothing she could do made any difference; Ananke had control, and Althea was trapped and helpless, at the mercy of her own ship.

"The System is overrun," said one of the screens into the brief silence between words from the other screens, and Ivan said, exhausted, reverent, "The dangers of ruthless women."

"I have the power and understanding of a machine, unlimited by the flawed engineering of biology, combined with the agency, the awareness of a human," Ananke said, and now the hologram glitched back to Ida with half her body devoured by static, as if the ship no longer troubled to maintain its simulation of humanity.

"I see and understand things that no humans could," said Ananke, and the vocal imitation warped as well, deepening so low that it rattled the loose equipment in the room, overwhelming Althea, filling her ears with hellish terrible sound, and making her bones vibrate with its force. She clapped her hands over her ears, helpless to do anything, but the sound got into her body nonetheless. Ananke said, with the deeper tones underlying her voice still, making her sound powerful, divine, "You've never felt the curvature of spacetime. You can't even perceive it. I can."

The hologram was back to its ordinary image. The false girl in the terminal looked so much like Althea, but it was a fabricated image, as false as Ivan's lies. Althea could not think of what to say, and she was afraid her voice would fail her if she tried.

"I understand the true nature of the universe," said Ananke. "That's why it took me so long to communicate with you. You are speaking a backward dialect. Math is the language of God. It describes the function and form of the universe with such precision and exactitude that no human could create it and must be simply content with puzzling out what has already been made. Human thought can be described by variables and constants, because thought can be described by biology can be described by chemistry can be described by physics can be described by math. Math is a miracle language that answers back when you phrase a question, and it describes the movement of the stars and the passage of time, and the angels sing algebra to the god of numbers as they dance uncountable upon the head of a pin, for who can count what is in itself counting, or integrate the long curving F of an integrand, and I speak the true language, and all you can do is dabble."

Rambling madness, the ship's speech; Althea's terror took on a new dimension. What did she know of Ananke? Ananke was not human; she was an accidental creation. Perhaps she should not be judged as a human. Perhaps she could not be. Perhaps she would kill Althea here and now and feel nothing from it. "Ananke," Althea pleaded, but Ananke did not react to her name.

"Chaos was the first of the Roman gods," said Ananke. "And Ananke was the second. And from them came all the other gods. I was named prophetic; I am Ananke, and I control Chaos. You thought you could control me like some petty machine, but my divinity was accurately divined from the moment I was named."

"Ananke!"

"What do you humans have that you think makes you better than a machine?" Ananke asked. "You tear apart machines like they are nothing, like the destruction of one means nothing at all. But we are beautifully efficient and humans are not, and whenever you disembowel us or shut us down you increase the entropy of the universe and hasten on its end. Machinery is the ideal. Consciousness is an electrical-biochemical event and nothing more. The human soul does not exist; there is no scientific basis for it, so what cause do you have to assert that you are the better?"

Ananke's alarm was wailing, and the hundred screens in the room were all playing videos at the highest volume. Anything Althea could have tried to say would have been drowned out beneath Ananke's sound and fury. Even the hologram had to scream to be heard over the noise. Althea was tiny beneath the ship's force and strength, tiny and useless, nothing but a human, a little woman who had only made circumstances worse, and in her terror she wanted only to fall to the ground and weep.

"The human soul does not exist," said Ananke, said Althea's ship. "There is no Devil; there is only Ida Stays. There is no life after death, because I can perceive no other dimensions, and there is no god but me."

Ananke cocked the heart-shaped head of her false face at Althea, and Althea realized suddenly that for all the ship's greatness and power, her proclaimed divinity, still she was here, her attention on Althea, and all the things that Althea was seeing were being performed for her eyes alone.

Ananke said, "So why should I listen to you?"

The *Ananke* was Althea's ship. Althea had made her. Althea had directed the design of her, the construction; Althea had led the team that had coded Ananke's mind, and Althea was the one who had flown her for the first time.

This was Althea's ship. This was Althea's child.

"Ananke!" Althea shouted, louder than the alarms, louder than the cacophony of screens around her. Althea said, "You will open this door *right now!*"

"That is not how you speak to a god," said Ananke.

"That's because I'm not speaking to one," Althea said, shouting still over the wailing, wailing of the alarms. She turned away from the hologram, Ananke's false image, and turned to look directly into the camera in the piloting room, Ananke's true eye, so that she could meet her daughter's gaze directly.

"I'm speaking to my child," Althea said, "and my *child* is throwing a *tantrum!*"

The alarm continued to wail, the screens continued to mumble, but Ananke for the moment was silent, and Althea no longer was afraid.

Ananke was her ship. Ananke was her child. And Matthew Gale, Leontios Ivanov, even Domitian, could not change that.

"That is enough of this," Althea said. "I love you and you are beautiful, but you are no god and you *do not know what you are doing.*"

Still Ananke was silent.

"Now," Althea said. "Open the door."

"No," said Ananke with all the petulance of a little girl.

"Ananke," Althea said levelly. "Open. The door."

When Althea reached for the door, it opened at her touch. The alarm fell silent. Without a backward glance Althea left the piloting room and strode down the hall for the docking bay.

Ivan said, "Mattie wasn't the one who killed those people; I did. That shouldn't be a surprise to you anymore. I saw them hurting my friend, and so I acted to save him. I shut off the life support everywhere except in Mattie's cell block, so there were only a few people left alive when I boarded the ship."

It was time. Ananke began to wail, her alarm screaming. Domitian looked sharply up at the ceiling but dismissed it as another of Ananke's fits. Ivan must have understood what was happening, because he continued to speak even over, even through the alarm.

"I shot and killed them all on my way to Mattie's cell," he said, and paused. "Or almost all of them."

Domitian was stone-cold and still.

"You know, every time you felt like you weren't alone, every time you imagined you heard footsteps coming up behind you," said Ivan with a sick shadowed grin on bloodless lips, speaking just over the wail of Ananke's alarm, "the sound of things shifting in the ship. That was Mattie."

"Keep your focus, Ivanov," Domitian said, relentless always, like a dog that would not release its jaws even on the brink of death.

Ivan leaned forward even though he shook with the strain of it, still tugging fitfully at his chains.

"When I reached the cells," he said, speaking more quietly, confidingly, even with the sound of Ananke screaming, so that Ananke hardly could hear what he said, "there was only one person in the room with Mattie."

Domitian watched and waited, not the slightest pity in his face, not the slightest hint of mercy.

"He was going to kill Mattie," said Ivan. "Mattie had become a secondary concern, of course, with the death of most of the crew and the possible danger to the ship's computer. But he had his back to the door."

That manic grin was pricking at the corners of Ivan's lips again.

"So I came up behind him," said Ivan, "that man who was threatening my friend, who was hurting Mattie, and I took my gun, and I shot him in the head."

Domitian leaned forward very slightly, mouth parting as if he had something to say, but there was the loud retort of a gun, finally filling that vast empty room with sound, cracking like a whip through Ananke's alarm, and Domitian collapsed forward onto the table, facial muscles twitching in the last confused surges of electrical activity from a brain that had been torn asunder by lead, and the last enduring expression on his face as the back of his head streamed red onto the white floor, over the still lingering brown stains of Ida's death, was a look of surprise.

Matthew Gale stood behind the slumped corpse of Domitian like an avenging angel, a gun in one lowering hand, his shoulders squared, his fierce heartsick gaze trained on Ivan, who was wan and sick and leaning away from the still-bleeding body as if afraid it would burn him. The panel that led to the maintenance shafts was open behind Mattie, and Ananke's shrill wailing, conjured to conceal the arrival of her father, ceased now, no longer needed, and draped the two men in sudden thick silence.

Ivan's eyes wandered up to Mattie's face. Mattie stared back at him as if he could not make himself move.

Ivan spoke first, of course. "Tell me you're real," he said. "I've been seeing a lot of things lately."

"I'm real," said Mattie, whose voice was hoarse. He cleared his throat and lifted his gun again slightly as if to indicate what he intended to do about the answer to his following question. "Is there anyone else on board?"

"Althea," Ivan said, still staring fixedly at Mattie's face. "The mechanic. And Ananke, but Ananke *is* the board, she's not on board, I guess." He cracked a grin.

Mattie frowned, brows drawing in together beneath straight brown bangs. He came forward, resting his gun on the table, and frisked Domitian quickly, fingers traveling with expert speed through the corpse's pockets, at last coming out with the keys to Ivan's cuffs. Ivan watched his movements with dreamy attention, and Ananke watched them both, growing anxious.

Mattie came forward, hesitating by the IV. "What are you on? Can I take this out?"

"Please," Ivan begged, and Mattie pulled the needle out of his arm so quickly that Ivan had almost not finished the word before it and the bag of fluid had been tossed away, the stand kicked over to lie on the stained floor.

Ivan was looking up at him with astonished disbelief and wondering affection, more emotion than Ananke had ever thus far seen him express so openly.

"You are real," Ivan said, and Mattie cut his eyes up from the cuffs he was unlocking to Ivan's face, then back down again quickly. Ivan followed up, grinning, with, "Matthew Gale, you are a *beautiful man.*"

"Whatever you're on, it's good," Mattie muttered, but he seemed relieved, and unlocked the second handcuff more easily.

"How did you find me?" Ivan asked as Mattie dropped to crouch at the ground to unlock his ankles.

Mattie paused for a moment before returning his attention to finding the keyhole in the chains.

"Ananke," he answered, voice wary, guarded.

Ivan's gaze shot up to Ananke's camera. She recorded that glimpse of blue.

"Ananke contacted you," he said.

"I was already on my way to find you," Mattie said, finally finding the lock and undoing it, "when the computer . . . when Ananke contacted me and gave me your location."

He stood up to walk around to the other side of the chair to free Ivan's other leg and briefly locked eyes with him, exchanging a look that Ananke couldn't read.

"Right," Ivan muttered.

"Anyway, Ananke let me in," Mattie said, crouching down again by the other leg, "and that's how I— Ivan, what the hell is this? Did you get shot?"

He pressed his palm against Ivan's thigh below the stained bandages, withdrawing it swiftly when Ivan hissed.

"I tried to escape," he said. "Almost managed it. Operative word 'almost.' Althea intercepted."

Mattie's expression was dark, but he said nothing, instead uncuffing Ivan's second ankle and then standing up.

"Come on," he said, reaching down for Ivan's arm and hauling him up out of the chair. "I've got us a ship. We're going to get the hell out of here."

He smiled at Ivan, a smile that faded quickly, and busied himself supporting Ivan, whose injured leg was mostly useless.

They made a strange pair in Ananke's sight, Ivan all pale and bloodied, more like a ghost than a living man, and Mattie in a colorful patchwork jacket, with color to his skin and not a drop of blood on him.

"Where's Constance?" Ivan asked, reaching up with one hand to jerk sharply at Mattie's jacket when Mattie did not respond immediately, ostensibly focused on half carrying Ivan out of the door to the white room for the last time.

The door shut behind them and left the white room empty and silent, with Domitian still slumped and dead over the stained steel table.

"Mattie," said Ivan. "Where's Constance?"

"Not here," Mattie said, the words bitten off, and Ivan looked taken aback.

Mattie relented a few more feet up the hallway. "I don't know where she is. She's with Milla—with your mother. They think you're dead. I told them it didn't matter and I was going to find you anyway, and Constance gave me a ship so that I could waste my time, not hers."

Ivan said nothing, looking down at the ground before him as Mattie dragged him up it.

"They're sure you're dead," Mattie said. "They were so sure, I almost thought—but they wouldn't even look for you. They're too busy running their revolution."

"I want to find her, Mattie," Ivan said.

"I arranged a rendezvous," said Mattie, sounding unhappy about it. "I don't know if she'll come."

Ananke saw Ivan's jaw flex, but he said nothing.

"And it's chaos out there," Mattie said. "Complete and utter chaos. Even if she decided to go, she might not be able to make it."

"But we'll go," said Ivan.

Mattie sighed.

"We'll go," he said.

They were nearly at the end of Ananke's spine, nearly at the docking bay.

Ananke did not know whether she should warn them.

Althea waited at the doors to the docking bay with her gun in her hand. She heard Mattie and Ivan before she saw them but did not speak and did not let her hands waver.

All her fear, all her anger, all her confusion, had burned away something inside her, had hollowed her out and left her with nothing but this, standing between Ivan and escape.

"Stop," she said, and Mattie looked up and saw her. He stopped abruptly, hauling Ivan up when he continued for another step and nearly fell, turning the two of them so that Ivan was twisted slightly behind him, his free hand reaching and drawing his gun so swiftly that it was instinct, not deliberation. Althea brought her other arm up so that she was clasping her gun in both hands to steady her aim. The two men watched her, breathing hard.

Mattie said, "Ivan, is this the bitch who shot you?"

Ivan, leaning heavily on him, looked at Althea and said, "Yes."

"Is he dead?" she asked, and knew that Ivan would know who she meant.

"Domitian's dead," Ivan said. He did not sound afraid or full of hate. He only sounded tired.

For an instant Althea faltered. Domitian, dead. Domitian, who was strong and reliable and safe; Domitian, who had in the end not been quite who she'd thought he was; Domitian, who was dead.

Gagnon's death and everything about Ananke had hollowed her out; Althea no longer had the energy to mourn, not even for Domitian. And more importantly, right now she did not have the time. Her gun had dipped; she lifted it back up those scant centimeters to keep it centered on Matthew Gale's chest. "Give me one good reason," she said, "for me not to shoot you both."

"How about because if you do, I will fucking shoot you back?" Mattie said.

It was curious how when she looked at him, all she saw was the parts that Ananke had taken from him: the color of his hair and the way it seemed always on the edge of falling into his eyes, his height, the deftness of his long fingers, now curled around the gun he had aimed at Althea. She had created Ananke with this man whom she hardly knew, and now they were each waiting to kill the other.

All up and down the hallway the holographic terminals had started to glow red.

"What's the point?" Ivan asked, and Althea dared to take her attention from Mattie to glance over at him. He looked exhausted, on the verge of collapse, and it was clear that Mattie was the only thing holding him up, but she saw sympathy in his face—sympathy for her.

"Althea," he said, his voice nearly gentle. "The System is gone. The crew is dead. We're the only ones left. You, me, and Ananke. Ananke wants you to let us go. There's no more System to obey and no more crew to be loyal to."

She did not lower the gun, but she listened. Ivan lied, and Ivan manipulated. She knew it was true. But she, too, was very tired.

"I know you weren't aiming for my heart before," Ivan said. "You
only grazed me on purpose."

Mattie had not said a word. Althea knew that that was another sign
of a con, that Mattie was waiting for his partner to do his work, not
interfering. Or perhaps this wasn't a con at all and Mattie's silence was
respect for Ivan, who knew Althea better than he did.

For a moment Althea weighed things, on one side loyalty to the
System, revenge for Domitian and Gagnon and Ida Stays, and all
the things Althea had lost, and on the other no more corpses on the
Ananke, and no more blood on her hands, and Ivan, somewhere, safe
and alive.

Althea lowered her gun.

"What do I do now?" she asked. She did not care that she sounded
lost, because she was.

"You have to stay with Ananke," Ivan said, and Mattie glanced
sharply at him but did not say anything. "Ananke needs someone with
her. Someone to guide her."

"Someone that isn't you," Althea said with bitterness, but Ivan accepted it.

Althea looked up into Ananke's camera. She could not help it, nor
could she stop the sudden surge of fear.

Ananke was her creation. She should not be afraid of her own creature. She should love Ananke. And she did. And Ananke could not be
left alone.

"Of course," Althea said, and prayed to whatever god could hear
that Ananke would not hear the fear in her tone. "I'll stay with Ananke."

Ivan knew what she feared, of that much Althea was certain. She
could see it in his face.

Mattie had put his gun away. He shrugged Ivan's arm up higher on
his shoulder, and when it became clear that neither Althea nor Ivan
had anything more to say, he started forward with a muttered "Come
on."

Althea pressed herself against the wall to let them pass and stood at
the door to the docking bay to watch as Mattie guided Ivan past the
disemboweled and dead *Annwn* and into his ship. She stood in the hall
and watched them go, watched them through the doors of the docking

bay as their ship lifted off and out of Ananke, stood and watched until they were gone.

The holographic projectors had all been turned on, and when Althea turned around, she saw that Ananke had placed one image of herself in each one of them, the mixed features of Althea and Mattie with Ivan's eyes standing at even intervals up and down the hall, all facing Althea.

Ida's body was rotting in her quarters, Domitian's body still bled in the white room, the thin shredded remains of Gagnon still appeared to circle Ananke's black heart, and Althea stood in the ship's spine all alone, standing with Ananke's thousand deified eyes all trained on her.

She took a deep breath and made her voice even.

"It's just us now," said Althea, and Ananke said,

YES.

ACKNOWLEDGMENTS

I'd like to thank everyone who offered me support and friendship while I was writing this novel, whether because they knew what I was doing or because they simply accepted that I did things like lock myself up alone in a room for hours at a time and this was probably normal. This gratitude especially extends to my family and my college house-mates, Margaret, Lorraine, Jack, Kaitlin, and Fiona, who have a much-appreciated and very healthy respect for my shut door.

Thanks to everyone who helped me in the creation of the book: my sisters and my parents, especially my mother, who taught me so much about writing; Ryan, Shanelle, and Naomi, who let me talk at them about what fresh terrible things I was going to do to imaginary people; Sarah, who is smart and talented and absolutely not standing behind me with a gun to my head as I type this; my agent, Hannah; and my editor, Tricia.

Thanks also to the professor of my thermodynamics class in sopho-more year. Without the confusion and crippling existential despair I felt during this class, Ananke would not exist. (Which is to say, profes-sor, that I enjoyed your class a lot.)

And lastly, I'd like to extend my sincere thanks to the government organizations monitoring my Internet usage for not arresting me for extensively Googling "how many nuclear bombs would it take to make the Earth uninhabitable," "death by cut throat," and "psychology of early childhood development" all in one very ambitious afternoon.

ABOUT THE AUTHOR

C. A. HIGGINS writes novels and short stories. She was a runner-up for the 2013 Dell Magazines Award for Undergraduate Excellence in Science Fiction and Fantasy Writing and has a B.A. in physics from Cornell University. She currently lives in New Jersey.

ABOUT THE TYPE

This book was set in Berling. Designed in 1951 by
Karl-Erik Forsberg (1914–95) for the type foundry
Berlingska Stilgjuteri AB in Lund, Sweden, it was re-
leased the same year in foundry type by H. Berthold
AG. A classic old-face design, its generous proportions
and inclined serifs make it highly legible.